JERI SMITH-READY

"... is one of my very favorite reads!"
—P. C. Cast, *New York Times* bestselling author of the
House of Night series

Bad to the Bone

Nominated for the Pearl Award

"Smith-Ready pours plenty of fun into her charming, fang-in-cheek urban fantasy."
—*Publishers Weekly* (starred review)

"Offbeat and hugely entertaining."
—*Romantic Times*

"Believable, captivating characters abound. . . . By turns funny, sexy, and gripping."
—*Library Journal*

"An entertaining, fast-paced, toothsome tale wrapped around an eclectic playlist of six decades' worth of hot music."
—The Green Man Review

"Equivalent to the best hot chocolate you have ever tasted. . . ."
—ParaNormal Romance (A Top Pick)

"*Bad to the Bone*'s action-packed plot, realistic characters, original vampire mythology, sinister secret societies, and shadowy government organizations make it a great read for both vampire fiction and urban fantasy fans."

"A solid and fast-moving

D0032200

"Filled with edge-of-your-seat suspense, hot love scenes, and plot twists that you never see coming. Jeri Smith-Ready has scored another hit."

—Bitten by Books

Wicked Game

Winner of the PRISM Award
A nominee for the American Library Association
Alex Award

"An addictive page-turner revving with red-hot sex, truly cool vampires, and rock 'n' roll soul."
—Kresley Cole, #1 *New York Times* bestselling author of *Pleasure of a Dark Prince*

"Smith-Ready's musical references are spot-on, as is her take on corporate radio's creeping hegemony. Add in the irrepressible Ciara, who grew up in a family of grifters, and the results rock."

—*Publishers Weekly*

"A colorful premise and engaging characters . . . a fun read."

—*Library Journal*

"Just when I think the vampire genre must be exhausted, just when I think if I read another clone I'll quit writing vampires myself, I read a book that refreshed my flagging interest. Jeri Smith-Ready's *Wicked Game* was consistently surprising and original . . . I highly recommend it."
—A "Book of the Week" pick by #1 *New York Times* bestselling author Charlaine Harris at charlaineharris.com

"This truly clever take on vampires is fresh and original."
—*Romantic Times*

"Jeri Smith-Ready has created a set of strikingly original, fascinating characters, rich with as much style and rhythm as the music her vampires love. Lyrical and uncompromising, *Wicked Game* is a winner I'll be reading again."
        —Rachel Caine, bestselling author of *Thin Air*

"*Wicked Game* is clever, funny, creative, and way too much fun. . . . A sure-fire winner."
        —The Green Man Review

"A wicked delight. . . . Urban fantasy that makes an irresistible playlist and an irresistible read."
        —C. E. Murphy, bestselling author of *Urban Shaman*

"Sharp and smart and definitely not flavor of the month, *Wicked Game* is wicked good. "
        —Laura Anne Gilman, bestselling author of *Flesh and Fire*

"Jeri Smith-Ready's vampire volume *Wicked Game* will make your corpuscles coagulate with corpulent incredulity. It's for young bloods and old jugulars alike. Whether you devour it on Sunday Bloody Sunday or just before Dinner with Drac, simply turn off the fifty-inch plasma, lay back, and 'Let It Bleed.' "
        —Weasel, WTGB 94.7 The Globe, Washington, DC

"Original and unique . . . a fantastically good read."
        —Love Vampires (Pick of the Month and
            one of 2008's Best Vampire Books)

"An imaginative tale that adds new dimension and limitations on the otherwise long-lived lives of vampires."
        —Darque Reviews

"A unique and lyrically entertaining story. . . . Excellent dialogue, skillfully crafted characters, and unique plot."
        —Romance Reviews Today

DON'T MISS THE SEXY BEGINNING TO CIARA'S TALE. . . .

Wicked Game
Bad to the Bone

Available from Pocket Books

BRING
ON THE
NIGHT

JERI SMITH-READY

POCKET BOOKS
New York London Toronto Sydney

The sale of this book without its cover is unauthorized. If you purchased this book without a cover, you should be aware that it was reported to the publisher as "unsold and destroyed." Neither the author nor the publisher has received payment for the sale of this "stripped book."

Pocket Books
A Division of Simon & Schuster, Inc.
1230 Avenue of the Americas
New York, NY 10020

This book is a work of fiction. Names, characters, places, and incidents either are products of the author's imagination or are used fictitiously. Any resemblance to actual events or locales or persons, living or dead, is entirely coincidental.

Copyright © 2010 by Jeri Smith-Ready

All rights reserved, including the right to reproduce this book or portions thereof in any form whatsoever. For information address Pocket Books Subsidiary Rights Department,
1230 Avenue of the Americas, New York, NY 10020.

First Pocket Books paperback edition August 2010

POCKET and colophon are registered trademarks of Simon & Schuster, Inc.

For information about special discounts for bulk purchases, please contact Simon & Schuster Special Sales at 1-866-506-1949 or business@simonandschuster.com.

The Simon & Schuster Speakers Bureau can bring authors to your live event. For more information or to book an event contact the Simon & Schuster Speakers Bureau at 1-866-248-3049 or visit our website at www.simonspeakers.com.

Cover illustration by Don Sipley

Manufactured in the United States of America

10 9 8 7 6 5 4 3 2 1

ISBN 978-1-4391-6348-1
ISBN 978-1-4391-6349-8 (ebook)

To my husband, Christian, who means more to me than the rest of the world put together

ACKNOWLEDGMENTS

Thanks as always to my family and friends, who continue to wait patiently for me not to be on deadline. Thanks to my beta readers—Patrice Michelle, Cecilia Ready, Rob Staeger, and Rob Usdin—for their honesty and sharp eyes. It's a foolish author who works alone.

A hundred and fifty (and counting) thank-yous to the WVMP Street Team, for their phenomenal support and enthusiasm.

Thanks to the hardworking folks at Pocket Books who brought *Bring on the Night* to life: Louise Burke, Erica Feldon, Don Sipley, Martha Schwartz, Renee Huff, Nancy Inglis, and Lisa Litwack.

Thanks to my brilliant editor, Jennifer Heddle, for keeping Ciara and her friends "alive" and well for more adventures, and to my agent, Ginger Clark, who is a rock star to her clients for a million damn good reasons. They deserve the best toffee and chocolate, respectively, the world has to offer.

Most of all, thanks to my husband, Christian Ready, for his love and patience and for getting me Subway when I'm on deadline. I don't need much, but I need him.

By the sad silence which
eternal reigns

O'er all the waste of these wide-
stretching plains;

Let me again Eurydice
receive,

Let Fate her quick-spun thread of
life re-weave.

—Ovid, *Metamorphoses*, Book X

PLAYLIST

"Looking After No. 1," Boomtown Rats
"Orange Crush," R.E.M.
"Bring on the Night," The Police
"See That My Grave Is Kept Clean," Dream Syndicate
"Sheena Is a Punk Rocker," The Ramones
"Here Comes Your Man," Pixies
"Clocks," Coldplay
"I'm an Asshole," Dennis Leary
"I Know I'll See You," A Place to Bury Strangers
"Goo Goo Muck," The Cramps
"When Doves Cry," Prince and the Revolution
"Bad Romance," Lady Gaga
"Sweet Dreams," Marilyn Manson
"Keep on the Sunny Side," The Carter Family
"6'1"," Liz Phair
"Otherside," Red Hot Chili Peppers
"Ripple," Grateful Dead
"Ciara," Luka Bloom
"Symphony number 7 (second movement)," Ludwig van Beethoven
"It's a Sunshine Day," The Brady Bunch
"Endless Sleep," Jody Reynolds
"Watusi Zombie," Jan Davis
"No, No, No," Dawn Penn
"Just Walkin' in the Rain," The Prisonaires
"Until the End of the World," U2
"Bitter Sweet Symphony," The Verve

1

My My, Hey Hey (Out of the Blue)

I'm okay now.
Just so you know.
I mean, just so *I* know.
Not that I wonder.
(deep breath)

2

Welcome to Paradise

I could smell my own fear, bitter and tangy as an overripe orange. I crept down the night-shrouded alley and wished for eyes in the back of my head. Even eyes on the sides of my head would've helped, though that would've required some strategic barrette placement.

Adrenaline spiked my senses. My eyes caught faint flaps of newspaper shreds tossed by the chill evening breeze. My ears filtered every scratch of twig and creak of plywood, singling them out from the background roar of the distant highway. My feet felt each pebble of industrial-grade gravel through the soles of my boots as I slunk toward the dark warehouse.

Beyond it lay freedom.

I'd been in the clutches of more than one vampire, so I knew what it was like to be prey. But I'd never been hunted. Never had a chance to escape, to match wits with my predator. To fight back.

At the end of the alley I passed an overstuffed Dumpster, where the odor of cat piss snagged my attention. I wrinkled my nose and glanced at the bin. The lid was clamped on a discarded pizza box, pinching it open to reveal a leftover slice inside.

My feet stopped, as if the brilliant (or possibly stupid) idea had passed through my toes on the way to my brain.

I opened the Dumpster, trying not to creak the rusty hinges. The grease-splattered pizza box slid off a stack of bulging, green-black trash bags. I trapped it against my leg to keep it from hitting the ground.

Before I could reconsider, I flipped up the cardboard top ("Enjoy your delicious moments!") and grabbed the remaining slice, grateful to be wearing gloves. I held it up to the moonlight leaking in between the charred brick buildings.

Jackpot: white pizza. Gooey splotches of ricotta oozed over a smooth layer of mozzarella. The whole affair was slathered in garlicky olive oil, with no tomato sauce to dilute the scent.

Holding my breath, I smeared the pizza slice over my throat and face, trying to convince myself the green stuff was oregano. I repeated the process on my arms, then my torso, keeping nervous ears and eyes out for an approaching attack.

Reeking like a frat house, I scurried to the warehouse door. It was ajar just far enough for me to slide inside without touching the frame.

The vampire was waiting.

I didn't see or hear him, just sensed him deep in my frightened little soul, the way a rabbit senses a fox. But unlike a rabbit, I couldn't outrun my hunter.

The door behind me slammed shut, its clang echoing

through the hangar-size warehouse. Above my head, the red Exit sign flickered, then dimmed.

I will not flee. I will not scream. Such panic could trigger the killer instincts of even the most serene vampire.

Cold sweat coated my skin, thickening my garlic aura. I stretched my fingers and willed them away from the sharp wooden stake in my hip holster. *Cooperation before coercion*, I chanted in my head like a mantra. *Cooperation before coercion.*

Something shifted on the far side of the warehouse. Something big.

The vampire shot forward in a dim blur, his long leather coat fanning out behind him, making him look like a linebacker with wings.

I stood my ground. (Or by some accounts, I froze like a deer in the proverbial headlights, but who's to quibble?) Before I could blink, he was almost upon me. My hands came up to defend my throat.

Then the bloodsucking behemoth slid to a stop. His nose crinkled. "What the—?"

"Hiyah!" A figure in black dropped between us, feet and fists blurring. Bone cracked against bone.

The vampire grunted and lurched back, then wiped his face and reset his stance. His attacker shrieked again, her black ponytail dancing behind her as she hand-springed into a double kick to his face.

He blocked her next blows easily. I sidled around them, waiting for her to distract him enough for me to escape.

Finally the vampire dropped his arms. "Okay, time out."

The girl leaped forward and stabbed his chest with her wooden stake. He gaped at it protruding from his shirt.

"I did it!" she gasped. "You're dead."

His thick brown hand flashed to her neck. "After you, sweetheart."

He drove her backward, her heels slipping on the concrete, until she slammed into the crate. She gurgled and squeaked, clawing at his wrist. Her eyes popped wide as her error no doubt dawned on her. Vampires don't die until you pull out the stake.

Which I *swear* I was about to do when the whistle blew.

Sergeant Kaplan stepped out from behind another crate, scribbling on her clipboard. Her slicked-back gray-blond hair glittered in the faint ceiling light.

"Recruit!" She stalked toward my partner Tina as the vampire released her. "What's the first precept of the Control?"

Tina massaged the front of her throat and coughed out her response. "Cooperation before coercion. But he was—"

"Were you asleep the day we taught defensive maneuvers?"

"I was defending *her*!" She pointed at me. "He was about to attack."

"Captain Fox was clearly slowing down. Your blows were sufficient to stop him, but the staking was overkill."

"Overkill without the kill." The hulking vampire yanked out the stake and tossed it at Tina's feet. Then Captain Fox unbuttoned his shirt to reveal a thick flak jacket. The first two-inch layer was penetrable, to simulate a real staking. A red oval was drawn on the dark gray vest, indicating the location of his heart. Tina's stake hole lay outside the oval. Swing and a miss.

In real life, she'd be dead. If I'd tried to pull out the stake to finish the kill, I'd be dead. But if I'd run while he was taking a victory sip, I'd probably have survived.

I was mentally filing this information when the sergeant turned to me. "Griffin." Kaplan scrunched up her face. "Good God, what's that smell?"

I offered my wrist to her nose. "This new Italian fragrance, all the rage in Milan."

Kaplan took a swift step back. "That's why Captain Fox slowed down as he approached you." She gave me a begrudging nod. "Good thinking."

Tina shook her finger at me as she spoke to the sergeant. "Agent Griffin didn't have her stake deployed."

"She's not an agent yet, recruit, and neither are you." Kaplan turned her ego-piercing gaze on me. "Why was your stake in its holster?"

I straightened my posture to answer, banishing all remnants of smirk. A little piece of me died every time I gave in to the quasi-military bullshit. But if I didn't fulfill my duties, they could take away a much bigger piece of me, the piece that made life complete.

"Sergeant," I said, "a direct threat can provoke an otherwise harmless vampire to attack. I lack the fighting skills to defeat him, so if we engaged in combat, I'd be killed. I therefore concluded that the best strategy would be to deter an attempt to drink my blood." I glanced at her. "Hence the pizza wipe."

"And if that strategy had failed?"

I paused. "Offer him a bib and a straw?"

"Yoosie lover," Tina hissed.

Captain Fox sent her a look that would freeze an open flame. I tried not to laugh at Tina's bureau slang for vampire. "UCE," pronounced "yoosie," stood for undead corporeal entity. She'd never used the slur when she and Captain Fox were secretly sleeping together, back before she joined the Control and he broke up with her, per agency rules.

"No one asked your opinion," Kaplan growled at Tina, then spoke to me again. "Your flippancy is not appreciated."

I resisted the urge to roll my eyes. After three and a half weeks of orientation with the Control (shorthand for the International Agency for the Control and Management of Undead Corporeal Entities), I had failed to give it a sense of humor.

"Furthermore," Kaplan continued speaking to me, "you abandoned your partner in the middle of a fight."

"I was just about to step in and—"

"Step in? He would've killed her before you could 'step in.' You must act without thinking. Defending your fellow agents must be a reflex, not a decision."

Tina and I exchanged a look, and I knew she'd never risk her ass for me unless she knew she'd get a medal. All the trust-building teamwork exercises in the world couldn't overcome the fact that she hated what I was—and what I wasn't.

"However," Kaplan continued, "you're right about one thing. Losing a bit of blood is better than losing your life." As Tina began to voice her disapproval, Kaplan cut her off. "Do you have a problem with our mission?"

That shut Tina up. For centuries, the Control had been little more than a band of vampire hunters, bent on extinguishing the undead. But since 1897 (according to the IACMUCE field manual), the agency's mission has been to balance the safety and well-being of humans *and* vampires.

By this point I'd realized that the Control's unofficial motto was "Whatever it takes." I admired their pragmatism—when it wasn't screwing over me or my loved ones.

Tina bowed her head, the corners of her mouth all twitchy tight. "I'm sorry for my mistake, Sergeant."

"Don't be sorry for your mistakes. You're here to learn." Kaplan closed her clipboard with a loud clack. "Be sorry for your pride."

A muscle in Tina's jaw jumped. "Yes, Sergeant."

"And you"—Kaplan pointed her pen at me—"take a shower."

I walked back to my dorm across the central commons of the Control's regional headquarters. The grass, which during the day mixed winter browns with spring greens, glowed in shades of gray in the moonlight.

The vampire Control agent Elijah, aka Captain Fox, strolled ten feet to my right, upwind. One of his strides equaled two of mine, so I had to hustle to keep up.

"Good thinking," he rumbled, "with the pizza."

"Next best thing to bug spray."

Garlic has no special powers, but a vampire's acute sense of smell means that any strong scent turns them off—chemical products being the worst.

"It wouldn't have stopped me if I was really thirsty." Elijah checked the buttons of his black uniform shirt. "But people like you already know that."

"People like me?"

"Yoosie lovers," he said with a scoff. "As your partner calls you."

If he thought Tina wouldn't tell anyone about their affair, he was naïve to the oversharing ways of women. While Tina and I weren't exactly buds, we'd hung out on occasion, since she was one of my best friend Lori's bridesmaids. As the maid of honor, I felt it my diplomatic duty to offer to be Tina's orientation roommate and training partner, though I knew we weren't exactly a match made in heaven. More like a match made in sitcoms.

Sure enough, the better we knew each other, the worse we got along. Between Tina's breakup with Elijah and her discovery that I pretty much believed in nothing, she'd been hell to live and work with.

"Not that it's any of your business," I told Elijah, "but I'm not my boyfriend's donor. I'm my boyfriend's girlfriend."

He angled a glance at me, the whites of his eyes flashing under his black cap. "Really?"

"Really."

"Huh." He turned down the path for the vampires' quarters. "Poor guy," I heard him mutter under his breath.

I watched him go, marveling at the grace and precision of his step despite his enormous bulk. Other than that brief fling with Tina, Elijah tended to keep a respectful distance from humans, no matter how they smelled. His size and strength meant he didn't need fangs to intimidate. He didn't just look like a linebacker—he'd actually been one for the Cleveland Browns before he was vamped in the late seventies.

I jogged the rest of the way to my dorm room so I could catch the aforementioned poor guy's show.

A clock radio sat on the nightstand between the twin beds. I switched it on to hear the closing strains of the Boomtown Rats' "Looking After No. 1." As usual, Regina's Goth/punk *Drastic Plastic* show was running over into her progeny Shane's midnight hour. I peeled off my dull black training jacket as the music faded.

"Happy Saturday, my friends." Shane's voice crawled out of the little speaker, so deep and soothing my knees turned to jelly. I sank onto the bed, forgetting my own reek. "It's two minutes past midnight here at 94.3 FM WVMP, the Lifeblood of Rock 'n' Roll. We've got forty-six degrees here in Sherwood, fifty in Baltimore, and fifty-two in Washington, with clear skies all over the map."

The mountains between the Control's regional headquarters and our hometown of Sherwood weakened the station's signal, but I still felt like he was speaking straight to me.

"The Easter Bunny has left the South Pole and will be heading your way in twenty-four hours—so, kids, behave yourselves. This next one goes out to all the secret agents. Give me a call and tell me a secret."

I was dialing his cell number before the opening bars of R.E.M.'s "Orange Crush" were even finished.

He picked up after the first ring. "Come home. Now."

"What's wrong?"

"Nothing in particular. Everything in general." He let out a long sigh, and I could picture him leaning back in his chair and propping his feet on the studio table. "I miss you, Ciara."

After almost three years, I still got that zing across the

back of my shoulders every time Shane said my name. Like it was created to be uttered by him, perfectly pronounced (*KEER*-ahh) with just the right amount of breath.

"I miss you, too, but the month is almost up. Besides, the way I smell, you're better off missing me." I described the unclassified parts of my latest training session.

"Sounds like you got high marks," he said.

"I ace strategic thinking." I massaged my shoulder, sore from yesterday's push-up marathon. "But I suck at teamwork and martial arts. I barely passed my tae kwon do final. On the plus side, I learned the Korean word for 'doofus.'"

His laughter came low and rich, making me twist the blanket with the desire to hear it in person. Preferably naked.

"How's Dexter?" I asked him.

"Same as usual. Cold and furry."

I missed my dog almost more than I missed my boyfriend. At least I could talk to Shane on the phone or get his messages. Dexter's vampirism—developed years ago in a Control laboratory—made him smarter than the average pooch, but he wasn't big on texting.

"He'll be psyched to see you Sunday night," Shane added. "You'd better wear a life jacket so you don't drown in drool."

I laughed at the image, to ease the stab of homesickness in my chest. "I can't wait to sleep in our bed again. And not sleep in it." When he didn't answer after a few moments, I prompted him. "Get it? Not sleep? In a bed? Hubba-hubba?"

"Sorry." His voice hushed. "Jim just walked by the studio."

"How did he look?"

"Bloody."

I rubbed my temple, where a headache the size and shape of a certain hippie vampire was forming. "What if a cop had seen him driving back from his donor's like that?"

"We've pointed that out, but he won't listen."

"If he doesn't knock it off, we'll have to get him some help."

Shane snorted. "Spoken like a true Control agent."

"Jim isn't just risking himself—his recklessness could blow everyone's cover and show the world that vampires exist. That means the end of all of you, and the station, too."

"I know." He let out a long sigh. "We'll try again. But Jim's not the best candidate for an intervention. It's more likely to drive him over the edge."

A key turned in the lock. Tina shoved open the door, banging it against the wall. Her face crumpled in disgust when she saw me. "You still haven't showered?"

I angled my shoulder away from her. "Shane, I gotta go wash up. See you soon."

"I'll wake you when I get home from work," he said, his voice rich with promise. "After three."

"Please do," I said after a long moment, when I could scrub my voice of all tension and speak of April 5 as if it were just another Monday. As if it were just the beginning of another work week.

As if it weren't the fifteenth anniversary of the death and resurrection of Shane McAllister.

After showering, I returned to my room to find Tina sitting up in bed, writing on a legal pad. Her heavy dark brows pinched together, and her lips folded under her teeth so hard I expected them to bleed.

I collapsed in bed with one of the textbooks for my History of Eastern Europe class, my last course at Sherwood College before graduation. My professor had let me off for Control orientation, and here I was repaying him by falling way behind in assigned reading.

Unfortunately, the rhythmic scratching of Tina's pen soon lulled me into drowsiness.

Just as I was falling asleep, she slapped down her notepad. "Goddamn fucking precepts."

When she left the room to go to the bathroom, I crept over to her bed and looked at the legal pad. So far she had written in long hand, "Cooperation before coercion" one hundred and seventy-three times. The repetitions grew shakier as they continued.

"Ouch," I muttered. "Not just old-school punishment. Grade school."

I took a small towel into the bathroom and soaked it at the faucet, avoiding Tina's glare in the mirror. She was using her left hand to brush her teeth, her right hand no doubt sore from scribbling.

In our dorm floor's kitchenette, I heated the towel in the tiny microwave. When I got back to our room, Tina was sitting on the bed again, listening to her MP3 player and gritting her teeth as she wrote. I held out the steaming towel.

She glared at me through a pair of taped-frame glasses, which she'd put on after taking out her contacts. "What the hell is that?"

"For your hand. Moist heat'll help the ache."

"What's the catch?"

"The catch is you have to pull that six-foot stake out of your ass and be a real person to me. Or neither of us will pass orientation."

Tina's mouth tightened, but she lowered her gaze to her legal pad. "I can't stop writing. Kaplan wants a thousand reps of this by 0600."

"Your fingers will fall off. Give it to me."

Another stunned look, but she shook her head. "It has to be in my handwriting."

"Not a problem."

Tina bit her lip, then traded me the pad and pen for the towel. "Thank you," she whispered. She placed the towel on the inside of her wrist and let out a groan of relief. "I'm not used to writing by hand. Haven't done it since sixth grade."

I wrote *Cooperation before coercion* in Slot 207 in a passable forgery of her handwriting.

She looked at the page with awe. "Where'd you learn to do that?"

"Parents taught me." I sat on my bed and kept writing. "They were professional fakers."

"Wow." She took out her earbuds. "Are they in jail?"

"Yep." *Two out of three of them*, I thought but didn't add out loud. I was hoping that a little openness on my part would thaw the chill between us, but as a rule I preferred to keep my personal details—both past and present—locked safely away.

"It makes sense now." Tina shifted her hand on the towel. "The way you are, I mean. Smart and jaded and . . . you know."

"Selfish?"

"Self-preservative."

We shared a laugh. I let my posture relax, relieved my gamble had paid off in goodwill.

Tina's humor faded, however, when she saw my Romanian history book.

"Why are you reading that?" she snapped.

I ordered my hackles to stay down, hoping to restore the brief harmony. "It's for school," I said, resisting the urge to add, *not everything is about you.* "Hey, since you're sort of Romanian, can you suggest a good paper topic?"

"I suggest you pick another country. You don't want to mess with my people."

"I'm not messing, I'm just researching."

"I mean it, Ciara. Blood is in our blood."

The way she uttered those words sent a chill down my back, which was probably her intended effect.

"It was crazy when I left." She winced as she flexed her hand. "My parents got me from an orphanage in Bucharest when I was five, right after the revolution."

"I didn't realize." Since she'd told me her parents here in the states were Romanian, I'd assumed they were her original mom and dad. "Your birth parents died?"

"Maybe by now they have." She tugged her black bangs to veil her eyes. "My father got taken away. Maybe he was a Communist. My mom couldn't afford to keep all her kids, so she dumped me and my little brother at two different orphanages. I think she got money for us."

I didn't know what to say. My biological mom couldn't take care of me either, but at least I'd ended up with my dad and the woman I'd thought was my mother for the first twenty-four of my twenty-six years before I found out the truth. "I'm really sorry."

Tina shrugged as she moved the hot towel atop her wrist. "She had to survive. And it was for the best." Her posture straightened into her usual haughtiness. "My adoptive parents picked me out of two hundred kids. You know why?"

The sharp look in her eyes told me there was definitely a right and wrong answer, so I just shook my head.

"They could tell I had magic."

"Huh." I'd perfected the noncommittal grunt through years of discussing Lori's fruitless ghost hunting with the Sherwood Paranormal Investigative Team (SPIT), of which Tina was the treasurer.

"I know you don't believe in that stuff," Tina said, "but that doesn't make it not true. I've spoken to the dead."

"I speak to the dead every day. They're called vampires."

"Not *un*dead. Dead dead."

"Do they talk back?"

Her gaze faltered, and she adjusted her glasses. "Not yet."

"Then how do you know they hear you?"

"It's in my blood." Her voice turned urgent. "My father—the one who adopted me—said that he could tell I was of noble Romanian heritage like him. He says there's more magic in the Carpathian Mountains than in the rest of the world put together."

"Ah." I went back to copying sentences, the politest response I could think of.

"Daddy would know. He's psychic." She rushed out the words as if their speed could overtake my skepticism. "Plus he and my mom are both high-level necromancers."

"Uh-huh." I wrote faster.

"And he's in charge of the Immanence Corps."

As I looked up, Tina gasped and clamped her hand over her mouth. I remembered a shaded triangle on the far edge of the Control organizational chart. "What is the Immanence Corps? None of the Control people will talk about it with recruits."

"Nothing," she said, but her hand muffled her voice, so it came out "Mumfig."

I suspected her slipup had been intentional, so I turned back to the legal pad and approached the question at an oblique angle, feigning ignorance. "What exactly does a necromancer do? Is it like the mediums on TV?"

She lowered her hand and took a deep breath, as if she'd been suffocating herself. "They communicate with the restless spirits of the dead."

"Let me guess: they're all restless." Or at least the ones with relatives who have more cents than sense.

"Actually, no. If a spirit's at peace, it takes a lot more skill to raise it and a lot more work. Besides, it goes against a necromancer's ethics to disturb those who've fully passed on."

I wanted to change the subject, but I wanted even more to find out about this Immanence Corps. Holding my metaphorical nose, I kept digging. "Do they do séances?"

"Sometimes, but most of the ritual is just for show."

"The show is everything. My parents used to be 'faith healers.'" I mimed the obligatory air quotes. "They would sing and pray and work the crowd into a money-giving frenzy."

"Did they really heal people?"

"They faked it. Some of the folks were shills we paid

to pretend they couldn't walk or see. I could've won an Oscar for my cute-crippled-kid act."

Tina stretched the fingers of her right hand, not wincing this time. "What about the regular people, the ones who weren't hired?"

"They felt better after my father touched them, but—"

"So they were healed."

"They were gullible. In the heat of the moment, people will believe anything that gives them hope. I'm sure once we left town, the pain and suffering came right back. Along with much lighter bank accounts."

Tina groaned. "Why won't you see?" She snatched the legal pad out of my hands. "Belief is a powerful force, Ciara. Just because your crooked parents made money off it doesn't mean it's not real." She plopped back on her bed, creaking the mattress, and reinserted her earbuds before scrawling out the next *Cooperation before coercion*.

I wanted to tell her that *dis*belief was just as powerful as belief. Thanks to my soul-deep skepticism (with a little genetics thrown in), one taste of my blood could heal vampires' holy-water burns or release them from traps sprung by religious artifacts. For the last two and a half years, I'd been donating blood samples to the Control so they could study this odd trait I'd inherited—in the most potent form ever seen—from my Irish Traveller ancestors. The agency hadn't shared any of their conclusions with me, but my con artist father said the strength of the anti-holiness lay in my capacity to create my own reality—and not buy into those that were fed to me.

Which meant that if I ever believed in anything, I'd lose my abilities.

I often wished I was normal, so I wouldn't have to

worry about becoming some crazy vampire's personal pharmacy. When I first started giving my blood to the Control, it was only to buy my double-crossing father some leniency. Then it was part of a deal—which included this year of service—to let Shane visit his human family, a privilege forbidden to nearly all vampires.

But I'd started to realize it wasn't just about me. It was about a world on the edge of another Dark Age, with superstition feeding the fires of hatred, and belief taking the place of thought. I couldn't stop nutcases from blowing up planes or shooting physicians, but maybe I could help answer a few questions about the nature of good and evil.

Because against the armies of zealots, the rational world needed more than convincing arguments. It needed its own magic.

3

Kryptonite

Sunday morning I sat on the non-colonel side of Lieutenant Colonel Winston Lanham's wide oak desk, waiting for my assignment. I counted the awards lined up along the wall and tried to convince myself that I didn't care where they put me. I could survive anything for a year.

Obviously they wouldn't assign me to Enforcement—I wasn't much for kicking ass, at least not with my muscles, which still ached from my final physical assessment test.

The Anonymity Division? Possibly, given my con artist expertise in forgeries. Maybe I'd get a job creating and arranging new identities for aging vampires.

My fiercest wish was to work for the Contemporary Awareness Division. Predominantly an internal branch, CAD had been created to counteract temporal adhesion, the tendency of vampires to remain stuck in the eras in which they were turned. CAD taught vampire Control agents how to live in the present—how to speak, dress, and act like twenty-first-century humans. Every Control vamp was required to report for regular CAD sessions and attend an annual two-week cultural immersion seminar.

I was musing on how I could wrangle funds to share CAD resources with non-Control vamps, when Colonel Lanham entered.

Instinctively I stood at attention, though as a contractor I didn't have to observe military customs and courtesies. Lanham exuded a mixture of hard-ass authority and cool competence that even I had to respect.

He was still wearing the ceremonial dress blacks from our graduation ceremony, a double-breasted uniform with a column of brilliant brass buttons. An array of medals on his chest reflected the recessed ceiling lights, as did his closely shaven head.

He nodded as he strode behind the desk. "Ms. Griffin."

"Sir." I sat when he did, resisting the urge to clear my throat.

He set down a hard black leather briefcase. "Congratulations on completing Indoc."

I grimaced at the official name for the Control's orientation program: Indoc, short for Indoctrination. "Thank you, sir."

His thumbs flashed over the combination locks, then snapped them open simultaneously. "My apologies for the delay." He pulled out a multicolored stack of file folders. "I needed one last high-level signature for your assignment. I think you'll agree this is worth the wait."

Lanham extracted a thick indigo file—the only one of its hue. He returned the other files to his briefcase, which he snapped shut and locked. Despite the efficiency of his movements, the colonel seemed to be dragging out the moment to torture me.

"The Immanence Corps is an elite special operations force within the Control." Lanham rested his hands atop the file. "Its composition is roughly half vampire, half human, but every IC human possesses paranormal abilities."

My heart slammed my breastbone. "What exactly is an 'immanence'?"

"The word has a variety of meanings. Theologically, it signifies the divine presence in our world. Among pagans, it refers to an event that occurs in the mind." His steel blue eyes studied my face, as though he were expecting a reaction. "But by its purest definition, it means 'inherent.' IC agents are born with their powers."

"I don't have any powers. I just have funky blood."

"We both know it's more than that." Lanham tapped his pen against his briefcase. "Though we're a secular agency, many of our weapons depend upon the faith of those who wield them. Others, such as holy water, are intrinsically powerful."

"And those are the ones I can neutralize."

He gave an almost imperceptible nod. "The Control would like to know which principle applies to the abilities of IC agents."

"That makes sense."

We sat there for a few moments, blinking at each other, before I grasped the connection. "Wait, wait, wait. You want to use me to experiment on my fellow agents? What am I, a chemical in a test tube?"

He shook his head calmly. "I assure you—"

"It's not enough just to study my blood. Now you want to throw me into a pool of alleged paranormals and see if I neutralize them just by hanging out?" I fought to keep the anger out of my voice. "When you recruited me, you said you wanted my brains and talent. But you just want to study my freakiness."

Lanham's face remained impassive. "You have a unique quality. You should share it with those who can best help you deploy it."

My spine chilled at the word "share." "If I join the Immanence Corps, I'll have to tell my colleagues why I'm qualified." I could see us all sitting in a circle on Day One: *Hi, my name is Ciara, and my magic is really anti-magic. Please don't bite and/or kill me.*

"Not to worry." Lanham leaned back in his chair, spreading his hands. "Immanence agents maintain absolute secrecy regarding one another's powers. You're not the only one whose abilities could be used for nefarious purposes by vampires or humans."

"Do I have a choice in assignment?"

"There's always a choice. But not if you want to maintain our agreement."

Two and a half years ago I'd signed a contract to join the Control after I finished college. In return, the agency would allow Shane to maintain contact with his human mom and sister in Ohio.

"So I join the Immanence Corps or you cut Shane off from his family."

Lanham tilted his chin down. "And since his family knows where to find him, the only option would be relocation."

My chest tightened. "You'd make him move? Away from me? Away from the job that saved his life?"

"I'm afraid we'd have no choice."

"There's always a choice." I repeated his words as a wave of heat rose from my neck. "You choose coercion."

"As a last resort." His fingers tapped the ends of the chair arms. "After we attempt cooperation."

"Your cooperation *is* coercion."

"Listen!" The colonel lunged forward to loom over me. "I've bent over so far backward for you, I could kick myself in the forehead." Fingers near my face, he counted off. "One measly year of obligation, no travel, no boot camp, and a starting salary thirty percent higher than average. So stop your bitching, or your boyfriend will find himself in Nome, Alaska, just in time for a long summer of midnight suns."

My mouth creaked open. I'd never seen Lanham's cool turn hot. Clearly he'd been saving it for this moment.

"Sign here." He shoved an embossed indigo binder across the desk and slapped it open to reveal a letter of appointment to the Immanence Corps.

I took it. I read it. I signed it.

Only one other car remained in the visitors' parking lot when I left. Colonel Lanham had made me his last assignment, probably because he knew I'd cause the biggest headache.

A woman with a dark ponytail sat behind the wheel of a silver BMW. Her face was in her hands, and her shoulders shook in a total bodyquake.

Tina.

I schlepped my bags over to her car and knocked on the window. She jumped, startled, and in the next moment a stake was pointed at me through the glass. Not exactly terrifying, but I admired her reflexes.

Tina grimaced and rolled down her window.

"What's wrong?" I asked her.

"They gave me Enforcement!" She shook a red binder at me and let loose another flood of tears.

"But that's great, isn't it? You're perfect for that." I hoped they could train some restraint into her.

"I wanted to be Immanence!" She wiped away a nostril bubble. "My mom and dad'll be so embarrassed."

"Maybe you can transfer later."

"It's no use. The Control can't see my magic, no matter how hard I try." She rummaged through her bag. "Maybe they're right. Maybe I am mundane."

"No, I'm sure you've got . . . something." I winced at the weakness of my reassurance.

"Don't patronize me." She dug harder in her purse.

I realized what she was looking for. I opened my messenger bag and reached into the inside pocket for my travel pack of tissues.

"Here." I held out the tissues. Her eyes went wide with horror.

She pointed at my bag and whispered. "You . . . of all people."

I looked down to see the edge of the indigo binder peeking from my bag.

"You don't even believe!" she said.

I stepped back, in case she decided to take out her rage on my face. "You think I'm happy? I had no more choice than you did. I tried to get out of it."

"Why didn't you tell me you had a paranormal ability?"

"Because it's a secret." I fumbled for a way to explain. "They've never made a TV show out of what I can do."

"Coward! How can you be so selfish? You were created special. The least you can do is use your God-given talents to help people."

Tina turned the key in her ignition. The engine screeched, having already been idling.

"Damn it!" she shrieked. As she drove away, she pounded her steering wheel with both fists.

I felt sorry for any vampire on the eventual receiving end of Tina's rage, but mostly I felt sorry for Tina.

As I walked to my car, I thought of my own parents—the woman who gave birth to me, as well as my father and the lady I thought of as my real mom. I wondered what they'd imagined their little girl would become. A ballerina? A business owner? A bullshit artist like them?

Living "in sin" with a vampire boyfriend and joining a paranormal paramilitary organization probably didn't make their wish list. But at least they'd let me have my own dreams. Tina could only dream of having her own dreams.

I watched her car disappear between the ivy-draped wire gates. "Good luck," I whispered.

4

How Many More Years

Night had fallen when I arrived at my apartment in downtown Sherwood. Since it was a holiday, the small town's historic district was nearly empty, so I found a parking spot in front of my building.

The place I'd shared with Shane for more than two years was a three-bedroom furnished basement apartment beneath a law office. It was more room than we needed, but it had two nonnegotiable features: it allowed pets, and it was dark.

Even indirect sunlight could burn a vampire's body, which was why they went underground at "civilian twilight"—roughly half an hour before sunrise and after sunset—when the sun was safely below the horizon. Not even my blood could heal a sunlight burn, since flashing out of existence in a burst of flames is an irreversible process.

I lugged my bags down the outside entry stairs, leaning against the wrought iron railing to keep my balance. The door jerked open.

"Ciara!"

Lori threw a strangling hug around my neck, yanking me close to her petite frame. The warm smell of cinnamon wafted out of the apartment.

Dexter shoved past her to circle my legs, panting and woofing. I grabbed his collar before he could run into the street. Despite his steady diet of doggie blood-bank leftovers, his instincts told him to hunt fresh pooches, such as the neighbor's shih tzu.

"I've been going crazy without you." Lori shut the door behind us and followed me into my living room.

"Something new with the wedding?" I asked as I slumped my exhausted body onto the sofa. Lori and I had been talking on the phone every night, and she'd kept me apprised of every detail, right down to the "Love Rocks" wedding favor boxes.

"David wants to elope."

I tried to ask "Why?" but Dexter had crawled all one hundred twenty pounds of undead beast into my lap. It gave me time to wonder if this was part of David's plan for Honeymoon Part Two—after a week in the Bahamas, he was surprising Lori with five days in Greece instead of coming home. He hadn't mentioned an elopement threat to me.

Lori explained. "He's afraid one of my relatives will find out the DJs are really vampires."

I held Dexter's big black square head and ruffled the short fur and baggy jowls. "David's spent his whole life in secret situations." David and his father had both been Control agents, and even after David's discharge, he had formed a vampire radio station with his ex-fiancee, Elizabeth Vasser. "Privacy is very important to him." I tilted up my face so Dexter could lick my chin instead of my mouth. "Yesh, it is," I added in a baby talk tone to the dog.

"I offered a compromise." Lori sat in Shane's favorite tattered green armchair, curling her legs under her. "I said we could just not invite the DJs."

I gaped at her over Dexter's head.

She bit her lip. "David gave me that same look. Shane can still come, since he's the best man. Besides, he's so young, it's easy for him to pass."

"Lori, the DJs are David's only friends, besides you and me."

"I know." She twisted a long lock of white-blond hair around her finger. "If they don't come, his side of the aisle will be almost empty."

"Besides, you can't change the guest list less than two weeks before the wedding. It's a rule." At least, I thought it was. "Stop stressing. Weddings are never as bad as the bride expects."

"How would you know? You've never even been to a wedding."

True. One of the side effects of living as a con artist and then a vampire wrangler was that I had few normal friends who did normal things like get married, or work during the day.

"But I've read all about them." I swept my hand toward the neat stack of inch-thick bridal magazines on the end table. Lori's narrowed eyes told me she'd noticed that their pages were uncreased and their spines unbroken. "Look, I'll talk to David, do some shuttle diplomacy."

"Thank you." She came over and hugged my head, the only part not smothered by Dexter. "I'm sorry I've become such a freak." She pranced off to the kitchen, her bridal bipolar state shifting back to manic. "David and I made cinnamon rolls for Easter brunch. We can eat the extras and have Irish coffees while you tell me about your Control assignment."

"It's classified." I felt an actual pain in my gut at keeping a secret from Lori.

"That's so exciting!" She poured coffee into a pair of glass mugs. "Ciara Griffin, secret agent."

"I'd rather be a marketing director for a radio station, or a college student. Oh wait, I'm those things, too."

"Not for long." She added whiskey to the glasses. "We'll throw you the biggest graduation party the academic world has ever seen."

"Proportional to my matriculation time." Lori and I had started at Sherwood College almost nine years ago, but she'd graduated in the standard four years.

"Speaking of graduating, Tina called me. She's *livid* over her assignment. She couldn't tell me which division she'd hoped for, said it was classified." Lori set the whiskey bottle down with a clonk. "Oh my God, you got the assignment she wanted?"

The phone rang, saving me from an ethical dilemma. I shoved Dexter off my lap and got up to check the caller ID. A number in northeast Ohio: Shane's mom.

"Happy Easter, Mrs. McAllister!"

"Happy Easter, dear." Her voice was warmer than my sweater. "And please call me Mom."

I already had two of those and had dutifully placed my holiday calls to them on the way home, but what the hell. "Okay. Mom."

I saw that Shane had left me a note on the refrigerator, as usual. His missives generally combined an affectionate sentiment with detailed instructions on how to stack the Tupperware containers or which angle the coffeemaker and toaster should be aligned. Obsessive-compulsive behavior is one of the quirkier aspects of vampirism.

I scanned the note as Mrs. McAllister told me about their Easter dinner. Shane's words made heat spread from the base of my spine out to the tips of my fingers and toes. The note was detailed, all right, but the only instructions were for me to be naked in bed when he got home.

"Ciara? Are you there?"

"Oh! Yes." I shoved the note in my pocket, my cheeks flaming. "What were you asking?"

"How was orientation?" Shane's mother and sister knew all about the Control, seeing as how the agency, along with me and the DJs, had saved their lives a few years ago.

"It was an adventure. I'm lucky to be in one piece."

"I've said it before, but I can't thank you enough." Her voice became muted. "If it weren't for your sacrifice, I'd never see my son again."

"It's no sacrifice. The pay is great." *Besides, you're not the only one who would lose him.*

"Should I call him tomorrow evening, for, you know . . ."

"He'd like that. But make it early. The DJs are throwing him a wake." I opened the refrigerator to get the water pitcher, which Shane had placed up front so I wouldn't have to reach past his emergency rations of human blood.

"How nice, I guess," she said, then cleared her throat. "Do you happen to know if he made it to Mass today?"

"You know he can't risk it. What if they sprinkle the crowd with holy water?" I retrieved a glass from the cabinet, noticing how perfectly they lined up. "Plus, it makes him sad."

"There's nothing wrong with sadness. I learned that in therapy after Shane's father passed away." Mrs. McAllister paused. "We shouldn't hide from real feelings. Life's too short, even for a vampire."

I poured myself a glass of water, unsure how to respond. I was a big fan of all the denials and self-deceptions that helped us get through the day with our sanity intact.

A beeping noise went off in the background. "Ooh, the tea is done," Shane's mom said. "I better go put out the pies. Dessert was late tonight because Jesse had to pick up his girlfriend from her dad's house in Canton."

"Is this the cheerleader girlfriend or the one who plays bass in his band?"

"This week it's the cheerleader. The other one, they're just friends."

Friends with benefits, no doubt. I wondered if Shane had been as popular and confident when he was seventeen as his older nephew was. I had a feeling he'd been shy like Jesse's little brother, Ryan.

After I hung up with Mrs. McAllister, I carried my cinnamon roll and Irish coffee into the living room to join Lori, who was staring at the engagement photo she carried in her wallet.

"Don't worry, you and David will grow old together." I licked the melted whipped cream off the top of my mug. "And you'll get disgustingly cuter with each passing year."

Her smile turned dreamy as she stared out the front window—or she would have, had it not been covered in blackout curtains. Then she ripped her gaze back to mine. "What about you?"

"I'll get cuter, too. It's what I do."

She blew on her coffee, which lacked whipped cream so she could fit into her wedding dress. "What about the future?"

"I don't think about the future," I said, and at the time it was true. "Or the past, for that matter."

"You and Shane can't go on forever like this. I see it in his eyes when he looks at you." She curled her hands around her mug. "He wants you to belong to him."

I laughed at her melodrama. "I do belong to him."

"Not officially."

"That's what's so great about it."

She lifted her cinnamon roll as if to lob it at my head. "How can you be so casual about true love?"

"I'm not casual, just realistic. Unlike him, I won't stay young forever."

"You really think he cares about that?"

"I care." I stirred the whipped cream to melt it into the steaming coffee. "Jeremy once said I'm with Shane because it doesn't threaten my independence, because one day we'll break up and I can blame it all on the human-vampire thing, not on my own inability to commit or be a good girlfriend."

"Let me guess: Jeremy's solution is for you to become a vampire."

"Pretty much." We shared a smirk at the expense of our morbid friend, the sole human DJ at WVMP. "That's his solution for everything, including static cling."

"But he might have a point. Not about you becoming a vampire but about your commitment phobia."

"He might." I sipped the Irish coffee, hoping its warmth would soothe my apprehension. "I never want to break up with Shane. But I couldn't stand losing him for normal reasons—because of something I did or because I wasn't good enough. So I know that eventually I'll start making a bigger deal about how different we are, until one day it's true, and we'll have proven that a vampire and a human can't go the distance together."

"If any human and vampire could, it would be you and Shane. If you ask me, it's better to have a few years or decades with someone who rocks your world than a whole lifetime with someone who makes you yawn." She studied my face. "What if he headed you off at the pass?"

"By breaking up with me?" Just uttering the thought made my voice squeak.

"By proposing."

I closed my eyes and imagined the moment. He'd come up with something clever and charming and sexy, like the hero of a romantic comedy movie. He'd be almost impossible to resist.

"I'd say no," I told her.

Maybe he'd ask again and again, and I'd say no again and again, and eventually he would give up.

And then the end would begin. He'd leave home earlier in the evening, start sleeping at the station. I'd be relieved to wake up alone.

Then, one night, he would leave for good. It would hurt him too much to know I couldn't give him forever.

Just imagining it made my lungs ache. But the alternative—marrying him, growing old, and finally dying while he stayed young—stopped my breath altogether.

In the battle over my state of consciousness, the whiskey kicked the coffee's ass, and I was asleep by eleven o'clock.

I barely had the presence of mind to take off my clothes before crawling under the covers.

I didn't know Shane was there until he slipped his arms around my waist and buried his face in the back of my neck. The soft scrape of his cotton shirt against my skin said he couldn't wait to hold me, not even long enough to undress.

I twined my fingers with his and kept my voice sleepy, as if my words were a reflex, which they never were. "I love you."

He sighed, deep and soft. I tightened my grip on his hand and tried not to picture him as he was fifteen years ago this moment, lying dead in his maker Regina's arms.

His next breath was nothing but my name. I turned to face him. In the dim glow of the nightlight, I could see the mix of joy and agony in his pale blue eyes. They were dry but crinkled and a little swollen around the edges, as if he had a head cold.

Though I longed to do much, much, much more, I simply kissed him softly on the tip of his perfect nose, then on his lips. I stroked the sharp angles of his cheek and jaw with the tips of my fingers, then slid my hand into the light brown hair that grazed his neck.

"Welcome home," I said.

He kissed me then, as gently as I had kissed him, but with lips parted, his tongue beckoning. The sudden wet contact shot a bolt of desire down my spine, pooling liquid heat in my core.

Despite our month-long separation, we didn't crash together in a desperate, grabby lustfest. We touched like we were sculpting glass in our bare hands, as if pieces of us would break off if we grasped too hard.

When his clothes were gone, he guided my leg over his hip and entered me. We lay side by side, facing each other, kissing deeper, saying nothing. I crested slowly, building higher and higher over what seemed like hours. Then suddenly I was clutching Shane's shoulder, my nails sinking deep into his skin to hold myself together.

He groaned against my neck and pressed his mouth hard to my flesh. Through his lips I felt his fangs and knew that part of him wanted to pierce me, taste my blood at its sweetest, at the height of my ecstasy.

But that would have made me something more and less than his beloved. We wanted to dwell in the fragile, *human* bliss we'd created.

So he just held my body tight to his as he came. Pulsing deep inside me, breathing warm against my skin, he had as much life as I'd ever need.

5

Destination Unknown

In a sure sign of the universe's cruelty, I had to go to work later that morning. I hated leaving Shane alone on his death-iversary, but at least Dexter would be there to cheer him up with random acts of laziness.

I dragged myself up the rickety stairs of the tiny station building and knocked on the front door. It unlocked and opened only from the inside, to prevent vampire flameouts.

The knob turned and the door popped open, sticking to the frame due to the foggy day's humidity. At that moment, I happened to be in the middle of a wide, uncovered yawn.

"Oh, that's attractive." Franklin, the sales director, waved me into the office. "Come inside before flies lay eggs under your tongue."

"Welcome home to you, too," I told him as I pushed past.

"I never left," he snapped.

"Maybe you should consider it."

"Love to, but then I'd miss all the free pie."

"What free—" I stopped as I approached my desk in the small, open main office area. On the surface sat a pie with a crumb topping and what looked like a homemade crust.

I looked back at Franklin. "Did you—"

"Don't get excited." He opened the credenza next to the bricked-up fireplace and pulled out a stack of paper plates and napkins with some plastic utensils. "Aaron hates rhubarb, so I used you as an excuse to make an extra pie for Easter."

I poked my finger through the crust. Apples, too. My all-time favorite. "Is that a candied walnut topping?"

"I used whatever was lying around the house." He slapped the plates, napkins, and utensils on my desk. "Candied walnuts, the crumbs at the bottom of the dog biscuit box . . ."

I grabbed a plastic knife and sliced the pie. "You are the worst coworker ever."

"You're the worst coworker in two or three evers," he said as he took the first piece.

It was as close as we'd ever come to saying "I missed you."

David's raised voice came from behind his office door, which was shut but so thin it might as well have been open.

"Mom, we're not really eloping. I would never do that to you." A pause. "No, I promise I'll talk Lori out of it."

I decided to save his butt, though after that fib, I was more interested in kicking it. I dialed an interior extension so his phone would ring.

"Mom, I gotta take this call," he said. "Love you. Bye."

He picked up the other line. "Agent Griffin, I presume."

"Got a minute for Control talk? Or an hour or a day?"

"Yep. Bring pie."

I was cutting David a slice when he opened his office door. He stopped at the threshold, where his sharp green eyes examined my frame. "Did you get taller?"

I hid a smile, secretly proud of my unprecedented level of physical fitness. "They stretched me on the rack until I told them where I hid Dracula's bones." I hooked my pinky through the loop of my thermos and carried our pie slices into his office.

David shut the door behind us and moved quickly out of my personal space to the other side of his desk. The minuscule general manager's office was lined with shelves of music books and filing cabinets of supernatural facts. As a result, it contained approximately five square feet of floor space.

He sat in his chair and straightened his sport coat. "How was Indoc?"

"It's all against my nature." I passed him his slice of pie. "Taking orders, working on a team—not to mention learning how to kill vampires." I poured myself a pre-sugared cup of coffee from my thermos. "But Lanham said I either did what they wanted or Shane would spend the rest of his unlife north of the Arctic Circle."

David let out a heavy sigh and picked up his fork. "They drive a hard bargain. But remember, the colonel's done a lot for you. A lot for *us*. He looked the other way while you were pretending to be Elizabeth so we could keep the station."

"I know," I said, in a junior-high sullen voice. After the station owner, Elizabeth, had died for good, I'd "borrowed" her identity to keep the station from being liqui-dated. Lanham and the Control had looked the other way.

"So where did they assign you?"

I hesitated. David knew about my "anti-holy" power, so my future work wouldn't be a secret to him. And he'd been close to the Control—when he wasn't actually *in* it—all his life. Maybe he could teach me how to keep my commanders happy without compromising my few moral principles.

"Something called the Immanence Corps."

His fork halted on the way to his mouth. The morsel of pie tumbled back to the plate.

"You're fucking kidding me."

I blinked. Unlike the rest of us, David rarely used pro-fanity. It was sort of adorable. It also let us know when he was really upset.

"Why would I kid about that?"

"I was afraid this would—" He slammed down his fork, flipping a shower of candied walnuts against his shirt. "What are they thinking?"

"I don't know. What are *you* thinking? What's wrong with the Immanence Corps, besides being a band of freaks?"

"They killed my father."

The pie's crumb topping turned to sawdust in my mouth. "He was assassinated?"

"Not directly." David set his elbows on the desk and rubbed his eyes, which had grown tight with tension. "More like driven to his death."

"I thought he was an enforcement agent like you were."

"He started out that way." David sank back into his squeaky office chair and rolled his palms over the curves of its arms. "When I was really young, I didn't know what he did for a living. But I knew he was happy." His expression softened as his gaze turned distant. "Sometimes he would dance with my mom even when there was no music playing."

I stabbed another bite of pie. "So what happened?"

"He got promoted into management. His command experience snagged him a high-level directorship."

"Of the Immanence Corps?"

"No. Internal Affairs."

I frowned around my fork. "Rat Patrol? That sounds like punishment, not promotion."

David lifted an eyebrow in assent. "So we settled down here. I started high school, and he started—" He drew a heavy hand through his dark brown hair. "The only word that fits is 'fading.' Like old vampires when the modern world becomes too much for them? My dad withdrew from us. He smoked and drank more than ever. Over the next seven years, Mom and I watched that job kill him."

Though my brain burned with a million questions, I forced myself to slow down and empathize. "I'm sorry. That must've been really rough."

He nodded, then seemed to go far away. I sensed he wasn't going to say more without prompting.

"But what's that got to do with the Immanence Corps?"

"He was investigating them when he began his . . ." David searched for the right word. "Descent."

"How do you know? Aren't those cases classified?"

"He made notes. I found them after he died."

His glance shot to the lowest drawer in his filing cabinet—the one that was always locked. I interpreted this as a hint that the notes were in there for the stealing. If I asked to see them, he'd say no, since that would be against Control rules. Then I'd be officially disobeying him by reading them. This way, we could both pretend he had scruples.

"I'll keep your warning in mind," I told David, "but I don't have a choice. And maybe things have changed. Maybe new management trends have made the IC more soul friendly. That was what, thirty years ago?"

His eyes narrowed. "Fifteen. I'm only thirty-five."

Ah, a chance to change the subject. "That's a long time for your poor mother to wait for her only child's marriage. The least you can do is give her a real wedding to cry at."

He opened his mouth, then closed it. "Lori told you I wanted to elope?"

"She tells me everything. It's a best friend rule."

"I thought *I* was her best friend."

"Girls can have more than one. That's another rule."

"Wait—she tells you *everything*?"

"As much as I can stomach." I stood, balancing the pie plate on top of my thermos lid. "I have a month's worth of trivial e-mail to read, so I really should—"

"Go. Yes." David shuffled random papers over his desk, avoiding my eyes. "I have, uh, things. To do."

I shut the door on my way out, satisfied. His mind had traveled far away from the Immanence Corps.

I wish I could've said the same for mine.

Before class that night, I went to the history department to meet my professor, who also happened to be Franklin's long-term boyfriend. In any normal universe, the younger and infinitely cuter Aaron Green would be way out of my coworker's league. But a normal universe wouldn't contain vampire DJs.

When I knocked on Aaron's open door, he looked up

from his notes, holding the rim of an empty Styrofoam cup in his mouth. "Hey, Ciara," came his muffled voice. He lowered the cup and gave me a distracted smile. "Welcome home."

"It's good to be back in the real world. Thanks for hating rhubarb so Franklin could bring me pie."

"I don't hate rhubarb." Aaron picked up our latest textbook and placed it in his open briefcase. "He made that pie because he missed you."

"Then I should go away more often, and Franklin would probably be the first person to agree with that."

A corner of Aaron's mouth twitched in response. His gaze traveled around the perimeter of his desk. "What was I . . ." He scratched the back of his head, tugging the soft waves of sable hair. "I needed something else for tonight's class."

He didn't normally fit the absentminded professor stereotype. "You okay?" I asked him. "Still jet-lagged?"

"No, it's been a week since I got back from Debrecen." Aaron's fingers trickled over the surface of his desk before reaching a stack of papers held together with an alligator clip. "Ah. Here."

Now that I had his full attention, I said, "Can I talk to you about my term paper on the way to class?"

"Sure." He shrugged on his dark brown leather jacket. "Did you plan to pick a topic before the end of the semester?"

"Ha-ha. Yes, I decided on the Legion of the Archangel Michael. The Romanian Iron Guard?"

"Oh, dear." He motioned for me to precede him out of his office. "You know, just because I'm Jewish doesn't mean you get extra points for Holocaust topics."

"That's not why I picked it." I kept pace with him down the polished floors of Craddock Hall, passing under a hand-painted banner supporting the Sherwood men's lacrosse team (Division III defending champions—go Bog Turtles!). "I picked it because out of all the fascist groups, the legion was the only one that used religion as the major motivator."

He lifted his chin. "Ah, so this is part of your crusade, so to speak, to demonstrate the evils of faith."

I ignored his jibe. "You know what was so fascinating about them? They didn't believe they'd find salvation through slaughter. They didn't think there'd be thirty virgins waiting for them in heaven, or that they'd be canonized for destroying the enemy." As we descended the marble steps outside the building, I pulled up my hood against the evening breeze. "They knew that the murders they committed were a sin, and they accepted their damnation. In their minds, they were sacrificing their souls for the sake of the fatherland. Isn't that wild?"

A grunt was his only response, so I continued. "Usually people like that rationalize their evil—they convince themselves it's what God wants. These fanatics were completely unapologetic."

As we crossed the grassy commons, Aaron looked to the right, into the dark woods surrounding the western edge of Sherwood College's campus.

I continued my well-rehearsed pitch. "Most religions are all about the next world. Not your religion, of course. But Christians, Muslims, Buddhists—their earthly lives are less important than the afterlife. So for the legionnaires to sacrifice eternal salvation, their patriotism must have verged on insanity."

Aaron craned his neck, still looking back into the woods.

To see if he was paying attention, I added, "Unless they thought they were already damned. Or that they were immortal."

No response. Aaron's face seemed unusually shadowed.

Wondering how long it would take him to notice, I riffed into the ridiculous. "Did you know they drank blood in their initiations? And hey, Romania. So put it all together, and what do you get? Vampires."

A few seconds later, Aaron finally turned his head to look at me. "Wait. What?"

"Or maybe they just used the vamps as hit men."

He stopped. "Are we still talking about the Iron Guard?"

"I don't know. Are we?" I gave him a playful smirk.

Aaron shook his head. "Sorry, it's been the weirdest day of my life, which is saying a lot." He tugged me off the path so the other students could hurry by. "This morning after my workout I was on the way to Craddock Hall. You know that path through the woods that leads from the gym?"

I nodded, though I'd never voluntarily gone near any venue of structured exercise.

"I was about halfway there" —he pointed toward the line of trees to our right— "when suddenly I caught this hideous smell, like scorched meat. It got so bad I almost turned back." He lowered his voice. "That's when I saw the body."

My gut tightened. "A human body?"

"Human shaped, what was left of it. The whole corpse was burned head to foot. No clothes, no hair, no shoes."

"Just a skeleton?"

"I wish." He rubbed the side of his nose. "Its flesh was—it was welded to the bones."

"How horrible."

"I say *its* flesh because I couldn't tell if it was a man or a woman." He dropped his hand from his face. "Whoever it was, they died screaming."

I remembered something I'd read in the paper. "Maybe they were murdered and then burned. Like in a gang killing? Maybe the fire stretched the face so it looked like it was screaming."

He stared at me for a moment. "I guess hanging out with vampires, you've seen a lot."

"Unfortunately." Too much of it had involved fire.

"But gangs, here in Sherwood?" Aaron spread his arms.

"The high schools have a major heroin problem. The kids usually go into Baltimore for the drugs, but maybe the dealers are coming out here now and fighting for territory. What did the cops say?"

"Not much. One of them threw up. They took my statement and let me go." He brushed his hand over his chest. "I had to shower again and change my clothes to get the smell out. But I swear it's still in my nostrils." He checked his watch. "And now that I'm done grossing you out, it's time for class."

We headed into the building without another word. I thought of a time years ago when our little world had gone up in flames and Lori's undead boyfriend Travis had been consumed.

And unlike that corpse in the woods, when vampires burn, nothing is left—no bones, no flesh, no skin. No ashes to ashes, dust to dust.

Nothing but nothing.

6

What Is and What Should Never Be

Shane's "wake" was just starting as he and I arrived at the station that night. Five vampire DJs (all but Monroe, who was on the air and avoided social gatherings, anyway) had gathered in the basement lounge. Cigarette smoke hovered thick, making the ceiling look like an overcast sky.

His maker Regina was slow dancing with Noah to the Police song blasting over the boom box—one of the crossover tunes between Regina's punk and Noah's reggae. Their relationship was off and on (mostly off, due to Noah's being a generally decent guy). I needed a baseball-style box score to keep up with their breakups and reconciliations.

Leaning her head on his shoulder, Regina twisted one of the dreadlocks cascading down his back, her ebony-lined eyes closed in contentment. Noah's eyes were open, probably so he could avoid stepping on the rug seams.

Fifties rockabilly DJ Spencer stood at the card table, which had been shoved to the wall to make room for dancing. The refreshments were all liquid, other than a bowl of crumbled tortilla chips and a store-bought ranch dip. Spencer shifted the bottles, arranging them in a configuration only he understood. As the oldest WVMP vampire (next to Monroe), his compulsions were the strongest. Most of his brain was stuck in 1959, like the ducktail in his dark red hair.

Jim stood alone in the corner, watching the rest of us. Tonight he wore traditional hippie garb—tie-dyed shirt and flowing white bell bottoms—instead of his usual Jim-Morrison-reanimated outfit of leather pants and black shirt open to the navel.

But what Shane had told me on the phone last week was spot-on. Despite his peace-and-love getup, Jim looked less balanced than ever. His gaze shifted between me and Jeremy—the only humans in the room—as if we were the two tastiest-looking entrées on a buffet, and he was deciding which to sample first.

There was a time when Jeremy would've jumped on the plate and handed Jim the fork. He'd been enthralled with the hippie vampire since the moment they met. But over the last six months, their relationship had cooled. Now it was positively subzero.

Jim sauntered over to where Jeremy was setting up his laptop on top of our new LCD projector. He slowly brushed back the bleached blond hair that swooped over Jeremy's face.

To Jeremy's credit, he didn't flinch or spook, knowing that sudden moves can make a vampire pounce. He simply pretended Jim wasn't there, even when the vampire's hand traveled down his back, over the belt loops of his black skinny jeans, then up under his vintage Jawbreaker

T-shirt. (Jeremy's classic emo garb, along with his black guyliner, fit his radio show, which featured the music of the recently deceased decade.)

"Look at me," Jim said to him.

"I'm busy."

"Look. At. Me."

Regina stopped dancing and turned to watch them, her nostrils twitching with worry. Noah kept his hands on her shoulders to hold her back. Jim was not only volatile but stronger than anyone else in the room, due to his age.

Stronger than anyone except Spencer, that is. But the older DJ was captivated by the task of pouring drinks. He squatted to bring his eyes level with the six glasses, making sure they contained an even amount of whiskey. Spencer frowned at the glass on the right, then used a set of tongs to add another ice cube.

"What's your hang-up, man?" Jim asked Jeremy. "I said I was sorry."

"No, you didn't."

"I'm sorry. There, I said it."

"You don't even know what you're sorry for." Jeremy was fighting to keep his voice down, though the battle for privacy was long lost.

Jim made no effort to lower the volume. "I'll make it up to you. What do you want? Dinner? Drugs?"

"Nothing."

"Nothing? That's not fair, when you give me so much." He grabbed Jeremy by the back of the neck and lifted him up on his toes. Then he pressed his mouth to Jeremy's throat.

We all gasped, and Regina stepped toward them. "Jim, knock it off!"

Feeding on Humans Rule Number One: always bite below the heart. If Jim sank his fangs into Jeremy's neck while he was standing up, it could cause an air embolism that could instantly kill him.

"It's just a game we play," he growled, as Jeremy's eyes flashed with fear. "Mind your own business. He's my donor."

"He's my donor, too," Regina said.

"Not anymore." He put a possessive arm around Jeremy's waist. "I don't want to share."

I looked at Spencer, who was dribbling a few more drops of whiskey into the left-hand glass.

"Jim, take it easy," Shane said. "We know you don't want to hurt anybody." His grip on my hand belied the calm in his voice. "That would defeat the purpose, right?"

Jim's eyes turned to dark slits. "Depends which purpose you're talking about."

"Donor loyalty. You keep messing with Jeremy's head, he might cut you off."

Jim turned back to Jeremy. "Is that true? You'll cut me off? Try it, and I'll cut you off." He drew his finger across Jeremy's throat. "I've done it before, and I'll—"

Spencer moved, his dress shirt a white blur. He grabbed Jim and pinned him face-first against the wall.

"Never. Threaten. A donor." Spencer's voice was low and even. "Hear me?"

Jim struggled in his grip, with as much success as a bug in a Venus flytrap. Jeremy stood next to the projector, rubbing his neck and breathing hard.

"I asked"—Spencer slammed Jim's forehead into the wall—"if you heard me. But I missed your answer. Maybe I'm goin' deaf."

"I heard you," Jim choked out. "I wasn't threatening—"

Slam! The wood paneling buckled under the impact of Jim's head.

"Okay, I was threatening him and I'll never do it again. Swear! Now let me go."

Spencer shoved Jim's knees into the floor, so hard the foundation seemed to shake. "How about you blow out of here, son. Take the night off."

Jim sprang to his feet, swaying. "I'm not your son. And this party is Dullsville, anyway." He stumbled for the door, snapping his fingers at Jeremy. "I'll wait for you in the car."

When he was gone, we let out a collective sigh of relief. Spencer went back to the table, then handed out the drinks he'd poured. I noticed there hadn't been enough glasses to include Jim if he'd stayed.

"You are not going with him, I hope?" Noah asked Jeremy.

"No way." He gave Regina a pleading look through his round, black-rimmed glasses. "Hey, if you turned me into a vampire, I could fight him off."

"No, you couldn't," she said. "He'd still have ten times your strength. And then you couldn't escape him during the day."

He made a noise like a little kid. "I turn twenty-seven next month. It'd be perfect timing."

The DJs were each twenty-seven when they were turned. We play up that fact to the public, comparing our jocks to the Club of 27, the long list of rock stars who left this world at that mythical age.

"You don't want to die on your birthday," I told Jeremy. "People will look at your tombstone and think it's a typo."

"Shut up," he snapped.

Regina patted Jeremy's cheek. "We've had this talk before, yeah?"

"Yeah." He glanced at Shane. "Guess I have to threaten suicide to get you to save me."

Her fingers tightened on his jaw, but her voice stayed sweet. "We'll discuss it later. Over a drink?" Her gaze on his neck told me what kind of drink she meant.

"Maybe." He pulled out of her grip, only because she let him. "Maybe not." He stalked out of the room toward the back hallway. He didn't take his coat, so he was probably just headed to the bathroom in as drama queeny a fashion as possible.

"What a child." Regina yanked a packet of cigarettes from her spike-heeled police boots. "He only thinks about himself. Not one fucking thought for what it would do to me." She lit the cigarette and sucked in a harsh puff.

"He doesn't understand what you've been through." Shane rubbed her shoulder, avoiding the long prongs of her studded leather collar.

Her face softened, and she almost leaned against him for support before straightening up and turning away.

If I didn't know her progenies' history, I'd think her momentary vulnerability was an act. The first was Shane, who made her the weapon of choice in his final suicide attempt; at the last moment she changed her mind and brought him back from death with her own blood. Later she turned a female friend to protect her from an abusive fiancé. That had ended in tragedy and almost got Regina, me, and several others killed by the vengeful aforementioned dickhead.

David and Lori entered the lounge from the back

door, each carrying two stacks of clear plastic food containers.

"Leftovers from our meeting with the wedding caterer." David set the food on the end of the card table.

"You're a godsend." I opened a dish of pasta-peanut salad. "Vampires suck at snacks. I think that ranch dip expired when Spencer was still human."

"Hi, Shane." Lori sent him a cheek-puffing, trying-too-hard smile. "Happy, um. You know."

"Thanks." He leaned over to kiss her cheek. "And thanks for feeding my girlfriend."

She nodded solemnly. "Ciara maintenance is my most important job."

"Funny, mine, too."

A loud double clap snapped the stuffy air. "Ladies and gentlemen—" Regina gestured toward Jeremy, who had gotten over his snit and was now manning the projector— "time to honor our boy before his big day ends." She squeezed Shane's arm and smiled at his inscrutable face. "Glad you made it through another year alive."

Someone switched off the ancient halogen lamp in the corner as the projection screen slowly faded up on a photo of Shane.

He was alive, but not. His eyes were more sunken than in his worst blood hunger. With gaunt cheeks and sallow skin, he looked ten years older than he did as we stood there.

But sunlight glinted off his light brown hair, something I'd never seen in real life. And never would.

Canned applause sounded as glittery red block letters scrolled across the bottom of the screen: THIS IS YOUR UN-LIFE. The non-Shane vampires and David laughed.

"I don't get it," Lori whispered.

"It was a TV show back in the old days," David told us. "*This Is Your Life*."

A song played, a cover of Blind Lemon Jefferson's "See That My Grave Is Kept Clean," but not the Bob Dylan version I knew. A new photo showed Shane in a tux, standing at a sound board. Tiny lights like those of a disco ball played over his face.

The photo slid to the left; on the right half of the screen, a video appeared, of Regina at her vampiest.

"Welcome. This is my tribute to the guy who means more to me than the rest of the world put together. Shane McAllister."

She raised her fists, and the room broke into whistles and catcalls. The real-life Regina hugged Shane around the waist in a way that once would have made me burn with jealousy, before I (sort of) came to understand the maker-progeny bond.

On the screen, Regina pointed her thumb to her right, toward the picture. "That was you the night we met. Not as happy as you looked."

I felt Shane tense beside me. "She wouldn't . . ."

The next photo shifted to the center, dark, and slowly came up in light. Shane sat at a table, writing on a piece of paper, balled-up pages scattered around him, his hand crumpling his hair and his eyes filled with agony.

"That stupid note," he said under his breath. I realized this was the last picture taken of him alive.

"Turn it off," he told Regina.

Her fingers dug into his arm. "Just watch the whole thing before you judge."

"Jeremy, turn it off, or I'll put your laptop through the wall."

Jeremy shrugged. "It's station property, not mine."

Shane heaved a tight sigh and crossed his arms, his face a study in silent simmering.

The photo faded, and the song crescendoed in the last verse. The black screen held nothing but a white caption: THE FOLLOWING NIGHT.

We gasped at the transformation. Shane wore the same clothes as in the previous shot, but his gaze had sharpened to an animal stare. His muscles now bulged his T-shirt in smooth lines. His body was no longer an enemy.

The photo shifted to the left again, and Regina's face reappeared.

"Foxy dude, huh?" She blew on her nails and rubbed them against her collar. "But things didn't go so well, and you ended up here."

A long, squat brick building appeared—a Control nursing home, where vampires go when their frozen minds can no longer handle this world. A place where they can live out their many years in "peace."

Peace for humans, that is. A confused vampire is an unstable vampire, a danger to the living. I wondered how long before Jim would end up in Control custody, assuming he let them take him alive.

Some nursing homes had rehab units for infant vampires who had trouble accepting their new "life." They'd be trapped there on suicide watch until deemed sufficiently stable. Shane had spent months in one.

The onscreen Regina continued. "But then came our savior."

A photo of David replaced the building. Unlike vampires, we humans age a lot in ten years.

Lori whistled. "Wow, David, you were hot!"

"Gee, thanks for the past tense." He ran a self-conscious hand over his stomach.

"You look better now," I told him. David gave me a grateful smile, which wasn't worth Lori's jealous glare. I had so little experience with truth telling, sometimes I let it out at inappropriate times.

"Enough of that guy," Regina continued in a voice-over. "Once we came here to WVMP, Shane's popularity skyrocketed, as demonstrated by this montage."

A series of photos flashed on the screen, all of beautiful young women. Shane shifted his weight uncomfortably, and I could've sworn he was blushing, but that could've just been the red light of the exit sign.

As the hot-chick montage continued, I asked him, "Are those all vampires?"

"Um, mostly. Well, not that one. Or that one. That one's a vampire."

"And they were your girlfriends?"

"Uh." He rubbed the back of his ear. "Not exactly. A couple of them." He looked at Regina. "Where'd you get all these pictures?"

"Various places." She tugged his shirt. "I can get you copies."

"No." He glanced at me, then at the screen. "When does this stop?"

She signaled to Jeremy, who hit a key to advance to a blank screen. "In keeping with *This Is Your Life*'s format, we have a special blast-from-the-past guest."

The music changed to a Ramones tune I couldn't place (they all sounded the same to me, frankly).

"No," Shane said. "No way."

A disembodied female voice said, "June 1998. Midnight. A Denny's outside Hagerstown. We were fattening up our donors before the feast. The moment our eyes met over our humans' Grand Slam breakfasts, we knew."

"Sheena," he whispered, just as the Ramones started to sing about the eponymous punk rocker.

"Sadly," Regina said, "Sheena was not a punk rocker, and to this day is still the dippy hippie we all know and love."

A tall, pale woman glided out of the hallway's shadows. Her hair cascaded past her waist in blood-red ringlets. Beside me, Lori let out a squeak.

"Shane!" The vampire was in his arms in a flash, straddling his waist with her gypsy-skirted legs. She planted a hard, tonguey kiss on his resistant lips.

With a heroic effort, he extracted himself from her embrace. "I can't believe it's you." Over her head he staked Regina through the heart with his eyes.

"Remember my VW microbus?" Sheena dragged her nails down his chest. "How many donors did we do in that little pink sweetheart?"

"Wow. I'd forgotten all about, uh . . ."

"Althea. Her name was Althea, after the Grateful Dead song." Sheena pouted. "Her carburetor gave out last year. Now I drive a 1970 Chevelle named Bertha." She grabbed his hand. "She's so cherry. You want to see?"

"No. Thanks." He pulled his hand away and put his arm around me. "Sheena, this is Ciara."

She gave my body an appreciative once-over. "Yummy. Is she your new favorite donor?"

"She's my girlfriend."

"His *live-in* girlfriend," Lori added.

"But . . . you're human," Sheena informed me.

"And loving it," I said with a smile. I would *not* let her get to me. Shane was mine now. Besides, this girl didn't have nearly the, uh . . . well, okay, she had everything I had, and more. Possibly I was a better speller.

Jeremy saved me by switching to the next tune. Regina looked startled, then said, "Okay, next guest! It turns out, Shane didn't spend all his time spinning records and shagging babes. He saved lives."

Shane reflected my bewilderment, until the man's voice came over the ceiling speaker. "When I called the suicide hotline that night, I thought I didn't want help. I thought I just wanted some company while I checked out, you know?"

"Whoa." Shane put a hand to his head. "Luis?"

"But you talked me down, man. I mean, literally talked me down off that roof. I can never repay you, *hermano*."

A man in his forties with close-cropped black hair stepped from the hallway. This time, Shane leaped forward to greet his guest. They shared a giant, backslapping embrace.

"Come here, I want you to meet my girlfriend." Shane dragged Luis over and introduced us.

Luis pointed at Shane. "This guy risked his life to save me, and I didn't even know it."

"What do you mean?" I asked him.

"I swore if Shane called the cops, I would jump. So he found where I was, got up on the roof with me, and we talked." He shook his head at Shane. "Almost until sunrise."

I stared at the man I thought I knew. "You never told me you worked a suicide hotline."

Shane looked away. "Then you would've asked why I

stopped. Besides, what I did for Luis was totally against protocol. We weren't supposed to contact clients." He turned to Luis. "So how *are* you?"

As the guys caught up on the last five years, Sheena took my arm and steered me into a corner, her ankle bracelets jangling with every step.

"Is this for real?" Her sharp voice nearly sliced my eardrum. "You and Shane are serious? How serious?"

"We have an apartment. And a dog."

"Wowsers." She chewed her lip. "So I probably can't borrow him for the night."

"You'd have to kill me first." I immediately wished I hadn't said that.

Sheena examined me some more, hands on her hips, then peered around the lounge. "Where's Jim? I saw his car outside. I used to love that Janis. Now there was a carburetor."

"I think he's actually sitting in Janis right now. Why don't you two go for a ride? I think you're just what he needs."

"Cool!" Her green eyes practically glowed. "If I'm not back in twenty, tell Shane I said happy death day, okeydokey?" She took a lock of my hair and sniffed it hard.

"Okey." I leaned away from her. "Dokey. Bye."

"Hmm, I like it." She yanked out a strand. My teeth rattled from the pain, but I held back a cry.

When she was gone, Lori handed me a glass of wine. "Can I make a BFF request? No matter which milestone birthday I reach, you will never do this for me."

I held out my hand. "Mutual request." We shook on it.

At midnight Shane returned to me and whispered, "We have to be somewhere soon."

"We definitely do." I thought he meant bed, and I

was glad to go. Watching Sheena's and Luis's testimonies made me realize, for completely different reasons, how lucky I was to have Shane.

The others were watching the closing chapters of his Unlife So Far when we snuck out. But as I closed the door, I saw David cast his gaze our way, then lift it toward the ceiling in the direction of his office.

Shane took the stairs three at a time. "Now for the real celebration." He tugged me toward the front door.

"First, I need you to work your magic for me." I led him into David's office.

He wrapped his hands around my waist. "Hmm, we've never done it on his desk."

"Your other magic." I pointed at the filing cabinet's bottom drawer.

"I don't have my lock-picking tools."

"You can't use a paper clip?"

Shane tweaked my nose. "You watch too many movies, but I'll try." He knelt before the bottom drawer, thumbed the switch, and pulled the handle. The drawer slid out with a squeak. "Ooh, magic."

David had left it unlocked. Ha—I knew he wanted me to read this stuff.

Halfway back—protruding above the other folders, no less—was a file labeled "Immanence Corps." He might as well have left it on my desk.

"What is that?" Shane whispered.

I tucked the folder under my arm and slid the drawer shut. "Hopefully not my future."

7

Sign Your Name

"Where are we going?" I asked Shane when I noticed our car speeding out of town instead of toward our apartment. I'd been trying to read the contents of the IC folder by the light of my cell phone screen, but it was making me carsick.

"We're going away. Take a nap." He softened the volume on Monroe's current song, a peppy little Asie Payton number called "Back to the Bridge."

"Away where?"

"Don't question."

"You know that's impossible."

He glanced at me, his face tense in the blue glow of the dashboard. "I can be stubborn a lot longer than you can be curious."

Outmatched, I frowned and looked out the window into pure black. We were heading due west, toward the mountains. Toward nothing.

As I drifted into a doze, the darkness gave way to a

bright afternoon sun shining on a grassy field. I recognized it as Sherwood College's football stadium, where the Baltimore Ravens had their summer training camp.

In front of me stood a row of tackle dummies. To the left and right, my Control cohorts were doing jumping jacks with stakes in their hands. I held one, too, but kept my feet on the ground and my sights on the dummies. Each had a red heart painted on its chest.

A whistle blew. My fellow agents and I assumed fighting stances. My muscles moved with such natural grace, I knew it must be a dream.

The tackle dummies morphed into human forms as they lumbered toward us on mechanical tracks. I struck.

The dummy lurched back and my blow fell short. While I was off balance, it surged again and knocked me down. I held onto the stake, jamming my finger against the wood when my hands broke my fall.

The dummy paused, then clickety-clacked forward, shuddering on its track. This time I feigned injury until it was almost upon me. Then I rolled to my feet and slammed the stake deep into its heart.

I screamed without sound. Not *its* heart. *His* heart.

The last thing I saw was the sun shining on Shane's hair. The last thing I heard was his sigh of relief as he pulled out the stake.

I woke when the car stopped. Rubbing my face, I peered through the windshield at a wide rustic porch lit by a warm yellow lamp near the door. In the gleam of Shane's headlights, a blue-and-white sign read INTO THE NIGHT BED AND BREAKFAST.

I got out of the car and gaped at the A-frame log cabin, its windows lit with electric candles. Woods surrounded us, and a chorus of spring peepers swelled from what must have been a nearby creek.

Shane collected our bag—which he had packed without my knowledge—and his guitar case from the trunk. I followed him up the wooden stairs to the front door. A pale blue porch swing rocked in the breeze.

The door opened to reveal a couple in their mid-thirties. Both short and lean, they beamed at us with no trace of sleepiness.

"You must be Shane!" the woman said.

"Brenda?" he replied as he shook her hand.

"No, I'm Brenda," the man behind her said with a laugh. "She's Mel. People make that mistake all the time."

I was so disoriented by the late/early hour and these people's chilling normalcy that for a moment I almost called him Brenda.

We walked through a short hallway into a kitchen with a center island. Beyond the kitchen, the house opened onto an enormous yet cozy living room. The walls, floor, and ceiling were all polished wood, with long thick cross-beams extending the length of the room. A woven tapestry showing wolves on a pine-strewn snowscape hung from the brick fireplace façade that extended to the high ceiling.

"Is this place for sale?" I asked Brenda.

She laughed. "I think it might be a little bright for your man's tastes. You two will be staying downstairs, of course." Brenda beckoned us to follow her.

Mel spoke up. "There's a fruit and cheese plate to go with the champagne. Figured you might be hungry."

"Champagne?" I looked at Shane, then at the proprietors.

Brenda held up her hands. "Don't ask us what it's for."

Shane gestured for me to precede him. A muscle twitched in his jaw as I passed.

At the bottom of the stairs, Brenda opened a door, then handed me a skeleton key. "This is the only copy, for security reasons, so don't lose it."

I nodded as I pocketed the key and followed her through a short passageway to a second door. A single key meant that no one could come in during the day, letting in sunlight that would fry Shane and ruin our—

Wow.

The bedroom beyond the second door took up almost the entire level. The ceiling featured long wooden beams amid swirling white plaster. A small fireplace held a virtual fire, safe for vampires.

To the left, a set of double doors opened into a large bathroom, where I could see a Jacuzzi tub big enough for a baseball team. My skin tingled at the sight.

On the right lay a king-size four-poster covered in a plush red comforter. Soft light suffused the entire room.

It was perfect. I couldn't wait for them to get the hell out.

"If this is suitable," Mel said, "we'll just leave you alone."

"We don't want to keep you up." I hoped the ceiling was soundproof.

"You won't," Brenda said. "The ceiling is soundproof."

With a final good night, Mel and Brenda made themselves scarce.

I went to the bed and grasped one of the posts. "Very sturdy. I hope you brought the handcuffs."

Without responding, Shane pulled his classical guitar from its case, then sat in the corner armchair and began to tune it.

"This is so cool—a vampire-friendly B and B!" I bopped over and gave him a quick kiss. "Talk about a niche market."

"Yeah. Let me focus for a second, okay?"

I pressed my lips together and piled a small plate with fruit, cheese, and slices of baguette, while behind me Shane tuned and fretted. Finally he took a pair of deep, slow breaths, muttering to himself in words I couldn't decipher.

"Come sit down," he said finally.

I moved to the brown-silk-upholstered ottoman in front of his chair, pulled it back a few feet to give him room, and sat with my plate upon my knees.

Fingers poised above the strings, he looked at me for a long moment. "I wrote this for you."

My heart halted, then sped up. He'd never written a song for me—never written a song, period. One effect of a vampire's temporal adhesion was difficulty learning new things, whether it was how to surf the Internet or how to love contemporary music. Shane's relative youth and his involvement with me helped him overcome the natural vampire stickiness, and while he wasn't exactly downloading the latest Kings of Leon tracks, he'd at least started playing music from the twenty-first century.

But concocting something new out of his own head and heart? Vampires didn't do that. Creation was an act of the living.

My food forgotten, I watched him play. I never tired of seeing his hands travel over the fretboard and the strings, imagining and remembering how they felt on my skin. He used no pick, only his nails and fingertips, stroking and coaxing beauty into existence.

When he started to sing, I closed my eyes.

First he sang of the past—our disastrous first encounter that almost ended in my death; our hands-off, one-hundred-percent-platonic first real date; and the first night we made love, after another vampire had almost taken my life. How Shane's own life had changed.

Then he moved to the present, extolling our mismatched, underground existence and making Dexter the first vampire dog to be immortalized in song. Shane sang of how he tried so hard to be normal.

The last verse told of the future, of silver hair and sallow skin. Of my deathbed and grave, and how he would be there, at my side. Until the end.

Tears squeezed out between my lids and rolled in swollen streams down my cheeks. I held back a sniffle, wanting this room to hear no sound but his promise.

He offered me his life, eternal youth, and timeless strength, wrapped in a love that would transcend the ravages of human fragility and vampire eccentricity.

We could do this, he was saying. He had faith in us. I'd never had faith in anything.

He stroked the last chord and let it echo against the wooden walls. Then he set down the guitar, leaning the headstock against the chair.

When he finally looked at me, his eyes held no fear.

"Do you know what comes next, Ciara?"

I opened my mouth, but could fit no words around my incoherent croak.

Shane sank to his knees before me, then reached into

the pocket of his flannel shirt. When his hand opened, it revealed a velvet jewelry box. Small. Black. Square.

My throat closed up.

He took my hand, and I met his gaze as he spoke. I'd been dreading this moment for years, the moment we'd move forward or fall apart. The beginning of the end.

"That song exhausted my supply of pretty words, so these are all I have left." He opened the box. "Ciara, will you marry me?"

I kept my eyes on his face and didn't even glance at the ring. It didn't matter how big or beautiful it was. My answer would be the same.

"Yes."

His eyes reflected my own shock. "Are you crazy? I mean, are you sure?"

"Yes. And yes."

I was sure. Sure this was insane. Sure it was unheard-of, for a million damn good reasons.

Sure it was what I wanted.

He looked at me sideways. "But are you sure you're sure?"

I hesitated, asking my gut if I was saying yes for fear of losing him or from the desire to make him happy or the rebellious urge to prove the world wrong.

My gut replied with a thousand celebratory butterflies.

"I want to be with you." I held his face between my trembling hands. "As long as I live."

The tension lines between his brows vanished. "Amazing," he whispered, then kissed me hard, with a deep, human sigh. I reveled in the feel of his lips against mine, and didn't care that they'd be the only lips I'd ever taste again. If I lived to be a hundred, my life with him would be too short.

He pulled away, face contorting into a half smile, half grimace. "I can't believe you said yes right away. I had this whole long argument planned out." His words tumbled over one another, his eyes gleaming with adrenaline. "I was going to keep you awake for days until you said yes out of sleep-deprivation-induced insanity."

I laughed, then finally looked down at the ring in his hand.

"Oh my God!" My plate flew off my lap, scattering fruit and cheese cubes across the rug. I snatched the jewelry box out of his hand. "Sapphires?" A pair of them, marquise cut, sat on either side of the round diamond. "They're my favorite."

"They are?"

"As of now."

Shane brushed my hair off my cheek. "I got them because they reminded me of your eyes." He winced. "Wow, that sounded cheesy. Can I take it back and say something macho like, 'They were on sale'?"

"Whatever." I reached for the ring, but he grabbed it first with supernatural speed.

"Uh-uh," he said. "I'm supposed to put it on you."

I stretched out the fingers of my left hand. "I didn't know you were such a stickler for tradition."

"I knelt, didn't I?"

"Yeah, but on both knees instead of one."

"I knew something was off." He shifted to set one foot down, then slid the ring onto the proper finger. "Anyway, happy engagement," he said with mock brusqueness.

I held the ring up to the fake firelight. It was a little loose. "Did you guess my size?"

"I borrowed its counterpart." He touched the silver

band with the Celtic knot on the third finger of my right hand. "Your left hand must have skinnier fingers."

"You stole my ring?" I smacked his chest. "You knew I was looking for it. My mom gave that to me."

"And I found it for you in the garbage disposal, remember?"

"Bad boy." I curled my fingers into the fabric of his shirt. "You're a bigger con artist than I am."

He took my right hand and slipped off the Celtic knot band.

"What are you doing?" I asked him.

"I want to see you wearing nothing but my ring." His fingers slid under my sweater, the thumb and pinky catching on the hem to lift it up. "Now."

"Shouldn't we open the champagne?"

"Champagne second. Naked first." He pulled the sweater over my head, then undid my belt. "Now's a really bad time to deliberate over sex like an old married couple."

My dread of normality jump-started a desperate desire. "Then it's a really good time to fuck me like a stranger."

Shane scooped me up, one arm under my knees, then rushed me to the bed like it was a medical emergency. He stripped off my pants, then his own clothes, with rough, urgent motions, his hands shaking with something more than desire.

He stretched out above me. I ran my hands up his lean, muscular back and opened myself to him, ready to chase away our fears with a bout of seriously savage sex.

But instead of beginning, he stopped and stared down at my face. Something passed between us, a silent acknowledgment that things had changed.

Under his gaze I felt more naked than ever, but I didn't look away. My fingertips brushed the underside of his jaw. "I love you."

His breath caught, the way it always did when I said those words first. Then he leaned down and kissed me softly, almost chastely. "I love you, too." He rolled onto his side next to me, then brought my left hand to his mouth. "We should have that champagne first."

"It is sort of a special occasion." I slid my ring finger between his lips. "But you have to drink it out of my belly button."

Morning twilight came at 6:16 a.m. I knew this not because I saw the approaching sun, since no shred of light crept past the shrouded window above our bed. I knew this because by necessity, the times were branded into our brains. Such was life with a vampire, and such would be my life forever.

After the poignant lovemaking, the celebratory Jacuzzi soak, then the dirty sex of jubilation, my muscles felt as liquid as the champagne, the last of which Shane was pouring into our glasses.

"I was sure you would say no." He clinked his half-full glass against mine. "I thought about offering you a choice between the ring and a wooden stake but figured that was a little macabre, even for me."

My hand tightened on the glass. "If you were convinced I'd say no, then why did you ask?" Maybe he didn't want to marry me after all.

"What can I say? I'm a dreamer." He trailed his fingertips, cold from the champagne bottle, along my arm. "Can we set a date?"

My chest constricted. An actual date would be a wall in the fourth dimension of time, beyond which lay the foggy valley of married life.

I took my first bold step toward that wall. "Whenever."

"I was thinking this winter, when the nights are long."

"But then I'll be working for the Control and we won't be able to go on a honeymoon."

"How about the next winter, after you're done?"

"That's almost two years from now."

"You in a hurry? Want to get it over with before you change your mind?"

"No, but I know from Lori that the longer a couple has to plan, the more complicated and expensive it gets. I do not want a three-day wedding extravaganza."

"No bridalpalooza, I promise." He rested his head on my pillow, close enough I could feel the sweep of his lashes against my temple. It seemed as if he were holding his breath, so I knew he was about to get serious again. "Ciara, you didn't say yes just to make me happy, did you?"

"I did it to make *me* happy. That's the good part about being with a selfish person. You know I'm never doing anything out of nobility, because I have none."

"Bullshit." He stroked the side of my hip. "You do a million things for me."

"Like what?"

"You keep your clothes organized in our closet so it doesn't distract me."

"Easier for me to find stuff. I'm half conscious when I get dressed for work."

"You never complain when I rearrange the spice rack in mysterious ways."

"Since all I ever use is salt and pepper, who cares?"

He went still again. "You risked your soul so I could have my family."

"Don't be dramatic." I skimmed my palm over his arm, as if I could brush away his concern. "The Control is just a job, not an adventure." I tried not to think of David's warning about the Immanence Corps and the folder of secrets in my overnight bag. "It'll be over before you know it, and I promise I'll bring my soul to our wedding."

There it went, that hitch in my throat again, at the sound of the word "wedding," but this time it wasn't fear. I felt a strange bubbly excitement at the thought of trying on gowns and tasting cakes and choosing a song for our first dance. Thus was the girly girl in me born.

I shoved her down and stepped on her face. "I'm not changing my name," I told Shane.

"I don't expect you to, especially since I'll have to change my identity one day."

"Ooh, can I help you pick a new name?"

"You can help, but I get final say. It's me we're naming, not a baby."

"Thank God."

His fingers tightened on my waist. "You don't care that we'll never have children? You're absolutely sure?"

"I've never wanted kids." I wove a lock of his hair through my fingers. "Except once when I went to a baby shower and saw how much stuff this girl got. But that feeling went away like an hour later."

He propped his head on his hand again and examined my face. "How can you not want kids?"

"Do you?"

"I would if I were human."

"Then it's a good thing you're a vampire, so we don't have to fight about that." I pressed my face into his chest. "Kinda funny. I'm not marrying you in spite of the undead thing, but partly because of it."

He ran his hand down between my shoulder blades, then across the planes of my lower back, stealing the last bit of tension in my muscles. Sleep tugged hard at my consciousness, slamming my eyelids shut.

"It's not funny," he whispered. "It's a miracle."

I meant to mumble, "I don't believe in miracles," my usual reflex on hearing that word. Maybe it was the exhaustion, or the champagne, or the press of Shane's lips against my cheek. But somehow, on the way out of my mouth, that familiar refrain lost the word "don't."

8

Gimme Some Truth

I woke around noon, due to the demands of various abdominal organs. My head informed me that I was not hungover—a rare feat where champagne was concerned. So I made myself a fruit, cheese, and bread plate, along with a pot of coffee, then settled down on the silk-embroidered sofa with the Immanence Corps file David had let me steal.

The report's findings were printed on Control Internal Affairs letterhead. The cover page contained the date (October 4, 1994), the author's name (Jonathan Fetter), and the title:

Immanence Corps' Project Blood Leash: Violation of Control Precept 1

"Cooperation before coercion," I mumbled by reflex.

The executive summary outlined the Internal Affairs's concerns. The Immanence Corps had been researching ways to secretly manipulate the movements of all vampires, including nonhostiles. Including vamps who worked for the Control.

In these efforts, the IC had deployed various sacred objects—religious artifacts and symbols like crosses and Stars of David; holy water, relics, etc. They'd hidden them in secret compartments incorporated into certain buildings at Control headquarters, then observed the vampires agents' reactions. Watched them as if they were rats in a maze.

Basically, Project Blood Leash had treated vampires like rabid animals instead of the rational individuals they'd proven themselves to be. And like any rational individuals, some vampires had taken issue with being treated like puppets. People had gotten hurt. Go figure.

Fetter's point was that the first precept wasn't a cozy, charitable impulse to be tossed aside when inconvenient. When dealing with dangerous creatures who could be reasoned with, it just plain worked. Due to their long history of being hunted and staked, vampires tended to get "up in arms" (I would've written "up in fangs") at any hint of organized repression.

I perused the report through two cups of coffee and three saucers of fruit and cheese. I was surprised to find that one of the Immanence Corps's primary missions was the development and deployment of holy weapons. So I was right. They wanted me only for my freakiness, not my brains or talents.

I couldn't wait to get out.

One of the report's final recommendations was to install a senior vampire to head the Immanence Corps, to ensure they never stepped out of bounds again. Tina had said her father was in that position but hadn't mentioned he was a vampire. Maybe the Control hadn't followed that recommendation.

Or maybe she didn't want to talk about it. I couldn't blame her. Being raised by people who never aged and drank human blood to survive had to be even weirder than being raised by a pair of con artists.

And if I was suspicious of all preachers because my dad was a bad one, maybe that explained Tina's hostility toward vampires. I dreaded meeting my new commander more than ever.

My coffee was cold and so was I, so I crawled back under the covers with Shane, bringing my cell phone with me.

He slid his arm around my waist. "You don't have to call the office," he murmured against the back of my shoulder. "David knew I was taking you away."

"I'm not calling anyone. I'm checking e-mail." I waited while the phone connected to the mobile messaging service. "Did David know you were proposing?"

"By now he probably knows. I told Lori."

"Why?"

"Your parents aren't around to ask for your hand."

I scrolled through my inbox. "Are you from the 1990s or the 1890s?"

"I wanted her opinion on whether you'd say yes."

I opened my mouth to ask him Lori's answer, but the subject line of the next e-mail froze my breath.

SAFETY ALERT: ASSAULT DEATH ON WEST CAMPUS

I tapped the e-mail to read it, assuming it was about the burned body Aaron had found.

Shane shifted against me. "Don't you want to know what she said?"

"Oh my God." I sat up.

"What's wrong?"

"One of my old professors was murdered yesterday morning on campus. I had her for freshman comp. She was so sweet."

"Freshman comp? What was her name?"

"Professor Haldeman. We called her Susan, because she was so close to our age. She couldn't have been much more than thirty when she died."

After a long, silent moment, Shane said, "She would have been thirty-one."

I turned to see his face illuminated by the white glow of my cell phone screen. "You knew her?"

"She's one of Jim's donors." He rolled onto his back and stared at the ceiling. "She used to be mine."

I caught my breath. "You traded her to Jim when we started going out?" Since the vampiric bite was such an intimate encounter, Shane had stopped seeing all of his female donors before becoming my boyfriend.

He nodded slowly. "How was she killed?"

My thumb shoved the text up and down on the screen. "It doesn't say how. I guess the police are withholding that—Whoa, wait a minute. Her body was in the woods where Aaron found that human torch yesterday." I dropped my hands into my lap. "I guess it wasn't a gang murder after all, unless she was a witness and they killed her to keep it quiet."

Shane covered his face with both hands. "I can't believe she's dead." His voice filled with pain.

I set my phone on the nightstand, then curled my arm over his chest. "I'm sorry." The vampire-donor bond was often intense. "Were you and Susan lovers?"

"Sometimes." He pulled me close. "She was with Jim, too, once she became his donor."

"When did you start, uh, biting her?"

"I found her in 2001, right after she moved here. We met at O'Leary's pub."

2001—the year I started college. A sick feeling oozed through my stomach as I realized that while she was teaching me about misplaced modifiers, she'd been giving blood to and sleeping with my future fiancé.

"Was it hard to give her up?"

"For you?" He stroked my arm. "Nothing was hard to give up."

I snuggled closer, wishing I could truly believe him. He'd sacrificed so much to be with me. And in return, I wouldn't even feed him. From now on, I would only get old and weak, every day drifting further from his immortality, until one night he'd wake to find me gone forever.

I'm told Lori's shriek could be heard all the way to Harrisburg.

"Ciara!" She hurled herself into my arms, knocking me back against the sharp edge of my desk. "I can't believe you said yes!"

"I sort of can't either." More than thirty-six hours later, our engagement still didn't feel real.

Her eyes bugged out as she lifted my left hand to her face. "This ring is soooo gorgeous. Tell me how it happened. Every. Last. Detail."

David poked his head out of his office. "You guys okay? I was on the phone and I heard screaming."

Lori yanked my hand in his direction, almost dislocating my shoulder. "She said yes! Ciara and Shane are getting married!"

For a moment his face froze, his gaze adhered to the ring. Then he blinked and gave a tortured smile. "Wow. That's . . ." He nodded. "That's great. I'm very happy for you." His voice was flat.

"I get to be maid of honor." Lori shook my arm. "Right?"

"Of course. But you'll be married by then, so technically you'll be a matron of honor."

"Ew, I feel old already. David, tell her you won't turn me into a matron."

He gave her a look of distracted affection, then turned back to me. "Did you hear about the murder on campus?"

Lori put her hands to her mouth. "Susan Haldeman—remember her, Ciara? Her comp class was where we first met."

I watched David's reaction, wondering if he knew Susan had been Jim's donor. "Have they said yet how she died?"

Lori shuddered. "I called my contact at the state police—you know, Travis's old friend?"

I nodded. Her late boyfriend had been a detective, and Lori had considered continuing his business before realizing she wasn't the sneaky sort. Instead she decided to become our full-time sales/marketing/office associate, aka godsend.

"It was massive trauma," she said. "Apparently she lost a lot of blood from what looked like bite wounds."

My knees shook. "Like a vampire bite?"

"They think it was a mountain lion, because—" Lori closed her eyes hard. "Oh God, it's awful."

"The bleeding wasn't just from the bites," David said. "It was from loss of limbs."

This time my knees gave out entirely. I sank into my office chair. "Does Sherwood even have mountain lions?"

"Not normally." He slid a comforting arm around Lori's shoulders. "There's a roadside zoo about an hour away."

My hackles rose. "That craphole that keeps animals in tiny cages? I thought they were under investigation for cruelty."

"The police are looking into whether an animal might have escaped," David said. "That place is so shady, they might not report it unless it was an exotic like an elephant or a wildebeest."

I crossed my arms. "So if a cougar escaped, no one would know until it killed somebody."

David glanced at the basement door, the one that led to the lounge, the studio, and the vampires' apartment. "Let's hope that's what happened."

Lori looked at her watch and sighed. "I have a sales call in Baltimore at ten." She gave David a quick kiss before picking up her purse and the client binder. "Remember, we're meeting the wedding DJ for lunch."

"Have you guys settled on a first dance song?" I asked.

"We did," David said, "but this time we're not telling anyone. No more wedding by committee."

Musical opinions at the radio station were as plentiful and heated as spices in a Thai kitchen. Shane and I would have to use the same tactic to keep the scoffers at bay.

When the front door closed behind Lori, David and I said nothing at first. I didn't know which secret to avoid harder—Jim's relationship to the murder victim, or the Project Blood Leash information David had funneled to me.

"Speaking of secrets," he said.

"Were we?"

"Lori made a sales appointment for the twenty-sixth."

Out of habit, I jumped out of my seat and moved closer, then remembered she was out of hearing range. "The day after she thinks you're getting back from the Bahamas?"

"Yep. So I need you to take the appointment for her, or at least reschedule it."

I bounced on my toes, a touch of wedding giddiness returning. "I wish I could see her face when she finds out you're going to Greece instead of coming home." I squeezed his arm. "You are the coolest fiancé ever."

He looked at my left hand. "Even now?"

"I'll let you know." I rotated the loose ring around my finger. "I wish Shane and I could go somewhere sunny for our honeymoon."

"Ciara." David reached for me, then seemed to think better of it. "You can't marry a vampire."

I put my hands on my hips, armed with the facts. "Legally, Shane's alive. He has his original social security number, he has a current driver's license, and he pays taxes. As far as the government is concerned, he's just a young-looking forty-two-year-old."

"It's not about the law, it's about reality. You'll age like a human, but he won't."

"He doesn't care about that. He says he'll love me when I'm wrinkly and incontinent, and I believe him."

"I believe him, too. But I watched Elizabeth change. She went from a warm, loving human to a cold shell of a monster."

"Shane is nothing like Elizabeth was. Besides, I've

only known him as a vampire, so there's no humanity for me to miss."

"You haven't known any of them long enough to understand what time does to them. Over the last decade, I've seen them fossilize. I've watched their compulsions get worse."

I folded my arms, giving in to defensiveness. "And I've lived with Shane for two years. I love his idiosyncrasies."

"It's only the beginning." David clenched his fists. "What will you do when he fades to Regina's level, or God forbid, Spencer's? What if he gets erratic like Jim? Have you thought of that?"

A shiver snaked up my spine at the thought of Shane drifting back and forth over the border of sanity. "Maybe he won't get that bad. Since he's been with me, he's learned a lot of new things. He even sends text messages. And last week he was listening to the Killers."

"Which CD?"

I shifted my weight. "*Hot Fuss*."

"That's six years old."

"But nine years newer than Shane's vampireness. You don't see Spencer listening to Jimi Hendrix, or Regina tuning into Limp Bizkit."

"Ciara, listen." David's voice dipped. "Be Shane's girlfriend, live with him as long as you can stand it, but don't take this step. If you could look ten or twenty years down the road, you'd see all the things he can't give you."

"Like kids? I don't want them. They scare me. So I can't babysit yours until they learn to change their own diapers."

"Maybe you feel that way now, but by the time you hit thirty—"

"I'll, what, hear my biological clock ticking? Why can't you understand that I don't want the same things other people want? Stop putting yourself in my place." I realized I was nearly yelling, so I softened my tone. "Whether you agree with my choice or not, please be a friend and support me."

"I wouldn't *be* a friend if I supported you. I admire your optimism, but between this and the Immanence Corps, you're coming off way too innocent."

"Me, innocent? You're talking to a former grifter. I get the world, David. I get how tricky it is." I went back to my desk. "Now if you'll excuse me—"

"You don't get anything. You think because you were a criminal, you've seen it all. You think you know all the ways people can be hurt." He stalked away, into his office. "But you have no idea."

9

Mr. Brightside

At lunchtime, I dug into my homemade sandwich, determined to plow through another dozen business e-mails now that I was finally alone.

Franklin appeared from behind his office door. He spoke on his cell phone as he put on his suit jacket. His voice pitched high and lilting in what he called his "faux faggot" act, which meant he was talking to a client.

"Oh, that would be fabulous!" He shifted the phone to his other ear and tried to find his other sleeve, while giving me an eye-rolling smirk. "I absolutely cannot wait to hear your ideas for the new spots. Of course we can talk bulk discounts. You know I live to please." He motioned firing a pistol to the side of his head. "See you at three . . . yes, with bells on!"

He slapped his phone shut and shoved his arm into the remaining sleeve. "Welcome back again. I hope at some point you'll consider working two days in a row."

I held up my sandwich. "I'm not even taking off for lunch."

"Good, because I'm meeting Aaron." He smoothed down his thinning blond hair. "How was your kidnapping?"

"Shane and I got engaged."

"Huh." Franklin turned to fetch his coat from the rack, which was currently a sturdy cardboard cutout of Jerry Garcia making a peace sign. "When's the wedding? I'm busy that night."

"I was hoping you'd be my maid of honor."

"Sorry, I'm allergic to taffeta," he said without missing a beat. "And what about Lori?"

"David will probably make her boycott the wedding."

"What do you mean?" Franklin asked in a flat voice that told me he didn't care—or at least wanted to give that impression.

"He kinda freaked about me marrying Shane. I don't know why."

Franklin stared at me. "You don't know why."

"No."

"There's a thing called an EQ—emotional quotient." He fished in his pocket for his keys. "EQ is like an IQ, but instead of intelligence, it measures how in touch you are with emotions. Your own, but especially others'."

"Yeah?"

A knock came at the front door, and Franklin moved toward it. "You're an emotional retard."

"That's impossible. I was a con artist. I know what makes people tick."

He put his key in the lock to open it. "Friends aren't people."

The phone rang. I looked at the screen. "Your line, and your favorite client."

He cursed as he opened the door for Aaron. "I gotta take a call. Don't let Ciara give you any ideas."

Aaron stepped in as Franklin hurried back to his office. "Nice to see you, too. Dearest darling."

Picking up his phone, Franklin gave his boyfriend the finger.

I locked the front door. "Remind me again why you put up with his crap?"

"Same reason you do. We know that his affection is inversely proportional to his courtesy." Aaron gasped and intercepted my hand. "What's this? You got engaged?"

"I did. To Shane, obviously."

His face lit up into a smile. "Congratulations!" He tugged me over to Lori's desk and examined the ring under her lamp. The stones shot blue and white sparks of light across the wall. "Your man has exquisite taste." He winked at me. "In rings, too."

"David thinks I'm crazy."

"He's just jealous."

"No way. He's totally in love with Lori."

"Not jealous of Shane. Wow, conceited much?" When I blanched, he gave me a playful tap on the shoulder. "I mean he's jealous of you. Didn't David used to have a vampire girlfriend?"

"Elizabeth." I looked into Franklin's office, which had once belonged to the former station owner. "She wasn't his girlfriend after she turned. More like his parasite."

"So it didn't work between them, but it's working for you and Shane. When David sees you two, he realizes he can't blame their breakup on the fact that she was a vampire. You've succeeded where he failed."

"So you don't think marrying Shane is crazy?"

"It's definitely crazy. But a good crazy, the kind most people wish they had the guts to be." Aaron moved to the whiteboard on the wall, where the day's morning and evening twilight times were written. "Let me tell you a little story." He uncapped two pens and sketched a yellow male symbol next to a green female symbol. "I spent the first two decades of my life letting the world tell me whom I should love. Did I find acceptance by dating women? You betcha." He drew a happy face next to the female symbol. "But did I find happiness? Hell, no." He drew a frowny face next to the male.

"Then one day when I was twenty years old, I got hit by a bus. Literally." He uncapped the black and red pens and started to draw. "Go ahead, laugh. I was riding my bike, not watching where I was going. Due to the immutable laws of Newtonian physics, I was transformed into a splotch on the pavement." He stepped back to reveal tire tracks drawn over the male symbol, with drops of blood spurting out.

"How horrible. Nice visuals, though."

"Thanks, they teach that at Yale. Anyway, I was in the hospital for ten months, a rehab facility for another year." He added a grimace to the frowny face. "Every moment when I could forget the pain, which was about three or four seconds a day, I vowed that if I survived, I wouldn't hide who I was anymore." With the blue pen, he sketched another male symbol next to the first and drew a happy face between them.

"Talk about clarity."

"We have to grab our happiness where we can, when we can, and let the future take care of itself." He tapped the board. "Because the future might come in the form of a Thirty-fourth Street crosstown."

"Lesson learned, professor." I lowered my voice. "Would you marry Franklin if you could? It's only a matter of time before they make it legal here."

He recapped the pens one by one and returned them to the board's aluminum shelf. "I'm up for tenure next year. If I don't get it, I'll have to find another job, which means moving, which means . . . asking him to come with me. Maybe."

"And if you do get tenure and don't have to move?"

"Then we'll probably grow old here the way we are." He smiled, but his eyes were tinged with sadness.

In his office, Franklin slammed the receiver into the cradle. "Fucking idiots!"

"What's wrong?" I asked him as he stormed into the main office.

"Nothing. I just like calling people that." He reached for Aaron's hand. "How are you? I'm a bitch today."

"I know." Aaron gave him a quick kiss as they headed out. "But you're my bitch."

"Ugh, you make it sound like we're in prison."

"Some days that's exactly how it feels."

"I walked right into that one, didn't I?"

Aaron turned to wave at me as Franklin unlocked the front door. "See you tonight. Congrats again."

"Don't encourage her," Franklin said. "Another year of centerpiece discussions and I'll shoot myself."

I watched them walk hand in hand to Aaron's car, arguing over whether to hit Panera Bread or try that new kebab shack on Main Street. Then I closed and locked the door, pondering the irony that I could marry a dead man but not a live woman.

Aaron's illustration caught my eye on the way back to my desk. Especially the part with the blood.

I called Shane, hoping he was still awake. To catch up on production work, he was spending the day in the DJs' apartment downstairs, where he still had his old room.

"Hey," he answered, "it's the future not Mrs. McAllister."

"Did I wake you?"

"I like when you wake me. Want to meet in the supply closet for a quickie?"

"In the abstract, yes. But I need you to look up something for me. You guys keep records of the donors you visit, right?"

He was silent for a moment. "I know what this is about."

"Can you tell me—"

"Got it," he said quickly. "Receipts from the last WVMP gig. They're around here somewhere."

"You can't talk?" I whispered.

"Right. I'll send you that information as soon as I find it."

"Just text it to me if you can't say it out loud."

He hung up. I continued to eat my sandwich, though I couldn't taste much.

Soon my phone vibrated with a text from Shane:

JIM W/SUSAN SUN NITE. B4 SHE DIED.

Before I could unfreeze my fingers to respond, another message followed.

LET US HANDLE IT.

10

There Is a Light That Never Goes Out

When I got to class that night, Aaron was sitting behind the desk, reading the newspaper.

"Good evening," I said in a bad Bela Lugosi impersonation. "Heh, get it? Because of my paper?"

He looked up and nodded. "Okay. Yeah." Then he put his head back on his hand and continued to peruse . . . the comics? His usual reading material was the *New York Times* international section, if not *The Economist*.

"Are you all right?"

"I think I'm getting a cold." He gave a wan smile that even in his muted state managed to score in the ninety-ninth percentile of Stunning. "You'd better stand back if you don't want to catch it."

I held my breath and hurried to a desk in the rear of the room. With Lori's bachelorette party in two days, I couldn't afford to be sick. Doing body shots and stuffing dollar bills in G-strings requires lots of stamina, or so I'd heard.

I reviewed the assigned reading, trying to blot Jim and

his possible heinous deed out of my thoughts, while the other students filed in.

"Where were you?" asked a sharp voice beside my desk.

I looked up to see Turner Jamison, who could've been the long-lost fourth Jonas Brother. He was leaning away from me like I might explode.

"Job training."

"Oh." He slumped behind the desk next to me. "I thought maybe you had the swine flu-monia."

"Nope. But thanks for caring." I turned back to the chapter on Montenegro.

"I guess you wouldn't be contagious anymore, anyway." He pulled an economy-size bottle of antiseptic gel from his book bag. "But just in case." He poured out a huge glop and rubbed it on his hands and forearms.

"Well, doctor, you're all prepped for surgery."

He glared at me. "You'd be germophobic, too, if your little brother almost died of the flu."

My face flushed hot. "Sorry. Is he okay now?"

"Finally. He spent a week in ICU."

Aaron cleared his throat at the front of the class. I turned toward him for the beginning of the lecture.

His voice rasped like an emery board across a broken fingernail. As he leaned on the podium, sweat beaded on his temples, turning his dark brown hair black against his paling skin.

"Last week—" He cleared his throat again and took a long draft from a water bottle. "Sorry. Last week we discussed the medieval roots of the Bosnian conflict. If you've read chapters three through six of—" He stopped, breathless, and wiped his forehead. Then he focused on the textbook on the podium. "Of the Berkower book, you'll note that he makes an interesting point about the stabilizing influence of the Ottoman Empire."

Aaron rounded the podium and began to speak in a stronger voice, though nothing near his usual animation. I shared a worried glance with Turner, then wrote down the gist of Aaron's point.

"But what Berkower misses," Aaron continued, his breath growing shallow, "is the very essence of the conflict. In my opinion . . . it would be inaccurate and . . . irresponsible to overlook the inherent . . ."

Thud! I looked up to see Aaron clutching the podium, trying to stay upright. His mouth opened and closed, gasping for breath.

I leaped out of my seat to help, but two students in the front row got there before me, breaking Aaron's fall as he collapsed.

"He's burning up," said Pamela, holding his head. "Krista, call 911. Allie, go get a cold cloth. Make that lots of cold cloths."

I pushed past the small crowd of classmates to kneel by Aaron's side. When I took his hand, it seemed to singe my skin, and I almost dropped it. "I'll call Franklin," I told him, "have him meet you at the hospital."

Aaron looked past me, as if my voice had come from across the room. "Hot."

"You, yes. Franklin, not so much." My attempt at an encouraging smile faded quickly.

"Ughhhh." Aaron jerked his hand out of mine and started to claw at his stomach like a flea-ridden dog. His other hand tugged at the collars of his V-necked sweater and button-down dress shirt beneath. His skin flamed as red as a sunburn.

"What's wrong with him?" asked Mark, the guy on his other side. "Pam, you got a clue?"

"I'm just a bio major," she snapped back at him. "I won't be a doctor for like five years."

"Let's think." I kept my voice steady. "He's itchy, has a high fever and a rash."

"Oh my God." Lauren covered her mouth. "This is just like I was sophomore year." She looked at her roommate. "When I had chicken pox, remember?"

I dropped Aaron's hand. "Chicken pox?"

"Help . . ." Aaron finally won the battle with his shirt, jerking it out of his waistband. He shoved it up and scratched deliriously. Across his taut abdomen lay a crooked line of red bumps, their centers swelling white.

"That looks like what I had." Lauren's voice shook. "But I didn't get every symptom the same day. By the time I got those spots, I didn't have a fever anymore."

I stood slowly, holding my breath.

"Maybe it's not chicken pox," Mark said. "Shit, maybe it's smallpox."

"Smallpox is extinct." Pamela placed her folded sweatshirt under Aaron's head.

"Terrorists might have it."

"And release it here in Sherwood instead of a big city? Brilliant tactic."

"It could be a test run. Or maybe he got it when he was in Hungary last week. They probably have terrorists there."

I backed away toward my seat, fear stiffening my limbs into slow-mo.

Krista slapped shut her phone. "Ambulance is on the way."

Mark turned to Lauren. "You didn't have chicken pox

until you were a sophomore in college? How is that possible?"

"I was homeschooled," she said, "and my parents thought vaccines cause autism or something. So I almost died."

"Shut up!" Pam hissed. "Professor Green's still conscious. He can probably hear you."

I finally reached my desk, where I fumbled in my bag for my cell phone.

Turner had already shoved his books into his backpack. "Good luck," he muttered to me as he hurried for the door.

I pressed the 4 key, Franklin's speed dial. He answered gruffly as always. "What?"

"Has Aaron ever had chicken pox?"

"I have no idea. Why?" He drew in a sharp breath. "Is he sick?"

"Fever, itching, rash. We called 911. Can you meet him at the ER?"

"I'm on my way." I heard the jingle of keys in the background. "Why do you think it's chicken pox?"

I told him what Lauren had said.

"I have no idea if he's had it." Franklin shifted the phone. "I thought everyone got it when they were kids."

My throat clenched around my words. "I haven't had it."

Through the front door of my apartment I heard the distinctive introductory riff of the Pixies' "Here Comes Your Man." Shane was rehearsing for his next gig with Vital Fluid, the band he'd formed with one of his donors and another human.

I stopped for a moment to listen, even though it was drizzling.

This season's swine flu outbreak had turned Shane into an overprotective monster. For weeks, if I went anywhere other than the radio station he'd equip me with a packet of alcohol wipes and a surgical mask. He did all the grocery shopping and dog walking, to minimize my contact with the public.

I hadn't worried then, despite the fatalities. But this was different. Aaron wasn't a statistic or a name in the newspaper. He was my friend, and he had collapsed into a shaking, sweating, scratching disaster.

I opened the front door. Dexter trotted over, wagging his long skinny tail. Shane looked up at me from the sofa and silenced his electric guitar, the pure white Gibson SG I'd given him three Christmases ago.

"You're early. Not that I'm complaining." He crossed the room to turn off the amp. "News on the Jim situation. He totally wigged when we asked him about Susan, but he claims to have an alibi. Regina's checking it out."

I dropped my book bag on the floor with a *thud*. The sound made him turn to face me.

"Jesus, what's wrong?" he said. "You look pale."

"Aaron's really sick." I sat on the edge of the sofa cushion, focusing on not falling over, and gave him a thirty-second replay of the events in class. "Franklin's going to call from the hospital when he knows something."

"I hope he's okay." Shane sat beside me and unplugged the cord from his guitar. "I've heard chicken pox can be really serious for adults."

I stroked Dexter's head when he shoved it against my chest. "I've never had it."

Shane froze for half a beat. "What about the shots?"

"It's a two-dose vaccine. I had an allergic reaction to

the first shot, so I couldn't get the second one." I sat back on the sofa to rest against the throw pillow. "They said it would give me partial immunity, but there was no guarantee. What if this is some kind of supervirus?" My hands were like ice, as if in rebellion against Aaron's heat. "If it's strong enough to give him every symptom at once, maybe it's strong enough to get us all. Not you, of course."

"And not you either. Don't even think it." He kissed my forehead. "Let me get you some tea to calm you down. Or would you rather have wine?"

I swallowed, and discovered my throat was dry and a little scratchy. Oh God, I was sick already. Or maybe it was just spring allergies.

"Tea, with lemon."

Shane crossed into the kitchen. I watched him over the breakfast bar as he filled the teakettle with steady hands. I wasn't sure whether his calm demeanor soothed or frightened me.

"Must be nice," I said, "never worrying about getting sick."

"True, we can't catch diseases." He pulled a pair of mugs out of the cupboard. "But we worry about starvation, about our safe supplies drying up. In a way, we're always teetering on the edge of illness."

He had a point. Vampires treasured their relationships with their donors, who were all that stood between them and annihilation. Without them, they'd have to drink nutritionally deficient bank blood. Or worse, they'd have to hunt, which usually led to a permanent death, courtesy of the Control.

Tea must have eventually made its way into my hand and down my throat, because next thing I knew the mug was empty. I watched the clock on the wall pass an hour, then another. To keep me sane, Shane even let me put on Coldplay, my musical Valium.

When the phone finally sang Franklin's assigned ringtone (Denis Leary's "I'm an Asshole"), I grabbed it so hard, I yanked the charger out of the wall.

"How's Aaron?"

"He came in on the ambulance." Franklin's voice sounded hollow. "They took him to the back and made me sit in the waiting room."

"Why? I thought domestic partners had visitation rights."

"That's not it. I had to wait because—he was in respiratory arrest."

I sat down hard. "Is he okay now?"

"They got him breathing again and put him in ICU on a machine. Finally I got to see him. The nurse was really nice."

In the three years I'd known Franklin, he'd never called anyone "really nice" except as an insult.

He continued. "He didn't even recognize me at first, the fever had him so delirious."

"What does he have?"

Shane put his hand on my shoulder, and I clutched it with my fingertips.

Franklin paused before answering. "The blood test says chicken pox. But it's such an odd pattern of symptoms, they're running more tests and calling in an infectious diseases expert from University of Maryland."

"Is Aaron stable now?"

"You could say that." Franklin's voice tightened. "He's in a coma."

11

Home of the Blues

When Shane went to the station at 3 a.m. to make up his missed shift, Dexter and I went with him. Not wanting to be alone, I planned to camp out on the couch in the downstairs lounge until my workday started.

Jeremy entered from the studio after turning the airwaves over to Shane. Unlike the vampires he had no stealth.

"Hey," I said.

"Sorry I woke you," he whispered, hurrying past the sofa to the small refrigerator.

"You didn't. I'm too wired." I untangled my legs from Dexter's so I could sit up. "Any water in there?"

"Yep." He fetched the drinks and sat at the other end of the sofa, removing his glasses as he sank into the cushion. Dexter shifted to put his head in Jeremy's lap. "Shane told me about Aaron. I can't believe it. He was one of my favorite professors."

"Don't say 'was.' He's not dead yet. I mean, he's not dead."

"Right, but his being my professor is still past tense." He rubbed Dexter's head in front of his ear, the spot that turned him into Liquid Dog. "You must be massively worried about yourself."

I took a long swig of water instead of replying.

"Have you thought about what you'll do if you get sick?" he asked me.

"Call my doctor." I propped my heels against the edge of the coffee table. "Maybe go to the hospital."

"What if they can't save you?"

I didn't even glance at him. "Shane looked it up online. He said 99.917 percent of people who get chicken pox survive."

"But what if you're in that 0.083 percent? Or what if this is a supervirulent strain?"

I turned on him. "What if for once you weren't so morbid?"

"I just think you should be prepared."

"If I die, I die."

"You can deal with that?" He waved his tattooed hand in a circle, encompassing the station. "Now, when you're so happy? You don't believe in heaven, right, so what've you got to look forward to after this life?"

I gave him a blank look, though I knew what he was getting at.

"Have you talked to Shane about it?" he asked.

"About dying?"

He rolled his eyes. "About immortality. Duh."

"Ohhhh." I put a finger to my chin as if it had never occurred to me. "Then we could be like he and Regina used to be. Toxic, incestuous, and doomed." I scratched Dexter's lower back, brushing away bits of dead gray winter undercoat. "Besides, Shane would never do it. It's against his religion."

"Right—he thinks vampires are damned. So quaint."

"He doesn't think vampires are damned. He thinks suicides are damned." I tempered the vehemence in my tone, surprised at how much Jeremy's assumption bugged me. "So if you get vamped against your will, it's not your fault. But if you ask for it—like you keep doing and like what you're saying I should do—that's killing yourself. Which is the ultimate Catholic sin."

"That's heartless. The last thing a depressed person needs is to be told they'd go to hell for ending their pain."

"I don't agree with their belief, but I understand the idea. Suicide is dissing God in the biggest way, saying you don't believe he can save you or that he even cares."

Jeremy stroked Dexter's ears. "It's hard to see God through the veil of despair."

"Believe me," I said softly, "Shane knows that better than anyone."

The door to the hallway opened, and Shane appeared. "More good news. Ninety percent of varicella virus sufferers who receive intensive care survive."

Varicella, I thought. *Sounds like it should be in a flowerpot in a hanging garden. Water your varicella every three to four days and pinch dead blossoms to ensure season-long beauty.*

I forced a smile. "Great odds." My chest felt heavy and tight. "Why would chicken pox put someone in a coma?"

Shane's eyes dimmed a bit. "Encephalitis. Inflammation and swelling of the brain."

I put my face in my hands. "Poor Aaron."

"Comas aren't painful," Shane said, and I wondered if he was speaking from experience. Then he patted the doorframe. "I gotta set up the next track. Let me know if you need anything."

When he was gone, I said to Jeremy, "See? He's not worried. If anything, he's kept me calm, arming me with facts."

"He's in denial. If Shane stopped to think about losing you, he would collapse to a quantum singularity."

A soft, steady knock came on the front door upstairs.

Jeremy and I looked at the swinging-hips Elvis wall clock—4:35. "Who the hell's that at this hour?" he said.

I forced my stiff legs to support me as we hurried upstairs to the front door.

Standing on the first step, Franklin squinted up at us, his face ghostly pale in the dim office light.

"Aaron never woke up," Franklin said slowly, each word crawling out of his mouth. He put his hand on the iron railing. "He's dead."

Instinct drove me to step forward and slide my arms around Franklin. It wasn't until I felt his hands on my back that I realized I'd never hugged him before.

He pulled tighter, one hand against my hair. "I better not lose you, too," he whispered.

I was so shocked that I let go. We both coughed, and Franklin rubbed his nose before adding, "It would make a lot of extra work for me."

I didn't laugh, though that would've been easier. "I'm so sorry, Franklin."

"Me, too," Jeremy said behind me. "Aaron was a great guy."

"Tell me about it. He was much more than I deserved." Franklin brushed past me on the way into the office.

I shut the door and locked it. "You're not here to work, are you?"

"I don't know why I'm here. I just couldn't go back to our house. Not yet."

"So what happened?" I asked softly.

He turned to us and shoved his hands into his jacket pockets. "At two sixteen, he went into respiratory arrest again, and they couldn't—" His voice caught, and he ran a hand through his hair so hard I thought he would pull half of it out. "His family's flying in from Colorado later today. My parents can't make it until tomorrow. Flagstaff had a late ice storm, and . . ." He stopped, his gaze flicking back and forth over the floor, as if his next words were carved into the rough hardwood surface.

Jeremy cleared his throat. "I didn't know you were from Arizona."

"I'm not," he said. "I'm from here. My parents retired there, because they love the Grand Canyon." He let out a harsh sigh and stared at the twelve-point deer head mounted on the wall. "Fuck. I promised Aaron I'd take him to see it." Franklin spat the word again, "Fuck!" and shook his head, eyes narrowed, as if he'd forgotten to pick up the dry cleaning.

I shifted my feet, barely holding back my tears. On the whiteboard behind Franklin, Aaron's cartoon tale remained.

"Want me to make coffee?" Jeremy said.

Franklin looked at him like he was speaking Swahili, then nodded slowly. "Okay. Thanks."

Jeremy hurried downstairs. Franklin shuffled toward his office, his posture that of an old man.

I followed him, stopping in the doorway as he eased himself into his office chair. "If you won't take time off, then let me do your appointments the next few days. Or longer."

"No!" He jerked up his head. "You can't go out in public. The doctor said anyone without immunity was in danger."

"But Aaron didn't cough or sneeze on me. Shane said that with chicken pox—"

"Ciara, this isn't normal chicken pox." Franklin's voice cracked as it rose. "We don't know what we're dealing with yet, but it's serious. It could be some kind of super-virus." His elbow on the desk, Franklin pointed a shaky finger at me. "And you could be next."

12

Dear Mr. Fantasy

I'd expected the county health department's decor to match its 1970s utilitarian exterior. Dull green linoleum floors, mustard yellow doorframes, beige walls covered with cracked-framed motivational posters exhorting employees to "Persevere."

Instead, the place where I was facing my biggest phobia radiated a contemporary touch. Soothing pastel walls conversed with freshly buffed, cream-colored floors. It almost looked like a hotel.

"Which room is it?" Lori asked as we stood before the building's directory.

I unfolded the sweat-dampened paper I'd been clutching. "106. Oh no, that's on this floor."

Lori seized my elbow before I could run. It had taken half an hour of pleading and ridiculing to get me out of the car.

"It's almost five o'clock," she said. "They'll be closing soon."

"Then we should come back tomorrow. I don't want

to bother them. Remember when you used to work at the bar, how much you hated people who came in two minutes before closing?"

"I was serving drinks, not saving lives." She tugged harder on my sweater, and I finally relented so that it wouldn't rip.

At 2 p.m., Sherwood College had sent an e-mail to all the students, faculty, and staff, notifying them of Aaron's death. The message implored those of us without chicken pox immunity to make tracks for the county health department, where medical staff would be giving out free varicella vaccines. Getting an injection within seventy-two hours of exposure was supposed to provide seventy percent immunity against the disease, and ninety-five percent immunity against a severe attack.

Of course, that applied to normal chicken pox.

As we walked down the shiny hall, I rubbed my shoulder, where I imagined the needle would stab me. "What if I have another allergic reaction?"

"The doctors can take precautions," Lori said. "Worse comes to worst, the hospital is next door."

"Great." I crumpled the e-mail message in my pocket, trying to think of anything but the sensation of a long, sharp implement penetrating my skin.

Just before we reached room 106, its door opened slowly. A young man with scraggly dark curls shuffled out, trailing a backpack listlessly behind him.

"Turner?"

My classmate saw me as he let the heavy door slam shut behind him. "Hey, uh . . . is it Kara?"

"Ciara, whatever." I looked at the door. "Chicken pox shot?"

"Yeah." He leaned his shoulder, then the side of his head, against the wall. "I figured after what happened to Professor Green, I better not take any chances." Turner swiped his sweaty hair back from his face. "I can't believe he's gone."

"He was one of the best," Lori said. "All the history majors loved him, even though he gave such hard exams."

"I really wanted to take his fall course on . . ." Turner ran a finger under the collar of his polo shirt. "On . . . uh . . . the Crimean War."

Lori whimpered. "That was my favorite class ever."

I stepped closer to him. "Turner, are you feeling okay?"

"I was." He put his hand on the brass plaque next to the door and traced the numbers 106, his eyes glazing over. "When I came here I was fine. Then I got the shot, and now I feel like utter crap."

I touched his arm. "Maybe you're allergic? I had a reaction when I was a kid."

"No, they tested me first." He leaned his forehead against the plaque. "I actually got the shot like . . . two hours ago, but I forgot my phone here and . . . had to come back. To get my phone. I forgot . . . I forgot my phone." Still slumped against the wall, he turned to me. "Do you think I'm hot?"

Lori reached out and felt his forehead. "My God, you're on fire."

Turner's lashes fluttered as he closed his eyes. "I thought so." He swayed, staggered one step to the left, then collapsed.

"Turner!" I caught his upper body before his head could hit the hard floor. "Lori, get the doctors!"

"Ciara?" Her voice pitched high with fear as she pointed.

Turner's shirt was riding up, revealing a band of lesions crawling across the pale skin of his abdomen.

I leaped back, my hands high in the air.

"Get out of here!" Lori whispered as she dug in her purse. "Here's my keys. Go wait in the car and use the wet wipes in the glove compartment. Don't touch your face!"

I took the keys from her trembling hand. "What about him?"

"I'll get the doctor. Run!" She jerked open the door to room 106.

As I backed away, Turner started to convulse.

I ran for my life.

Fifteen excruciating minutes later, Lori sank into the driver's seat next to me.

"What'd they say?" I asked her.

She spoke slowly, as if the words prickled her tongue on the way out. "That guy from your class had no symptoms of chicken pox when he walked in, but two hours later he's on his way to ICU. Just like Aaron." Her voice choked on our professor's name.

"So what does that mean? Did the vaccine give him the disease, or did he already have it and the shot made it worse?"

"They don't know." She shoved her hands against her face and swept her hair up off her temples. "They don't know anything, and that's what's so scary. They're calling the state health department and then maybe the CDC."

My heart felt like it was trying to kick out my ribs.

The federal Centers for Disease Control would want Aaron's class roster, would maybe even quarantine all of us who couldn't prove we'd either had chicken pox or the vaccine. And now the vaccine not only couldn't help but maybe even made the disease strike faster and harder.

My options were limited, to say the least. All I had left were hope and luck. And the beginnings of a plan.

My voluntary quarantine forced us to move Lori's Friday night bachelorette party to my apartment. After Aaron's death, we weren't in a festive mood, but her wedding was in a week, so there was no room for postponement

Turner was in critical condition, according to the hospital, but still alive twenty-seven hours after collapsing— much longer than Aaron had lasted. Maybe Turner's vaccine was working. If so, maybe the first dose of vaccine I'd gotten fifteen years ago would be enough to fight it off.

Shane's online research suggested that this was no ordinary chicken pox. The incubation period should have been ten to twenty days, but Turner had gotten sick only a day after exposure. Then again, he and Aaron could have gotten it from the same source, someone they'd been around while I was off in the mountains playing Control agent.

I was confused, and tired of making conjectures based on crap information. I was ready to get drunk and be a girl.

"I love you." Shane attached Dexter's leash to the dog's collar and kissed me good night. "Now eat, drink, and be merry."

"For tomorrow I will die? Isn't that the rest of the quote?"

He blanched. "Oh. Uh, well, I think it's—"

A knock came at the door. He opened it to reveal Regina, who held up her hand and said, "Tag team Ciara supervision."

He slapped her palm as he and Dexter escaped to an allegedly low-key bachelor party for David.

At the kitchen counter, Regina picked up two multi-colored penis straws and butted their heads. "So lifelike." She poured herself a glass of tequila.

I pointed to the fridge. "The margarita mix is—never mind," I added as she downed the tequila in one gulp.

She smacked her lips. "I'm taking notes for your bachelorette party. Assuming you survive to see it."

My chest tightened, but I emitted a shaky laugh. "That's not much incentive to live."

Another knock. I hurried to answer it, relieved to avoid the subject of my mortality. "It's probably Tina. Be nice."

Sure enough, my recent roomie gave a forced smile when I opened the door. "Hey."

"Hey! It's great to see you again." I stepped back so she could enter. "How have you been since orientation?"

"Indoc," she corrected. "It's only been five days. How do you think I've been?" As Tina stepped across the threshold, she fixed her eyes on Regina. "You're kidding me. A yoosie bridesmaid?"

"Don't worry." The DJ lifted her glass, newly tequilaed. "I'm only drinking booze tonight."

"Speaking of which, what can we get you?" I tugged off Tina's fur-lined suede coat to encourage her to stay, despite the undead presence. As her arms slipped out of the sleeves, I saw a long bandage running up her inner forearm. "Did you cut yourself?"

"No." Tina pulled down her shirtsleeve, then folded her arms over her chest. "I'll have a white wine spritzer."

"Brilliant." Regina picked up four bottles in two hands. "Zombies all around!"

Tina sighed and turned to me. "I'm sorry about your professor. Lori said he was great."

"He was. Chicken pox, of all things. Lori told me you've already had it."

"My adoption papers said I had immunity, so I guess I caught chicken pox when I was little, back in Romania." She smoothed the static out of her long dark hair. "Lori said Aaron was in Hungary last week for research. He probably caught it there. I've heard it's a filthy place."

Clearly the Romania/Hungary rivalry was alive and well in the twenty-first century.

"The state health department says it's investigating," I told Tina, "which probably means they're as clueless as we are."

"Don't think—drink!" Regina scooted to the other side of the breakfast bar and passed out her cherry-garnished concoctions. "That's tonight's motto. Now pick your penis straw, and we'll toast Aaron's spirit."

I examined the tall glass, wishing I was in the mood to drink. Someone knocked on the front door. Reminding myself of my duty to show Lori a good time despite the circumstances, I hurried to the door and swung it open with a flourish. "Surprise!"

Lori laughed through her gauzy white veil. "You remember Maggie, one of my friends from SPIT? She's my vice president now."

"Congratulations." I hugged the thirtyish woman and planted a kiss on her perky red bob of hair. "I'm glad that if anything happens to Lori, someone will be there to step in. Constitutionally speaking, I mean."

Regina was already lining up three more glasses. She gave Maggie a "Hey" when introduced but looked slightly past the newcomer instead of meeting her gaze. Direct eye contact with vampires can throw the uninitiated off balance.

"How was Aaron's funeral?" I asked Lori.

"Very sad." She slid off her coat and straightened her veil. "The History Department canceled class and chartered a bus to take students and alumni down to the burial in Baltimore. Franklin held it together, but you could tell he was heartbroken."

The thought of his pain produced an ache of my own. "I wish I could've gone to the funeral without endangering the world."

She pulled back her veil to examine my face, as if looking for the Grim Reaper's shadow. "How do you feel?"

"Fine." I waved my hand at the clock. "It's been forty-eight hours. I bet I'm safe." I grabbed her hand. "Help me celebrate life and shit like that."

I cranked up the music, and we all danced like a bunch of death-defying freaks.

Lori and Maggie were jamming on the couch, halfway through their second zombies, when a knock came at the door.

"Pizza!" I seized the remote control, switched CDs, and pressed Pause. "Lori, answer that while I put out plates. It's all paid for."

She boogied over to the door and opened it to a man who looked like a younger, cuter Keanu Reeves. He held a pair of pizza boxes in a insulating red bag.

He glided in, casting a smile over Lori on his way past. She returned it, smoothing her hair in an unconscious gesture of *OMG hot!*

Ken—for that was his name—deposited the pizza on the table and winked at me. I hit Play on the remote control.

The opening guitar riff of Prince and the Revolution's "When Doves Cry" squealed out of the speakers. Ken turned to Lori with an intent gaze.

She took a step back, eyes crinkling in confusion. "Didn't Ciara pay you?"

He circled her like a cat with its prey, stalking in time to the music. I snuck up behind Lori and shoved a roll of dollar bills into her hand, which was already damp with sweat.

She looked down at the bundle of ones, then at Ken as he tore open his plain brown delivery shirt to reveal a tight red silk vest.

Lori's eyes grew wide as softballs. "You got me a private stripper?"

She looked horrified. My mind played back our entire friendship in one moment, like a drowning person's life. Maybe I didn't know her as well as I thought.

Lori threw her arms around my neck. "I love you!" she shouted over Prince's moans.

I grabbed the zombie out of her hand so she could dance with Ken without spilling. When I set the drink on the counter, I noticed Regina watching the spectacle from the kitchen. Her eyes never left Ken, and the hunger within them made me shiver.

Then he was in front of me, naked but for a dark blue G-string that set off his tan. As we began to dance,

I couldn't help thinking that Aaron would definitely approve.

"You're the best idea I ever had." I trailed the end of a rolled-up dollar bill down the glistening skin of his chest, finally folding it into his G-string.

He spun me around to face away from him. We bumped and ground for another verse of Lady Gaga's "Bad Romance," and I took mental notes for my next striptease for Shane.

All too soon, Ken moved on to perform a lap dance for Maggie, whose face turned as red as her hair. Then Ken proceeded to Tina and held his composure in the face of her seizure of giggles.

The music took a darker turn with Marilyn Manson's cover of "Sweet Dreams." Ken finally turned to Regina.

For the first time that night, their eyes met, and for the first time that night, Ken's steps faltered.

She didn't budge as he swayed toward her, hips and shoulders off rhythm. He stopped a few inches away, his eyes glued to hers. She traced the tip of one long, black-lacquered fingernail up his arm, from wrist to shoulder, then finally arcing down to his heart. He shuddered.

The rest of us watched, released from his spell, as he turned his head to expose his neck.

"Stop that." Regina gave his face a gentle slap. "Dance for me."

He jolted as if from a trance, then did as she asked. His self-possession had vanished, replaced by a desperate, almost doglike desire to please. Regina's gaze roamed over his sinewy frame, as he knelt before her, twisting his body in a pathetic pantomime of lust.

By the last chorus, he was writhing on his belly, like

Roman slave dancers I'd seen in movies. As the song ended, he laid his head on her foot and stretched out his tongue to lick her boot.

"No!" Regina stepped back and looked away. He crawled after her, bobbing his whole body to stay within her vision, a puppy begging for attention.

She leaped over him and dashed for the bedroom. With a strangled noise, Ken lunged to follow her, but she'd slammed the door and locked it behind her before he could take a step.

Ken turned to me, eyes heavy lidded with longing. "What's wrong with her?"

"For starters, she's not the bachelorette." I motioned to Lori. "See the veil? Dance for the veil."

But Lori shook her head. "I think we're done." After a short, awkward silence, she started applauding. We all joined in, though it sounded more polite than appreciative.

"I'm so sorry." Ken collected his clothes and hurried off to the bathroom, dropping a sock on the way.

"So." I unzipped the insulated pizza bag. "Who's hungry?"

"Nakedness and pizza." Lori grabbed a slice with olives and sweet peppers. "Perfect man."

"Sorry he went all Igor there at the end," I whispered.

"I'm sure it'll seem really funny ten years from now." She stepped out of the way for Maggie and Tina. "Do you think he stuffs his G-string?"

"Definitely," Maggie said. "No way that's real." Tina and I just snickered. Silence fell over the kitchen as we devoured the pizza with hormone-enhanced hunger.

Ken hobbled out of the bathroom wearing one shoe. "Oh, there's my other sock."

"You want to stay for a drink?" I said.

His eyes turned to the bedroom door with a distant, cloudy awareness.

"Of alcohol," I added. "Or soda."

"Oh." His face relaxed into a boyish smile. "No thanks. I have another, um, delivery."

"Where'd you get the pizza?" Maggie asked. "It's amazing."

"My dad's restaurant."

Lori gasped. "You're actually a delivery guy?"

"No, I'm a dancer." He sat at the table to put on his remaining sock and shoe. "The pizza is one of my gimmicks."

"So if I'd picked the fireman stripper," I said, "he would've brought his giant hose?"

Tina choked on her laughter, but since her face turned red instead of blue, I decided she didn't need the Heimlich.

When Ken was fully dressed and had collected his props, I led him to the front door. "Thanks for an unforgettable experience."

He reached into his pocket. "Can you give that black-haired girl my card?"

"Isn't dating a client's friend kind of unprofessional?"

His hand remained steady as it held out the card, poking its corner into the webbing between my thumb and forefinger.

Figuring it was none of my business (and really wanting to return to the pizza before it got cold), I took his card and shooed him out.

"Should we bring Regina some pizza?" Maggie asked me.

"She's lactose intolerant, but I'll check." I picked up our half-full zombies, went to the bedroom door, and tapped it softly with my foot.

"It's open!" she called.

I found Regina on our bed, smoking a cigarette and reading my latest issue of *Under the Radar*. I was so high on alcohol, saturated fat, and naked-man endorphins I didn't care how I would get the smoke out of my duvet.

"I heard him leave, so I unlocked the door." She flipped the page and frowned at it. "Thought I'd stay here until your little friends defreaked."

"I think you're the most freaked of all."

She slapped shut the indie music magazine. "That guy was so hot."

"He was pretty cute."

"I don't mean cute. I mean, hot. Sweaty." She eyed my neck a little too intently. "When a human's temperature rises, the blood moves to the surface of the skin. He smelled incredible." She hugged the throw pillow to her chest and kneaded its soft fabric. "I wanted to put my hands all over him. I wanted to keep him."

I set her drink on the nightstand. "He would've let you." I dropped Ken's card in her lap.

She stared at it as if it were a winning lottery ticket coated in holy water. "Give it to Shane. He always needs guys, thanks to your little arrangement."

"But Ken liked you. Why not call him? You can end it if he seems unstable."

"And then he stalks me, and things get messy. Breaking in a new donor isn't worth the novelty of fresh blood. So unless I'm desperate, I try to keep things status quo." She rested her chin on the corner of the pillow and scowled. "It pisses me off, looking at 99.9 percent of the male population and knowing I can't fuck them—at least not without risking the thing that makes fucking them worthwhile."

I didn't envy Regina or other female vampires. Their, uh, interior muscles could ruin the life of a human male. But male vampires could sleep with female humans. Monumentally unfair.

"Still." I took the card and stuffed it into her hand. "I think it would make Ken's day—and yours—if you called him."

Someone knocked softly on the door, then Lori opened it. "Sorry to interrupt. Tina just had the spookiest idea."

13

Girl Power

The Sherwood cemetery was less than a half-mile walk from my apartment. It was almost midnight, and the streets of the small town were empty. So we figured as long as I didn't cough on any permeable surfaces, I wouldn't be a public health hazard.

The three ladies of the Sherwood Paranormal Investigative Team walked down the cemetery lane ahead of Regina and me, examining their *Star Trek*y EMF readers, which they all kept in their car trunks for ghost-hunting emergencies.

"If we get caught trespassing, I'm running away," Regina told me as she lit a cigarette. "Remember, jails have windows."

"Speaking of windows . . ." I raised my voice. "Lori?"

She turned, then looked where I was pointing. A small stone building sat at the top of the hill, in the center of the cemetery. A light was on in the upper window.

"It's commemorative." Her drunken lips tripped over the word. "That chapel was a stop on the Underground

Railroad. They'd leave a light in the top window to show it was a safe haven for runaway slaves. So there's always a lamp lit at night. Cool, huh?"

I kept my eyes on the glow, expecting a shadowy figure to pass before it. This was only my second time in a cemetery; most of my experience with them came from horror movies.

The fact that Susan Haldeman's body had been found nearby should have made this outing seem stupid. But I was accompanied by a vampire and a soon-to-be Control Enforcement agent. As bridal parties went, this one had high ass-kicking potential.

To lower the creep factor, I kept Lori talking. "So the Underground Railroad went through Sherwood?"

"It went through everywhere. It was so secret that most of the places still aren't known. This one's been confirmed." She drew an imaginary line from the chapel toward town. "It had an actual tunnel that led to one of the churches in Sherwood."

"Is the tunnel still there?" Regina asked.

"It's sealed off. Probably collapsed by now."

"Shh!" Tina glared at us, apparently having sobered up during the walk to the cemetery. "Ghosts prefer quiet."

"Nuh-uh." Regina clapped her hands together, cupped for maximum volume. "I saw *Poltergeist* a million times. Those ghosts were loud."

Tina flapped her arms. "Poltergeists haunt houses. The ones in cemeteries prefer to be left in peace."

My skin prickled. "If I believed in ghosts, I would say that maybe peace is where we should leave them."

Lori caught up to her fellow SPITters. They whispered among themselves, sweeping their EMF readers, each covering a different sector or whatever.

At least it had stopped raining. The blacktop of the cemetery lane still glistened, and I had to weave to avoid soaking my pink high-tops in the puddles.

A breeze stirred the bare-branched trees scattered throughout the cemetery. I unbuttoned my jacket to let the cool, damp night air soak the skin of my neck. A week from now, I could be in my own grave after my brain swelled out of my skull and my body baked from the inside, like a potato in a microwave.

The thought made me giggle, partly at the image of a giant microwave and partly with the euphoria of being not yet dead.

"I've never seen you this pissed," Regina said.

I turned to face her, walking backward. "I'm not mad."

"'Pissed' means 'drunk' in England."

"We're in America." I raised my arms to encompass the glorious nation. "And you're Canadian. When are you going to start talking like one?"

"I'm a citizen of the world, and I can talk any way I bloody well want."

"Legally, yes, but if you don't want people to laugh at you, then—"

My voice cut off. Someone was coming. Fast.

I pointed past Regina. "Look out!"

But she had already spun to face the gray-skinned figure lumbering in our direction. Behind me, Lori screamed.

He—*it?*—moved with the speed of a vampire but none of the grace. He stumbled toward us in a blur, making no sound but the *thwap!* of his torn shoes and the swish of his ragged, muddy clothes. Oddest of all, he seemed to be wearing sunglasses.

My Control training kicked in, and I whirled to look for other attackers, in case he was a diversion.

Nothing. I turned toward him again and stifled my own scream.

He wasn't wearing sunglasses. His eyes were holes.

"It's a vampire!" Tina pulled a stake from her inside jacket pocket.

Regina lunged, punching the man on the left cheek. He stumbled back and almost fell. She flicked away her cigarette and planted her feet, hands up in a fighter's pose.

When he straightened up from the blow, his neck was torn, almost broken. Flaps of skin hung over his collarbone.

I yanked Tina back. "That's not a vampire."

The creature stepped forward, and Regina planted another punch in the middle of its chin. This time the head flew off, as cleanly as a Wiffle ball from a tee. It bounced across the wet grass, eye sockets flashing twin black spots, and came to rest against the back of a tombstone.

The body toppled forward. Regina stepped out of the way.

We stood there for a long moment, four of us wondering if the head would get sucked back into the creature's body as it curled into itself. But unlike a vampire, this thing didn't disappear, and it seemed to contain no blood. It reeked, though, like the ancient food at the back of my refrigerator.

"What. The. Fuck. Just. Happened." Maggie stared at Regina, then at the body, then back at Regina.

I sighed. Debriefing hyperventilating civilians wasn't one of my fortes.

Lori took Maggie's hand. "Um, Regina's a vampire. But it's okay—she's a nice one."

"Hey!" Regina rubbed her knuckles against her Hüsker Dü T-shirt. "I am not nice."

"Sorry." Lori turned back to Maggie. "She's actually a bitch, but she doesn't kill people."

"Doesn't kill people!?" Maggie's voice verged on hysteria. "She just knocked that guy's head off!"

"That wasn't a guy." Regina knelt beside the body. "Well, it used to be. But he was definitely dead before I hit him."

Tina pocketed her stake and brought out her cell phone. "I'll send a picture to my dad. I bet he'll know what it is."

I scowled at her, wondering who brings a wooden stake to a bachelorette party, then squatted next to Regina, hands in my pockets. "Have you ever seen anything like this before?" I whispered.

"Hell, no. People joke about us being walking corpses, but it's bollocks. We're reanimated at the moment of death. We don't die long enough for a coffee break, much less a burial." She poked at the mud caked on the man's clothes, then pointed to his hands. "His fingers and knuckles are all torn up. He must have clawed and punched his way out of his coffin." She looked around the cemetery. "Assuming that's where he came from."

I pulled out my cell phone and plugged my ear to block Tina's excited chatter: "Daddy, you'll never believe what I just saw! I just sent you the photo—is it another kind of yoosie?"

I dialed Colonel Lanham's office, not expecting him to answer this time of night.

He picked up on the first ring. "Lanham."

"Sir, it's Ciara Griffin. Something weird just happened here in Sherwood." I looked at Regina, who was holding the corpse's head in a Hamlet-like pose. "Weirder than usual."

14

Who Will the Next Fool Be

Colonel Lanham was the only person I knew who could look parade rigid while hunched over a corpse. Face hidden by a light blue surgical mask and the bill of his black cap, he scoured the putrid ex-human with the quick, methodical strokes of a flashlight beam.

Around him, black-clad Control agents were securing the area—far away, at the cemetery's front and back gates, and close by, taping off the path from the creature's grave to its final-final resting place. All the agents were either vampires or had chicken pox immunity (I made Lanham check).

A female agent with graying brown hair and a kind smile was sitting on a bench with Maggie, who was still trembling an hour after the attack. I first met civilian liaison Major Ricketts more than two years ago, after a band of fanatics had kidnapped me and Jeremy, who had needed lots of counseling after his hard impact with the truth about vampires.

Ricketts laid a hand on Maggie's shoulder and offered her a fresh cup of cocoa. A tough debriefing—Maggie had to accept the existence of vampires and maybe-zombies in one night. It was hard enough for the rest of us to deal with the latter.

Colonel Lanham straightened his jacket as he stepped away from the corpse. Then he tugged off his mask and placed a call on his cell phone. I inched closer to hear, but a young agent stopped me before I could get near the orange barricade tape.

If curiosity was killing me, it was carrying Tina to hell and back. She bounced between me and Lori. "This is so amazing! I wish I could've been the one to take it down. If only that vampire hadn't gotten in the way."

I glanced at Regina, leaning against a nearby tree as an agent in a gray uniform interviewed her. She cleaned under her fingernails with her thumbnail, as if she'd been gardening.

"If that vampire hadn't gotten in the way," I told Tina, "we'd all be dead."

"Yeah," Lori added. "Regina totally made up for stealing my stripper."

I tried to smile at her attempt to lighten the mood. Usually that was my job. But my buzz had faded into a headache, and the corpse was a painful reminder of human mortality. Like poor Aaron's. Like mine.

Lanham ended his phone call and spoke to two of the sentries. "A cleanup crew will be here in ten minutes. This is a biohazard, so please continue to not touch it." He peeled off his latex gloves and stuffed them into a red plastic receptacle one of the agents held out for him, then stepped over to us. "You've all given your statements?"

"Yes, sir." Tina cut in before I could speak. "We told Major Ricketts everything."

He gave her a crisp nod. "Good. Please leave."

I smirked before realizing he meant all of us, not just Tina. "You're not going to explain this?" I asked him. "We just got attacked by a zombie!"

He winced as he held up a hand. "We call them *cadaveris accurrens*, Latin for 'running carcasses' or, more precisely, 'attacking carcasses.'"

I turned the words over in my mouth. "Cadaver whats?"

"*Cadaveris accurrens.* CAs for short."

"Looks like a zombie to me," Lori muttered.

"There are no such things as zombies," he told her, "not as pop culture has portrayed them. The *cadaveris* don't infect the people they attack. They often don't even bite."

"Then how do they kill their prey?" Tina asked, and I could tell she was wishing for a pen and notebook.

"Their victims most often die from trauma associated with tissue disruption."

"Huh?" we all said in unison.

"They get ripped apart."

I took a step back. "Why didn't we learn this in orientation?"

"Indoc," he corrected. "It's been over seventy years since the last *cadaveris* walked the earth, so we consider them extinct, like polio or smallpox. They're practically a footnote."

"A footnote?" My voice rose in uncontrollable insubordination. "That footnote almost disrupted the five of us! If they're extinct, then this cemetery is Jurassic Park."

Lanham sighed. "Didn't you ever wonder why we're

the International Agency for the Control and Management of Undead Corporeal Entities, not the International Agency for the Control and Management of Vampires?"

"I figured it was the bureaucratic inability to be straightforward." One of my orientation papers had been returned for a rewrite because the language was too "readable."

"I can't believe my dad never told me," Tina said.

I snorted. "I can't believe he didn't see this coming. He's supposed to be psychic."

Instead of sniping back at me, Tina stared at the corpse and rubbed her left arm—the one with the bandage. I felt a stab of sympathy. Whether someone had cut her or she'd cut herself, clearly things weren't right in Tina's world.

"Sorry," I told her, but she ignored me, so I turned back to Lanham. "Is this supposed to be a secret? Does David know?"

"No and no," he replied. "For all intents and purposes, the *cadaveris* are nonexistent. The Control keeps a small interdivisional team to handle the rare cases. Most of the time the agents serve in their usual functions in Enforcement or other divisions."

Lori cleared her throat. "Um, back to the zombies? If they're supposed to be extinct, where did this one come from? Where do any of them come from?"

"From the grave," he said. "Raised by a necromancer to do his or her bidding."

I looked at Tina, whose shoulders hunched at the sound of her father's alleged power.

Lanham continued. "Many Control scholars—especially vampires—have argued that CAs shouldn't even be classified as undead."

"Then what are they?" Lori asked.

"Dead," said a familiar voice from behind. We turned to see Elijah sauntering toward us in a gray field uniform like the one worn by the agent interviewing Regina.

Beside me, Tina stiffened and stepped back. When Elijah approached us, he nodded to Lori and me, but his gaze skimmed over Tina's face without making eye contact.

Definitely a post-breakup vibe there. Elijah and Tina had surely crossed the human-vampire divide with abundant fluid exchange. Maybe they'd had a blood/booty call this week, and that's why she needed the bandage.

Lanham returned Elijah's salute. "Captain Fox, your haste is commendable."

"Thank you, sir." The vampire rubbed his hands together. "I'm all over my first real live CA." He looked at me as he pulled out a small notepad. "Well, not *real live*, but you know what I mean."

Lanham turned to us. "Captain Fox leads a trio of platoons in the interdivisional team I spoke of."

"The ZC, we call ourselves. Zombie Company." Ignoring Lanham's frown of disapproval, Elijah ducked under the orange tape—not an easy feat given his height. "Who killed this sucker?"

"I did." Regina swaggered past me, bumping my elbow. "Two punches. It was easy."

Elijah's eyes almost glowed at the sight of her. Tina let out a faint whimper that she probably thought no one could hear.

"How old are you?" Elijah asked Regina. "In vampire years."

"That's a personal question." She lit a cigarette and flicked the match into a puddle. "I like personal questions."

He bobbed his eyebrows. "I like personal answers."

"I'm twenty-three. It was 1987. I was in London, and—"

"That's plenty, thanks." Elijah jotted a note on his pad as he turned away. "So they can be killed by an unarmed vampire of average strength."

"I'm not average," Regina grumbled.

Colonel Lanham pocketed his phone. "Captain Fox, when you're finished there, please brief these witnesses on the CAs." He took a deep breath. "I need to speak to the cemetery manager."

A portly man with a mustache the size of a small ferret was arguing with one of the agents and pointing to an open grave several rows over. I could've sworn he said something about, "Second time this week."

I wondered how much Lanham would pay the caretaker to keep quiet. *Cooperation before coercion* applied to humans as well as vampires.

Lori had crept up to stand beside Regina. "So, um, Captain Fox, is it?"

"You're a civilian." He gave her a gleaming grin. "You get to call me Elijah."

"Elijah. How do these necromancer people raise—what do you call them—?"

"*Cadaveris*, but if you wanna call 'em zombies, go right ahead. The necromancers raise them with blood magic—usually their own blood, but not always." He squatted beside the corpse and poked its gelatinous belly. I swallowed hard, glad we were several yards away. "Same basic mojo that makes us vampires. But like I said, they're not *un*-dead, they're dead." He tapped the end of his pen against his temple. "When a person dies, see, their brain is history. A few weeks later, it turns to liquid and leaks out their ears. So these things can't think, they just move."

I was too busy trying not to retch to think of questions, but Lori thankfully kept her head (and stomach).

"How do they move without a brain?" she asked.

He drew an imaginary line along the length of the corpse. "If a body has any nervous system tissue left, even just a few neurons, the blood magic can make it grow a new spinal cord, which lets it reanimate. At least, that's what they told me." Elijah put his hands to his head and gave a wide smile. "Wow, a real *cadaveri accurrens*. I'm so cranked! I've trained for this for ten years, but I never thought I'd see one." He slapped his knee and let out a sudden laugh. "Guess they won't be cutting our budget now. Dyno-mite!"

His exuberance was cracking the veneer of timelessness that the vampire Control agents maintained, with the help of the Contemporary Awareness Division. I would have smiled at his use of seventies slang if the reason for it hadn't been so creepy.

"How do you kill them?" asked Tina in a cold voice. "Can they be staked like vampires?"

"No." He answered without looking at her. "The CA's life force—if we can call it that—is in its spinal cord, not its heart, so they have to be cut in half or decapitated." He gently jiggled the corpse, causing a tarry liquid to ooze out of its side. "Lucky for us, they get less dense as they rot."

I willed my slice of pizza and the one and a half zombies (oh, I just got that—ha!) to stay in my stomach.

"Colonel Lanham said they're not contagious," I said. "So no zombie apocalypse?"

"Right. That's another big difference between vampires and *cadaveris*. We can both take life." He looked at Regina. "But only vampires can give it back."

She gave him a slow, sad nod, and they shared a moment before Elijah glanced my way again.

"Plus," he said, "they burn up in the sun like we do, but they don't know enough to take cover, so their rampages only last until morning twilight." He shook his head. "But they can do a hell of a lot of damage in just a few hours. They're superstrong—hell, they punch through a steel casket and dig out six feet of dirt. And when they're attacked, they get all turbocharged. So just because they won't take over the world doesn't mean they can't kill a shitload of humans."

"But not vampires?" Regina asked.

"They can't use weapons." He toed the zombie's torn fingers. "So the only way they can kill us is by ripping off our heads."

I stared at the zombie despite myself, and imagined it poofing into nothing at the first light of day, the way my vampire friends would. Then again, considering the "life" of a zombie, a quick flameout was probably a blessing.

Unless . . . wait a minute. I forced my booze-soaked brain to connect a few dots.

"Captain Fox?" I raised my hand like a kid in class. "When you say they burn up, do you mean like vampires do, all flash-papery?"

Elijah grimaced at the corpse in front of him. "I wish it was that clean. No, if we left this thing here, come sunrise it'd roast like a piece of chicken someone forgot to take off the grill. Look a lot like it, too."

"Aaron's body!"

Lori gave me a horrified stare. "Ciara, what are you—"

"Aaron discovered a burned-up body Monday morning," I said. "That was two days before he got sick."

"For real?" Elijah whipped out his notepad. "Where was this?"

I pointed toward the Sherwood campus. "Past the other side of those woods. And a professor was found killed near the same spot." I swept my hair back hard against my scalp. "Holy crap, maybe it wasn't Jim after all."

"I assume the police were called?" Elijah asked me.

"Yeah, but I think they were keeping the details under wraps until they'd identified the body."

Lori put a vise grip on my elbow. "Do you know what this means? Maybe Aaron was poisoned by the corpse he found. Colonel Lanham said their remains were toxic."

"Which means—" I gasped. "Maybe Aaron didn't have chicken pox." Then my hope died as soon as it was born. "But the blood tests said he did."

"Maybe they were wrong."

"Then what about Turner?"

"Maybe he was in the same area at the same time as Aaron." Lori pulled on my arm. "The important thing is that you weren't anywhere near it."

We turned our heads to look at tonight's corpse. "Near the first one, at least."

Lori and I took a long step back from the orange tape separating us from the zombie remains. I bumped into Tina, who had her phone to her ear. She frowned at me when I trod on her foot.

"Where is he?" she mumbled as she glared at her phone.

At the moment, even Tina's Ms. Grumblepants routine couldn't mute my sudden surge of hope. If Aaron hadn't been killed by chicken pox, that meant I might not die. As a bonus, one of the station's star DJs might not be a murderer.

"Daddy!"

I turned to see Tina saluting a wiry man moving toward us with the controlled grace and power of a panther. This person she called "Daddy" looked no older than us.

So the Control had taken Jonathan Fetter's recommendation and put a vampire in charge of the Immanence Corps. Nice to know they read their memos.

From the corner of my eye, I saw Colonel Lanham's posture stiffen, which I didn't think possible. He left the cemetery manager mid-sentence and strode over to intercept the newcomer.

"Colonel Petrea." His voice was a low growl as they saluted simultaneously. "What brings you here?"

"My daughter called me," Petrea said, though the piercing look he gave Tina was far from filial. "Said there was a *cadaveris accurrens* sighting."

"In my jurisdiction, yes."

"With all due respect, Colonel, CAs can only be summoned by a necromancer." His Romanian accent was faint but unmistakable. "Involvement of a person with paranormal abilities makes it my jurisdiction as well."

Lanham waited a moment before lifting the orange tape. "Very well." As Petrea was about to enter the restricted area, Lanham turned to me. "Ms. Griffin, Lieutenant Colonel Petrea here will be your Immanence Corps commander."

Tina let out a huff. "Could my night suck any more?"

"You're Ciara Griffin?" Petrea's sharp brown gaze raked my frame as he looked down his perfectly straight nose at me.

"I am." I put my hands on my hips so that my jacket parted to reveal my MAID-OF-HO camisole. "How you doin'?"

He raised his eyes to meet mine, and I suddenly wished I was wearing sunglasses, or better yet, a welder's mask. I felt a cold tickle behind my forehead, as if something were scratching around my brain like a cat in a litter box. It was more than the usual vampire magnet eyes.

But I didn't look away. If Petrea didn't like my attitude (aura, whatever), maybe he'd kick me out of IC. Then I could serve out my term in the Control behind a cozy desk in a climate-controlled office, concocting fake passports for aging vampires.

Petrea's eyes narrowed to little rat beads. "*Smecher.*"

My mouth dropped open. "What did you call me?"

He glanced at Tina and Lori. "Miss Griffin, let us speak in private."

"An excellent idea." Colonel Lanham's eyes crinkled at the edges, the closest he would allow any expression of irony. No doubt he was glad to get Petrea and me out of his nonexistent hair.

Pivoting with precision, the vampire colonel beckoned me to follow him.

"What does *smecher* mean?" I asked Tina.

"It's Romanian for 'con artist.'" She tilted her head. "Still think he's a charlatan?"

"Now more than ever."

I followed Petrea along the damp blacktop lane. He stopped next to a modest-size mausoleum (if there is such a thing). I kept several feet of open air between us as he spoke.

"I understand your trait is unique within the ranks of the Control."

I almost corrected him. My father and birth mother—who each had a diluted version of my anti-holy blood—had spent time as undercover Control agents. For all I knew, my mother was back in their ranks, though she claimed to be working as a phlebotomist in her native South Carolina.

But then I remembered the meaning of the word "undercover." So I just nodded.

"Unfortunately," he said, "I don't regard your neutralization as a real ability. To me, you're nothing more than a metaphysical bucket of bleach, a walking bit of nothing. You have nothing to contribute to the corps."

"Is this reverse psychology?" I asked him. "Trying to make me all gung ho to prove you wrong? We can skip that. If you don't want my service, then have Lanham reassign me."

"You think we have a choice? This isn't a corporation where you can just skip from one department to another if you don't like your boss or if your boss hates you."

"Why do you hate me? You don't even know me."

"I see inside you." He stepped closer, and I fought not to retreat from the brain-skewering power of his gaze. "I see the lies that make up the fiber of your mind." He shook his head slowly. "I see nothing I can work with, because there's nothing there." He shrugged. "Nothing but Gypsy scum."

"You didn't read me, you read my file. Found out I used to be a con artist and that my family are Irish Travellers—who hate the name 'Gypsy,' by the way." I halved the distance between us, showing him I wasn't afraid. "I know all about your kind—mediums, psychics, communicators. You gather a little intel on someone, then pretend to speak to their dead loved one or tell their fortune. To them it feels real, because they want to believe."

His eyes grew suddenly haunted, and the manufactured spookiness pissed me off.

I lifted my chin. "But you can't predict the future any more than David Copperfield can make the White House disappear. It's all smoke and mirrors. It's all bullshit."

Petrea remained silent, his unfocused gaze pointing at me.

"So what do we do?" I asked him finally. When he still didn't answer, I prompted him. "About my assignment?"

His gaze fell, and his voice softened. "It doesn't matter."

"Why not?"

"Because, Miss Griffin, you are wrong. I can see people's futures." He looked into my eyes. "And you don't have one."

15

Going Under

"It can't be true." Huddled on our sofa, I smooshed myself against Shane's solid frame, but couldn't stop shivering. "Petrea's making it all up."

"Of course he is," Shane said, his arms steady around my body. "He probably found out about the chicken pox and was fucking with your mind. Maybe mental torture is part of the Control hazing process. You know how these charlatans operate, playing on people's fears."

His words and touch soothed me, until I remembered Jeremy's words—that Shane was in denial. But hope was my only path to sanity.

"You're probably right. He didn't know about the theory that the zombie poisoned Aaron, because we had just come up with it right before he got there."

It seemed like such a brilliant theory at the time. But really, what were the chances that Turner had gotten his illness straight from the zombie? The police had cordoned off the area as soon as they arrived, so they would've seen him—unless he'd found the body before Aaron and run off without calling the cops. He *was* sort of skittish.

"Speaking of which," Shane said, "tell me more about this zombie. You sure it wasn't a hoax?"

I knew he was trying to distract me, but he was probably also insanely curious. The CAs would be a worldview-shattering development for a vampire.

"He was real, as far as I could tell. Reeked like rotten flesh, and the way he ran . . ." I shivered again and pulled the sofa's fuzzy green blanket tighter around me. "It reminded me of you guys, except for the stumbling."

"I guess if blood magic can create vampires, it could create one of those . . . things."

"It wasn't a thing. It was a person, or at least he used to be." My breath eased, as I focused on something other than my possibly imminent demise. "I'm glad we were there. If it had gotten loose, it might've killed people. Plus, this way the Control can study it, maybe even figure out who summoned it."

"I'm not glad you were there," he said, "but if you had to be, I'm glad Regina was with you."

"Yeah, otherwise Tina would've staked the zombie and gotten—um, what was the word Lanham used?— 'disrupted.' And it would've poisoned the rest of us, and then I would be dying. If I'm not already."

"You're not dying." Shane tightened his embrace.

Dexter shoved his face against my knee as he walked by, not stopping for a pat on his way to pick up a chew bone he'd left behind the chair.

"See?" Shane said. "Dexter doesn't think you're on your way out. Animals can sense these things better than stupid old psychics can."

"Just because I'm not dying yet doesn't mean the virus isn't inside me."

"Shh." Shane drew his fingers down my cheek and along my jawline. "If it is, remember, you had half the vaccine. So even if you get sick, it won't be that bad. Worst that'll happen is you miss Lori and David's wedding."

"Lori said they'd postpone rather than do it without me."

"Then there's nothing to worry about."

"Her grandparents are coming from Finland."

"And they'll deal. Finns are a practical people, or so I've heard."

I sighed and closed my eyes. "Shane, I'm scared. Can't you be scared with me, or do you have to be Denial Dude?"

"Hey." He took my face between his hands. "I'm worried, yes. But not scared. I have faith."

"In what? Statistics?"

"Yes, but also in God. It's in his hands."

I stifled a groan. "Why would God care if I live or die? I'm just one person. I'm not even a very good person, and even if I were, bad things happen to good people all the time, so what does that prove?"

"Nothing."

"Exactly! So how can you find comfort in that?"

"It's hard to explain. You either get it or you don't."

"I want to get it." I grasped the front of his shirt. "Help me get it."

"I'll try." He pulled me to sit across his lap, then wrapped his arms around me. "You know how when you think about us as a couple—I mean really think about us—the future seems totally impossible? Hell, even our present defies the odds."

"So?"

"So why not give up? Why stay together?"

I opened my mouth to give the easy answer: *Because we love each other.* Well, duh.

"Because losing you now would definitely hurt a lot," I told him. "Any future hurt is purely speculative. In finance we call that discounting. Only the present value matters."

"But by not breaking up now, we could be making our eventual disintegration that much worse."

"I don't care." I held up a finger. "See? I'm discounting."

"Maybe that's why I have faith in your life. The thought of you—not making it . . . I can't even wrap my mind around the concept." His arms tensed. "So I just believe."

"Must be nice." My whisper curled into a hiss. "To have such an easy mental exit."

"I didn't say it was easy."

"A lot easier than facing reality."

His left eye twitched, a sign I'd pissed him off. "What do you want me to do, Ciara?" he said softly. "Freak out and cry and beg you not to leave me? Would it make you feel better to watch me self-destruct? Or would you rather have someone to lean on?"

I considered for a long moment. "Are those my only options—drama queen or stoic soldier?"

He nodded solemnly. "Unless you want me to get a sex change."

I sank down in his lap, nestling my head under his chin and fighting back tears. "I don't want you to get an anything change."

"I take it back. You're definitely sick, because you're

getting all corny and cute on me. Better call the priest for last rites."

I giggled sleepily. "He can leave the holy water at home, since it won't work on me. Besides, you might accidentally chug it, and I wouldn't be around to heal you with a quick sip."

Shane started to stroke my hair again. "If you weren't around, no pain of mine would matter. Nothing would matter."

My stomach plummeted, hard and heavy. I was afraid to ask if he meant that the way it sounded: when my life ended, whether tomorrow or decades from now, he would follow me into the great unknown. It would mean losing not only his unlife but, according to his own beliefs, his very soul.

I couldn't let that happen.

I must have fallen asleep in Shane's arms, because the phone woke us hours later. I checked the living room wall clock, which said ten after ten—a.m., I assumed, though the blackout curtains kept me from confirming.

I crawled out from under Shane's left arm and leg and stumbled for the phone, my feet half asleep. Dexter moved out of the way just in time to avoid being tripped over.

"Thank God you're home," Lori said when I answered. "How are you feeling?"

"How are *you* feeling?" I attempted a smile, though she wasn't there to see it. "Hungover?"

"Turner's dead."

Shane sat up suddenly. His sensitive ears must have heard that.

"Oh." My knees turned cold and weak. I sat on the breakfast barstool so I didn't end up on the floor. "That poor guy." I pressed the heel of my hand against my temple. "If I hadn't been so needle phobic, I would've gotten the shot like he did. I could be dead, too."

"I'm sorry I tried to make you get it. But you feel okay?"

"Yeah." I swallowed quickly. "Other than a major case of cotton mouth. I'm never letting Regina make me a drink again."

Shane went to the fridge and pulled out a cold bottle of water. He set it on the counter beside me, then disappeared into the bathroom, where I heard the creak of the medicine cabinet.

Lori's words rushed out. "But you don't feel feverish?"

"No. Maybe the incubation period is over and I'm not going to get sick." I mouthed a thanks to Shane as he placed two aspirin next to the water bottle.

"Ciara, that's not all." Lori's voice shook, and after a deep breath, it shook even more. "David called from the station. The *Baltimore Sun* sent out a breaking news e-mail fifteen minutes ago."

The skin across my shoulder blades prickled. "About what?"

"Two more Sherwood students went to the hospital last night with this chicken pox supervirus."

I gripped the edge of the counter as Shane slid his arm around my waist to steady me. "What's their condition?"

"Critical. They're in comas."

My mind scrambled for another explanation, even as the cold fear threatened to halt all brain cell activity. Dexter sniffed my ankles and uttered a soft whine.

"Are they sure it's chicken pox?" I asked her. "Meningitis happens a lot with kids living in dorms."

"The symptoms are all the same as chicken pox, except they appear at the same time and they're way more severe than usual. And everyone who's gotten sick had never had the disease or the shots." She didn't need to add, *They were all like you, Ciara.*

"What are they doing about it?"

"Sherwood canceled classes indefinitely, and they're thinking of shutting down school for the semester and sending the residents home. But the CDC might force a quarantine and not let anybody leave. So the college is telling everyone without immunity to stay inside, avoid anyone you're not absolutely sure has immunity."

"I'm already doing that. What else can I do? Don't they have medicine or something?"

"That's the worst part. On those two new cases, the antiviral drugs did the same thing the vaccine did to Turner—they just sped up the disease." Lori let out a sob that split my heart. "There's no treatment and no cure."

"Okay," I said, my mouth on autopilot as my mind began to numb. "Remember, I had one shot. It's probably all I needed."

"There's a blood test you can take to see if you're immune."

"But if I fail it, they'll put me in quarantine. If there's nothing the doctors can do for me, I might as well stay here and—" And what? Die in the comfort of my own home?

I looked up into Shane's eyes.

"Do you want me to come over?" Lori asked.

"Not now," I whispered. "Maybe tonight."

"Ciara, promise you'll call me if you feel sick before then. Shane can't take you to the hospital during the day."

"The hospital can't help me." My voice rang hollow inside my head.

"They could make it—I don't know"—she sniffled—"easier."

A peaceful voyage to the other side, courtesy of the U.S.S. *Morphine*. So it wouldn't have to hurt. There was that, at least.

"All right." My hand gripped the phone so tight, I didn't know how I would let go. "I love you."

"I love you, too." I think that's what she said; it was hard to tell around the sobbing.

I pressed the End button slowly, as if disconnecting myself from a lifeline. Shane took the phone and laid it on the counter, then drew me so close to his chest I couldn't breathe.

"What do you want to do?" he whispered. "What can I do for you?"

Save me, I shouted in my mind. *Make me live forever. I don't care how much it hurts to bleed, to die, to be born again. I don't want to leave you.* I drew in a breath to make my thoughts come alive.

But I knew what he'd say. No matter how much he loved me and wanted to keep me around, he'd consider himself a murderer and me a suicide, damned forever. He wouldn't destroy my eternal soul to save my transitory life. He would tell me no.

Then if I survived, my resentment would demolish us, especially since his conviction came from a faith I didn't understand. If I didn't survive, our last few hours together would be filled with sadness and strife and guilt.

So I said, "Marry me."

He drew me to arm's length, his eyes wide. "What, today?"

"Do you have other plans?"

Shane let out a hard breath that was half laugh. "Let's do it. Maybe a justice of the peace will make a house call." He zoomed into the kitchen and yanked open the corner drawer. Two seconds later, he was flipping through the blue pages at the front of the phone book.

"Internet might be faster." I woke up my laptop and opened a new browser tab, ignoring the WebMD chicken pox page. After typing in the search terms, I clicked on the first result, the Maryland state court Web site.

Shane read the screen over my shoulder. "A forty-eight-hour waiting period?"

I brought up another site that had a grid with each state's marriage license laws. "Virginia has no waiting period and no residency requirements. We can get to Leesburg in an hour and a half."

"Can we go tonight?"

I clicked on the link for the county clerk's office. "They're only open eight-thirty to four on weekdays."

"Of course." Shane sank onto the couch and put his head in his hands.

"Don't worry. It says only one of us needs to show up. So I can just bring your ID with me when I pick up the license. After the quarantine."

He said nothing, and I could almost hear the sound of his faith toppling. He thought there would be no "after the quarantine." He thought I was going to die.

I bounced over to him to show off my vitality. "Or we could drive to Vegas next winter, when there's lots of night." I sat in his lap. "Stay at hotels without windows, or more of those vampire-friendly B and Bs. It'll be an adventure."

"Yeah." Shane pressed his forehead against mine. "I'm sorry. I want to be strong for you."

"You are."

He held me so tight against him, my bones seemed to creak. "I can't live without you."

So don't.

"Shane . . ." I eased my head away so I could meet his gaze. "If I get sick, and it looks like I'm not going to make it, there's something I want you to do."

I expected his expression to turn guarded, but he just nodded, eyes sad but earnest. "Whatever you need."

Maybe he hadn't considered turning me to save my life. Or if he had, he'd thought I wouldn't want it—because of the hundreds of times I'd said so—or that I would never ask him.

I had to ask.

"I'm not ready to die," I said.

His fingertips grazed my cheek. "I understand."

"Do you?"

"You're so young." He traced the line of my jaw with his thumb.

"Exactly." My heart started to race with hope and fear. "Too young."

"Why would someone your age plan for this sort of thing?" He nodded slowly. "If you need me to make arrangements, for your family, or your—your funeral—" His voice caught.

I gripped his shoulders, wanting to shake him. How could he not understand?

I stared at him as the terrible truth soaked my heart. Shane did understand. He just couldn't say it out loud, and neither could I. If I asked him straight out, *make me a vampire*, he would say no. This was his way of saying *don't ask*.

The phone rang. As we turned our heads to face it, the sound seemed to stretch out, growing lower and garbled like a warped cassette tape. Dexter snorted and lifted his massive head off the sofa's other arm, aroused from sleep.

"I'll get it." Shane slowly slid out from under me and moved toward the kitchen counter. He looked at the phone handset. "David's number. Maybe it's station business." He waited another ring before punching the talk button. "Hello?"

I held my breath and stared at his face, as if David's words were scrolling on a marquee across his cheeks and nose.

"Okay, thanks," he murmured after what seemed like hours. "I'll let her know." He paused again. "Maybe later. We'll call you."

He hung up. I rubbed my chest to keep my heart beating.

"Those other students didn't make it." Shane turned and spoke to a point beyond my head. "The CDC has shut down the university. David said Homeland Security might get involved, in case it's bioterrorism."

I took two deep breaths. "But it's only four people so far on the whole campus of, what, fifteen hundred?"

"No." His lips pressed together. "Five other students and another professor have gotten sick with this supervirus. None of them had immunity."

I pulled the throw pillow into my lap and clutched it tight to my chest. "It's really happening. We're under a plague. If this gets out of Sherwood, think how many people could die."

He knelt by my side. "You might not get it. You had half the vaccine."

"Maybe it's just delaying the inevitable."

"Or maybe it'll give you the strength to beat it if you do get sick. David said none of the people who died had gotten any shots at all."

"Okay. Hope. I'll try hope." I started to rock, with the pillow still in my lap. "I'm not like everybody else. Maybe my special blood will fight off the infection."

He went to the counter and picked up the phone. "You should call your parents."

I gasped. "Yes! Maybe they'll remember me getting the second shot."

"Right, but I meant, you should call them to . . ." He dropped his gaze to the floor. "You know."

I did know. I should call them to say good-bye.

After navigating the prison's labyrinthine switchboard, I finally reached a guard.

"Hi, honey!" came my mom's voice half a minute later. Immediately I pictured her as she'd looked when I'd visited last Christmas—on the thin, pale side, but spirited as ever, like a canary in a cage.

"How are you?" My voice sounded hollow and far away, as if I were on the phone with myself. I watched Shane pour boiling water into a pot of mint tea.

"Excited. Counting down to my parole hearing."

My lower lip trembled. With good behavior, she'd be released by the end of the year. If I died of chicken pox, I would've just missed her. I wanted to hurl the phone across the room at the unfairness.

"Ooh, I have news!" she said. "They're letting me lead the prison choir."

I forced myself to speak. "Congratulations."

"There are far too many altos. Perhaps there's a connection between vocal pitch and criminal behavior. What do you think?"

"Uh, it's possible. I think testosterone affects how low your voice is and how much risk you're willing to take."

"That makes sense. My little girl is so smart. So that's my entire recent life in a nutshell. What about you?"

"Uh . . . are you sitting down?"

"Yes, they give us chairs. Why? Is it—" She sucked in a squeaky breath. "Are you pregnant?"

"No." She didn't know that was impossible, since she didn't know Shane was a vampire.

"Oh, thank goodness. Engaged?"

I slipped my thumb over my diamond and sapphire ring. "Yes, but that's not why—"

"Ciara, that's wonderful! Is it Shane?"

"Of course it's Shane." I tilted my head toward the bedroom. He nodded, then quietly slipped away to give me privacy. "But, Mom, that's not why I called."

"Something bigger than an engagement? Do spill."

I sat on the couch. "One of my professors died this week." I paused while she expressed her high-strung sorrow. "The thing is, he died of chicken pox."

"Oh," my mother said in a faint whisper. "Oh, no."

With those words, my last hope died.

"I never had it, did I? What about the shot? Did I ever get both parts?"

Her voice came fast and tight. "We were always on the move. I homeschooled you, you weren't around enough little kids to catch it. And then when the vaccine came out, it gave you all those hives, so we never . . ." She paused. "Oh my Lord, I'm so sorry."

Dexter shoved his head into my lap, grunting. I clutched the thick folds of fur and skin at his neck.

"Do you feel sick?" Mom asked me.

"No. But not everyone has come down with it at the same time."

"What do you mean, everyone?"

"Eight other students and another professor have gotten chicken pox. Three died. So far no one's recovered. The shots and the medicine make it worse."

"Oh my goodness." She took a deep, shaky breath. "Maybe you won't get it. Or maybe you'll get better. There could be other cases where people didn't get sick enough to go to the hospital, and you just don't know about them yet."

I closed my eyes. She and Shane were trying their best to give me hope, but I needed so much more.

"Mom . . . just in case. I want you to know that I love you." My chest grew tight, so I hurried on to practical matters. "And you're one of the beneficiaries of my life insurance. Shane gets the other half."

"Oh, Ciara." She started sobbing. "I love you, too. You must be so scared. I wish I could hold your hand and tell you everything will be okay. I wish I could hug you like when you were a little girl." She sniffled hard. "I wish I could come and be your mom."

That did it. Tears spilled out of my eyes, tears of anger and bitterness and defiance. And with them, a resolution.

I wiped my sleeve across my nose. "I wish you could be here, too. I hope if anything happens, they let you out so you can come." I couldn't add the words "to my funeral."

She sobbed again. "Have you called your father?"

"I was going to do that next."

"Go. Do it now before it's too late."

"Is there anything you want me to tell him?"

"Just that . . . if he wants to contact me, afterward, not to worry that I'm angry. I'll forgive him. He shouldn't have to go through this alone."

"Neither of you should."

"Go," she said quickly, and I sensed she was on the verge of breaking down.

We hung up. I put on my coat, buttoning it over Shane's baggy shirt, then knocked on the bedroom door.

"I'm going outside," I said, "to get better reception on my cell when I call my dad, then Luann. I don't want them knowing our home number."

He opened the door, his face tight with worry. "Are you sure?"

"I won't go far, I promise." I put a hand on his chest. "I'll stay where people can see me."

"Come here." He pulled me against him and kissed me. I could feel the fear in his lips, but let him have me as long as he wanted. I wasn't afraid anymore.

When he finally released me, I gave him a slight push. "Get in while I open the door."

"Hurry back." He clapped his hands. "Dexter, come!"

As soon as they were safe inside the bedroom, I opened

the front door. The spring day was unseasonably warm, with sunlight so bright it stabbed my eyes.

I took a deep breath, inhaling the heady scent of my neighbor's pink hyacinths. The streets of Sherwood were emptier than usual for a Saturday afternoon, no doubt due to news of the chicken pox plague. A breeze stirred the cherry trees lining the street, shivering their white flowers. The forsythia bushes next to the bank's drive-through gleamed like clusters of suns—it almost hurt to look at the bright yellow blossoms.

Across the street, the coffee shop door was propped open, and I could smell fresh-baked chocolate croissants. My stomach growled, but I didn't dare enter the shop, for fear of infecting an innocent coffee drinker. Yet there was something else over there I needed.

I crossed when the light changed, hurrying, as if the thing in question could save my life.

When I reached the opposite curb, I turned left and walked, humming "Keep on the Sunny Side" to myself— probably off-key, not that I could tell.

The golden rays warmed my face and gilded the hair that blew in my eyes. I shivered with the sensation of sudden warmth.

I pulled out my phone, but didn't dial my father or my birth mother. Instead I switched it to camera mode, turned it around, and gave myself an enormous, squinty-eyed grin before pressing the button.

I checked out my photo. A bit off center, as usual, but at least it got my head and my hair, shining in the sun.

I turned off the camera and made another call, to someone who would understand.

16

Until I Fall Away

I knocked on the apartment door and waited half a minute before entering, to give Shane and Dexter time to hide from the light.

The moment I shut the door behind me, they appeared from the bedroom.

"I was worried." Shane helped me take off my coat. "I almost called David to go find you."

"I took a walk. It felt good." The apartment seemed dismal now compared to the sunlit afternoon. "You should get some sleep. It's the middle of the day."

"How am I supposed to sleep?"

"Shane, I need some time alone, okay? I promise I'll come to bed soon." I looked at my computer. "There are people I should say good-bye to, just in case. And some financial stuff to clean up." When he started to protest, I cut him off. "And then I can relax and be with you, with a clear head."

"I understand." He kissed me quickly, then picked up

his cell phone from the counter. "I'm setting my alarm for an hour, and then I'm dragging you off to bed."

I watched him go into the bedroom and shut the door. Then I went to my CD rack, faced with that desert island question: If I could only listen to one album the rest of my life, which would it be?

Nirvana's *Unplugged* concert, the first thing Shane and I ever listened to? No, I wanted something for me alone. Red Hot Chili Peppers' *Californication*, my favorite CD in the world? Nah, too upbeat for the occasion. I needed something that would make me feel strong.

I pulled out Liz Phair's debut, *Exile in Guyville*. I was ten years old when it came out. I shoplifted the cassette from a used record store—not to avoid paying for it, but because my parents would have thrown it away if they knew I had it. I'd listen to it late at night under the covers with my Walkman. It made me believe I could do anything, and I didn't have to be perfect or well behaved. It made me happy to be a girl.

At the sound of the first solo guitar chords of "6'1"," I knew I'd made the right choice. I stood in the center of the room, eyes closed, feeling my resolve grow with every measure.

When the maracas faded and the second song kicked off, I looked around. Dexter wagged his tail at me from the couch, where he had stretched out with his head on his paws.

I plopped down next to him, and he wriggled his upper body into my lap. I stroked the soft thick fur on his face, tracing the old battle scars he must have gotten in his regular dog days, before the Control made him what he was. Then I nudged Dexter until he sat up, groaning, so I could wrap my arms around his neck and broad chest. He rubbed the side of his head against my hair, hugging me back.

"I swore I'd never leave you. But that might change. You have to be a good boy for Daddy. Don't let him be sad, okay? I mean, he can be sad, but not enough to—" I didn't dare voice the thought, not even for Dexter. "Give him someone who needs him," I whispered. "Give him something to live for."

Dexter licked my ear. I took that as an okay.

I extricated myself from his long legs and went to the breakfast bar for my laptop. I poured a second cup of tea from the pot Shane had made and carried it and the computer back to the sofa. Dexter resnuggled as soon as I settled in.

I logged into the Web sites of my banks, offshore and onshore. With a series of clicks and passwords, I transferred all but a few dollars from my accounts—enough to keep them open—into the joint checking account I shared with Shane.

Then I wrote e-mails to Lori, David, Franklin, my dad, Luann, and my foster parents, and saved them in my drafts folder. Shane would send them In the Event Of.

Thinking of him sitting here alone tomorrow, hunched over my computer releasing my last missives, made my chest tighten and crumble. The tears came again, drenching my cheeks. Dexter licked them away, making my face even wetter.

When the music faded, I turned off the power on the stereo. Then I told Dexter to stay.

"You had two minutes left," Shane said as I entered the bedroom. "Good choice of album."

I stripped down to my camisole and underwear. "I want to take a shower, so I won't smell bad if I go to the hospital." The phrase "Live fast, die young, and leave a beautiful corpse" flashed through my mind as I stepped onto the smooth, cool threshold of the master bathroom.

He got out of bed. "I'm not waiting for an invitation."

"Good."

Shane's mouth met mine with an achingly familiar urgency. My fingers tightened on his shoulders as he pressed me back against the doorjamb. He bent his legs, and one of his hands descended to my thigh, lifting it up and around his waist. We kissed harder, our bodies straining against each other.

Finally he moved his mouth to my ear. "Get in the shower."

I reached for the hem of my camisole to pull it over my head.

Shane caught my hand. "Keep it on." He led me to the tub and helped me step over the side. "For now."

Soon he stood naked outside the tub. "Hold still." With the shower attachment pointed at the tub's floor, he turned the water to a steady trickle and checked the temperature. Once the steam began to rise, he angled the soft spray on my top, soaking the thin cotton layer and turning it heavy against my skin. My nipples hardened. He leaned forward and suckled me through the cloth, as if he were thirsty and I was the only source of water.

Shane rubbed the trickling showerhead lower, soaking my panties. He climbed into the tub with me and got to his knees.

He brought his head between my thighs and stroked me with his tongue through the wet material. My knees shook, and I arched my hips against him. He ran the showerhead up and down my legs, slowly, the warm water setting my nerves on maximum tingle. I moaned and clutched at the slick wall behind me, trying to memorize each sensation.

With his other hand, Shane drew down my panties and tossed them away. He lifted one of my feet to rest on the side of the tub, then handed me the showerhead.

When he tasted me, his groan echoed against the walls. His fingers explored my depths, moving with fascination, as if it were the first time he'd ever touched me instead of possibly the last. I sent the water rushing down the back of his neck and watched it stream over the lean muscles of his shoulders and torso.

A sudden rising ecstasy shot through me. I dropped the showerhead. It clattered on the porcelain surface, and its leaping, pulsing spray was the last thing I saw before I closed my eyes and succumbed to the pounding orgasm. When my legs grew too weak to hold my weight, I dropped to my knees.

Shane picked up the showerhead, then tilted my head back. "Close your eyes."

I obeyed, and shivered when the warm water flowed over my scalp, trickling to the back of my shoulders. Then his mouth was at my neck, teeth grazing, then nipping without fangs, never breaking the skin.

This could be our last chance. But I still didn't want pain and blood between us.

Unless it was the only way to save my life. I clutched his back, biting my own lip to hold in my plea.

Shane stood and reattached the showerhead to the hook so that it flowed over both of us. He started to rejoin me on the floor of the tub, but I stopped him. I wanted to give him everything, maybe one last time.

As hard as he was in my hand, he stiffened further when I took him in my mouth, deep and tight. He responded instantly, rocking his hips, palms braced against the wall above my head. The water streamed over his back, soaking my hands as they grasped the tightening muscles of his ass.

"Yes," he breathed. "Oh, God. God, God, God . . ." The way he intoned the name of the deity he loved and feared so fiercely threatened to make me a believer again myself.

Finally he went still, sighing my name. I let go of him, and he leaned back, tilting his head into the rush of water.

Shane helped me to my feet, then peeled off my wet top and tossed it over the shower curtain rod. As I shampooed, he lathered my body with soap, his hands coasting warm and slippery over my skin.

I rinsed my hair, then returned the favor, cleansing every inch of him. By the time I finished, he was fully aroused again. Our slick flesh slid together with a heat that told me we weren't nearly done.

The water, on the other hand, was out of heat. Shane shut it off, then stepped out to fetch my favorite fluffy red towel. He wrapped it around both of us and kissed me again as he dried my back. When we were still damp but not dripping, he helped me out of the tub and led me into the bedroom.

As we stood next to the bed, I gazed up at him, his wet hair glistening in the soft lamplight, flat against his head, giving him a boyish, vulnerable look.

"This isn't the last time," I told him.

He wiped a rivulet of water from the side of my face, then let the towel drop at our feet.

We didn't speak any more that afternoon, not even to say what we wanted to do. We didn't need words when we could read each other's bodies so well.

I was right—that wasn't the last time. Neither was the next time, an hour later; or the next, a half hour after that. We made love in an endless cycle of kissing, touching, and fucking, until the clock told me the sun was on its way out.

I got dressed and dragged my exhausted body up the fire escape to the roof of our building. One last sunset, maybe, a gift to myself.

The red orb flared as it descended below the horizon. Tendrils of scarlet and tangerine spread themselves across the sky, like the fingers of a child's brightly colored glove.

"Good-bye," I whispered to the vanishing sun. "Thanks for all the great tans in the summer, and for warming my car in the winter, and the free vitamin D."

As if in reply, the last rays burst into sharp beams against the clouds. My own personal laser show.

A breeze tousled my hair, which was still a bit damp from the shower. I drew my jacket tighter across my chest, expecting a chill.

Instead, a wave of heat broke over me, curling up from my feet as if I'd been standing over a subway grate.

I glanced around for the source of the hot air. The panorama of building tops blurred, their lights swirling and spinning. It was like looking out from the center of a merry-go-round.

"What the—"

The pain hit me like a steel spike to the temple. I

stumbled, fingers splayed, lungs too cramped to scream. I thudded to my hands and knees, the fine-gravel surface jabbing my palms. If I'd been near the roof's edge, I would have fallen and splatted on the sidewalk. But at least the pain would have ended.

I began to crawl.

The railing of the fire escape protruded above the roof's edge. I kept my eyes on it, though craning my neck sent imaginary foot-long needles into my skull. The roof felt ice-cold against my burning palms.

"God, please . . ." If I could get down . . . somehow . . . then maybe thirty steps to the front door. By then it might be twilight already, and Shane could drive me to the ER.

Wait. That wasn't right. I was supposed to . . . what?

I tried to remember, but the pain bent my thoughts into origami angles. Had to lie down . . . but not yet. Somewhere else.

I reached the fire escape, where my elbows and knees gave way. I rolled onto my side, pressing my face into the rusty but blissfully cold iron surface.

The chill cleared my thoughts long enough for one name.

Jeremy.

I slapped my pockets for my cell phone. It was in the left one, the side I was lying on. Figures. I rolled onto my back, and the motion made my stomach pitch and twist. I closed my eyes until the nausea swept on, then shoved my hand into my pocket.

The moment my fingers brushed my ribs, the itching began. "Ungh!" I forgot everything but the need to scratch. It obliterated the ache in my head and the sick in my stomach.

Whimpering, I raked my nails over my belly, but the itch spread around my waist to my spine. Desperation gave me the strength to arch my back against the fire escape rail, trying to rub off the millions of tiny pins pricking my skin.

My skin. That was it. Too much skin. My nails could only scrape. But a knife could flay it off. We had knives in our kitchen. *How do I get to the kitchen?*

Go down.

I rolled so that my head was over the edge of the stairs. Too weak to stand, I grabbed the railings on either side and pulled.

I slid down headfirst, belly-flop style. Each stair jarred my ribs and breasts, but I didn't care. Nothing mattered but finding the knives. And ice. And—

I hit the landing and flipped onto my back, helpless as a turtle. Breathing hard, then hardly breathing, I stared at the darkening sky, which slowly, gracefully, turned to black.

"Ciara, can you hear me? *Ciara!*"

I tried to open my eyes, move a finger, or anything to let Shane know that his voice had reached me, that I could feel his cool hand on my face. But the darkness pulled so hard.

A sharp motion jerked my body to the right. The sound of squealing tires forced me awake, but I couldn't open my eyes.

I made my lips move. "Where?"

"We're in David's car," he said. "I called him as soon as you left the apartment to see the sunset. I had a bad feeling, I thought I was being paranoid, but thank God. He and Lori found you on the fire escape."

"Lori?"

"I'm right here." Her voice came from my right, from the front passenger's seat. Beneath my head, something shifted. Shane's leg.

He smoothed the hair out of my face. "We're taking you to the ER. They'll give you some fluids and try to get this fever down."

The ER. What's an ER? Something scary. Instinct tried to tell my fever-fuzzed brain why that was a terrible idea. It dug for dormant associations.

They canceled the show ER. *You don't want to be canceled, do you?*

It wasn't canceled, I told Instinct. *Its time had come. Maybe my time has come, too.* I snuggled into Shane's lap. *To everything, turn turn turn, there is a season . . .*

Yes, Instinct said, *and now is the time of the season for living.*

"Living"? I thought the line was "loving." Did I get that wrong, too, the way I always thought the guy in the Radiohead song "Creep" was a widow instead of a weirdo?

Instinct went for the direct approach. *WAKE. THE. FUCK. UP!!*

Shane spoke, interrupting my interior dialogue. "David, I'm staying with her every minute, I don't care what they say."

"Fine, but you get back home or to the station before sunup. I'm not losing you, too."

"Do you want me to call the station?" Lori said. "Let them know what happened?"

"Thanks," David said. "Ask Jeremy to do Shane's midnight show."

Jeremy.

"Stop the car!" I screamed.

David slammed on the brakes, spiking the pain through my lurching body. "Shit, you scared me. We can't stop."

"But I have to throw up!"

"Throw up on the floor. We're almost there."

"Please." I made my voice as pathetic as I felt. "Just for a sec. Won't make a difference."

I felt the car drift, then rumble as it hit the shoulder of the road. Shane lifted me to sit up, and I tried to siphon his immense strength with the nonexistent power of my mind.

The car stopped. He jerked open the door and helped me lean out over his lap.

I gagged and spat as loud as I could. One hand clutched the car door handle while the other one snuck my cell phone out of my pocket and pressed the screen to unlock it. Moaning with all-too-authentic pain, I opened my draft messages. At the top of the list sat the one-word text:

NOW.

Off it went, my last chance to live.

I shoved the door wider to see the dark glistening waters of the Sherwood community pond. Beyond it lay the farm museum and agricultural center, where we went for fireworks last Fourth of July. That meant . . .

The hospital loomed behind me, on the town's highest hill. David was right. We were almost there.

No! I kicked against the seat and spilled myself out of the car.

"Ciara!" Shane grabbed me as I tried to crawl away

across the shoulder's rough pavement. "Where are you going? We have to take you to the hospital."

"Not yet!" I scrabbled at his arms like a feral cat. The pain and itching and dizziness faded into the background, subsumed by fear and the drive to survive.

"She's delirious." Shane's pained voice turned back to me. "Shh, listen. Calm down. You'll make your fever worse. It's gonna be okay."

"No!" I clutched at his shirt. "I don't want to lose you. I love you. Just hold me."

"Okay, okay." He stroked my hair and rocked my body slowly. "I love you, too, with everything I have. With every last fucking piece of me, I love you."

"I never meant to hurt you," I whispered into his chin.

"Now you're really goofy." He kissed my forehead. "You've never hurt me."

I started to cry. Shane loosened his hold so my lungs could heave and sob.

After a few moments he said, "Can we get back in the car now?" His voice was soft but urgent. "The meter is running."

"Ha-ha." I drew out each syllable, buying time. We would never be like this again. "Hey, let's get married right now."

"Okay." He laced his right hand with my left one. "We're married."

"Yay." I giggled as the delirium soaked my brain like a bath of boiling acid. "Congratulations, Mr. Griffin."

"Ciara, please." Lori's voice shot from the car, loaded with tears. "Come back. We love you so much."

Her sadness broke my heart. I let myself go limp.

Shane lifted me into the car, and we were on our way. I

felt the incline of the giant hill. The emergency room was on the far side of the hospital campus from this entrance, through a maze of lanes that David was taking at top speed.

After two more violent turns, which made me want to puke for real, we screeched to a stop. The back door opened, and Shane lifted me into David's arms.

I whimpered and tried one last time to fight. Too late. It hadn't worked. I'd be dead by morning.

Then, like the trumpet clarion of an approaching cavalry, I heard it: the bowel-shaking roar of a 426 Hemi V-8 engine.

David's arms tensed around my shoulders and knees. "That looks like Jim's car."

Shane slid out of the backseat and stood next to us. "It is. What's he doing here?"

I lifted my chin to see the bright white ER sign reflected in the midnight blue hood of a '69 Dodge Charger.

Both doors of the muscle car opened. From the driver's side emerged the world's most unlikely pair of saviors.

"Let her go," Jim said.

"She's coming with us," Regina added as she crawled out of the backseat behind him.

"What are you talking about?" Shane planted himself in front of me. "She's dying."

"Yes, she is." Regina's combat boots thumped the pavement as she strode forward. "But not like this."

"This is crazy!" He backed up to shield me, pressing my body between his and David's. "She needs a doctor."

"She needs a vampire." Regina shoved Shane aside and held him against the frame of David's car.

"Shane, let me go," I managed to croak. "I want to live."

"Bullshit!" He looked at Regina. "She doesn't know what she wants. She's not in her right mind."

"She was today."

Everyone turned in response to Jeremy's voice. He stood on the curb beside the Charger's passenger door.

"She called me this afternoon," he said to Shane. "We arranged it."

I almost wished the coma would take me right then, so I wouldn't have to see Shane's face.

He turned to me, eyes filled with hurt and bewilderment. "You asked them to do this?"

I couldn't speak past the thickness in my throat, so I just nodded. Inside David's car, Lori started to cry.

"And you didn't tell me." Shane looked at me as if I were a stranger who'd murdered the love of his life. Which I guess I had.

"Don't do this," he whispered. "You could still live. You had half the vaccine."

"I can't take that chance." Tears garbled my words. "I can't leave you."

His eyes softened, and for a moment I thought he would acquiesce.

Then Regina said, "She's made up her mind. Get over it already."

Shane's shoulders tensed. His narrow gaze shifted from David and me to Regina, then back again. He was no doubt calculating whether he could overcome her long enough for David to carry me inside the ER. Given his determination, he probably could.

"Let her go."

I jolted at the sound of Monroe's voice. He stood a few feet behind Regina, his clothes and skin as dark as the shadows enveloping his frame. His hands were in the pockets of his Sunday best suit, but we all knew he could tear out Shane's throat in half a heartbeat.

The hope drained from Shane's face, and he turned his eyes back to me one last time.

"Please . . ."

I shook my head.

David spoke behind my ear. "Ciara, are you sure about this?"

I focused on keeping my voice strong and steady, for at least two words. "I'm sure."

His grip loosened. "Then go." He stepped forward and laid me in Regina's arms.

I fumbled for Shane, but he was out of reach. "Forgive me."

He stared at me, hands folded under his elbows.

"Come with me," I pleaded.

"There's no room in the car," Regina said, "but he can follow if he wants."

As she hurried me away, I reached out to Shane again. "Please! Or I'll let myself die."

Regina stopped, her dark gaze piercing me. "You won't do this without him? You mean that?"

"Yes." At least I think I did. Looking back, I might've been partly bluffing. But at that moment, I didn't want a life—or unlife—without Shane, and I sensed that what I had done could break us in two forever.

His face crumpled. "Fuck," he said through gritted teeth. He clenched his fists and pressed them to his temples for a long moment, then dropped them.

Without looking at me, he nodded to David. "Let's follow them."

* * *

"You're not gonna upchuck in my car, are you?"

"Bite me," I said to Jim from the backseat. The two-word sentence exhausted me.

"You heard it, folks." Jim slapped the steering wheel. "She picked me. I knew it."

"Did not." I tried and failed to raise my head from Regina's shoulder. Her arm wrapped tight around me, steadying my body against the car's lurching.

Monroe sat on my other side, silent as ever.

"Ciara, it's all set," Jeremy said from the front passenger seat. "They got everything ready at the station after you called me today."

"Thanks," I whispered, not sure he could hear me.

"Have you decided who you want to make you?" Regina asked me quietly. "We're all up for it except Noah. He's like Shane—religious precepts against killing. Simple-minded boys."

"S'okay," I slurred. "I respect that."

The ultimate question. Whose life would I connect with my own forever? Definitely not crazy Jim's. And picking Regina would make me Shane's blood sister—*ew*.

That left Spencer and Monroe. Could Spencer pass his poker skills through his blood? The thought would've made me laugh if it didn't hurt to breathe.

I opened my eyes. Even now, the impenetrable, ancient Monroe wouldn't meet my gaze. A cultural thing, David once told me, from Monroe's days in the Jim Crow South. Black men had been lynched for much less intimate contact with white women than what a turning would involve.

Maybe he was just being polite in offering to make me a vampire, assuming I'd say no. Maybe he'd be scared, and I'd die while he got up the nerve to drain me.

We turned onto the station's long gravel driveway, where the only illumination came from the headlights and dashboard. I stared at Monroe across the dark car as we rumbled down the quarter-mile lane. I thought about the way he played guitar, the mystery he wove with his hands and voice in a way that made even Shane sound as mundane as an *American Idol* reject. Monroe was magic.

I whispered his name. After a long moment, he turned his head slowly and met my gaze.

His eyes held no trace of civility. They challenged me. Was I strong enough? Did I want this for the right reason? Or was I playing with blood and fire and life itself?

My blinks came faster, but I forced my eyes to hold still. A thousand tests lay ahead of me. I wanted to pass the first.

Monroe dipped his head.

"Thank you," I said. My heart twisted with fierce hope—that I would make him proud, that I would be worthy of my maker.

That I would live.

17

Famous Last Words

I'd wanted to see the vampires' apartment ever since I met them, but they enforced a strict No Humans Allowed policy. Even Jeremy, their fellow DJ, had never been admitted.

"Huh," he said behind me as we entered through the heavy steel door. "Not what I expected."

In Regina's arms, I could see nothing but her cascade of black hair—and beyond it, the dropped ceiling's white tiles. I tried to turn my head to look around, but the motion had become impossible. My headache was now more of a me-ache. The only parts that didn't hurt were the parts I could no longer feel.

"It's all ready," I heard Spencer say in his calm, steady drawl.

Regina laid me on a bed in the middle of what I assumed was the common room, since we hadn't gone through any other doors. The mattress felt thin and creaky, like that of a pullout couch.

Spencer appeared in my dimming vision with a large

sippy cup. "Here, darlin', try to drink something. Being hydrated makes you easier to bite."

Regina rolled me so I could put my lips around the end of the straw. It tasted like blue Gatorade, the world's coldest drink. I whimpered in gratitude.

"Easy. Go slow." Spencer sat on the edge of the bed and wiped my forehead with a cool wet cloth. I wondered if I'd made a mistake in not choosing him to turn me—his maternal qualities would have been comforting.

Then I saw Monroe standing behind him, and I knew we were right. Like my blood already called to him, and his to mine.

He passed a clipboard to Spencer, who held it out to me. On it was a sheet of paper with the Control sun logo in the top left corner.

The infamous VBC form. Vampire by Choice.

By signing it I was consenting to be killed and (hopefully) resurrected. Without a VBC, the Control could prosecute Monroe for murder.

I scanned the form, though it hurt to move my eyeballs. The others must have known I didn't want to be a vampire, that I just didn't want to be dead. But they were willing to create a monster to keep me around. I could never repay them.

"Regina, it's quarter to nine," Jeremy said. "If you want, I can do your show. I'm doing Shane's as it is."

"If you spend nine hours straight on the air, OSHA will be on our ass for worker abuse." She pointed to the end of the bed. "Stay there. You need to see this."

I gripped the pen so hard my knuckles cracked. Regina wanted Jeremy to witness the horror of vamping, so he would stop wanting it so much for himself. He needed to see that no one with a choice would ever do this.

I signed the form and slipped into darkness.

"Open your eyes, ma'am."

I wrenched my lids apart to see Monroe, his body stretched out next to mine.

"You ready?" he said.

"Where's Shane?"

Spencer spoke from my right. "He'll be here any minute, sweetheart." He rested a light hand on my forehead.

"Lori just called," Jeremy said from the end of the bed. "David got pulled over for speeding. She managed to convince Shane not to eat the cop, so they're on their way."

I looked at Monroe, wanting to ask if we could wait for Shane. I wanted my lover's face to be my last sight.

But Monroe's ink-black eyes were the ones I fell into.

It was like soaring into another galaxy, like those movie shots where they enter hyperspace and the stars around them stretch and shimmer. My pain faded, and even the itch felt like it belonged to someone else's body.

Then my fever spiked, the heat spreading over my scalp and through my skull until it seemed like my brain would roast. The tunnel of my vision constricted to a point.

From a distance, I heard Spencer draw in a sharp breath. Then Noah asked him, "What's wrong?"

He didn't answer, only said, "Monroe, you better start now."

I felt them all draw closer but saw nothing except the eternity in my maker's eyes. Caught between freezing and burning, I reached out.

Monroe took my hand, touching me for the first time ever. "Say your prayers if you got 'em."

I closed my eyes and sent a mind-whispered message out to whatever force in the universe had brought me to this moment: *Please end this pain.* (Either way, it would soon, so I was hedging my bets, prayerwise.)

Monroe's lips touched my throat, as soft and cold as dry ice. They parted, and I felt his tongue flick against my skin, searching for the heat of my pulse.

A familiar hand slipped against my empty palm. "I'm here," Shane said. "I love you."

The same words were on my lips when Monroe's fangs sank into my flesh, his teeth like twin hot pokers.

I let out a strangled shriek. My muscles seized as I fought the instinct to shove him away. Every cell in my body screamed *No!* and if I'd been anything but near comatose I'd have pounded Monroe's face until my fists shattered.

"Ciara, breathe," Shane whispered, his thumb caressing the side of my hand. I focused on the pressure of his warm skin, and on the rhythm of my breath.

In, one, two, three, four. Out, one, two, three, four, five, six, seven, eight. A distant yoga class memory told me the exhale should be twice as long as the inhale. Was my life flashing before my eyes? If so, why not any of the fun parts?

The stabbing pain subsided as Monroe withdrew his fangs.

"I'm so sorry," he said.

"No, I'm sorry," I told him. "You're doing fine."

Everyone seemed to find this funny, or maybe they just really needed a laugh.

"Shh." Monroe motioned to the rest of them, who silenced instantly. Then he wrapped his arm around my waist and raised my torso. His other hand slid behind my head, supporting my neck, and just like that, I was suspended in his embrace. He lowered his mouth to my neck, where the blood flowed in a hot, steady trickle.

He drank. I closed my eyes and dropped Shane's hand.

The room fell silent, and my world shrank to nothing but me and Monroe. I clutched his back until I had no more strength, then let my hands fall where they would, onto his right hip and the crook of his left arm.

The pain in my neck was a pinprick next to the bellowing agony of my swelling brain. The virus had stepped up its attack, as if realizing something else might have the privilege of stealing my life. It felt like my carcass was being tugged in half by two wild beasts, and I had to choose which would win.

You won't take me, you itchy little bastard. I tried to bleed harder.

But Monroe's swallows were slowing. Blood was escaping his lips and running down to the back of my hairline.

Finally he let out an exhale and pulled his mouth away, holding me in the same position, head below my heart.

"Why y'stop?" I slurred.

"A belly can only take so much. You have to do the rest on your own." His thumb grazed the wound, making me hiss with pain. "It'll come."

So I wait to bleed to death, I thought. *This is happening. It's happening now.* My heartbeat and breath slowed as my body tried to delay its decline. "When?"

"Not long, child."

Shane choked back a sob. Under his breath, he began to recite a Hail Mary, the words tumbling over one another. In a far corner I heard Noah praying, too. Their faith felt like a shield between me and permanent death.

I let Shane get through a few more Hail Marys, a couple of Kyrie Eleisons, and an Our Father before using my last bit of strength to touch his hand.

"Play for me," I whispered. "Anything."

He cleared his throat as if struggling to speak. "My guitar's back at the apartment."

"Use mine," Monroe said.

I heard a collective gasp around me. No one ever touched Monroe's guitar.

Shane didn't wait for a second invitation. "Thank you."

A few moments later he was back at my side. I heard the rich wooden echo of the guitar as he sat down. I could picture the instrument's polished crimson surface.

Shane took a few tentative strums, then let out a breath of quiet admiration. He started with my favorite song: Red Hot Chili Peppers' "Otherside," then moved on to "Ripple" by the Grateful Dead. Finally he played my song: Luka Bloom's "Ciara," the first thing he'd ever played for me on the guitar, on our first date, which seemed like a pile of eternities ago.

By the end of the song, my vision had turned black, and the room was filled with weeping. Monroe's tears fell hot on my neck as he held me.

I drifted for minutes that seemed like hours. My body felt warm in its core but cold on the surface. With each passing moment, the surface thickened.

At the end of the dark tunnel of my vision, I glimpsed a bright white light.

Well, I'll be damned, I thought. *Or not.* Peace swept aside the feeling of foolishness. It was nice to be wrong, or at least wrongish. All in all, this whole dying thing hadn't been too bad.

Until the convulsions.

They started in my lungs, gripped by a sudden icy fist. Then the shudders spread all over, seizing every muscle. I bit my tongue and tasted blood.

"This ain't right," Monroe said.

Shane dropped the guitar with a hollow *dong!* "What's happening to her?"

A palm splayed across my chest. "She's dying," Spencer said in a shaky voice, "but not the way we want her to."

Inhale, one, two, three, four. It wasn't happening. The words "respiratory arrest" bounced around my brain, fed by the tale of Aaron's death.

An arrest, for sure. Cop, kneeling on my chest, shoving a nightstick against my windpipe. Tasing the ever-living breath out of me.

My hands flopped and my fingers stretched, as if they could grasp the air and suck it into my body through the skin of my palms.

"Feed her!" Shane's voice rang out above me. "Feed her now."

"Shane, listen." Spencer's hand lay on my quaking form, rattling his words. "She ain't dead yet. We don't know what bringing her back will do, what she'll become."

"It's the only chance she has. Feed her!"

The beam of white light, which had been sauntering toward me with the leisure of a Sunday driver, suddenly surged forward like a charging lion. It devoured the blackness until the light was all I could see. My mind shrieked one last defiance.

Everything stopped.

No screaming, no crying, no singing. No breathing, no choking, no thumping heart. No white, no black, no color in between.

It was just . . . over.

18

Dust in the Wind

I waited. I thought of nothing.

No one came to greet me—no St. Peter or Satan's minion with a pen and clipboard to declare my eternal fate. For one long moment, I was alone.

And then, I was with everything and everybody who had ever lived. We were all held together in . . . something. Something good.

I reached out so It could gather me into Its eternal embrace.

Then the nape of my neck began to tickle, and I realized I had a neck with a nape to tickle. But by what? Not a finger or other solid object.

It was the music. From another world a melody curled out and called to the one within me, a song I didn't even know I had. Half alive, they reached for each other, blocked by the walls of this realm I'd entered.

I had to go back, unite the two melodies into one harmony. I grasped for the other's music, but it was as thin as a thread and just as fragile. It couldn't hold me, it could only lead me—if I found the strength to follow.

I let the song within guide me, but the journey back was like walking through chunky peanut butter. The . . . something . . . wanted me to stay forever. It offered one last chance at this thing called peace.

I turned away.

Darkness wrapped around me again. Pain spiked my neck as someone rolled me onto my side. A hot substance filled my mouth, a liquid thick as cotton.

To keep from smothering, I swallowed.

Light and heat flared inside me, as if I'd swallowed the sun. The space blazed out, filling my bones and muscles with life. I remembered who I was and where I belonged. Here. Basement, WVMP Radio, Highway 97, Sherwood, Maryland, United States, North America.

Earth.

The pain vanished, and I became thirst.

My hand locked around Monroe's forearm. My tongue sucked and lapped, and my teeth ground into his flesh, urging the blood from his veins. I was pure instinct, an instinct I had no strength to fight.

Under the noise of my harsh gulps and needy moans came the sound of a single guitar. As the chaotic roar in my ears quieted to a steady thrum, I discerned the lilting melody.

Shane was singing the song he wrote for me, the song that convinced me to marry him, the song that had now called me back to life. I had followed his voice straight out of . . . heaven? Hell? Didn't matter. I only wanted to be here, drinking, listening, feeling. Living.

Monroe's essence flowed into me, ancient and cold and silent, but with a glimmer of the Ciara I had been. It was like finding a better, stronger version of myself and taking it deep, making me a part of me again.

Just as the song ended, I hit my last swallow. No one told me to stop, but I knew it was enough.

I let go of Monroe and opened my eyes. My vision was blurry, as if my corneas were coated in Vaseline. Was I going to be the world's first visually impaired vampire?

"You're not done yet, child." Monroe stroked my cheek, filling my nose with the heady scent of his blood. "But we'll be here. Don't you forget—"

My scream sliced his words.

My bones were stretching. *Bones. Stretching!* Impossible. True. Every muscle, tendon, ligament was twisting, hardening, fusing, all grinding against the frayed ends of my pain nerves.

Imagine every weapon at the Inquisition's fingertips: the rack, hot pokers, thumbscrews, the iron maiden. Then imagine enduring them all at once. Multiply by twenty.

I writhed on the bed, shrieking and cursing, begging for death, despising the Ciara (fool!) of ten minutes ago, the one who had turned down eternal peace and painlessness.

The vampires took turns holding me so I didn't shatter myself or the furniture. I'm pretty sure I broke Shane's arm, but he didn't let go.

Finally a slow flood of relief started in my gut and oozed out into my limbs. My fingers and toes were the last to stop twitching.

I opened my eyes. The room had brightened, but not because someone had turned on more lights. I lay curled in the fetal position on the torn, bloodstained sheets.

"Ciara?" Shane said. "Can you hear me?"

I blinked twice for yes, then realized we'd never established an unspoken code. "That sucked."

Relieved laughter echoed throughout the room. Noah said, "Praise Jah!"

"You ain't kidding," Jim added. "This calls for a party."

My breath was still coming hard and fast, like I'd finished a triathlon. My muscles felt limp as string cheese.

I rolled onto my back. Shane was lying beside me, his gaze traveling over my broken, mended body. His hand reached out—tentatively, as if it might go straight through me, as if I were a hologram.

He touched my face, and a shiver passed between us.

"I need to explain," I whispered. "I need to tell you why I did this without you."

"You tried to ask me, I realize that now. But I couldn't hear you. I wouldn't listen."

"I thought you'd say no."

His eyes turned sad. "I gave you a million reasons to believe that. And maybe you were right."

My heartbeat stuttered. Did he hate what I'd become? Had I gained my life only to lose the best part of it?

"Maybe I would've said no." His whisper softened. "But then I would've said yes. Even if I hated myself forever for it, I couldn't have watched you die."

My fingers curled into the front of his shirt. Whatever happened, I'd never let him go.

"Folks, she needs some quiet time," Spencer said. "And you'd better go, son."

"Is she going to be okay?" came another voice, one that sounded thicker than the others. Juicier.

"You need to leave now." Spencer's tone was urgent. "Please."

My new muscles tensed, jolting into tight cords. I waited for Jeremy to pass the bed on his way to the door. Then I sprang.

I was halfway through the air, launching myself over the back of the couch, on a direct trajectory with Jeremy's neck, when a great weight tackled me. My body slammed to the ground.

Jeremy screamed as he ran. I snarled and kicked under Spencer's weight. The steel door opened, then slammed shut.

"Ain't no doubt now the change worked." Spencer got off me, then helped me to my feet, where I swayed, unsteady.

"I was just playing." The gob of drool on my chin made me a liar. "When's he coming back?"

"Judging by the look on his face?" Shane came up behind me. "Never."

"Ciara, we thought we had lost you." Noah stripped the bloody sheets off the bed. "We thought we were too late."

"Almost." I leaned against Shane's solid frame. "The virus was definitely catching up to Monroe in, well, killing me." I looked at my maker, who stood at the foot of the bed, hands in pockets, already wearing a clean shirt. "I was in the light."

They stared at me.

"What do you mean," Spencer said, "*in* the light? You saw the white light from far away, right?"

"At first, but then it swallowed me up." I looked at their shocked faces. "Did I do it wrong?"

They exchanged worried glances, but then Jim spoke up.

"Doesn't mean anything. Everyone has a different experience." He grinned at me. "So was it a trip or was it a trip?"

"It was something."

He put on a wistful look. "I wish I could do it all over again."

I would never understand him.

"How do you feel?" Shane asked me.

"Alive." My voice resonated, as if my head were an arena. "What time is it? Can we go out? I want to hunt and drive fast and hurdle cars."

I took two steps toward the door before my knees folded. A pair of strong arms caught me. I gaped at the carpet, which was two inches from having my nose embedded in it.

"Easy there." Bearing most of my weight, Shane helped me shuffle to the closest armchair.

Behind me, Jim snickered. "Not ready for prime time."

The door to the hallway opened. I craned my neck as I sat, my mouth watering at the thought of Jeremy.

Regina stood there, hands pressed to her cheeks. "You did it. You're alive." She rushed over to take me in her arms, pressing my face to her sharp collarbone. "I'm so much happier than I thought I'd be."

"Thanks. I think."

She let go of me and sniffed my mouth. "You guys haven't fed her yet? What the fuck is wrong with you?"

After a short, oddly uncomfortable pause, Spencer said, "I was just about to do that."

Regina peered at my face. "How do you feel?"

"Everyone keeps asking me that. I'm fine."

"You're not fine." She touched my arm, with more gentleness than I thought she possessed. "You died and came back to life."

"And what was the alternative? Dying and not coming back to life. So all things considered, I feel pretty damn lucky."

I rolled my shoulders, then stretched my arms above my head. My muscles sang. The shift of fabric against my skin was almost painful, and I had a mad desire to tear off my clothes. I resisted.

I looked around the apartment for the first time. The brown-and-oatmeal-striped sofa bed sat in the center of the common area, flanked by matching comfy chairs and a set of teak end tables with black-tipped legs. Every horizontal surface contained at least one smoked-glass ashtray.

Were it not for the bloody sheets, it could have been any 1970s basement family room. (Not that I had direct experience, but I've seen *That '70s Show*.) The only thing that didn't fit was a long chain of dark blue beads on the table beside the sofa bed.

The kitchen area looked comparatively modern, which made sense, since the apartment itself was built in the mid-nineties. A pale yellow counter stretched along the wall behind me, ending at a cream-colored refrigerator. A microwave was built into the cabinets over the gleaming white stove.

Surrounding the common area were six closed doors—leading to the DJs' bedrooms, I assumed. A dim corridor led off from the kitchen. I wondered what mysteries hid there.

Spencer came out of the kitchen area with a shiny green insulated coffee mug. "Drink."

I opened the little hatch on top and crinkled my nose at the stale scent, then took the bendy straw Spencer offered me. "You don't all have to stare."

"At least one of us does, to make sure you drink it." Shane gave me a crooked smile. "Probably more than one, considering your sleight-of-hand abilities."

I put the straw in my mouth and sipped a few drops. Then I swallowed quickly, banishing the warm, salty metallic substance from my tongue. *This is all I'll ever eat again*. My stomach sank with this piece of reality.

They stood surrounding me, their eyes on mine, waiting for my verdict. I felt like a judge on *Iron Chef*, but I didn't bother saying so, since they wouldn't get the reference.

My stomach dropped further. In five or ten years, I might not understand pop culture references either. In twenty-five years, I might still be making *Iron Chef* jokes. This was it, this was as far as I'd evolve without serious professional help.

But I couldn't show my doubts now, not after what they'd done for me. I lifted my cup. "Nummy."

Shane's head took on a skeptical tilt. "No, it's not. Bank blood is like hospital food. It doesn't do much except fill you up and keep you alive."

I sipped again, relieved my underwhelmedness didn't mean there was something wrong with me. The tang that had pierced the back of my throat since Jeremy's escape faded with each sip.

"After you finish," Shane said, "we'll get you cleaned up."

I touched my neck and grimaced at the drying-paint stickiness. The wound made me think of Monroe, and I turned to thank him for saving my life.

He was gone.

I looked at the floor near the sofa bed, where I'd heard Shane drop the guitar. The instrument was missing, too.

"Monroe's run out for a bit," Spencer said.

"Run out for what?" Maybe he was getting me a present. Maybe a glad-you're-not-dead flower bouquet or a tasty young man with a shy smile and thin skin.

Spencer gave the others a look that verged on warning. "Best leave him alone, honey."

The back of my neck chilled. "Leave him alone for tonight? For tonight, right? Not . . . forever?"

Spencer turned away to fold up the futon. "Noah, don't forget to wash this mattress pad."

I sat frozen, clutching my first meal. Monroe had walked out on me. What about our blood bond?

"Why did he leave?" I looked at Shane and Regina, kneeling on either side of my chair. "Was it something I did?"

"Don't think that." Shane rubbed my back. "You haven't done anything."

"We'll take care of you," Regina said. "And we'll also hunt down that callous prick Monroe and bring him back."

"Tomorrow night," Spencer added. "Give the man some time."

I turned to face him. "If you had made me, would you have run out? Would you need time?"

"I'm not Monroe." He leaned over my shoulder and

pulled the cup toward my mouth. "Drink up now, so we can stop frettin'."

I took another sip, swallowing past the lump in my throat. The rest of them, even the schizoid Jim, made me feel safe and cared for, like an orphan puppy brought in from a snowstorm.

But it wasn't enough. I needed my maker. What if he never came back, or came back but acted as if nothing had changed? My heart twisted at the thought.

The sensation distracted me. I put a hand to my chest to feel the organ beating beneath my skin. I was alive, re-animated. Moreover, my body still reacted to unpleasant emotional states such as *total fucking abandonment*.

Wondering what else my body did, I ran my thumb along my teeth. "Did I fang out when I tried to pounce on Jeremy?"

"I saw no fangs." Noah carried the armful of bloody linens into the mysterious dark corridor off the kitchen. Oh. It was the laundry room. So much for mystique.

"Believe me, you'll feel it when it happens." Jim lit a cigarette and took a pensive puff. "But like I said, everyone's different. Your fangs'll pop soon. Probably next time you see a human."

"How long before I can control it? In time for Lori's wedding?" I imagined writing to the etiquette column of *Bride* magazine: *Are saber teeth an acceptable maid of honor accessory? Or should I stick with a string of Swarovski pearls?*

"They've postponed the wedding," Shane said. "Guests had started canceling because of the plague."

I felt a sudden, stabbing sadness for the chicken pox victims who didn't have vampires to deliver them from the clutches of an untimely death. Chastened, I finished my first blood mug without further self-pity. I vowed to remind myself that no matter what happened, there was no such thing as a fate worse than death.

Our shower together was nothing like the last one. Shane washed the blood from my hair and neck and chest, as tenderly as a mother cleansing an infant. My skin felt extrasensitive, as if it had been stretched and reshaped.

I examined my arm, beaded with water drops. "What's happening to me?"

"You're growing extra nerve endings." He turned off the water and picked up a WVMP Lifeblood of Rock 'n' Roll beach towel. "Actually, you have the same number of nerves, but the ones that feel pain are changing to feel other things, like hot or cold or touch. Your whole body will feel like a cat's whiskers until you get used to it. Some vampires notice the sensitive eyes or ears or nose first. I guess for you it's touch." He held out the towel for me to step into. "Like it was for me."

"So that's why you're ticklish." The terry cloth scraped like sandpaper, and I swallowed a hiss of not quite pain.

I stepped toward the foggy mirror. Using a dry washrag, Shane wiped a large circle in the condensation so I could see.

I was still Ciara. Same blue eyes, prominent nose, and dark blond hair. I trailed my fingers over my neck. The gash in my throat—the one that had robbed and restored my life—had disappeared.

"What do you think?" he said.

"I thought I'd look different."

"You will soon. Even better than before, if that's possible."

"No more zits?"

"You never had zits."

"I had a huge one last October." I pointed to the edge of my jaw. "Right here."

"Oh yeah, that was hideous. I almost moved out."

I smacked him in the chest in my usual playful manner. This time he staggered back and held up his hands.

"Watch the hitting, until you learn your strength."

"Sorry." I pulled the towel tight around me, up to my chin, wondering why he hadn't kissed me yet. Maybe he was hurt and angry about my betrayal, despite what he'd said in front of the others.

Might as well get this out of the way, naked or not. "Do you think I'm going to hell?"

He put his arms into his shirt and didn't answer until he'd fastened two buttons. "I guess that's up to God."

"But what do *you* think? In your best theological opinion."

"Unlike me, you saw the white light." His voice was taut, as if he strained to keep it steady. "You saw heaven."

"If that's what it was."

"Did it feel like it?"

"It felt . . . blah. But good blah, like vanilla ice cream, or a rice cake."

He stared at me, mid-button. "The afterlife felt like a rice cake?"

"Not the plain ones that taste like cardboard. More like the cheddar-cheese or barbecue-flavored ones." In an effort to fit into my maid of honor dress, I'd become a connoisseur of low-calorie treats. "It felt comforting. But not something I'd want to make a habit of. So thanks for calling me back." When he kept staring at me, I added, "With my song."

His eyes widened. "You heard that? While you were dead?"

"I felt it."

"I pulled you back to life?"

"No. I had to make the effort. But the song showed me the way back to this world." I summoned all my courage and took a step forward. "Back to you."

Shane raised his trembling hands like he wanted to seize me. But instead he rested them gently, one on each of my cheeks.

"Ciara." He bent low and brushed my lips with nothing but his breath. "I'd have kicked God's own ass to get you back with me."

In my shock, I released the towel. The air met my naked, cooling skin, tightening it into a thousand goose bumps.

Before I could marvel at the fact that I could still get goose bumps, Shane kissed me, and the thousand turned into a million.

19

Jesus Don't Want Me for a Sunbeam

Inside Shane's old room, a faint cream-colored lampshade spread soft illumination over the blue walls, which were mostly covered in posters of rock icons.

"I know—it looks like a 1994 dorm room," he said, "but I never thought I'd be bringing a girl here."

Wrapped in the towel, I sat on his twin bed while he turned on the clock radio on the nightstand. Just like at home, it was tuned to the D.C. classical music station, which helped him sleep during the day.

I watched him open a drawer in a beat-up wooden dresser. "Now what?"

"Sleep." He handed me a plain white T-shirt and a pair of gray running shorts with a small Pittsburgh Steelers logo.

I glanced at the pillow, and had to admit it looked as tempting as chocolate mousse. Regret stabbed me as I realized that from now on, chocolate mousse would taste like styling mousse.

I put on Shane's clothes, sighing at the feel of the soft cotton after the towel's scrubby terry cloth. Then I crawled under the covers, which smelled faintly of Shane. It had been half a week since he had last spent the day here, but my nose picked up his scent.

He slipped the chain of blue beads out of his pocket and hung it on the doorknob of his closet, where it rattled against the wooden surface. I noticed that beads at certain intervals had pieces of tape on them.

"What's with the Mardi Gras swag?" I asked him.

"I use it as a rosary." He stripped off his shirt and tossed it into a hamper in the corner. "Obviously I can't use real ones, since they have crucifixes."

"I thought sacred items only hurt vampires when wielded by a believer." Holy water, on the other hand, was intrinsically sacred and could burn vampires no matter who splashed it.

He spread his arms as if to gesture to himself.

"I know you believe," I said, "but you wouldn't use it against yourself. There has to be intent."

"Best to play it safe. Like humans not leaving a loaded gun in the house." He peeled off his jeans and sat on the edge of the bed to remove them, looking as weary as I felt.

I shifted next to the wall to give him room. Over the head of the bed hung the classic poster of Kurt Cobain, with him staring straight into the camera, unsmiling. The photo was in black and white, but my imagination filled in the sharp blue of the dead man's eyes. They held a haunted quality that Shane's gaze often approached, but with a harder, desperate edge I'd never seen in my lover.

Shane slipped under the covers beside me. As his arm wrapped around my waist, I laced my fingers with his, absorbing his strength. I wondered how he could have willingly given up this world.

"Did you know, deep down, that Regina wouldn't kill you like you asked her to? That she'd make you a vampire instead?"

His breath stilled. "I don't think anyone knows what they know deep down."

"If she'd been good for you, the way you are for me, then you would've wanted to stick around and get more of her. Alive or undead."

"It's not that simple." He sighed. "You can't understand. You were blessed with good brain chemistry, not to mention a personality that finds a way around every problem, rather than wallowing in it."

"Hey, being shallow is hard work."

"You're not shallow," he said. "You're strong."

"Not compared to you. Which is why I can't imagine you wanting to end it all."

"First of all, it's not a matter of strength. And second, I've changed since I was alive." His arms tensed, and I wondered if we shared the same thought.

"Will I change?"

"Yes. The question is how."

I had no illusions about the quality of my character. I'd spent years as a professional con artist—a different kind of predator. My new vampire vibe would give me even more power to manipulate people's desires and actions.

I could be dangerous—and worse, unlovable.

"For now, just sleep." Shane took his hand out of mine and reached for the bedside lamp.

"Leave it on. Please?"

"Okay," he said without hesitating, as if it were perfectly normal for a vampire to be afraid of the dark. He shifted close to me again, his body stretched against mine.

I turned my head to see his eyes open, staring at the wall on the other side of me. "Aren't you going to sleep, too?"

"I need to watch over you. Feed you. Keep you warm."

"Is there something I should—"

"Sleep." He threaded his fingers through my hair, over and over, like he used to do when I had insomnia before a big exam.

I drifted off, too exhausted to indulge my fears. I slept without dreams, but when I woke again, it was like swimming up through cold quicksand.

Shane was shaking my shoulder. "You need to drink."

"No. Sleep." I put my arm over my eyes to blot out the light. "More blankets."

"Blood, not blankets."

"Monroe come back yet?"

"Not yet. Here, drink." A warm, smooth surface rested against the back of my hand. I latched onto the travel mug with nearly numb fingers.

Shane tilted up my head so I could sip. Cold burned in my core like a fire fueled by ice cubes. My neck was so stiff, it felt like it would snap.

But by the time my straw gurgled at the bottom of the mug, warmth flowed through every cell. My mind cleared, enough to wish with all my heart that my maker was the one feeding me. The stab of pain made me long for the cold numbness again.

Maybe if I pretended nothing was wrong, nothing would be wrong. "Thank you," I murmured to Shane. "Check, please."

I lay down again, weighed by fatigue and a new, crushing dread: I was now an addict. Blood wasn't like air or water or the endlessly interchangeable food I once ate. It had a very specific source, one that now had complete power over me.

Before drifting off, I swept my tongue across my teeth, in a fruitless search for fangs.

The next time I woke, I heard Shane's voice, but from a few feet away rather than the pillow beside my head. He spoke in an urgent, breathy whisper. No one answered.

" . . . grant to the souls of thy servants and handmaidens departed, the remission of all their sins . . ."

I parted my eyelids to see him kneeling on the floor next to his dresser. His eyes were squeezed shut. The Mardi Gras rosary beads lay in a pile on the thin carpet beside him.

Finally he said, "Amen," then tilted his chin up to gaze at the ceiling with more agony than I'd ever seen in his eyes.

"What was that?" I whispered.

He started. "Did I wake you?"

"It sounded like you were reciting, not making it up."

Shane collected the rosary from the floor. "It's a novena for the souls of the departed."

"Departed? Are you praying for me or for the ones who died for good?"

"All of you," he said without looking at me.

My heart wanted to rip in half. "So you are worried about my soul."

He folded the rosary into his palm, where the beads spilled like water over the edges. "I'm worried about your soul, for giving up when there was a tiny chance you could survive. I'm worried about Jeremy's soul and the souls of the other DJs, for conspiring to end your life." He lowered his gaze to the floor in front of him. "And I'm worried about my own soul, for being glad they did."

I let myself breathe a little. "Then you're not sorry I'm a vampire?"

"I'm not sorry, but I should be." He shifted over to kneel by the bedside. "You were so young, and so alive." He ran a strand of my hair through his fingertips. "You were like walking sunshine."

"Except for the burning-you-into-a-puff-of-nothing part."

"You have no idea how much you're going to miss. The little things will creep up and slam you when you least expect it. We can be there to help you cope, but in the end, each of us has to make this dark journey alone."

I squirmed a little at his uncharacteristic melodrama. "I managed okay."

He shook his head sadly. "Death is just the beginning."

I picked at the lint on the blue blanket, searching for my optimism. "But it'll be an adventure, right? There'll be good parts? Assuming I ever have the strength to get out of bed."

His eyes glinted as they gazed into mine. "There'll be very good parts."

"Like sex?"

"Yes, like sex. But you're a long way from that now."

"I know, I've never been so out of the mood." I rubbed my face, which felt like it was made of clay, then let my hand drop onto his. "Why didn't you bring your rosary with you when you moved in with me?"

Shane sighed as he crossed his legs to sit on the floor beside the bed. "I didn't think it'd fit."

"You know I respect your beliefs."

"You say you do." He stroked my knuckles with his fingertips, soft enough to soothe yet firm enough not to tweak my nerves. "But it came between us last night. You made an end run around me because you didn't trust me to save you. You shut me out of the most important decision you could ever make."

The pain in his eyes twisted my innards. "I'm so sorry."

"I know you are. We'll have to deal with this one day." He tugged the covers up over my shoulders and tucked them under my chin. "Not tonight, of course."

No, tonight was for survival. But one day I'd make it up to him.

I had no idea how.

20

Big Empty

"Ciara . . ." Shane gently shook my shoulder, which felt like solid rust.

"Eggs over easy and white toast," I slurred. "Coffee, three sugars."

"You have a visitor."

"Monroe?" I sat up so fast, the room tilted, sending a flash of nausea up my throat.

"Sorry, darlin'. Just me."

My vision cleared to see Spencer sitting in Shane's desk chair, ankle crossed over his knee.

"Oh." I looked at the clock. 7:30—long past sunrise. "Is Monroe here?"

Spencer shook his head. "But don't worry about him—we've all got backup hidey holes. He's probably at a donor's house."

"I wasn't worried about him. I was worried about me."

"How do you feel?" Shane asked.

I did a quick inventory. "No better. But no worse, either."

"I'll get you another meal." He headed for the door. "And some coffee."

I wanted to lie down, but not with Spencer watching me. So I pulled the pillow up and sat back against the wall. It took every bit of concentration to stay upright.

"I should've picked you," I said.

He shrugged. "Grass is always greener, ain't it? I wouldn't be a perfect maker either."

"You'd be here. Wouldn't you?"

"We're all here. We'll all take care of you." Staring at the wall, Spencer smoothed his hair back on both sides. "And if you're in danger, Monroe'll come back."

"How will he know I'm in danger?"

Spencer dropped his hands to his lap. "You already know vampires can feel when their maker is killed or in pain. But what you might not know is that with some, the connection goes both ways."

"Why would it be that way with me and Monroe?"

"Because he saved your life by turning you—far as we know, anyhow."

I nodded, not wanting to think about the possibility that I could've survived in the hospital. It was too late.

Spencer continued. "He stole you away from death and pain, so your pain is a part of him now. Monroe will always know when you're in trouble."

But would he care?

"I was like you," Spencer said without prompting. "I didn't want to be a vampire. Hell, I didn't even know they were real until that night. I just wanted to live."

"Were you sick?"

He gave a gruff chuckle. "Not unless there's a shiv-in-the-stomach disease."

"Someone stabbed you? Was it a mugging?"

"No, I just made the wrong enemies. What I'm telling you is, my maker always knew when I was in danger." A grim smile crossed his face. "Which was a lot of the time. I wasn't real . . . careful."

I blinked in astonishment. The Spencer I knew was the epitome of cool calculation. I'd never seen him have so much as a flyaway hair, much less a complete loss of control. Despite his eternally youthful appearance, it was easy to forget he was once young for real.

I was also amazed that he was telling me a portion, however small, of his turning story. According to Shane, vampires never shared this tale with anyone they didn't trust with their lives.

I was one of them now.

Shane continued to feed me throughout the day. In late afternoon, when I was coherent enough to string two sentences together, he left me alone so I could call Lori.

"Ciara . . ." She sounded like she was holding back tears. "Are you okay?"

"Tired."

"Is that normal?"

"There is no normal. Shane says I'm weak because I was so sick. How's Dexter?"

"He ran up and down the hall for a few hours, and then collapsed. He wouldn't touch his breakfast. Speaking of which, are you, uh—"

"Drinking blood? Yeah. It's nothing to write home about. And no fangs yet."

"Wild." She took a deep breath and when she released

it, her words spilled out, almost faster than I could comprehend. "It was so scary. David and I sat in the lounge—well, we didn't really sit. Mostly we paced, like when someone's having a baby? Noah kept coming out and giving us updates, but there was one part where we didn't hear anything for like half an hour. Shane had his cell phone off, obviously." She finally inhaled, long enough for me to get a word in.

"I'm sorry I didn't tell you my plans. I didn't want Shane to be the last to know. He was hurt enough as it was."

"I know. You should've seen him on the way from the hospital to the station. I think he went through every stage of mourning five times over. How was he when, you know, it happened?"

"He was perfect." I told her how the music had called me back from the other side.

She let out a wistful sigh. "That's so unbelievably romantic. He was like Orpheus, only successful."

"Is that the dream guy from those comics you and David love so much?"

"No, that's Morpheus. Orpheus was from Greek mythology. When his wife Eurydice died, he went to Hades and sang this mournful song that made everyone in the underworld cry. So they made an exception and said Orpheus could lead Eurydice back to earth—back to life—with his lyre and his voice."

"So why wasn't he successful?"

"They told him not to look back until they were both on earth, or he would lose Eurydice again. He had to trust that she was following. Of course, as soon as he reached earth, he got all excited and looked back too soon. So she died again, this time for good."

"Harsh." I hoped Shane's resemblance to Orpheus ended with the pretty music. "Speaking of tragedy, I'm almost afraid to ask, but—any more news on those students?"

"Oh, Ciara, it's horrible. Six out of the seven have died, plus the professor. The last one's in a coma."

"God." I put a shaky hand to my forehead.

"Another student plus a professor are in the hospital. If anyone carried the infection out of town, it could be a national disaster. Of course all the big news stations are lurking around campus."

I rubbed my eyes, feeling lucky all over again. "I better call my mom and let her know I'm okay."

Lori let out a long breath. "I'm sorry you're a vampire, because I know it wasn't what you wanted, but I'm so glad you're not dead."

"Me, too." Suddenly fatigued, I curled up on my side. "Call you later."

I hung up, then dialed my mom, hoping the prison would let me speak to her two days in a row.

"*Ciara!?*" My mother screamed into the phone, blasting my newly sensitive ears.

"Ow." I turned down the speaker volume.

"What do you mean, 'ow'? Are you in pain?"

"No, I'm fine. That's why I called, to let you know I'm not going to die." Technically that was true, since I had already died. Such is the magic of verb tenses.

She gasped. "That's wonderful, honey! Did they find a cure?"

"No, but—"

"Did you get sick and then recover? No, that's silly—I just talked to you yesterday and you were fine."

"That's not it." No doubt all calls to and from the prison were monitored. If anyone knew that I had survived the disease, I'd be in a CDC laboratory—with windows, no doubt—in a matter of hours.

I spoke slowly so she would have time to pick up on my signal. "I talked to Dad, and he said I had chicken pox that one time you went home to visit Grandmom. Remember? I was four years old."

My mother said nothing. I could almost hear the wheels turning in her head a thousand miles away. My grandmother died when I was two, and Mom knew I knew that.

"Ohhhh." She gave a high titter. "That's right! I remember, I was so worried and wanted to be there to take care of you. But it was a pretty mild case, right? That must have been why we both forgot."

"Yeah, Dad said the same thing." My shoulders relaxed. Living in a family of liars had its advantages.

"So how is everything otherwise? Besides finding out you can't catch a deadly plague?" Her laughter was breathless, and I could only imagine how her heart must be pounding. When she got out of jail, I owed her an in-person truth—or at least a plausible story.

I tried to think of a topic that wasn't off-limits. *I'm a vampire? I was attacked by a zombie? I'm training to work for a paranormal paramilitary organization?*

The engagement. Assuming there still was one.

I told her all the nonvamp details of Shane's proposal, and she gushed at the appropriate moments.

"So when's the date? Will you wait for me to get out?"

I hesitated, then realized that even if she weren't paroled this year, Shane and I no longer needed to hurry. We were both immortal now. "Sure, Mom."

"Hooray! And if you wait until next year, your father might be out of prison, too."

"Maybe." I knew he wouldn't. He'd violated the trust his liberators (the Control) had placed in him, and in turn they'd sent him back to federal prison to finish his original term. It would be at least another six or seven years before he saw the outside. But Mom didn't know that, and I couldn't tell her, because it was classified.

"My time's almost up, honey." Her voice fluttered again, making my throat tighten.

"I'll see you next month."

"I'm afraid to hope." The phone went silent, as if she'd pressed her lips together to keep all sound inside. "I love you, Ciara."

"I love you, too, Mom," I whispered.

I hung up, then stared at the screen for a long moment. The phone's wallpaper was currently a shot of me and Shane at our favorite bar, the Smoking Pig. It was New Year's, and in the photo I'm pointing an orange blowout party favor straight at the camera, while he gazes at my puffed-out face like it's the most amazing thing he's ever seen.

Disobeying my brain, my thumb tabbed the screen to bring up my gallery of photos. The first to come up was the last one I took. In it, I'm standing on the sidewalk across the street from my apartment. The sun glints off my hair, making the blond highlights gleam. Deep lines form around my eyes from squinting and bad sleep. One day they would have been wrinkles.

The doorknob turned, and I switched off the phone. Shane walked in carrying a red three-ring binder. I couldn't even lift my head from the pillow.

"Still tired?" He sat beside me on the bed. "You've been drinking and sleeping all night and day."

"Not real blood, though."

"Bank blood is real blood."

"It's nutritionally deficient, right?"

"In the long run, if you drink nothing else. But for one day it should make you strong."

I rolled onto my back and stared at the ceiling. "I want to go home."

"You're too dangerous. You could attack the neighbors as easily as Dexter could attack their shih tzus."

"Ew, no. The Hendersons probably taste awful."

Shane didn't laugh. "Believe me, you wouldn't care."

"So when can I go home?"

"When we know you're safe. Could be days . . . or weeks."

"No way! You guys don't even have high-def cable." I hugged the extra pillow to my chest. "How can I prove I'm safe?"

"By controlling yourself around a human."

"Then let's go see one, and I'll try not to eat him. Or her," I added. "Can it be a him? Please? Just for starters?"

"That's why I brought this." He opened the binder so I could see the pages. "Donor directory."

"Like a catalog?" I pointed to a photo of a handsome young Middle Eastern guy. "I want that one."

"Hamed is one of Spencer's, who might be willing to share." Shane flipped the page to the other side, which contained a series of neatly printed dates and notes on the lined paper. It reminded me of the cards that used to be tucked into the back of library books. "But Hamed just donated two weeks ago, so that won't work."

"All the donor information is stuck in this binder?"

"It's very organized." He slid his finger over the color-coded divider tabs.

"This should be in a password-protected database, with an offsite backup. What if it gets lost?"

"Nothing gets lost here."

I decided to fight that battle later, when I had the energy. "Can I borrow one of your donors?"

"Probably not." He flipped to the back of the binder. "Since I'm the youngest—or at least I was until last night—I have to drink most often. My donors are on a tight rotation." He paged backward through the sheets. "Nope. Nope. Nope." He reached the front of his section, then turned to Regina's.

I pointed to the donor on her last page.

Shane looked at me. "Fifty bucks says he tells you no."

I thought he'd be afraid.

Maybe it was the two vampires holding me back. Maybe it was my continued fanglessness (God, how embarrassing). Maybe it was the fact that I looked tiny in Shane's extra-large flannel shirt.

Regardless, Jeremy didn't hesitate as he crossed the room toward me.

I sat on the couch between Noah and Spencer. I tried not to dwell on the fact that Monroe should have shared this experience with me. *He should be finding me fresh blood. He should be holding me the moment that first taste touches my tongue. He should be* here.

At least Jim was in the studio, not here watching. When I'd seen him earlier that evening, he'd looked at me like I was next in line to board his Love Train.

But the moment Jeremy stood before me, close enough I could hear his heart pound, everyone else faded from my mind. I breathed through my mouth so the scent of blood beneath his skin wouldn't turn me into a quivering mass of want.

He slid his gray long-sleeved Jimmy Eat World T-shirt over his head, revealing a pale chest that was more solid than I would have guessed.

Noah squeezed my arm. "How are you?"

"So far so good!" I chirped with more certainty than I felt.

"Go ahead," Spencer said to Jeremy.

The nonvampire DJ went to the kitchen sink, where he scrubbed his left arm with soap and water. Steam rose around him, and I licked my lips as the thirst filled my throat.

Jeremy approached again, Shane at his side. I took long, deep breaths, trying to keep my muscles from tensing like I wanted to jump him.

Mind over matter. That would be my vampire motto. *Mind over matter.* Concise, if not original.

Two feet away, Shane knelt and turned Jeremy's bare forearm to face me. I stared at the familiar tattoo as if seeing it for the first time—a depiction of a slit wrist, complete with drops of blood flowing over the smooth white skin toward his elbow.

Shane gave me one last cautionary look. His fangs were out.

Jeremy closed his eyes and let his head fall back. When his skin was pierced, he released a half sigh, half moan. He sounded like prey.

The scent of his blood swamped my sinuses, and my throat uttered an answering moan. The vampires' grips tightened.

"Easy there," Spencer murmured in my right ear. "Wait your turn."

My turn came. When the blood was flowing down Jeremy's arm, real drops over the inked ones, he stepped forward, offering. I kept my eyes on his, marveling at the trust within.

"Remember, don't suck," Shane said. "Just lick."

I closed my eyes and drank.

To say it was better than bank blood is like saying a glass of Châteauneuf du Pape is better than a swig of Thunderbird. The moment my tongue touched his skin, it adhered like a magnet to iron. I didn't know how to pull away, and I soon ceased to care.

Even after dying and going to that . . . place, I still hadn't believed in heaven. Until the moment I tasted Jeremy's blood.

Then I believed. Believed that there was a reason for everything, that some loving, divine hand had guided me to this moment. How else to explain this union of body, mind, and soul that made the best sex of my life seem as mundane as preparing my taxes?

And then, I pictured myself drinking him, lips and tongue chasing every drop. Like Dexter cleaning his dog bowl. If they hadn't held me back, I'd have been on my knees before Jeremy, hands everywhere, so crazed with bloodlust I'd have signed away my last possession to become his eternal slave.

I hated it.

(Not *it*, of course. I could never hate the blood.)

I hated what it made me. Helpless. Needy. It wasn't sexy or trippy or sacred. It was pathetic.

I pulled away, but Jeremy didn't step back. He opened his eyes and held out his arm to my lips.

"Go on," he said. "You hardly had any."

"I'm done. Thank you." I tilted my chin to avoid his eyes. "Thank you very much."

"You sure?"

"I need to lie down." *Under a rock. And die.* "I'm really tired."

"If you're tired," Shane said, "you should drink more."

"I don't want to." I lowered my head further, letting my hair veil my burning face. "Please let me stop."

Jeremy held up his arm. "What am I supposed to do?"

"Hang on." Shane knelt in front of me. "Ciara, what's wrong?"

I tried to move my tongue to speak without re-tasting the blood in my mouth. "I just. Don't. Want to."

"Okay. I'll take you back to our room."

"I can walk on my own."

"You sure?" When I nodded, he said, "Guys, let her go."

They released me, and I stood slowly, looking away from everyone, especially Jeremy. One false move and I'd be tackled.

In Shane's room I crawled into bed and tugged the covers up to my nose. The radio was playing at a low volume, something Beethoveny. I stared at the brand name on the front of the display and mentally rearranged it to make words of at least four letters.

SPAN

SPIN

COIN

COINS (if adding an *s* wasn't cheating)
SCAN
CANS
NIPS
SOAP

And of course, SONIC, but that was definitely cheating. Zero points.

I groaned as I realized that I'd never had thoughts like this before, anything that could remotely be considered obsessive. It was starting already.

I rolled on my back so I couldn't see the clock and pressed the heels of my hands into my eyes. *I will not cry.* The water dribbled out my nose instead.

A soft knock came at the door, which then creaked open.

"I'm fine," I told Shane before he could ask. "Situation normal."

"Situation the polar opposite of normal." He sat at the end of the bed, after feeling for my feet so he wouldn't crush them. "I've never seen a vampire react like that to their first taste of a human."

"Clearly I suck at this." I was too depressed to acknowledge the unintentional pun. "I have no fangs, no bloodlust."

"You had the bloodlust. I saw you shudder."

"Ugh." I yanked the covers up over my head, creating a seal against the outside world like I did when was a kid, to make a fortress against monsters. But now the only monster was under the covers.

"It's not unusual to feel ambivalent," Shane went on. "It's a big change."

"I like change." The blanket cave flattened my tone. "Change is fun."

"So what's wrong?"

"I hate myself." Words I thought I'd never say.

"Ciara . . ." He put a hand on my knee through the blanket. "You're not hurting anyone. Jeremy was happy to do it."

"Of course he was. It gives him power." I brushed back a lock of hair that was itching my cheek. "Now I get why some humans like to be bitten. They want to be needed."

He sighed with what sounded like relief. "Okay, this is making sense now. You hate to need anything."

"I'm scared." I curled back into the fetal position. "What if I can't get blood? I'll die slow and painful."

"We'll make sure you have blood." He shifted to rest his hand on my hip. "This is why there are so few lone vampires. We take care of each other."

The situation was wrapping around my throat like a fist. I was living the con artist's worst nightmare—trapped in a place I could never leave, with people I would always need.

I tried to tell myself I hadn't had such isolation and independence for years. I'd stuck around when things were tough—with the station, with school, with Shane. I no longer had a bag packed and ready to go with half a minute's notice.

My mind knew this. But my soul clung to those old reflexes. *Get up!* it screamed at me. *Run!* My body started to shake, fighting the urge to flee.

Shane rubbed my back. "Can I get you anything?"

I searched my dimming memory and imagination for one thing that would make me happy. But my brain felt wrapped in cotton, with a new layer added every hour.

So I just shrugged.

"Never mind," he said. "I know exactly what you need."

The car keys jangled in his hand as he swept them off his dresser.

Were I still alive, I'd think he was on a quest for Ben & Jerry's Chubby Hubby ice cream. But that would never taste like anything again.

The door closed behind him, and I let myself cry. I'd never seen any of the other vampires so much as sniffle, except when I died. They were all so tough.

Maybe I wasn't a real vampire. I'd gone all the way into the light—maybe I'd left part of myself there. I certainly felt half dead, half undead. Maybe I was incomplete. Maybe that's why Monroe left. He could tell I was defective.

The void inside me widened as I thought of my maker. It spread from my gut, out into my limbs and my head until I was nothing but one gaping, gnawing emptiness.

Whatever I was, I hated it. Not out of bitterness over the life I'd lost. Because I hadn't just lost my life. I'd lost myself.

I was still crying when the door opened. A *woof* boomed off the walls, then one hundred twenty pounds of fur and flesh landed atop my body.

I wiped my eyes as a huge black muzzle appeared under the covers, making frantic wuffling noises.

Dexter stopped, nostrils quivering, sensing the monumental change in me. I held my breath. Would he still want me to be his mom?

I threw back the blanket and stared up into my dog's deep brown eyes. Cautiously he stretched his neck forward and licked my chin. Shane stood watching in the doorway.

Dexter cocked his head. His eyebrows popped up, giving him a look of scandalous surprise.

"Hey, boy, it's me."

He whined, then turned away. My heart thudded to a halt.

Then Dexter began to sniff me, head to toe. He lingered on my hands, wetting them with drool. I made no move to pet him.

Finally he grunted, then, without ceremony, plopped next to me on the edge of the single bed, as if we'd always lived here. He gave a wide yawn, then set his head on his paws, kicking out his back legs in an unsubtle hint for me to move my feet.

"See?" Shane crossed his arms and leaned against the doorway. "You're not the only one who needs."

I curled my arm around Dexter and buried my face in the folds of furry skin at the back of his neck.

"If you're thirsty," he added, "Jeremy donated some blood."

Leftovers. I nodded without looking at him. "Thanks."

From a cup it would be just another drink. No intimacy, no connection, no need. I'd spent most of my life fooling others, so why not fool myself? I could pretend the blood was Hawaiian Punch. I could pretend I was driving around the Sonoma Valley sampling the latest Cabernets.

I could pretend I had a choice.

21

Pardon Me

That night, Shane and Regina took me home to collect my belongings, in preparation for a long recovery. Jeremy's blood had given me the strength to walk in a straight line, at least temporarily.

Outside, the shadows had gained nuance and depth, as if yesterday the world had held only two and a half dimensions and was now appearing in true 3-D. I stared out the car window, eyes devouring the familiar new landscape with one burning new purpose: blood.

The Smoking Pig had become a hunting ground. In the bar's dark, empty interior, the exit lights leaked red over a forest of upside-down chairs perched atop tables. As we passed the wide front window, I searched the chairs' shiny wooden legs for reflected movement.

I fingered the car's electric window switch, longing for a whiff of night air. The switch clicked, but the window didn't budge.

I looked at Shane, sitting beside me in the backseat.

He shook his head and tightened his grip on my wrist.

Regina glanced at me in the rearview mirror. "You're lucky we let you come with us at all."

I sighed and turned back to the window. The thought of drinking from a willing donor like Jeremy still made me feel gross and subservient. But the thought of tracking, hunting, and bringing down my own prey made the tips of my fingers and tongue tingle.

I pressed my nose to the cool glass. Sherwood might as well have been a ghost town—Sunday night plus a chicken pox scare meant there was nothing to see, move along now. But surely someone yummy would be walking a dog. Maybe my superstrength could force open the car door. Regina and Shane would catch up to me, but not before I had a taste.

Oh, who was I kidding? I didn't even have fangs.

When I entered our apartment, my melancholy returned along with the last memories of my life as a human.

I slipped into the bedroom alone, leaving the door open. I set my open suitcase on the bed, where the sheets were still rumpled from sex and sleep. I wondered if I'd ever again feel like doing the former and would ever stop wanting to do the latter. Even now I wanted to sink onto the bed and let the dark steal my consciousness.

I wanted to be alone, something I would never truly be again.

On my nightstand lay two of the books I'd been using for my Eastern European History term paper. I slipped them into my suitcase, determined to finish the assignment. Even if I never graduated, I needed to do it for Aaron.

I turned away from the bed and went to the dresser.

Shane entered the room as I was giving my underwear drawer a dull, unseeing stare.

"Need some help?" His voice and posture were one of a calculated calm, the way one acts around someone on the verge of a nervous breakdown.

I ran my hands through the silk nightgowns and lace teddies. My hypersensitive skin tingled at the feel, awakening memories of the material sliding between me and Shane. "Should I bring any of this?"

"Only for private viewing, right?"

"Of course. You think I'm going to turn all horndog on the other vampires?"

"It's part of the process."

"Clearly I'm not following the process." I rested my forehead on the edge of the drawer. "I still feel so human, but only in the bad ways. And I only have the bad parts of being a vampire—the need for blood, the over-the-top angst."

"It happens slower for some than others. Be patient." He kissed my temple. "And leave the hot stuff here, for my sanity's sake."

"But what about us?"

"When you're ready, we can make love without the help of Victoria's Secret." His hand slipped under the back of my shirt.

I jumped at his touch. "Your hands are hot."

"I grabbed a snack from our fridge, so my core temperature is probably higher than yours now." He stroked the curve of my lower back. "You used to feel this way to me sometimes."

My heart grew heavy, as if injected with liquid lead. "Will you still want me now that I'm chilly?"

He gave a thorough sigh, then tugged me gently to rest against his chest. "Do I need to sing that song again?"

"Which song?"

"The one I wrote for you. I said I'd be with you when you were old, so why wouldn't I be with you when you're cold?" He winced with his breath. "I swear I didn't mean that to rhyme."

I felt the heat of his muscles pulse through his shirt. "So much has changed."

"But not us." He held me at arm's length and stared into my eyes. "Right?"

"I betrayed you. I didn't trust you to save my life." The tears came again, blurring his face. "Can you forgive me?"

He brushed his thumbs over my eyes, so hot I expected my tears to turn to steam.

"If you need me to forgive you," he whispered, "then I forgive you."

He kissed me, and the sick sensation in my gut broke apart. For a moment I felt worse, like I would spew all over Shane's battered Chuck Taylors. Then it dissipated, floating away through my veins, diluting until I couldn't feel it anymore.

I slid my arms around Shane's neck and kissed him back, shoving aside the fears of a forever future.

We hurried down the sidewalk, Shane holding my suitcase and my left hand. Regina flanked me on the right. They swiveled their heads in a continuous scan for humans.

Though the streets were empty, a thousand scents lingered in the humid, pollen-thick spring air. A woman with a talcum-coated baby, a man with a sharp aftershave that clashed with the natural sweetness of his skin. My neighbor's shih tzu, having taken a dump on the sidewalk.

Our car was parked across the street from St. Michael's, the tiny old Catholic Church. Most Catholics in Sherwood went to the enormous St. Luke's on the outside of town, where they could always find a seat and a parking space. St. Michael's parishioners were mostly elderly ladies who still covered their heads when they entered. I'd heard that they even did a Mass in Latin once a week.

As I stared at the front door with the smoky glass window, something in my gut screamed at me to *Run!* Not away from the church, like I'd expected. Toward it.

I checked the street. No traffic.

Shane dug the keys out of his pocket, then let go of my hand to force open the trunk, which always stuck.

I ran.

Regina and Shane released panicked shouts, but I couldn't stop until I reached the front door, where Shane caught up to me. Regina stopped at the bottom of the porch's brick stairs.

"Are you mental?" she hissed. "You can't go in there."

"I have to. I can't explain it."

"No." Shane seized my wrists before I could touch the doorknob. "Churches get consecrated after they're built. The building could burn you."

"This place is over two hundred years old. It must have worn off by now." My eyes pleaded with him. "I need to go in there."

"Why?"

"I don't know. Just trust me, okay?" It was a lot to ask, considering I hadn't shown him that same trust yesterday.

Shane didn't let go, but his grip loosened a fraction. Using a Control self-defense maneuver, I rotated my arms, twisting my wrists out of his hands.

"Hey!"

Before he could stop me again, I grabbed the iron doorknob. Shane and Regina shared a strangled gasp.

The knob was cool to the touch. "See?" I opened the door.

"Ciara, please." Shane reached for me, but stopped, as if my body could conduct holiness like electricity. "Don't do this."

I swung the door open wide enough that he could get through without touching the frame. "Are you coming or not?"

He folded his arms, shoving his bare hands into the crooks of his elbows, and inched sideways through the doorway, sparing me a killer glare as he passed.

"I'll wait in the car," Regina said.

I followed Shane through the vestibule, which contained a coat rack and two confessional booths, and through a set of open doors into the darkened sanctuary, which was no larger than the common room of the vampires' apartment. The rough wooden pews looked like they could seat maybe two hundred people. The wall sconces were dimmed to a minimum, but my eyes adjusted easily.

"I'm surprised it's open," I whispered to Shane. "They could get robbed."

"It's Church policy. These places are refuges for those in need."

I felt a stab of guilt, then realized that I was, in fact, in need. But of what? What had drawn me here?

I looked for a clue in my surroundings—the crucifix beyond the altar, the statue of Mary in a cubbyhole to its left, and a series of small wooden dioramas placed at intervals on the walls.

I pointed to the closest of the dioramas, which showed Jesus' crucified body lying in a woman's arms.

"What are those?" I asked Shane.

"The Stations of the Cross. Don't touch them."

"I won't," I said, though I very much wanted to. "They're so sad."

"Yeah, well . . ." Shane shoved his hands deep into the pockets of his denim jacket. "Life is sad."

In the far corner of the sanctuary, to the right of the altar, the floor became an open space, maybe a staircase leading down to a lower level. Its darkness drew me forward. I took a few steps down the center aisle, then stopped when an astonishing sight caught my eyes.

Looming over the sanctuary was a huge stained glass window. A wrathful angel with golden wings stood atop the throat of a writhing red dragon. His wooden spear pierced the monster through the heart.

"St. Michael the Archangel defeating Satan," Shane said.

"What are the words on his sash?"

"*Quis ut deus.* 'Who is like God?' It's what the name Michael means. But I've heard it's also supposed to be a rhetorical question that St. Michael is asking the dragon as he defeats him. 'Who is like God?' The answer is obviously 'no one,' except God himself."

"So it's Latin for 'Who's your daddy?'"

Shane smirked. "I guess."

A homework flashback hit me. "Dracula means 'son

of the dragon.' Dracula's dad was part of the Order of the Dragon, so he took the name for himself. Aaron told us that in modern Romanian, *dracul* just means 'devil.'"

"Well, there you have it."

"What?"

"If a picture's worth a thousand words, a stained glass is worth a million. Dracula, devils, vampires, St. Michael the righteous warrior." He cast a mournful glance around us. "We don't belong here. We never will."

The rational part of my brain reminded me that the Romanian prince Vlad "the Impaler" Dracula wasn't really a vampire, but rather a power-hungry ruler who put the "evil" in "medieval." Bram Stoker just recycled the name because it sounded cool. So this image had nothing to do with us.

But my gaze fixed on the thwarted dragon struggling beneath the angel's boot. The bright light from St. Michael's halo seemed to blind the creature. Light like the sun, something Shane and I would never see again except as a pale, cold reflection in the face of the moon. Or just after our last breath, when the world became too much for us.

Banished from the sun. Burned by holy objects. Filled with the urge to kill.

Maybe we *were* evil.

I backed up, fast enough to stumble, unable to tear my gaze from the pain and rage in the dragon's eyes. Dizziness swamped my head. Thirst cramped my stomach. At that moment, I was little more than a mindless monster.

My heel hit something solid. I jerked my chin down to see a marble pedestal. The sudden motion spiked my vertigo.

"Whoa." I wavered, hands splayed for balance.

I reached out to grasp the pedestal's reassuring solidness. My left hand slid forward over a slick shiny surface and down into—

"Ciara, no!"

The hiss of singed flesh mingled with Shane's shout. Steam rose from the steel bowl atop the pedestal.

Under the clear water, my hand turned black.

Shane yanked my elbow, pulling my hand from the holy water. Drops flew in all directions, singeing my face. He howled my name again.

I stared at my hand. My teeth gnashed as my lungs seized, trapping my scream of agony.

Impossible. Holy water had no power over me. I wouldn't let it—not then as a human, not now as a vampire.

Not ever.

"Ciara . . ." Shane's words came in gasps. "Oh God . . . what have you done?"

"It's only water. It's not real." I clutched my wrist and focused my mind on the charred skin and twisted fingers. By now it had stopped hurting. My hand was permanently dead.

No. I gritted my teeth and tried again. "It's. Only. Water."

The healing began at the edges of the burn. Pink crawled over my flesh, obliterating the black. Like a leather glove disintegrating to reveal the hand beneath, the burn shrank as I coaxed my mind and body to deny centuries of vampire truth.

In less than half a minute, my fingers were whole and clean and smooth.

"It worked." I touched my cheek, where I'd felt the water hit me, then turned to Shane. "Is it gone from my—"

My breath stopped when I saw his face. He was staring at my hand with one eye open.

The other eye was welded shut. Melted black flesh formed an oozing patch over his left socket.

"Shane . . ." I took a step forward, stumbling. "What did I do?"

He touched his eye. "Uh-oh."

I shoved up my sleeve. "Drink from me." I'd healed his holy-water burns before, as a human. I didn't know if my blood still worked that way, but we had to try.

"Not here," he said.

We dashed out of the church's front door. Regina was in the driver's seat, in getaway position, so she couldn't see us until we got in the car.

"I'll handle her," Shane told me as he opened the back door and pushed me in.

"What the fuck were you thinking, Ciara?" She turned to Shane. "And what was all the— Holy shit!"

"Just drive," he said. "You can freak out when we're home safe."

She pointed a long black nail at me. "You'd better fix this."

I strapped on my seat belt (habit) and kept silent all the way to the station, afraid to look at Shane. He didn't reach for my hand—in fact, he sat as far away from me as he could.

My thoughts ran in a circle. If I could heal myself, maybe I could heal Shane. Maybe my blood hadn't changed when I died.

But when I was human, holy water hadn't turned my

fingers into matchsticks. Standing in that church, looking at the angel and the dragon, had I let myself believe the hype? Was I finally ready to see vampires as evil, now that I was one?

Maybe the anti-holy wasn't in my blood anymore. Maybe it was only in my mind. And what lurked in the depths of that mind? Years of sitting primly in an itchy white dress while my father preached fire and brimstone. It didn't matter that I'd grown up to figure out the scam. That fear would always be a part of me.

You can take the girl out of the church, but you can't take the church out of the girl.

Regina skidded to a halt in the middle of the station parking lot, sending a spray of gravel onto the grass.

"Go!" she said without putting it in park. "Suck her dry if you have to."

Shane and I sprinted around the station and through the back door. As we passed the studio, Spencer gaped at us through the glass wall from his seat in the booth. My misery spiked as I realized he was covering Monroe's shift, which meant my maker still wasn't home.

When we reached Shane's room, I tore off my coat, then scrambled to unbutton my sleeves, trying not to stare at the monstrosity of flesh that was once his left eye.

"I'm so sorry," I said, though I knew it would never be enough. "It was an accident."

"I know. I saw you stumble." He ripped off his jacket. "But why weren't you careful? Why were you so close to the font in the first place?"

"I didn't see it! I've never been in a Catholic church before. I didn't know they kept weapons out on display."

He hurled his jacket into the corner. "You could've

lost your hand. And then what? How would you pass for a human with a blackened stump at the end of your arm?" He grabbed my shoulders. "It could've been the end of everything."

"But it wasn't. I fixed myself, and I can fix you, if you just believe. Or stop believing."

Shane let go of me and took my hand, the one that had burned. His own hand trembled, but his touch stayed gentle.

He shook his head as he examined my unblemished skin in the light. "Fuck." From his mouth, the word sounded like a prayer.

I brushed my healed hand over his burned eye. This was what separated us. He couldn't stop believing any more than he could stop breathing. Which meant I couldn't heal him with words alone.

"Hurry," I whispered. "Drink."

Shane yanked me against his chest, slid his arm around my back, and gripped the back of my head. Before I could breathe, he pressed his mouth to my neck. I stiffened in his grip, though I knew it was safe now. No embolism could stop my heart.

His breath came warm against my skin. "It won't hurt now that you're a vampire. I promise."

His lips moved down my throat. I took a deep breath and rested my weight against him, sinking into his strength.

A sharp pain pierced my neck. My hands clamped onto Shane's shoulders, but I couldn't catch enough breath to cry out. He groaned and clutched me tighter, lifting me off the floor. My feet kicked helplessly with the instinct to flee.

Shane's fangs withdrew, but his mouth burned my skin. Every twitch of his tongue sent another wave of pain through my body, straight to my toes and out, like an electric shock.

My head started to swim. With my last scrap of consciousness, I gasped his name.

Then it all went black. Again. Damn it.

My ears woke before my eyes. I heard voices near the end of whatever surface I was lying on—the bed, I presumed, from the scent.

"It's very odd, her fainting." Noah's voice was full of concern. "Perhaps she is some type of half vampire?"

Regina scoffed. "Half-*assed* vampire is more like it. I could kill Monroe. If he were here taking care of her, she'd be strong enough to handle a little bite without passing out."

I whimpered at the sound of my maker's name.

"Ciara?" Shane sat on the bed next to me and laid a cool cloth on my forehead. "Are you okay?"

"I am now." I rubbed my eyes, then forced them open. Shane was gazing down at me.

With one eye.

"Oh, no." I flailed my hand to touch his face, but he grabbed it and set it on the bed.

"I thought of a solution," he said.

"A pirate patch?"

"No. Well, yeah, that's Plan B."

"What's Plan A?"

He pressed my cell phone into my palm. "You're Plan A."

* * *

This was the call I'd dreaded more than any other. To the person who would be most dismayed with my change in metaphysical status. The human with the most power to make my unlife miserable.

His middle-of-the-night voice was as crisp as midday's. "Lanham."

I gave Shane, Regina, and Noah a grim thumbs-up. "Um, hi, sir. It's Ciara Griffin."

"I know."

"David told you what happened?" Relief flooded my veins—at least I didn't have to break the news.

"He told me nothing. I meant that I know it's you. I have caller ID." He exhaled, as if he were getting out of bed. I tried not to imagine what he wore to sleep. Too late—my mind formed an image of Air-Force-blue pajamas.

In the background, I heard the click of what sounded like a ballpoint pen. "Has there been another CA sighting?" he asked.

"No, it's not about that. It's about the fact that I'm sort of a vampire."

After a long pause, he simply said, "What do you mean, 'sort of'?"

"Okay, not sort of." I explained as quickly and steadily as I could. He grunted acknowledgment at appropriate intervals, and I found myself calmed by his unemotional reaction.

"So you see our dilemma," I said after I told him about that evening's misadventures. "But I figured that since I gave you so many samples of blood over the years—you know, for free, so you could do vampire-saving research—that maybe I could borrow a vial so Shane can get his eye back."

"Borrow?"

"Have." I glanced at Shane straddling his desk chair,

then at Regina and Noah standing in the doorway. "We could meet you somewhere for the handoff, wherever's convenient for—"

"I'll think about it." Lanham hung up.

"What the—" I hit Send again, but my call went straight to his voice mail. "Son of a bitch."

"He said no?" Shane's voice curdled with anger. "How could he say no? That's your blood."

"It's the Control's blood. I gave it to them." I tapped my phone against my chin. "He's figuring out what he wants from me in exchange."

"They'll experiment on you because you are different," Noah said to me. "They'll want to know why you could heal yourself, and why you don't yet have fangs."

"I might know," Regina said quietly. The other two vampires exchanged a surprised and worried look. "Not about the self-healing, but the fangs."

"Regina," Shane said, "I'm not sure if—"

"She should know what can happen," she snapped. "She should have all the facts."

"What facts?" I pushed myself to sit up and leaned back against the wall for support. "What can happen?"

"When I was turned, I wasn't alone." Regina looked me in the eye. "My husband joined me."

"You were married?"

Her face hardened. "Is that so tough to believe?"

I shut my mouth.

"Anyway," she continued, "Jack wasn't the healthiest person when he died. And the vamping didn't really take."

"He didn't survive the change?" I asked her.

"He became a vampire. But he didn't have fangs, and he felt as much pain as a human. Like you." She drew in a deep breath, then let it out. "He . . . withered, and he died permanently three weeks later. The blood didn't nourish him the way it should have. Or maybe he didn't get enough. I don't know."

Noah laid his hand on her shoulder, and she leaned into him, just a bit.

"I'm so sorry." My hand clutched the pillow. "There was nothing anyone could do?"

"We didn't have a big enough donor base. And back then it was harder to get bank blood. I did what I could."

Noah took his hand off her, and Shane looked away. By their reactions, I realized what Regina meant—she'd killed people to keep her husband alive.

"Are you saying I could still die?" I asked her.

"No." Shane stood and moved to my side. "We won't let that happen. We'll make sure you're fed. And we'll find Monroe and get him back here, even if we have to shoot him with a tranq gun." He looked at the clock, then tore his jacket from the back of the chair. "Fuck it, let's go now. We know where his donors live."

Regina held up a hand. "Wait a second, Elephant Man. You can't go knocking on doors at three a.m. looking like that."

"You are pretty melty," I told him.

Noah stepped forward. "Regina and I will go."

"I'm coming with you." I threw back the covers. "Maybe Monroe and I can sense each other."

"You should come," Regina said. "You're one of us now."

I reached for my shoes, trying not to blurt out the words *I don't want to be one of you*.

Because I wanted even less to die.

22

The Maker

It was 3:15 when we arrived at the home of Monroe's favorite donor, who lived on—swear to God—Sunshine Way. Which would have been funny if it hadn't resulted in me getting the Brady Bunch's "Sunshine Day" stuck in my head, along with another twinge of bitterness at the permanent loss of said shine.

We eyed the darkened ranch home through the windshield of Noah's car. Regina sat in the back with me. Once again, the power windows and locks were on child mode so that only the driver could control them.

"Perhaps we should have called first," Noah whispered.

"And give Monroe time to run?" Regina said. "Come on, let's hurry. He could be heading out the back door right now."

They each held one of my elbows as we went up the brick walkway to the porch. Regina counted rapidly under her breath, and Noah stepped carefully so that his feet fell only on the bricks that were pointing forward.

I tried to heighten my maker radar (assuming there was such a thing), tuning my mental divining rod to find Monroe. I sensed nothing beyond the overwhelming scent of freshly turned soil. My first thought was of zombies, before realizing it was just flowers.

"Seventeen red and twenty-nine white," Regina said when we reached the porch. "God, that bugs the crap out of me. Why can't they plant an even number of each color?"

"Maybe a few red plants died," Noah said.

"I'll ask her." Regina knocked firmly on the door. The porch light winked on over our heads, and I braced myself to resist the urge to attack.

No eating people. Not even a little. Not even at all.

The door opened to reveal a guy in his late thirties, a gray Orioles T-shirt stretched across his broad chest. He yawned as he ruffled his short blond hair.

"I admire your ambition." He looked straight at me. "And since you got up so early to beat the competition, put me down for three boxes of thin mints."

I was confused. Troubled, even.

What I was not, however, was thirsty, despite the fact that this guy was twice as hot as Jeremy.

Regina glanced at her handwritten notes. "You must be Brad. Can we speak to Sandy?"

"Is this about Monroe?"

I quaked a little at the sound of my maker's name. "Is he here?"

Brad shook his head. "Haven't seen him in months. He and Sandy were supposed to meet the other night, but he never showed up or called."

Regina shifted forward. "We really should speak to your wife."

I blinked. This guy's wife was Monroe's donor, and he was cool with that?

"I'll get her." He glanced at us in turn. "Don't be offended if I ask you to stay on the porch, okay? Have a good night. Or day, or whatever you call it." He shut the door and turned the deadbolt.

Once again I was struck by the creepy banality of suburban vampirehood. "Your world is so weird," I observed.

"It's your world now, too," Regina said.

"But I totally didn't want to bite that guy. No bloodlust whatsoever. Or maybe I'm learning to control it." I tried to tug my arms out of their grip. "Which means you can let go."

Noah and Regina laughed. "What you don't understand," Noah said, "is that you had no thirst for that man because he—"

The door opened, and my world turned red.

I don't even remember what she looked like, this Sandy person. I just remember how she smelled—like my favorite takeout dinner, chicken tenders and waffle fries.

Okay, really she just smelled like blood. But it had the same effect as a whiff of fast food on an empty stomach—instant craving beyond all rational need.

I lunged. Noah and Regina yanked me back like my arms were the leashes of a vicious dog. Which I guess I was.

"Please!" I cried as the woman slammed the door. "Just a little. I won't hurt you. I can't hurt you, I don't even have—"

Regina crammed a hand over my mouth. "Shut up before the neighbors call the cops!"

I shut up, but I kept struggling, hunger giving me super-super-super-*duper* human strength.

"Noah, take her back to the car."

He picked me up fireman style and flung me over his shoulder. The world spun and tilted, and then we were rushing across the lawn toward the driveway, my eyes at the level of his butt. I pounded on his back and sides, hoping he would drop me so I could make one more plea to Sandy. If Monroe hadn't bitten her lately, she must be full of blood. Hot, tangy, plasma-licious blood.

The rear door on the driver side had wisely been left open. Noah dumped me onto the backseat, then followed me inside and slammed the door behind us.

He shoved a balled-up sweatshirt against my face. "Now you may scream."

I howled into the thick fabric, and when I ran out of breath, I gnawed it like a teething puppy. (I am not proud of this.)

And then I realized that like a teething puppy, I had a very sore mouth. My gums ached with a sense of fullness, as if ready to give birth.

I dropped the sweatshirt into Noah's lap. "Do I have fangs?"

He leaned close as I stretched my lips up. "Not that I can see."

I ran my thumb across my top eyeteeth. Dull and duller. The pregnant gums sensation was already fading.

"So close." I covered my face, squishing the tears back into my eyes. "What's wrong with me?"

"You're thirty hours old." Noah tugged me into a soothing, brotherly embrace. "That's what's wrong with you."

"Travis had fangs when he was thirty seconds old."

"Everyone is different. Remember, Travis was a babbling fool his first two days."

"True." I wiped my nose as he let go of me. "I wish Travis was still around. We could form an Abandoned by Maker club."

"It would have many members." Noah sighed. "Including me."

"What happened to your maker? Did he die? Or she?"

"He is still alive," Noah replied. "I would know, of course, if he had been destroyed. I would feel all his pain, and then some."

I held back a shiver, remembering the way Travis had suffered and almost died when his maker was killed by Shane (with my help). If Monroe died now, it would probably kill me.

"Why did your maker leave?" I asked Noah.

"I failed him. I would not kill. Not on purpose."

"Because of your religion."

He bowed his head in a semi-nod. "If you want to call it that."

"What do you call it?"

"A way. A path. One that may lead to wisdom, if I and I will it."

I and I—one of the Rasta terms for God. "Do you think Monroe is gone for good?"

"Hard to say." He stared out the window toward the porch, where Regina was still interviewing Sandy.

"Why did Monroe leave me? Did I fail him?"

Noah eyed me over the rim of his glasses. "How could you fail him? You have done nothing."

I rested my cheek on the back of the seat. "I exist."

"As they say, it's not you, it is him. Give him time, he'll come back. He has a job."

"But what if he doesn't come back? What will the station do? What will I do?"

"We will all survive."

"Monroe didn't have to make me. It could have been Spencer or Jim or Regina. If he didn't want me, why did he sign my VBC form?"

"Perhaps he didn't know how hard it would be, to kill and resurrect."

"Have you ever done it?"

Noah shook his head. "I do not kill."

"On purpose."

His eyes turned down at their corners as he averted his gaze. I hurried to change the subject.

"How come I wanted to bite Sandy so much, but not her husband?"

"The man is not a donor and does not want to be. Non-donors smell different to us." He drew a smooth brown finger across the side window. "Think of the flowers. Some of them have scents that attract bees or butterflies, and some don't."

"That makes sense." I chuckled. "Get it? Sense? Scents?"

Noah lifted one corner of his mouth, indulging my new obsession with wordplay.

I continued, sans lameness. "Shane knew Jeremy was a willing donor the first time they met. Jeremy didn't even know vampires were real, but he wanted to be bitten."

"A fervent donor can make us thirsty even if we've just fed." He picked up my travel mug and shook it. "There are still a few sips."

I took it with less reluctance than usual. The bank blood was a million times better than nothing.

Regina opened the door and slid into the driver's seat. Noah handed her the keys. "Any information?"

"Pretty much what her husband said. Monroe never showed up for their donor date." She started the car. "But at least now we have help looking for him. Sandy'll check out all Monroe's favorite bars tonight and ask if anyone's seen him since Saturday." She put the car in reverse and tossed a sheet of paper into the backseat. "Do we have time to visit another donor?"

Noah looked at the sheet, then at the dashboard clock. "It's not far over the border into Pennsylvania. We'll make it no problem."

Regina gunned the engine, and we lurched down Sunshine Way. "Mason-Dixon line, here we come!"

As we headed out of town, I finished my meal with my face pressed against the window's cool glass, my eyes fixed on the low hills of the eastern horizon. In two hours, they would be dark silhouettes against the pale blue light of dawn. My skin seemed to shrivel at the thought.

By then I would be underground, safe from what would be the second in an eternally long line of missed sunrises. Maybe if I hadn't taken this path, I'd be lying in a hospital bed right now, recovering from chicken pox, staring out a temporarily dark window, waiting for a delicious breakfast of lime Jell-O, stale toast, and rubbery eggs.

I would never know.

23

Will You Love Me Tomorrow

I stayed in the car while Regina and Noah took turns interviewing the next two donors, who had even less information than Scrumptious Sandy. They hadn't heard from him since their last appointments, which had been two and three months ago, respectively.

"What if he wants to come home but can't?" I asked them as we turned down the station's long gravel driveway. "What if someone's holding him?"

"You mean captive?" Regina snorted, eyeing me in the rearview mirror. "Just because you're always at the center of a hostage crisis doesn't mean that's what happened to him."

"Monroe is too strong to capture," Noah pointed out. "No one could take him alive."

"And you'd know if he died." Regina thumped her fist against her chest.

I remained silent for a moment, knowing how they would react to my idea. Finally I said, "Maybe we should ask for help in finding him."

"His donors are helping," Regina said.

"I was thinking more along the lines of professional help."

She slammed the brakes. I sailed forward, smacking my chin on the back of the driver seat.

Regina turned to face me. "Don't even think about calling the Control. If they declare him a rogue vampire, they'll be the ones locking him up. We may never see him again."

"But if he's in danger—"

"He'd rather die than be in the hands of the Control. Got it?"

I nodded, though I didn't get it. I'd seen the damage done by zealous, unsanctioned hunters who scorned the Control's "cooperation before coercion" precept. For them, it was more like "torture before kill"—the vampires were trapped, starved, burned, and finally staked when they became as weak and fragile as moths. The Control cracked down on these antivampire vigilantes, so to me, the agency seemed like the lesser of two evils.

Regina's icy glare told me that any argument to that effect would be useless. She turned forward and drove faster than ever. When we got back to the station, a familiar black sedan was parked outside.

Regina hit the brakes too hard again. "Speaking of pigs."

I picked myself off the floor where I had landed during her abrupt stop, deciding to keep wearing a seat belt after all. "Let's hope he's here to help."

We went in through the back door, which led to a long hallway to the lounge. My nose told me who else was there, and hope quickened my pace.

"Shane . . ."

I opened the lounge door to see him standing near the opposite wall, glaring at Colonel Lanham. With one eye.

"Ms. Griffin." From his seat at the card table, Colonel Lanham nodded at Regina and Noah. "I need to speak with these two privately."

Regina rolled her eyes. "Oh, can't we please stay to hear the bureaucratic bullshit?"

"No." He turned back to me and Shane, who reached out to draw me close to him.

"Any luck finding Monroe?" Shane whispered in my ear.

"No, but I almost got fangs."

Lanham pulled a padded envelope from his briefcase as the apartment door closed behind Noah and Regina. "I have a proposition," he said.

I sat at the opposite end of the table from him. Though I didn't want to bite Lanham, it was a struggle to maintain my composure. I needed mind over matter, to save Shane's face—literally.

"What do you want from me?" I asked him glumly. How many more years would he add to my contract? Would he switch me from the Immanence Corps to the Enforcement Division? Just because I was now physically strong didn't mean I had any desire to dispatch my fellow vampires.

But I would've done it. I would've been a Control toilet cleaner—the best damn one they'd ever seen—if it meant healing Shane's wounds.

"Not you." Colonel Lanham looked at Shane. "You."

Shane's remaining eye widened. "What?"

"We want you to work for us."

Shane started to step back, then seemed to catch himself. "No way. After what I went through in that hellhole rehab center of yours, I can't believe you'd even ask."

Lanham folded his hands over the padded envelope, which I assumed contained a sample of my human blood. "I have something you need."

"I don't need two eyes to live. And I'm not vain, so don't try that tactic."

"You're not the one who has to look at you."

Shane put both hands on my shoulders. "She doesn't care either. She's not shallow."

"Perhaps not. But she is capable of substantial guilt, especially for a sociopath."

I kept my gaze on the package, waiting for the chance to steal it in the event of a distraction.

"Think about it, Mr. McAllister. Now that the two of you could have a long life together, do you want to burden her with a constant reminder of a simple but costly mistake?"

Shane took his hands off me and shoved them in his pockets. "We don't even know if the blood would work."

"Trust me. It will work."

Lanham's confidence told me they'd already used it in experiments, or maybe even administered it in the field. I wondered how much they charged for this Anti-Holy Wonder Salve (apply internally).

"Trust *you*?" Shane scoffed at Lanham. "That's a good one."

"Then trust this contract." He leaned over to reach into his briefcase, taking his hand off the package.

I pounced.

As my hand hit the padded envelope, Lanham grabbed my arm and yanked me toward him, flipping me onto my back. His elbow crooked around my neck. I gaped at the ceiling as something sharp pressed against my chest.

"Don't move," he said, as calmly as if he were requesting cream with his coffee. "Either of you."

I held my breath, certain that inhaling would drive the tip of the wooden stake through my blouse and into my skin.

Two feet away, Shane raised his hands in surrender. He'd been on the verge of attacking Lanham to protect me.

"Back off," I gasped, staring at the ebony stake that shone as smooth and polished as Lanham's scalp. I'd never seen a stake tip so needle sharp.

As soon as Shane reached the far wall, Lanham rolled me off the table in one smooth motion. When my feet touched the floor, he let go, then tucked the stake back in his—well, actually, I have no idea where he kept it. It disappeared as quickly as it had appeared.

I straightened my shirt, keeping my eyes on Lanham's expressionless face.

"Now." He leaned over to his briefcase again, this time releasing the package even longer than before, as if to test us. My fingers didn't even twitch—on the outside, at least.

Lanham brought out a folder and opened it to reveal three copies of a contract like the one I'd signed two and a half years ago. "All terms are negotiable, so let's begin."

"I don't have time for another job," Shane said. "I've got WVMP—"

"Every other night, for three hours."

"Plus my satellite radio gig."

"Which is weekly. That leaves eleven free days a month."

"Being a DJ isn't just the time spent on the air."

"David is willing to hire voice talent to take over your production work."

Shane's nostrils quivered in a sure tell. He hated recording promo spots for the station or commercials for whatever product our advertisers were hawking that week. He died a little inside each time he had to plug the latest lawn tractor—as if he'd ever had a lawn.

He looked away, at the door to their apartment. "No. I'm not a species traitor."

"Is that what you think Ms. Griffin is? A species traitor?"

"Of course not. She joined when she was human, and she did it for me."

"Then perhaps you can return the favor."

Shane's posture stiffened. Lanham had clearly struck a nerve, reminding Shane of the sacrifice I'd made.

"Would you excuse us for a few minutes?" I asked the colonel.

"Absolutely." He stood, leaving the contracts on the table but not the blood. He stuffed the package back in his briefcase and carried it upstairs, shutting the door behind him.

Shane didn't move from the wall or even shift his position. "Don't try to talk me into this. I already have a job."

"You can't do your current job without two eyes. Not if you ever plan to leave the booth."

"I can wear a patch to public appearances."

"A patch'll be torn off sooner or later. People like to get close to you."

"So I'll tell the truth—I got burned."

"Human burns don't scar like that."

Shane gave a harsh sigh and lowered his head, rubbing

the bridge of his nose between his thumb and forefinger. "There must be another way to get your human blood. It's bad enough that you're part of that soul-sucking agency."

I saw my ace in the hole, as if spotlights shone upon it and trumpets blared on either side. "If you join up, you can keep an eye on me, make sure I remain unmolested and uncorrupted."

He jerked his head to look at me. I put my hands behind my back in a poor imitation of innocence.

"Fuck." He shoved himself away from the wall and started to pace.

I sensed he needed time alone to come to grips with it all, and that any more pushing would be counterproductive.

I shifted toward the door. "I'm famished after being around all those donors, so I better—"

"Go ahead." Concern flitted across his face, diluting the anger for a half second. "I'll be along."

I was in bed dozing off, empty cup on the nightstand, when the door opened. I sat up quickly to see Shane.

He gazed straight at me with two perfect, pale blue eyes.

My lips started to curve into a relieved smile, but it faded at the look on his face.

"It's done." He turned away, slid off his shirt, and threw it over the back of the desk chair. His jeans followed but not his boxers.

I scooted over to make room. He got into bed without looking at me, then turned away and switched off the light.

With my back pressed against the wall, I waited for him to shift to face me. He gave his pillow one last punch and settled in with a sigh.

"I'm sorry you had to do that." I touched the back of his shoulder, which felt still as stone. "I screwed up, and you had to pay the price."

"We've been through this already." His voice was smooth and tight. "It was an accident, remember?"

I waited a few moments before asking, "Did Lanham tell you about the Immanence Corps?"

"He thought it would be a good match for me."

Now I wouldn't have to leave Shane behind to do my job. We could fight—or investigate or whatever it is the Immanence Corps does—as a team. Together.

"When do you start orientation?"

"I start class work in two weeks. Correspondence, obviously, because I have you to take care of here. One of the local agents will train me in combat basics."

"So you won't have to leave." I squeezed his shoulder. "That's great."

"In the fall I go to training camp for eight weeks."

My brow furrowed. "You mean four weeks. Only enforcement agents do eight weeks."

He was silent for a long moment. "I know."

I sat up. "Lanham made you join Enforcement?"

"I chose the assignment." His eyes stayed shut. "Let's not talk about it right now."

"Why would you do that? Of all the assignments—"

He put his hand up to silence me. "Not now."

I nodded feebly, though he couldn't see me. My throat was too thick for speech. I lay back down and pulled my hand under the covers to keep from trying to touch him again.

Why would he join the division he hated most, the one that did the most direct antivampire work? Why become one of those thugs? To punish me, or to punish himself?

I didn't understand, and I couldn't make him make me understand. Shane and I had always been different. But before, I could blame most of this difference on the human-vampire divide.

Now that we're the same, we're not the same.

A week ago we lay together in the bed-and-breakfast, dreaming about our future. Now that that future could be longer than we ever imagined, it seemed to be melting, then freezing, then melting again in our hands as we tried to sculpt it into something we could recognize.

Something that would last.

I was lying awake, listening to Shane sleep, when our door creaked open at 5 p.m.

Jim stepped in, waving a travel mug. "Pre-breakfast. I think you'll like this flavor."

I sat up halfway and took the drink from him. The bank blood tasted more powerful than usual. "This is fresh from a human, isn't it?"

"I wasn't very thirsty last night," he said, "but I hate to break a donor date, so I brought home a doggie bag. Not that you're a dog."

I gulped the rest of my meal, feeling the blood's warmth pulse through me faster than any since Jeremy's.

"Been pretty quiet in here." Jim glanced at the sleeping Shane. "How's it going?"

Sensing his loaded question, I pulled the covers up farther, even though I was dressed. "Great."

Jim parted his lips as he nodded with a knowing look. "Let me know if you need anything, okay? If you get thirsty or . . . curious."

As a human, I'd been as susceptible as anyone to the lure of a vampire's eyes, and Jim had used that power to mesmerize me into letting him go too far. Shane had attacked him for it, which could've gotten him killed by the older, stronger vampire.

Though Jim's gaze no longer made me feel helpless as a kitten on muscle relaxants, it pulled me in a different way. Flush with new blood, my body began to simmer, as if his eyes held a blowtorch against my skin.

Bad news. Very bad news. No wonder Shane wanted me to leave the Victoria's Secret at home.

"No, thanks." I broke eye contact to look past him. "I'm good."

His brows popped in surprise. "I bet you are."

"No! I meant, I'm fine. 'I'm good,' it's new slang. Newish." I set the cup on the nightstand and turned away. "Thanks for the snack. See you later."

"Yes." Just before he closed the door behind him, I heard him say, "You will."

I pressed my forehead against the wall, vowing never to be alone with Jim. If Shane caught him making a move on me, they'd fight. And this time Shane would die.

He turned onto his back with a sleepy groan. "Who was that?"

I couldn't say Jim's name. "Early breakfast."

"Good." He rolled over and slipped an arm over my waist. "Mmm, you're warm." His hand slid under my sleep shirt.

I squirmed against him, fitting my back tight to his

front. He kissed the nape of my neck, then the curve of my ear as his hand moved up to cup my breast.

I let out a gasp. "What brings this on?" I suspected it was Jim, even if Shane had sensed his visit only subconsciously.

"Does it matter?"

It mattered, but my body craved his touch—and my soul his acceptance—much more than my mind craved the truth.

"Do you want me to stop?" he said.

"No." I ground against him again, making him groan. "I'm dying for you."

Shane rolled my nipple between his thumb and forefinger, and I almost screamed at the shock of pleasure. I felt all my nerves reconnect at once, reforming a body that responded to him even more intensely than it had in life.

He pulled my shirt over my head. The feel of his smooth bare chest against my back made me writhe. I let my pounding pulse drown out the voices of doubt. If we could be like this again, maybe the rest would work. Maybe we could find a way forward together.

I turned my head for the kind of deep, long, wet kiss I'd almost forgotten existed, though it had only been a few days. His hand slipped between my legs, then stilled.

"Tell me if it hurts," he said. "You might not be ready."

"I'm ready." I didn't care how much it hurt. Nothing was stopping me from taking him.

With his arm snaked around my waist, he caressed me in soft torture through the silk of my panties. He kissed me again, giving me his tongue in a way that made me imagine how it would feel down there. I moaned again, hoping the sound traveled. Let them all hear we were together, and would stay together. Let them hear him claim me.

Shane tugged off my underwear, then caressed my legs, his fingers drifting closer and closer until I was practically snarling with urgency.

He turned me on my back and opened my thighs to his touch. At the first press of his fingers, I caught my breath so hard I almost choked.

"Sorry," he said, and started to pull away.

"No." I grabbed his wrist. "Don't stop unless I tell you. Don't try to read my mind." *You don't want to know what I'm thinking.* I laid his hand where I needed it most. "Just read my body."

He closed his eyes and touched me, his own breath drawing in fast and sharp when he discovered how slick I was in need of him.

"God . . ." He dragged his teeth across my collarbone. "You feel so good."

"Yes." I arched my back, ignoring the twinges of pain. "More."

"I won't hurt you." He brushed his lips against mine before shifting down to my neck. "I won't let anyone hurt you." He slowly swept his tongue over my nipple. "Ever again." Another long, lingering lick.

I fought to decipher his words through my haze of desire. They held the key to an important question.

More warm, wet circles, and my mind blanked at the flood of sensation. I stopped caring why he said or did anything then, as long as he didn't pull away.

The next time he spoke, his breath was warming my inner thighs. "No one will touch you, ever again."

Suddenly I understood. "Is that why?" I gasped.

He stopped, his mouth hot and taunting. "Why what?"

"Why you joined Enforcement? To learn how to protect me? To keep other vampires from—" I struggled for the right word. "Having me?"

Shane paused for the longest moment in either of my lives. "Whatever it takes."

His tongue flicked out, once, and I exploded.

I screamed from the blinding, violent orgasms that built and burst as he didn't let up, didn't let go. I screamed from the fear that we would never again touch each other's souls. I screamed from the sorrow that almost stole my breath.

When my screams faded to gasps and then finally to silence, Shane laid his head on my belly, facing the wall. We held perfectly still, not speaking. I stared at the ceiling, where a spider huddled in the far corner.

Though nothing separated our bodies, we'd never been so far apart. I didn't know which words, if any, could begin to close that gap.

A knock came at the door. There was a whole world out there that cared nothing for our despair.

"Emergency," came Regina's voice, flat as ever despite her word. "We've got zombies."

24

Ants Marching

I yanked on my sweatpants and threw Shane's shirt over my head before answering the door.

"Zombies?" My hand almost pulled off the doorknob. "As in plural?"

She looked at my face, then past me at Shane, who now lay half under the sheets. "I waited until the screaming stopped."

"Where are the zombies?" he asked her, his voice tight with tension that had little to do with walking corpses.

"In the cemetery, where else?"

I looked at the clock: 5:25. "But it's still daylight."

"Yeah, they had even worse timing than me."

"I don't get it."

She spoke slowly, as if we were dim-witted—which I guess we were. "The Control saw three zombies climb out of their graves just before sunrise this morning. The agents chopped them in half, but even if they hadn't, they said the zombies wouldn't have made it to the cemetery gates before they roasted." She turned back to me. "Lanham says there could be more tonight. He wants you both in the cemetery by 2030, whenever that is."

"When is 2030?" Shane asked me.

I subtracted twelve from twenty as I shut the door. "Eight thirty."

He glanced at the bed beside him. "Three hours."

I took a small step forward, wishing that zombies were the scariest thing in my life.

The door opened again.

"But first—" Regina stuck her head in the room "—briefing in the lounge in five minutes."

"What did you say to him?" I asked Lanham when I entered the lounge two minutes later, without Shane. "Why is he joining Enforcement?"

The colonel glanced up from the table where he sat with his open laptop. Rather than feigning innocence, he said, "I pointed out the reality of your new condition."

"What about my 'condition' means Shane has to become the thing he hates most? What's forcing him to be a vampire hunter?"

"He's forced to do nothing." Lanham calmly shifted his mouse, then double clicked. "Unless he wants to keep you."

"Vampires aren't animals. They're not going to suddenly start ripping each other's throats out over me."

"Perhaps not all of them. But it only takes one."

I held back a groan, knowing he was probably right. "Why did Shane get to choose his assignment? I didn't." My voice's petulance made me flinch. "Neither did Tina."

"He didn't choose. He only thinks he did." Lanham picked up the laptop and set it on the projector. "By the way, you and Agent McAllister are temporarily activated until the *cadaveris accurrens* threat is eliminated." He turned to me. "Under my command."

"Fine." I glared at him, hands on my hips, until his meaning sunk in. "Oh." I straightened my posture. "I mean, yes, sir."

Shane entered then, precisely on time. "Good evening, sir." His lips twisted as he uttered the words, as if they had a sour taste.

I glared at him. "Sucking up to your commander doesn't make you an instant badass."

"That is correct, Agent Griffin." Lanham nodded at Shane. "But it's a fine start." He switched on the LCD projector. "Let's begin."

Shane and I sat on opposite sides of the table. A Flash video in sepia tones was frozen on the screen.

"The rest of your squad—all vampires, of course—are being briefed at other locations. We will depart the station in—" he looked at his watch "—one hour twenty-eight minutes. You'll receive rudimentary training on site, but since you lack experience, you'll be asked to stay back and document the event. You will receive weapons and protective gear, in case your aid is needed."

"What kind of weapons?" Shane asked, his testosterone no doubt kicking in at the mention.

"Mostly katana swords." Lanham reached under the table and pulled out a long carrying case. He set it on the table and unlatched it. "What you would probably call a samurai sword." He lifted out the long, gleaming weapon. "With vampires it's usually used for decapitation."

"I know," Shane said.

"Of course. You once destroyed one with a weapon like this."

Shane met his gaze. "It was self-defense."

But his fingers twitched as he looked at the sword. I wondered whose head he imagined liberating from its body.

Lanham turned to the projector. "We have footage of this continent's last known CA attack, from the late 1920s, in Michigan's Upper Peninsula." He put the cursor over the Play arrow. "Keep in mind, this event was filmed at normal speed." He started the video.

"Jesus." Shane turned to me. "The one you saw moved that fast?"

I couldn't answer right away, because my jaw was stuck in the holy-crap position. Dozens of zombies—CAs, whatever—streamed past the stationary camera like a swarm of giant, meth-addled cockroaches.

Like the creature I'd seen in the Sherwood cemetery, they didn't swerve to avoid headstones and shrubbery. On the contrary, every obstacle sent them spinning ass over teakettle. They used the momentum to lurch to their feet and continue running toward . . . what exactly, I couldn't tell. But their prey must have been tasty, based on the gnashing and twisting of the holes that had once been their mouths.

I almost envied their unabashed hunger. They wanted blood, but didn't need it. I needed blood, but couldn't bring myself to want it.

I'd never seen so many vampires in one place. They arranged themselves like fence posts around the perimeter of the Sherwood cemetery. Most wore solid black with the red patch of the Enforcement Division. In front of them, several squads of vampire agents wore the gray uniforms of the nearly defunct but newly revived Zombie Company. A few scattered agents wore the midnight blue garb of the Immanence Corps.

Since Shane and I were contractors, we could wear civilian garb along with a special leather jacket and cap. Shane grumbled at the latter, saying that hats made him look like Kid Rock. I tried not to look at him at all, so I wouldn't see the red patch on his shoulder and be reminded of why he wore it.

Captain Fox oversaw our brief weapons training. While he lectured us, he paced before a pair of shiny green torsos. Elijah was clearly in his glory now that zombies were an official crisis.

"These dummies are made of a special gelatinous compound that approximates the consistency of human flesh. I want you to both find out what it feels like to cut a body in half." He indicated the space above the collarbone. "In the same way that gunmen are trained to aim for the center mass instead of the head, I want you to swing down and across. Simple decapitation isn't so simple with a moving target. But it's hard to miss the entire body."

Elijah pointed to me. "Ladies first, Griffin."

I gripped my katana sword in both hands, as I'd been trained, and stepped forward, remembering to put my momentum into the swing without committing so far forward I lost my balance.

Zing! Thwap!

The blade sang through the torso as easily as—well, as easily as a sword through Jell-O. I tried to hide my gasp of surprise, but apparently failed, based on the titters I heard from a pair of veteran agents passing by.

"Perfect," Elijah said, "except for one thing. While you were admiring your handiwork, another zombie came up and ripped your damn head off. So slice and search." He turned to Shane. "Slice and search. Go."

Shane didn't hesitate. He blurred forward, and by the time the torso fell into two pieces at his feet, he had returned to his fighting stance.

I had to admit: it was hot.

They stationed the two of us in the back of an open box truck across the street from the cemetery. We were far enough away to have a good vantage point for filming, yet close enough to be deployed as a last resort.

Unfortunately, they left us alone, which at the moment seemed more dangerous than being at the center of a zombie pileup.

"This'll probably be the only time we get to work together in the Control," I said as I finished setting up the video camera on its tripod, "since we're in different divisions."

"Uh-huh." He didn't look up from the digital camera's instruction book, which he'd been perusing for almost an hour.

"How many times are you going to read that?"

"Until I understand it. These things are after my time." He flipped it upside down and backward. "Besides, I need to brush up on my Spanish."

"In case the jackbooted thugs deploy you to Mexico?"

"Yep." He kept reading.

I sighed and peered down the street. Outside the cemetery, a perimeter had been established by what looked like the Department of Homeland Security but was no doubt the Control in one of its federal guises. They coordinated at the highest levels with the agencies of the United States and other countries. As long as the Control kept human-vampire peace, governments were happy to spare a few vehicles and uniforms.

The hours crawled by. I ate my lunch early, so Shane wouldn't have to remind me. To pass the time and keep from thinking about our disintegration, I made a list of four-plus-letter words from the letters in the Sherwood cemetery sign.

I checked my watch at midnight. "You're missing your show," I told Shane, who was lying on his back just inside the box truck. "Who's subbing for you tonight?"

His whole body tensed. "Jim," he said without opening his mouth.

I knew then for sure that Shane had been awake that morning when the hippie DJ had visited. Maybe Lanham was right—Shane needed combat skills to make up for his youth, skills only the Control could give him.

A shout came from the cemetery. I lifted my binoculars to see several ZC agents waving their arms. They pointed to the ground in the high center section, near the chapel and adjoining mausoleum. The rounded, treeless area held several tall, elaborate headstones.

"Something's happening." I woke up the video camera and focused on the earth where the agents were pointing. I heard Shane sit up beside me, grabbing his own camera.

Beside a headstone, a hand shot up through the ground. I stifled a yelp.

Another hand shoved into the air in a geyser of soil. Then, wriggling like a grub, the corpse burst from the ground. Clumps of gray-brown grass cascaded from its head and shoulders.

"Whoa." Shane gave a low whistle. I pointed at my camera, then put a finger to my lips to hush him.

Another zombie, at almost the same point in its "birth," left its own grave a few rows behind the first. I zoomed out to see a third, then a fourth.

The earth gave up its dead. One after another they pulled themselves from the ground, their bodies straining, arms flailing, legs kicking. Mouths screamed without sound.

According to the Control, zombies had no souls, no awareness, no pain. They felt less than a bug feels. Yet as I watched them struggle like wounded animals, I wanted to strangle the sadistic bastard who'd raised them from the peace of their graves.

The vampires on the perimeter of the cemetery readied their weapons. Orders were to hold off on destroying the zombies until they could be observed. The IC hoped to discern a pattern that could lead them to the necromancer.

But the zombies didn't run. Instead they stood, heads lolling on too-flexible necks, clothes mud-streaked and torn, flesh in various states of decay. A woman in a pink dress and pale, scraggly hair touched her face to discover she was missing the lower half of her jaw. My heart ached as I imagined her long-ago beauty.

I knew my sympathy would evaporate the moment the zombies attacked. Any moment now, I thought, their instincts will kick in. They'll catch a distant scent of human blood.

The *cadaveris* moved, slowly at first, and entirely with-out rampage. They milled about like people at a party where no one knows each other.

Two skeletal males bumped shoulders, then froze. They aimed their hollow eye sockets at each other's skulls. I wondered if a challenge had been issued. Would we see a duel?

As I watched them, my eyelids grew suddenly heavy. I placed my hand on the truck's interior wall to steady myself.

The two zombies turned away and walked deliberately toward the others. Each collided with a new one, who stopped and "stared" for a few seconds before setting off to touch another.

"Reminds me of a game kids used to play in the neighborhood," Shane whispered. "Like freeze tag, but the opposite. I always thought we made it up."

I rubbed my eyes as the dizzy feeling cleared. "How do you win?"

"I don't remember." His camera clicked and whirred. "It was just an excuse to run around shoving each other."

When all twelve zombies had been touched, they turned as one toward the path. I held my breath as their pace increased to a stumbling jog. Their speed didn't approach the full-fledged gallop I'd seen last Friday or on the film tonight. But they moved with a sense of purpose that chilled my bones.

When they stopped together, I muted the video camera. "Something's weird."

"You still have a baseline for weird?"

"Zombies don't cooperate." My pulse sped up as the ramifications hit me. "What if this is a different kind of zombie? What if they've evolved? Wouldn't they be a lot more dangerous if they could think and act together?"

"All we've seen them do is rub against each other and shuffle in the same direction. Not exactly Michael Jackson's 'Thriller.'" He sucked in a quick breath. "What the hell?"

I looked through the video camera. Four of the male zombies had dropped to their hands and knees, side by side. Three more males climbed on their backs, also on their hands and knees.

My eyes widened so hard they hurt. "Is that what I think it is?"

"It can't be," Shane whispered. "That's just . . ."

"Weird."

The zombie pyramid was shaky but held steady—until two female zombies attempted to climb aboard to create the next level. Their added weight made the formation sway and shudder.

My head filled with clouds again, like my blood lunch had been spiked with sedatives. I tried to remember who'd prepared my meal and realized it was me.

An arm snapped off one of the first-level zombies, and the pyramid collapsed. They tumbled into a pile of heaving, writhing bodies, limbs sticking out in all directions. If they made a noise, I couldn't hear it, but their mouths spread wide, their expressions as garish as clown faces.

They tried again, arranging the pyramid in as random a fashion as the first time.

"They're doing it wrong." My voice sounded far away, as if I were listening to myself from the back of a lecture hall. "The bases should be working together to lift the mid-bases so the flyer has a stable structure to work with. And they don't have any spotters."

"The huh?" Shane said.

"Someone should show them how it's done." The compulsion tugged hard at my gut, like someone had hooked one of my intestines.

I rubbed my stomach and got to my feet, hopping off the end of the van.

Shane grabbed my arm. "Where are you going?"

I turned to him, and a fog seemed to lift from my brain. "I don't know. What was I saying?"

"Something about bases."

I glanced at the zombies trying to reassemble their pyramid. "Must've sparked high school cheerleading memories."

I climbed back into the van and checked out the zombies' progress. The one with the broken arm—which seemed to cause no pain—was hanging back while the others formed the first two levels.

My thoughts slowed to a crawl again, worse than ever. It was like those chunky-peanut-butter moments trying to get out of the white place. It was like being dead again, except this time there was no music to call me out. No thread, no lifeline. Just . . . nothing.

"I can't believe you were a cheerleader," Shane said, startling me.

I rubbed the heel of my hand against my temple. "It was a small school. They weren't very selective."

"No, I mean I can't believe you wanted to be a cheerleader."

I knew I should bristle at his comment, but the conversation seemed like my only link to sanity. "My foster parents gave me two years' worth of normal life. I was going to milk it for all it was worth."

The corpse in the middle disintegrated, the foot of the man above him plunging through his back. The pyramid collapsed again.

"I know cheerleaders are an auto-uncool in your grunge-boy book," I told Shane, "and you never would've looked at me twice. At football games you would've been too busy getting stoned under the bleachers with your ironic friends, making fun of everyone with school spirit."

He didn't answer at first, and I worried I'd driven home too hard the painful truth that we were different.

The CAs had picked themselves up, dusted themselves off (in a manner of speaking), and started all over again, with dogged, unthinking determination. These were no highly evolved creatures.

As I watched, I felt my own brain devolve back into a bug.

Say something, I begged Shane without speaking. *Say anything. Or zombie cheerleading coach will be the last job of my unlife.*

"I would've looked at you," Shane said finally. "A lot more than twice."

I sent him a smile, but he didn't see it, so I took it back and saved it for later.

The zombies had finally completed the third row of the pyramid. All that remained was the top person, and if I recalled correctly, the placement of that person didn't involve climbing.

Oh no. The broken-armed zombie backed up, then stumbled full speed toward the two who remained on the ground behind the pyramid. When he reached them, they caught him up and tossed him to the top.

Where he sailed over, about ten feet too high, then

landed on the ground with a splat that even I, with my infant vampire ears, could hear from two blocks away.

Shane gave an audible wince.

"They don't feel pain." I was reminding myself as much as him.

As if to prove my point, the zombie wrenched himself off the ground, looking much the worse for his misadventure, having broken his fall with his face. The other members of the pyramid, who had had no reaction to his belly flop, didn't watch his excruciating journey back to the launch point. They stared straight ahead, empty as marionettes waiting for the show to begin.

The image made me wonder: was the person—or people—who controlled them sending them signals now, or had they preprogrammed the zombies? And why?

"What's the point of this?" I had to focus extra hard to get the words out, as the brain fog set in again. Definitely needed more blood. Or sleep. Or—I don't know—maybe my goddamn maker in my life.

"Warfare practice?" Shane said. "If someone can make them do a complicated maneuver like a pyramid, maybe they can coordinate them into a synchronized attack. Maybe the necromancer is perfecting his zombie-controlling techniques."

"Or her. Or . . ." A thought was forming, but it was crazy. *Maybe it's not about the zombies.*

"So ten years ago, you were doing your splits and twirls and pom-pom shakes, and here you are, ready to wield a samurai sword against a plague of incompetent zombie cheerleaders."

"That I would not have predicted. I sure as hell thought I'd have my bachelor's degree by now." I bit my lip, but it didn't stop my final thought from coming out. "I also thought I'd be alive."

He gave me a sympathetic glance, but it turned gloomy. "When I was seventeen, I was already so fucked up, I knew I'd be dead in ten years."

"And so you were." I fought to keep the bitterness from my tone. At least he'd had a choice.

The broken-armed, flat-faced zombie shambled toward his launchers at a speed an old lady with a walker could have outpaced. They waited for him, arms outstretched, and when he arrived, they boosted him up, up, up.

He tumbled cartwheel style through the air. The zombies on top snagged his legs and yanked him back down to land on their shoulders, limbs splayed.

For a moment, the entire pyramid wavered under the shock and sway of the new weight. Then the top zombie spread his arms, broken and whole, in a macabre simulation of exultation.

I wanted to cheer. Or cry. Or both.

"Well." Shane clicked his tongue. "That's something you don't see every day."

After a few triumphant seconds, the zombies on the bottom of the pyramid gave way, and the whole structure came down in a silent cascade of flesh and bone and rags.

This time, when the zombies picked themselves up, they did not brush themselves off and start all over again.

They ran.

Rampaging in all directions, they seemed to have forgotten one another and the odd directive from their mysterious pep rally coordinator. They had returned to form.

The ZC agents were ready for them. They fanned out, encircling the zombies and wielding long, gleaming katana swords or heavy battle-axes. A few held weapons that looked like giant hammers with stubbled surfaces, like those found on meat tenderizers.

One-on-one, the zombies might have put up a fight with their speed and strength. Certainly against humans they'd be a tough match. Against unarmed humans they'd be unstoppable.

But the vampire ZC agents had them outnumbered four to one. Their weapons made short work of them, hacking off heads or slicing bodies in half.

I'd seen humans die, killed in a battle with vampires. No one ever really "dropped dead," falling by pure gravity. No matter how they died, for a few moments their muscles remained rigid, resisting their body's plummet to the earth.

Not these bodies. They went down as heavy and unresponsive as bags of laundry. Fluid spilled from their cavities, leaking like a toppled milk carton, not spurting like a human would.

They weren't even animals. They were just animated objects, with no more feeling than a windup doll.

Or at least I tried to tell myself that as I watched the ZC agents close in on the last few zombies, the ones whose pyramid mishaps left them unable to run. They crawled through the mud, the ground sloughing off the last remaining rags of what was once their Sunday best.

The agents acted with brutal efficiency, reminding me of videos I'd seen as a kid, of hunters clubbing baby harp seals.

The broken-armed guy was last. He couldn't even crawl, only slither on his belly, using hips and elbows to drag himself toward the distant scent of blood. His neck could no longer support his head, so he lay facedown, oblivious to his approaching annihilation.

Two agents stepped up to him. One pressed on the man's back with the end of his giant hammer, holding him still. The other agent raised his sword.

A moment later, it was all over.

Silence shrouded the cemetery. Shane turned off his camera and set it beside him. We didn't speak. It felt like that moment just before the credits roll at the end of an emotional gut-punching movie. But this was no movie.

My hands shook as I picked up what was left of my second lunch. My head spun from what I hoped was only thirst and not a complete emotional breakdown.

"What are you doing here?" said a man with a light foreign accent.

I turned to see Lieutenant Colonel Petrea approaching the van, with four human agents flanking him.

"Working," I said. "For Lanham."

He stopped a few feet away—which was far too close for my tastes—his dark eyes raking my frame. "You were made only two days ago, correct?" When I nodded, he said, "You should be resting." He turned to Shane. "Is this your maker?"

"No, he's my—um, this is Agent Shane McAllister."

Shane folded his hands under his arms. "You're the one who told her she would die." He glared at Petrea. "Still think she has no future?"

The IC commander swiveled his head to meet my gaze. "The future is always in flux."

Shane scoffed. "Then you can never be wrong. How convenient."

"I saw darkness and death on your path," he told me in his ethereal voice. "Was I incorrect?"

"You saw her file," Shane interjected. "You knew she'd never had chicken pox, that she had Aaron Green as a professor, and that she'd probably be dead in a few days. Brilliant deduction."

Petrea turned his whole body to face me. "I need no powers to know that you should not be out at your age. I only need memory. You should be with your maker."

I looked away, partly because the angles of his face hurt my eyes, but mostly because it seemed like it would soon become impossible. He seemed to have me in some sort of prehypnotic state. "I've been activated. I have a duty to perform."

Petrea stepped closer, and I could feel his gaze sear my face. "Your maker has left you, hasn't he?"

My mind raced for an answer that wouldn't reveal too much. How did he know my maker was a man? Was he bluffing, or had the details of my turning already been added to my file?

Shane shouldered his way between us. "It's none of your business," he told my commander. I pulled in a sharp breath at his insubordination. He had a lot to learn about Control agent conduct.

"You are dismissed." Petrea's gesture encompassed Shane and his own agents. "Now."

The others obeyed instantly, but Shane stayed where he was.

"Go," I told him. Much as I disliked Petrea, I didn't want Shane to get punished for pissing him off. Besides, his overprotectiveness was getting on my nerves.

With a heavy sigh, Shane picked up his camera and

the video assembly. "I'll take this to the ZC commander and then start helping them clean up. The sooner we do that, the sooner we can leave." He gave Petrea a glower before stalking off.

"Sit," Petrea told me, as controlled as ever despite Shane's behavior. "Are you getting enough to drink?"

"I think so." I sat on the tailgate of the truck, confused by his sudden concern. But he wouldn't be the first vampire to treat me differently now that I was one of them.

"You have other vampires in your support system, besides this—" he waved his hand in the direction of Shane "—friend of yours?"

I nodded. "They take good care of me. Keep me out of trouble." I scratched the back of my neck, feeling like I was talking to a high school guidance counselor. "If that's all, sir, I should probably go see—"

"My maker did not care for me either."

I blinked, taken aback by his sudden change in demeanor. "They didn't feed you?"

"He fed me too well." Petrea's gaze went cloudy. "As soon as I was made, he took me home to help him kill my family."

"Oh. Wow." That put my troubles in perspective. "Did you—go through with it?"

"I was crazed with thirst. I drank them all."

I didn't know what to say. Would I have devoured my own family in those first moments of insatiable hunger? If Spencer hadn't tackled me, I would've killed Jeremy, who in one hour had gone from friend to prey.

"When I woke later," Petrea continued, "and the bloodlust had faded, I saw what I had done to my father and mother and"—he bowed his head —"and my wife and daughter. My rage and grief drove me to stake my maker through the heart."

I gasped, imagining the pain he'd brought on himself.

"I did not know, of course, the agony it would cause my own flesh." He touched his chest, brushing the edge of the rows of rectangular metal ribbons. "But I would have done it nonetheless. It was a righteous act." He adjusted the already straight jacket of his midnight blue uniform. "My survival, however, was an act of cowardice. I should have had the courage to destroy myself, to pay for my sins."

"It wasn't your fault. Your maker took advantage of your weakness." My con artist info-digging instincts kicked in. "Why did he want to kill your family?"

"Vengeance. My father was a vampire hunter. He'd killed my maker's wife. Or so the monster claimed before I pulled the stake from his heart."

"How did you survive without your maker?"

"Like you, I found a coven that took me in. Vampires who band together like us, they live longer and kill fewer humans." His face hardened. "It is the rogues like my maker whom we must guard against."

Why was he telling me this? Petrea struck me as the type who didn't give away anything without expecting something in return.

"Why do you think your maker left you?" he asked.

Ah, there we go. "I never said he did."

"Perhaps the Control can help find him. We have many resources at our fingertips."

I'll bet. No doubt they had entire squads devoted to hunting down rogue vampires. Not that Monroe was rogue.

"That's not really necessary," I said.

"Of course. Unless he's been taken captive. We know where the unlicensed vampire hunters have their nests."

My throat tightened at the memory of the torture I'd once witnessed, the ashen faces crisscrossed with holy water burns. The thought of Monroe in the hands of the latest band of sadistic zealots made me squirm.

But still I told Petrea nothing. If the details of my turning were in my file, he already had enough information to make me feel vulnerable. My life of secrecy and subterfuge had ended when I signed that contract with the Control.

I wouldn't let it go without a fight.

25

Breaking Us in Two

An hour before morning twilight, Shane and I headed back to the station—muddy, exhausted, and reeking of putrid flesh.

I reached into the glove compartment and pulled out a fast-food napkin to blow my nose. "I'll never get this smell out of my nostrils."

Shane grunted a reply and clicked on the radio. Before I could conjure a tension-lowering topic of conversation, the wild surf-jam song ended.

Jim's laconic tone came from the speakers. "94.3 WVMP Sherwood, Maryland. It's 5:06 a.m., and that was Jan Davis with 'Watusi Zombie.'"

I would have chuckled at the title if the sound of his voice hadn't dropped the temperature in the car ten degrees.

"I have an important governmental type announcement for all you crazy early risers, so listen up."

I glanced at Shane, who returned my worried look.

"In a joint order of the United States Centers for Disease Control and Department of Homeland Security, a mandatory curfew has been imposed for the town of Sherwood. Beginning at 1900 hours today, Tuesday, April thirteenth—that's seven p.m. for us civilian non-pig types—all residents are to return to their homes until further notice. That means no leaving your house after seven tonight. Not tomorrow morning or the next morning, not at all until they say it's okay."

"An indefinite curfew?" Shane said. "I've never heard of that."

"Probably has more to do with zombies than chicken pox. But of course they can't tell people that."

Jim continued, "Sherwood residents are permitted today to acquire any necessary items to facilitate this extended quarantine. Area grocers have been instructed to ration certain items to ensure that no citizen lacks amenities." He chuckled. "That means no one gets to hog all the Fritos and toilet paper."

He read the notice in a mock-official voice. "Residents and nonresidents will be required to remain in Sherwood as of the time of this announcement. National Guard troops have been deployed to enforce this quarantine order."

"They're trapping everyone inside the town," I whispered.

"The federal government hopes to return the town of Sherwood to normal operations within a week. To expedite this process, any persons susceptible to the chicken pox virus should report immediately to the county health department at 991 Center Street in Sherwood, where CDC officials will provide all necessary tests and health care provisions at no charge. Susceptible persons are those eighteen months and older who have neither contracted the virus previously nor received the vaccination.

"This is where it gets interesting, folks." Jim returned to the edict. "The CDC, along with the state and county health departments, will conduct interviews with all residents to determine the identity of susceptible persons. Cooperation will be rewarded. Failure to voluntarily subject oneself or one's dependent child to testing and quarantine, or withholding information regarding susceptible persons, may result in arrest for obstruction of justice."

I shivered, as if someone had drawn the tip of an icicle down my spine. "They're getting people to rat each other out."

"Shh." Shane raised the volume.

"Oh, here's a bonus," Jim said. "The IRS will provide no-penalty filing extensions to all those affected by the quarantine, seeing as you won't be able to get out Thursday to send in your taxes." Jim paused, and when he spoke again his voice was dead serious. "Just to be crystal? You can't leave town. As of tonight, you can't leave your house, maybe for several days. If there's the least chance you could get sick with this plague, turn yourself in, or you'll spend your dying day in a jail cell. They are not messing around."

He gave the phone number and Web site URL for people to get more information, then read the whole order again, this time without editorial comment.

"I'll repeat the announcement every fifteen minutes through the end of my shift, at which point someone else will have that unsavory duty. WVMP 94.3 will be the official source of emergency services information." He recited the station phone number twice. "Let's stick together, okay? Don't go all every man for himself. See if your neighbors need anything. Look out for each other, and let's get through this with as little drama as possible. Peace."

Shane turned off the radio. "Who knows you never had chicken pox?"

"Outside of the Control and the radio station, just Lori, Tina, and Maggie. I had to make sure they couldn't catch it from me at the bachelorette party."

"Lori and Tina know not to say anything. And Maggie was debriefed after the first zombie attack, right?"

I pulled out my cell phone. "I'll tell Lori to let her know what happened to me. I'm sure Major Ricketts made Maggie understand how important it is to keep vampires a secret." And what would happen to her if she spilled.

Lori answered my call right away. "Hey."

"Did I wake you?"

"Jim called at four thirty to tell us about the curfew." She stifled a yawn. "David just left for the station."

I told her all about the zombie "attack," including the cheerleading antics.

"Oh my God, how bizarre," she said. "That sucks you had to help shovel it up, what with your new sense of smell."

"Eau de zombie will be the least of my problems if Maggie or Tina tells the authorities I never had chicken pox. Can you get to them and explain what happened?"

"I'll call them right now."

"Are you coming to the station with David until the end of the quarantine?"

"No, I better stay here with Antoine."

"Bring him. Dexter would love to see his old kitty buddy. And I'd love to see you."

She spoke slowly, the way I was getting really tired of people speaking to me. "I don't think it's a good idea for us to hang out right now."

My chest turned cold. "Are you afraid of me?"

"Shouldn't I be?"

"I'm your best friend." My voice trembled. "I would never hurt you."

"Not on purpose."

"Not at all."

"Travis once told me what he was like when he first turned. All crazy and out of control."

"I'm not like Travis." I looked at Shane for confirmation, but he kept his eyes on the road.

Then I thought of how much I'd wanted to eat Jeremy, and Monroe's donor Sandy.

Lori spoke again. "I'll think about it. It would be great to see you, check out your new vampire bod."

"No." I pressed the phone hard against my cheek. "Stay home. Just for a while. I promise eventually everything will be the same."

Lori was quiet for so long that I checked to see if the phone connection was intact.

"Ciara," she said finally. "I don't think anything will ever be the same."

A chorus of *ewww*'s greeted our arrival in the common room. Even Dexter ran away whimpering.

"God, you reek!" Regina said.

Noah grabbed a pair of towels from the hall linen closet and hurled them at us. "Strip, then shower."

Shane let me shower first while he shaved over the sink. We didn't speak, either from exhaustion or the left-over tension of this evening, renewed by our nudity.

When I reentered the common room, still in a towel, Regina was alone, standing in the kitchen area.

"That was fast," she said. "I figured you two would be in there for days."

"I've seen Shane wet and naked before."

"Novelty worn off?"

I forced a beleaguered smile. "I spent the last two hours scraping up viscera. Right now, a harem of porn kings couldn't keep me from a nap."

She snickered as she pulled a serving-size package of blood out of the fridge. I checked the clock and frowned, realizing it was meant for me.

"Speaking of naked men." She set the plastic container in the microwave. "I'm going to call that stripper guy."

"Ken? I thought you weren't interested."

"We need to expand our resources. You'll be sharing our donors, so until you find your own we should each get a new one, just to be safe."

Safe. Who knew how much effort dead people had to put into surviving?

"I'm glad you took Ken's card from our apartment. There wouldn't have been time to go back today, what with the quar—" I stopped. A troubling fact tickled the back of my brain. Not did-I-leave-the-iron-on? troubling. More like a-piano-is-falling-on-my-head! troubling.

"What's wrong?" Regina said. "You look paler than that zombie."

"Ken." I sat on the arm of the sofa, so hard it jarred my spine. "Ken."

"What about him?"

"He knows I haven't had chicken pox. I asked him before the bachelorette party, in case he was suspect—susceptamble." My dry tongue couldn't pronounce the word. "In case he could catch it."

"Did you ask him directly, or did you ask someone at the stripper company?"

I rubbed my scalp hard, trying to remember. It seemed like months ago, and yet it hadn't even been a week. "He texted me the playlist Wednesday night so I could burn a CD for his performance. I asked him then. Aaron hadn't died yet, but we already knew it might be some kind of chicken pox." I covered my mouth. "He'll tell the authorities. What am I going to do? I can't escape during the day."

"Calm down." She marched over to me and took my hands. "It's going to be all right, I promise."

"How?"

"We're going to take care of Ken, you and me." She rubbed my cold hands in her warm ones. "We'll make sure he never tells a soul."

"I don't know about this." I frowned at my image in Regina's full-length mirror. She had turned me into a blond version of herself—complete with strapless, silver-studded black leather corset, long fingerless black lace gloves, and thigh-high boots that approached the hem of my black leather miniskirt. "I'm every vamp cliché in one package."

"Ken likes this look," she said.

"How do you know? You weren't dressed like this when you met him."

"I know the type." She handed me her makeup bag. "You can do this part, I trust, while I get dressed?"

I sat at a small table in the corner of her black-curtain-draped room, in front of a magnifying mirror. The clock said 7:45 a.m. "It's past time for my snack. I never got it out of the microwave."

"I want you thirsty when he gets here at eight thirty. Damn, I left my favorite garters in Noah's room. Be right back."

I uncapped a tube of black liquid eyeliner, then leaned close to the mirror. Only then did I notice my hands were shaking.

"I can do this. It's like the badger game, but with more clothes and no stealing." After a pair of deep breaths, my hand steadied, so I tried again.

The door slammed open. My arm jerked, and the eyeliner brush poked me in the eye.

"Ow!" I glared at Shane. "Knock first?"

He shoved the door shut behind him. "What's she doing to you?"

"We're having a new donor." I explained how we met Ken and why he needed to be corralled.

Shane listened with his arms folded, his jaw working into a near cramp. "So what's with the *Rocky Horror* reject outfit?"

I wished for a cardigan. "She says he needs to bond with me so he'll be willing to break the law to protect my life. I'm supposed to drink him."

"And that's it?"

"She said she'd do the rest."

His eyes turned to slits. "The rest?"

I twisted the eyeliner tube open and closed. "I guess she'll get him off."

"With you watching." His voice was flat and hard.

"I don't have to watch. I can just hang out, and then drink when he—you know."

"When he comes."

"You told me that blood tastes better during the donor's orgasm."

"Yeah, but I don't want you to—" He put his hands to his head. "Oh God, this is your life now."

"It's okay." Other than the ick factor of seeing Regina in action, I was pretty curious.

"It's not okay." Shane started to pace. "You have no idea how not okay this is."

"I've done worse."

"That was when you were a crook." He slammed his hand against his chest. "That was before me."

"I won't do anything with Ken. Regina's the one he likes."

"What guy in a room with two hot chicks is only going to want to touch one of them?"

He had a point. "I'll tell him no."

"No, you won't. He has all the power. He could end your life with one phone call." Shane was on the verge of hyperventilating. "You'll do whatever he wants."

I caught the accusation. "Because I have no principles?"

"Because you want to survive. It's what you're best at."

"Isn't that what you want?"

He sank onto Regina's bed. "I never wanted this for you."

My insides curdled. He hated what I'd become. "You'd rather I died."

"No."

"Yes. It would've been perfect. I'd be a beautiful corpse you could howl and scream over, like Mary with Jesus in that Station of the Cross thing. Then you could waste away mourning me, wallowing in your misery like the tragic figure you always wanted to be. Maybe even follow me and end it all. This time for good."

He stared at me, his face an impassive mask, and when he spoke, it was in a low growl. "I'm mourning you now, Ciara."

My breath stopped, and I wondered if it would ever start again. That novena he prayed was for real. I was dead to him.

I stood slowly and slipped off my engagement ring. "Here."

He gaped at it without taking it. "You don't want to get married?"

"I'm not the person you proposed to. Ask me again." I grabbed his wrist and slapped the ring into his palm. "Ask me when I'm a vampire."

As if by reflex, he took my left hand. "Will you marry—"

"Don't ask now." I stepped back, out of his grip. "Ask when I'm a real vampire, and you can live with what I've become."

Before he could speak again, Regina entered. "What are you doing?" she said to him. "She's not nervous enough, you have to lay a guilt trip on her?"

I rose to his defense. "You expect him to be happy I'm prostituting myself?"

"I don't expect anyone to be happy about anything. I

expect obedience. That's what will save you." Her tone softened a bit. "Besides, you're just role-playing."

"Playing the role of a prostitute."

Regina ground her teeth but kept her voice level. "When you were a con artist, you played make-believe to trick people out of money. Isn't keeping yourself out of government custody—keeping yourself *alive*—worth more than money?" She clutched her hands together, maybe to keep them off our throats. "Ciara, I want you to live. I want that more than anything in the world right now." She glanced between us, looking embarrassed at her display of emotion. "Except maybe that Bauhaus *Burning from the Inside* vinyl import."

Despite her attempt at levity, pain filled her dark eyes. No doubt she was remembering her poor husband dying a second, permanent death.

"She's not Jack." Shane got to his feet to face her. "And she's not doing this."

"I already told Ken it would be both of us," she said. "We can't risk disappointing him."

"Then I'll go in her place."

"Great idea. 'Hi, I'm the fiancé of one of the girls you want to shag. Let's talk.' He'd be gone in a heartbeat, assuming his heart still worked." She brightened. "But if it turns out he swings both ways, we'll call you in. How's that sound? Compromise?"

"No compromise. She's not going."

"Shane." Regina said his name in a steel-spike voice. "You know what that blood-sex connection does to a donor. It's not enough for him to be in thrall to me and have me tell him not to rat her out. A direct bond is the only way to guarantee Ken's silence."

"No," he whispered. "Not the only way."

Regina and I each took a step back from him.

"Are you saying—" My voice shook. "No, you can't be saying that."

"He is." Regina stared into his eyes. "Girl, what have you done to him?"

"Just get Ken here," Shane growled. "Have him come through the back door so David doesn't see." His fingers clenched into claws. "I'll take care of the rest."

"No!" I wobbled forward on the spiked heels. "This is insane. You can't kill him." In his fifteen years as a vampire, Shane had never taken a life, on purpose or by accident. Hell, sometimes he went hungry instead of biting his donors when they had a cold.

Regina scratched her head, as if considering it. "She's right, you can't kill Ken. There's a paper trail."

"And hey—murder?" My voice pitched up. "It's wrong." I pointed at him. "Plus, it's a sin."

The darkness in his eyes told me he didn't care. "My soul means nothing next to your life."

We stared at each other for a long moment, then Regina cleared her throat.

"On that romantic note, Shane, can I talk to you out in the common room? I think I have a solution."

He broke our gaze with what looked like a great effort, then stalked ahead of Regina out the door.

Behind his back, she pointed to the makeup case in my hand, then at my face. At the last moment, she reached around the door into her closet. She snagged something shiny off a hook on the wall.

Handcuffs.

"Wait." I stepped toward her.

"Sorry." She slipped out of the room.

I lunged for the door. It was locked, or someone very strong was holding it from the other side.

I planted my feet and pulled the knob with every muscle in my body. My hands slipped, landing me flat on my butt.

Shouts erupted from the common room, followed by a crash. Shane yelled a long string of profanities, which were suddenly cut off. Everything went quiet, except Dexter's frantic barks coming from our room.

"Shane!" I threw myself at the door, but it wouldn't budge. "Let me out!"

I stepped back to get momentum, squared my shoulders, and made one last run at the door. On my way there, it opened. I crashed into Regina, who caught me before I fell.

She set me on my feet. "Let's get you made up. Nice and dark. Zero points for subtlety."

"Where's Shane?" I asked her over the sound of Dexter's howls.

She rubbed her arms. "He's getting really strong. Usually I can handle him myself."

"Where is he?"

"Noah and Spencer are keeping him safe." She set me down in the chair in front of the mirror. "You know this is for the best, right?"

"I don't want him to kill Ken, but—"

"So you do know. Good." Regina picked up the liquid eyeliner. "Now shut your eyes and prepare to be vamped."

26

Last Resort

Ken was supposed to meet us at the station at 8:30 a.m., before the CDC and health departments started their door-to-door interviews. But to wipe the record pristine, we needed an accomplice.

The moment Regina opened the lounge door leading up to the office, a new, delicious scent hit me.

David.

Undiluted by the ventilation system, he smelled incredible, like when my mom used to make French toast and bacon, and the RV would fill with cinnamon and sugar and salt and meat.

He smelled like breakfast.

I stopped on the bottom step, hand over my nose. "I can't go up there."

"Don't be a doofus." Regina led me up the stairs, gripping my arm so hard it would've bruised if I'd still been human. The main office was empty, but the light in David's office was on.

I hid from his sight while she spoke. I couldn't look at him. I definitely couldn't have him looking at me.

"David," she said, "there'll be a young man knocking on the door soon. He's our guest, a new donor."

"You guys can't bring donors to the station. That jeopardizes everything—"

"Save it," she said. "There's no choice and no time. We need you to, uh . . . Ciara, explain the phone part."

She dragged me into the doorway. Despite my intentions, my eyes met David's.

"Oh God," he said. Not an "oh God" of shock or dismay, but the kind of "oh God" a guy makes when a woman strokes him in the happiest place possible.

He rose from his seat, and for a moment I thought he'd crawl over his desk. His eyes burned with the same hunger I felt in my own throat.

"Guys . . ." Regina said. "This really isn't the time."

Her voice sounded far away, drowned by the blood rushing in my ears. David's blood, thumping through his arteries, cruising through his veins, squeezing through his capillaries. I could hear it, smell it, taste it through his skin. My mouth opened—

—and spiked with sudden, shrieking pain, like getting my teeth pulled without novocaine. I doubled over, clutching Regina's arm to keep from falling. A sound like an air-raid siren squealed from my throat as the pain spread through my jaw and around my head.

This is it, I'm dying for good. No one told me my brain could explode from bloodlust.

The pain faded as fast as it had appeared. I touched my jaw, my ears, and my forehead, searching for the source of the sensation before remembering where it had started.

My teeth.

Regina whistled. "About time. Bitchin' fangs."

David wavered, eyes heavy lidded. "They are truly bitchin'," he slurred. "Come closer so I can see."

I did not need to be asked twice.

Regina moved between us and slapped him across the face. "Snap out of it! You're our boss, not our breakfast."

I carefully examined the two protruding teeth with my thumb. "Will it always hurt that much when they come in?"

"First time is the worst," Regina said. "Eventually it'll be like blinking." She tilted my chin and peered in my mouth. "Of course it hurt you more than most, since you're a wimp."

I pulled away from her and turned to David. Regina promptly stepped between us again.

"Explain the phone thing," she told me. "Without looking at him."

I dropped my gaze to the pointed steel toes of my boots. "His name's Ken." Thrilled that I didn't lisp even my first sentences with the new fangs, I continued. "Tell him to leave his cell phone up here, that we're extra cautious about being recorded or photographed."

I rubbed my right ear in a futile attempt to block the sound of David's blood. His pulse was still racing, flushing his extremities—yes, *all* his extremities.

"Who is this guy?" he asked.

"He's a—a dancer." I wiped my forehead, still looking at the floor. "Last Thursday we texted about Lori's bachelorette party, and I told him I might have chicken pox."

Lori. Crap. How could I look at her knowing how

much I wanted sink my teeth into her fiancé and lick every drop of whatever came out?

"Ohhh. I see." His pulse slowed, probably since he was focusing on my safety instead of my fangs. "Wait— you hired Lori a stripper?"

"Good," Regina said, "you still remember her. Moving on." She poked my arm. "Tell him what to do."

"Delete my text message, obviously," I told the rip in the rug, "and any replies in his outbox."

"Right." David paused. "What are you two going to do to him?"

"Don't worry," Regina said. "He'll be happy. And more important, quiet."

"Ciara, you okay with this?" he asked in a gentle voice.

I felt so miserable, I needed to see the eyes of a friend. A human friend.

I raised my gaze to meet David's. And knew, with a sudden, crashing heartbreak, that we could not be friends.

He moved as if to rush toward me, the way a lover rushes toward one he's lost and found again. My mouth watered and every muscle tensed to spring.

Regina jerked me back into the main office and slammed David's door. "Easy there, pet. Ken'll take that edge off."

"I don't want Ken," I whined. "I want David."

"You can't have David right now. You'd tear his throat out."

"What about in an emergency? He does that for the rest of you." My speech sped up as she led me down the stairs, away from my one true meal. "He let Shane bite him once, when Shane's donors were all busy or sick."

"We'll cross that bridge when—" She stopped suddenly and cocked her head to listen. "Ken's early. Very good sign."

I heard it then, too, the approach of a car engine and the rumble of wheels against gravel. My stomach clenched in anticipation. David had awakened a major case of the munchies.

Regina secured us in the lounge, where a rubber seal on the door's bottom edge kept out every photon of light.

"Let's relax for a second and chat." She led me to the couch and sat beside me.

Close beside me.

With her hand resting inside my right thigh.

I looked at it, then at her face. "What are you—"

"Shh." She leaned over and brought her lips near my ear. "If you're a good girl and do what I say, I'll show you what Shane saw in me for so many years."

"But I'm not—I don't—"

"What? Like girls?" She took my face between her hands. "Welcome to the jungle, cutie pie. This is your life now, so get with the program. You have to touch and kiss and fondle people who make you want to puke. You do it so you can survive. Shane will learn to live with it, and so will you."

"He doesn't hook up with his donors anymore. Why should I?"

"He's spent years building trust with those people. He can afford to be choosy. You don't have that luxury." She kissed me on the forehead, soft as a mother. "There are a million reasons why so few girl vamps survive, but I'll teach you everything. How to stay safe, how to say no when things get dodgy. How to live with yourself." Her grip on my head tightened. "But you have to trust me, okay?"

My eyes grew hot, and I wanted to run away and cry in Shane's arms, have him stroke my hair and tell me it would all be easy, that being a vampire meant a few minor inconveniences instead of these soul-killing compromises.

But I'd chosen this so-called life, like every life I'd had up to this point. I had more experience as a predator than most fledglings; instead of denying that past, I could use it as a source of strength. I could use it to survive.

I met Regina's dark, formidable gaze. "Okay."

A knock came on the outside door upstairs. David's footsteps crossed the ceiling, and my muscles tensed again as my thirst surged.

Soon the stairs creaked and the door opened. David and Ken stood together. I noticed the superficial resemblance—the soft, dark brown hair, the animated green eyes, the perennial tan. But I felt nothing when I looked at Ken and everything when I looked at David.

David gripped the doorframe as if to keep himself from lunging forward. "I'll be upstairs. Call if you need anything."

He disappeared, shutting the door behind him. Dismay stabbed the back of my throat, making me whimper.

Regina closed her hand over mine. "Hey there, Ken."

His gaze fixed on her face. "I thought about you all weekend. At my next assignment, I pretended I was dancing for you. I got the most tips ever in my life."

"Lovely." She scooted over to make room between us. "Come sit."

Ken did as she said, as automatically as a remote-controlled robot. When he passed in front of me, he bumped my knee, then looked at my face for the first time.

"You're that girl who hired me." He took in my outfit. "You look different."

"I am different." I held out my hand. "That's what we need to discuss."

He grasped my hand, and I tried not to flinch as his flesh almost singed me. How many hours had it been since I'd drunk? I got cold so quickly.

When he sat between us, I slid my hand over his chest to warm my freezing palm. His pulse was already pounding, and his pores emitted desire with a faint, bitter taint of fear, like a pinch of hot curry powder. The red of his shirt (Regina's request) made my mouth water.

His eyelashes flickered as he tried to play it cool. "So, um, what did you want to talk about?"

"Kenneth." Regina rested her elbow on the back of the couch and set her chin atop her folded hands, a few inches from his face. "Do you mind if I call you Kenneth?"

"No." He breathed harder, like his full name turned him on. "Please."

"Kenneth, you know what we are, don't you?"

"Um, a couple of major hotties?"

With one long-nailed fingertip, she turned his chin to face her. "We're vampires."

He laughed. "Right, the radio thing. Hey, I've been thinking about adding a vampire routine to my dancing repertoire. Girls love that."

"Brilliant," Regina purred. "I'd love to see it." She drew the *l*s over her tongue in a way that made me want to take notes, then smiled to display her fangs.

"Whoa." Ken pulled away from her, turned to me, then saw my fangs as I gave a similar wide smile. "Where'd you guys get those? They look real."

"That's because they are real." My fingers slid up the

buttons of his polo shirt as I fought the urge to rip the whole thing off. "Do you want to feel them?"

He reached forward eagerly and brushed his thumb against my mouth. The scents of soap and yeast wafted from his open palm. Had he been up early making Sherwood's last prequarantine pizzas?

"Ow!" He jerked his hand away and gaped at the bright spot of blood on his thumb. Without thinking I leaned forward and licked it. He moaned, lashes fluttering. The sound and taste tipped my brain into a death spiral of bloodlust.

"Good," Regina murmured as she ran one hand through his hair. "You believe us now?"

"Mmm." He closed his eyes at the sensation of her nails against his scalp. "I don't care."

"Even better." She turned his head and gave him a light, teasing kiss that brushed her tongue against his lips. His breath seized, and I could hear the blood surge south.

"Wait," he said, "if you're vampires, how come you're awake after sunrise?"

Her chuckle almost hid her annoyance. "Do you fall asleep at sunset?" she asked as she drew her mouth along his earlobe, tugging with her human teeth.

"No, but—"

"If you can stay up at night, we can stay up at day." She slid her hand under his shirt. "All day, if necessary."

"Whatever." He slid one hand behind her neck and pulled her into a deeper kiss, letting his other hand fall to my thigh. It was so warm, I didn't care when his fingers dug under the elastic of my stockings and stroked the bare flesh beneath.

Still, I was glad when he kept his focus on Regina,

dragging her to straddle his lap and peeling open her leather vest to fill his hands with her black-lace-covered breasts.

Boom. Boom. The pounding of his blood blotted out all other sound, even the rolling reggae tune playing over the ceiling speaker.

Boom. Boom. My fangs seemed to quiver in perfect rhythm, pulsing with the need to pierce his flesh.

Regina peeled off his shirt, then slid her hand between their bodies and unfastened his jeans. He panted harder as she stroked him.

Boom. Boom. The sound pummeled my lungs and heart, like a giant woofer speaker at a rock concert with the bass overcranked. It was almost too much to bear.

Regina bent over to bite his arm.

"No," he gasped. "Not there. Do the neck."

She looked up at him, her fangs an inch from his skin. "Why?"

"It'll leave a mark." He wiped his mouth, struggling for breath. "On my neck I can cover it up."

"How?"

"I have a waiter's costume with a bow tie."

"Necks are more romantic, anyway, don't you think?" She slid off him onto her feet. "But you have to lie down or it could kill you."

Ken seemed happy to take orders from her. Which was good—the air embolism explanation always made me queasy.

He hurried to stretch out on his back, using my thigh as a pillow. He smiled up at me as she stripped off his pants and boxers. "Are you going to watch us fuck?"

I glanced at Regina, not wanting to be the one to

break it to him. So far he seemed content, without me having to do much more than look cute, and much less than what Ken did in his own allegedly non-slutty job. I'd managed not to even check out his goods, thanks to the careful drape of my hair over that side of my face.

Regina pinned his bare legs together with her stocking-clad knees. "Sorry, Kenneth," she said with heartbreaking sincerity as she tiptoed her fingers up his chest. "We can't fuck. I don't want to hurt you." He started to protest, and she laid a finger on his lips. "We can do anything else. Anything you want."

His face turned blank and panicky, like a kid on Santa's lap who forgot what he wanted for Christmas.

She slid her tongue up his chest to the hollow of his neck. "What's it gonna be, boy?"

He remained frozen, hands on her elbows. In my thirst and impatience, I must have sighed, because his attention shifted to me. His face lit up.

"I wanna see y'all make out."

27

Sick of Myself

Somewhere in my mind, a little voice said, "I told you so." The voice sounded a lot like Shane. Men know men.

I jumped to my feet, dumping Ken's head against the cushion. "I don't think so."

"Aw, come on," he said. "You promised me anything."

Regina looked down at him. "That's all you need this time?"

I gave her a sharp glare she didn't see.

Ken's eyes widened. "*This* time? I can come back?"

"If you behave yourself." She drew her fingernail over his cheek, then down his neck. "If we can drink you."

I waved frantically at her, out of his peripheral vision, but she ignored me.

"Then, yeah, that's all. You two go at it. I'll take care of the rest." His hand slid down to grip his—*Whoa*. He had definitely not stuffed that G-string.

I forced myself to look at Regina. She was gazing up at

me through ink-black lashes. Her head tilted, motioning me to sit on the floor next to the couch.

Ken was watching me, too. I hoped he took my hesitation for some reluctant-lesbian act. If he knew how much I wanted to run, cry, or puke (or all three at once), he'd leave right now and never come back. If they interviewed him, he'd tell them I never had chicken pox, and I'd be quarantined in a place where I'd see one last sunrise.

Slowly I knelt beside them. Regina's eyes held mine, hypnotizing me like a snake with its prey.

"First we drink." She bent over Ken's neck.

His body seized as she bit him, and a strangled gasp flew from his throat. A moment later, the sweet, coppery scent reached my nose.

Regina moved aside, her mouth barely stained.

"Brains before beauty," she whispered.

I drank. The neck *was* different, so close to his thumping heart, his heaving lungs, his rumbling throat, all vibrating against my lips and tongue. I slid one hand into his hair, the soft strands tickling my sensitive palms, and the other over his baby-smooth chest. His blood tasted no better than Jeremy's or Jim's doggie-bag donor, but the feel of his body made me want to cry.

Pathetic.

I sat back on my heels and gave her a quick nod, hoping it came across as politeness instead of revulsion.

Regina spread herself over his chest and drank, her fingers kneading his flesh like a nursing kitten's. Ken ran his hands over her body, sweeping across skin and leather and lace.

Then she lifted her face and saw me, sickened by my

own need and ready to run. She snatched my head and pulled me to kiss her.

At the touch of her lips I jerked back. Her hold on my neck slipped.

"She's new at this," Regina told Ken. "Give us a minute, hmm?"

"Yeah." His voice was breathless.

Regina slid onto the floor, her back against the couch and her legs out straight. "Come here. I won't hurt you." She tugged my waist, maneuvering me to straddle her lap. I winced as her studded belt bit into the sensitive skin of my abdomen.

Regina stroked my hair. "Breathe," she whispered.

I closed my eyes and inhaled, drawing the smell of blood into my head, where it curled around my brain like incense smoke around a lamp. This need was part of me now, and I had to accept it or die.

I opened my eyes and stared down into Regina's liquid brown gaze, letting myself forget who I was, who I belonged with, who I'd ever been.

It was time to become a vampire.

Regina tipped my chin down and kissed me with a tenderness I never thought she possessed. I focused on the scent of Ken's blood on her breath. Her lips were warm and almost unbearably soft, like rose petals.

She held the sweet, chaste kiss for several moments. Finally my shoulders lowered as the tension dripped out of them.

Her tongue flicked against the underside of my upper lip. My gasp opened my mouth a fraction of an inch. She deepened the kiss.

I tried to let myself become nothing but Body, tried

to let Regina's tongue coax my lips apart, let her hips arch beneath me, spreading my thighs around them. Let her have me.

"Oh yeah," Ken whispered. "You girls are so hot together."

My body tensed. I wanted to claw out his eyes so he'd stop watching, to rip off his hands so he'd stop stroking.

But he could end my life with five words: *she never had chicken pox.*

"Come on." Ken's voice tightened. Skin shifted against skin in a quickening rhythm. "That's it, yeah. Show me more."

Everything inside me crumbled. "No . . ." I shoved against Regina. Her grip loosened, and I toppled backward, knocking my head on the table leg.

"What's wrong?" She kept her voice sweet, but her eyes held a deadly warning.

"I can't do this."

"Yes, you can," she said through gritted teeth.

"I can't." I turned to Ken, who had frozen mid-stroke. "Listen, I wasn't a vampire last week. I was human. I was alive. Then I got chicken pox and would've died if my friends hadn't turned me into this." I lifted my arms, then let them fall to my side. "Now I'm trying to make the best of it."

He gaped at me. To his credit, he had mostly lost his erection (not that I looked). "Man, that sucks. I'm sorry for, um, for your loss." He dragged a hand through his hair. "That was lame. How do you offer condolences to a dead person?"

Perversely, I felt bad for embarrassing him. "I'm not dead anymore, if that helps."

He looked up at me. "But what's that got to do with this?"

"The health department and the CDC want to quarantine everyone without chicken pox immunity."

"Yeah, I heard something about that." He glanced around. Figuring he wanted to get dressed, I handed him the pair of boxers near my feet, ignoring Regina's simmer. "Thanks," he said, covering himself with them rather than putting them on (clearly he still had hope).

Regina sighed. "They're offering rewards to people who contribute to the list. So if the health department knocks on your door, what will you tell them about Ciara here?"

"Nothing." He looked between us. "Really, I swear."

I didn't believe him. He probably knew on some level we wouldn't let him leave without a promise to hide my secret. That didn't mean he would keep it. But surely there was a solution I could live with, literally and figuratively.

Ken sat up. "Is that what this was all about? Buying my silence with sex?"

"That's not all it was about," Regina said. "Ciara needs blood, preferably directly from a human, preferably while that human is having an orgasm."

Ken was starting to look seriously weirded out. "Why?"

"It tastes better that way. She's having issues."

He turned to her. "What about you?"

"I have no issues."

"Yeah, right," I muttered.

"That's not what I meant," he told her. "I mean, do you need blood? While . . . you know." He glanced down at himself.

Her lashes lowered as she gazed at him. "I am in the market for a new donor, yes. If you're nice and sane."

His eyes unfocused, mesmerized. "I could be sane for you."

I sensed my opportunity to escape and let Regina seal the deal, so to speak, on her own. I took a step toward the door to the apartment, then stopped and looked at the door to the upstairs. I longed to run to Shane, but would he even want to look at me after I'd returned his ring and caressed another man?

Shame—and let's face it, lingering hunger and curiosity—propelled me up the stairs, back to David.

"Be careful," Regina warned as I retreated.

David was hunched over my desk with his back to me. "Hi."

He jumped a foot in the air. "Ciara! Jesus, you gave me a heart attack."

We eyed each other warily. The tug definitely remained, me for his blood and him for my fangs (which were still out). But thanks to the dose of Ken, the edge was gone. I didn't feel an urge to pounce—well, not an uncontrollable urge.

I saw the unfamiliar phone on my desk. "Did you find the text messages?"

He nodded, so vigorously I thought he'd pull a neck muscle. "Luckily his phone wasn't password protected."

"He'll be down there for at least a few more minutes. Enough time for me to double-check."

David handed me the phone, then stepped back to put my desk between us. "Everything go okay?

I just shrugged and turned my attention to Ken's phone. The messages were indeed deleted, so I set the phone on the edge of my desk.

David touched his chin. "By the way, you have a little . . ." He handed me a tissue.

Confused, I wiped my face. Blood streaked the tissue. "Gross. Can I tell you a secret?"

"You hate being a vampire?"

"It's that obvious?"

"No, but the fact that your engagement ring is gone tells me that there's no joy in Bloodville."

"It doesn't fit anymore." I splayed the fingers of my left hand. "I guess because my body temp has gone down. Doesn't that cause shrinkage?"

"Your other ring is still there."

"My right hand has fatter fingers."

"Ciara, I don't think your problem is shrinkage."

Veering away from him, I crossed the office to Lori's desk, where I slumped into her chair. "You were wrong. Shane and I would've been happy forever as human and vampire—as much forever as we could give each other. But now I'm someone he doesn't recognize. Maybe someone he can't love. It doesn't matter how much time we have in front of us if he can't stand who I am." I twisted my hands in my lap, trying not to notice David drifting closer. "I always said vampires and con artists were a lot alike. But he never knew me as a hard-core criminal, only a recovering one."

"He'll come around." David took another step, closing to within a few feet of the desk.

"Maybe." I scooted my chair away several inches, backing its wheels up against the wall. "I had to give him a chance to reconsider marrying me. Otherwise it's a bait and switch."

"Ciara, people change a lot over their lives." He moved

closer, his fingers trailing along the back of the chair beside Lori's desk, which held a precarious stack of papers. "I told you what happened to my dad after he got promoted."

"He got bitter and self-destructive." I rubbed my mouth to keep the drool inside. "Why should that make me feel better?"

"The point is, my mother still loved him just as much. When you commit to someone, it's for better and worse, richer and poorer, in sickness and in health."

"Until death do us part for three or four minutes. The thing is, Shane and I haven't said those vows yet."

He reached the edge of the desk, so close I could grab him. "Do you need to?"

"My dad never married my mom—the woman who raised me, I mean, not my biological mother." I swiveled my chair so I faced the front wall. "He abandoned her after they went to prison. I know now that it was because of his undercover work with the Control, but she doesn't know that."

From the corner of my eye, I saw David's hand drift to his shirt collar.

"If they were married," I continued, "she could've joined him in witness protection, rather than rotting away in prison wondering why the love of her life forgot her. So yeah, marriage matters." I focused on the floor at my feet. "Ew, that sounds so family values."

He stood right behind my shoulder. "You don't look very family values right now."

I heard the shift of skin against cloth and plastic as he undid the top button of his shirt.

My eyes squeezed shut, and I held my breath, repeating Regina's words to myself.

Boss, not breakfast. Boss, not breakfast.

My only weapon left was a blunt one.

"Can I bite you?"

"What?" he said with a nervous laugh.

"Not now, necessarily. I'm making a list, and since you have experience, I thought you'd be a good place to start. Pull up my appointment calendar on the intranet and pencil yourself in when it's convenient. Use a red font so I know it's for bloodletting instead of business." I stood and turned to face him. "Or we could do it now. If you want."

Eyes wide, he backed away slowly. Halfway to his office, he stopped. "You're kidding, right?"

I skewered him with my gaze. "I am absolutely one hundred percent kidding. If I ever put one fang on you, Lori would kill us both."

"You're right." He rubbed his face, then hurried to redo the unfastened button. "I better warn her about you. You've got a powerful vibe for such a young vampire."

"It's because I'm hungry." I checked my mouth. "As you can tell from the fangs."

He nodded. "A vampire's hunger can trigger a donor's, um, willingness. And vice versa. Like a positive feedback loop."

He turned his back and entered his office. Cornered. Vulnerable. My body shuddered with the predatory instinct. I could still smell his, um, willingness.

I took a step—okay, three or four steps—toward his office.

The door at the bottom of the stairs jerked open. Ken hurried up, followed by—*uh-oh*.

Followed by Shane. He had his hand on Ken's back, guiding him past me.

"Bye, Ciara!" Ken grabbed his cell phone from the surface of my desk.

Shane stared at me and David. "You guys are up here alone together?"

"David was a Control Enforcement agent," I pointed out. "He can defend himself against li'l old me."

"Assuming he wants to."

"Hey, guess what?" I smiled to show him my fangs, hoping it would distract him from thoughts of me and David.

A click came from behind us. "See you guys later!"

I turned to see Ken pocketing his phone, waving the other hand before putting it on the doorknob.

"That won't open," I told him, "without the . . ."

Key.

Which was in the lock.

Already turned.

"No!"

Instinct made me leap forward to stop him. Shane grabbed me around the waist and yanked me into David's office just as a shaft of sunlight swept inside the station.

I screamed.

Shane and I landed on the floor, his body covering mine. David leaped over us into the main room and slammed the office door shut behind him.

The fire swept up my arms, spiking a million tiny daggers into my skin. I shrieked and writhed beneath Shane. "Put it out! Put it out!"

"Shh. Shh." Shane pulled me close. "Ciara, you're okay."

"It's on my hands. My face!" I sobbed, my lungs tight with agony. "Make it stop."

"There's no fire. It just feels like it." He shifted enough to pull up my arm. "See?"

My skin wasn't even red. "It hurts so bad." My voice choked with tears. "That wasn't even direct sunlight."

"I know. Indirect stings like a motherfucker, huh?"

I looked at his face, tight and contorted. His pain was probably worse than mine, since he'd been on top.

I touched his cheek. "Would it have killed us?"

"Not for another half a minute or so. Problem is, the pain is so debilitating, most vampires can't escape. We're lucky David's office was here."

The door swung open. My arm shot up to shield my face, but no heat blasted us. The outside door was closed.

"You guys all right?" David knelt beside us. "Ken must've grabbed the key from on top of your desk when he picked up his phone."

I wiped my nose. "He was probably in a hurry to not get killed by Shane." The pain was fading from my face and arms.

"Good thing it's a cloudy day and the door opens north." David stood up. "Stay here while I get water."

Nothing had ever sounded so good. My mouth was sticky and sour from my last meal, and my throat was singed from the brush with permanent death.

Shane caressed my face. "That ends any doubts about you being a real vampire."

The corners of my mouth trembled. "Sorry."

"No, I'm sorry." He tightened his arms and rocked me gently. "I'm so sorry."

I clung to him, mumbling a weak protest. I was tired of our apologies. I just wanted to be happy again.

David brought us each a water bottle, so cold they sweated. I gulped half of mine before speaking to him. "You need any help in the office?"

He shook his head. "You've been through enough this morning. Anyway, Jeremy's coming in soon to stay until this quarantine is over. Frank, too."

"Is Franklin okay to work?" Shane asked him.

"He says he's going crazy sitting around his and Aaron's house. He doesn't want to be stuck there during the curfew, not when there'll be so much to do here with the emergency services info network."

I downed the rest of my water, forcing it past the lump of dread in my throat. The Lifeblood of Rock 'n' Roll was about to become the Lifeline of the Siege of Sherwood.

But what bothered me more than anything? For two or three milliseconds, as that front door opened, I was glad to see the sun.

28

All That Heaven Will Allow

"I need another shower," I told Shane as we entered the empty common room of the DJs' apartment. Dexter ran up to me and sniffed my hands with voracious breaths and what sounded like huffs of disapproval, or maybe I was just projecting.

"Go ahead. I'll put some clean clothes inside the bathroom for when you get out."

"Thanks." I chewed my bottom lip, then stopped when my fang stabbed it. "Um, where should I go afterward?"

His voice was solemn. "Where do you want to go?"

I hesitated, then settled on honesty. "Wherever you are."

"I'll be in our room."

My gut fluttered at the sound of the word "our." Maybe there was hope for us.

But once I was in the shower, the Ken/Regina episode replayed itself behind my eyelids. I scrubbed my skin so hard it would have bled had I still been human. I lathered and rinsed my hair and body five times before the water lost its heat. Then over the sink I brushed my teeth for ten minutes, stopping only to gargle and spit and start again.

Finally I dried my hair and dressed, then headed to our room.

Shane was waiting for me under the covers, dressed in a T-shirt. I crawled over him to my spot next to the wall. We lay facing each other for a long moment, until I worked up the courage to speak.

"Did Regina tell you I wussed out?"

"She said you would tell me all about it." He shifted his head on the pillow. "But if you're not ready to talk . . ."

I brought my knees toward my chest, wishing I could hide. "Being a vampire is so fucked up." I drew deep breaths to keep the sobs from bubbling out of my chest. Tears dribbled from my eyes.

"Tell me what happened."

"I can't."

"Ciara, nothing could shock me."

"Do you promise never to kill Ken or Regina?"

"I promise never to kill Regina. If only to avoid hurting myself."

I wiped my face. "You were right. It wasn't enough for him to be with her, and me just watching."

Shane's jaw clenched. "He wanted a threesome?"

"Not exactly." My face flamed at the memory. "He wanted us to make out while he jerked off."

He blew out a deep breath and turned on his back. "And Regina was okay with this?"

"She acted like I had no choice."

Shane threw back the covers. "I'm going to kill her. I don't care how much it hurts me."

I put a hand on his arm. "I'm sure she believed my life depended on it."

"No, she didn't. But she has to cover every base to keep us from being exposed, whatever the cost, whether it's taking someone's life or just their dignity."

"They didn't take my dignity. They borrowed it." I squeezed his arm to calm him. "Please don't make it worse with more fighting."

His shoulders sagged, and he shook his head sadly. "Being a vampire doesn't always have to be this fucked up. You'll see."

"When? When will things be normal? When will I be normal?" My voice started to choke with tears again. "Do I really need to drink someone during an orgasm? I can't think of anyone I could stand to do that to."

Shane lay beside me again and wiped the wetness from my cheek. "Not even me?"

A sharp thrill zinged through my body. "I thought vampire blood couldn't nourish me."

"No, but just like with human food, sometimes it's not about nutrients." His fingertips brushed my lips. "It's about pleasure."

My pulse thumped in my ears, and in other places that were thrilled to be alive. "Can I taste you?"

He slipped his middle finger against my left fang and pressed hard. Tooth slid through skin, into flesh. A single drop of blood hit my tongue.

I moaned as I drew his finger into my mouth and sucked hard. He closed his eyes, his lips parting.

It tasted better than anything in this life or the other. Nothing had ever felt so right inside me. And all without shame. I didn't need this blood, so I lost no power in taking it.

His wound had healed already. "More," I said, letting go of his finger before I could gnaw it off.

He sat up to remove his shirt. "You can bite me anywhere." His eyes were lit with a new fire. "You can't hurt me."

I touched the curve of his neck, where it met his shoulder. "Will you feel pain?"

"Just the right amount." His mouth quirked. "You know I like it a little rough."

I knew everything he liked. But as I ran my hand along the planes of his chest, I wanted to learn him all over again. "Let's do this right. Let's make love."

He exhaled hard, desire mixed with tension. "Are you sure? You've been through a lot. Dying, becoming a vampire, almost getting fried by the sun."

"Not to mention zombies."

"I'm not sure we should put sex on top of all that."

"I want to feel like me again." I stroked his cheek with the back of my fingers. "Making love with you is normal."

"It won't feel normal. You've changed."

I looked down at my body. "Everything works, right?"

He nodded. "But just like you've had to get used to your new skin and eyes and ears, you have to get used to your new muscles."

The muscles that could totally ruin a human male's day. "Will it hurt?"

"It might. Like when you lost your virginity."

"I meant, will it hurt you?"

He gave a gentle laugh and brushed the hair out of my eyes. "You're so sweet. No, it won't hurt me. And you'll be okay once you relax."

"Then what are we waiting for?"

Instead of answering, Shane kissed me deep and slow, until I was melted wax molded against him. Then he pulled away a few inches and looked into my eyes.

"I'll beg if I have to," I whispered. "I'm not proud."

His expression eased into a smile. "Sorry. It's just that I've almost lost you too many times not to get overwhelmed at the sight of your face."

Now I was melted all the way through. "If you think my face is overwhelming . . ."

In ten seconds flat I was naked. In twenty seconds, I had him in the same state. We kissed and stroked and explored each other's bodies as if for the first time, reconsecrating our connection.

Finally he eased me to lie on top of his smooth, hard chest. "Go as slow as you need," he said. "We can stop anytime."

Trying not to hold my breath, I opened myself and guided him inside.

He was right—it hurt. I felt sixteen again, wondering if I could go through with it, if pleasure awaited me on the other side of such gut-rippling pain.

But I wasn't sixteen, I was twenty-six. I wasn't with an awkward, self-absorbed boy. I had a man of infinite patience and understanding.

Shane kissed me with a tenderness that eased the ache inside. "We can try again later."

"I don't want to wait." I eased my hips down, but the pain shot back up my gut, making me grit my teeth. "I don't suppose you have a smaller penis we could use."

"Sorry, the mini version's been in the shop for about thirty years. I probably lost the receipt by now."

I laughed, and my muscles loosened. Shane stroked

my lower back, relaxing me further. His hands crept around behind my thighs, then he slipped a single exploring finger between my cheeks.

As in life, my new body responded instantly to that most intimate touch. I quivered as a sudden warmth flooded within, allowing him to move deeper inside me.

He let me control the pace, and I went slow, savoring the new sensations. The way his palms lit up the surface of my skin, the way his tongue scraped and rolled my nipples, the way his muscles coiled beneath my hands—it all helped ease the hot, hard pain and turn it into a building, blinding pleasure.

"I love you," he murmured in a shaky breath as I came—with deep, quiet cries—wrapped in his arms. Then he pressed my face to his neck and said, "Do it now."

I opened my mouth wide and gave in to instinct.

His body seized with the first bite, and his arms tightened around me. But no blood came.

"Harder," he gasped. "My skin's tougher than a human's."

"I don't want to hit an artery." The last thing we needed was blood on the ceiling.

"You can't. Your fangs aren't long enough." He turned us over to put himself on top. Then he slid a hand behind my head and pulled my mouth to his neck. "Do it."

I stabbed hard. The blood came, and I licked it eagerly before the wound could heal. His taste flooded my senses. I finally understood why this act was described with words like delicious, sexy, trippy. Sacred.

"Yes." He pressed against my mouth as he thrust deep. "Do it again. Now." He gave a long, shuddering groan as his orgasm pulsed within me. I could feel it stronger than ever and realized I was close to the edge again myself.

I bit him, so hard it jarred my jaw.

Oh. My. Gooooooood.

He tasted like liquid fireworks coated in spiced honey, like lightning basted in barbecue sauce, like heaven and hell suspended in maple syrup.

My moan mingled with his as white heat slammed through my body. The fire shot from my tongue, down my throat, all the way to my core and back again. I met his thrusts with new strength, every muscle flaring with the electricity that arced between us.

Shane clutched me close, filling me with himself, until I knew he'd never let me go. Until I knew that this Ciara—the cold, undead, less-perfect-than-ever Ciara—was the one he loved.

We came to a stop, letting our breath slow, without parting even an inch. My fangs had receded, but I kept my mouth against his skin, tasting his sweat and the last drops of blood. His own mouth was pressed to my hair.

Finally he turned his head and stared down at me, as if seeing me for the first time. "Now I know why you always said I was alive."

"Why?"

"You're alive, Ciara." He ran his hand down my body, following the curves of my waist and hip. "You're even sweating."

"No different from the way you always were with me."

"That's what I mean." He brushed his lips over my forehead. "With you, I've lived. Without you . . ."

"There is no without me. You're stuck."

If I survive, I added mentally. If I ever got over my hang-ups about drinking from humans. If one day it didn't feel like whoring myself or turning off part of my soul.

But lying there with Shane's arms around me, hearing his familiar quiet breath as he slid into sleep, I felt like I'd taken the first step. He'd shown me that it could be beautiful, something no one else could have done.

And even if I never felt that way with anyone else, even if every human's blood turned my stomach and withered my soul, I would do whatever it took not to leave Shane and this world behind.

I would live.

29

Waiting in Vain

I woke at 5 p.m. with a mad need to pee, thanks to that bottle of water. I crawled across Shane, trying not to knee him in the groin in the process.

"Where you going?" Eyes slitted, he tried to tug me back into bed.

"Bathroom. Urgent." I shoved against his chest. "Ack!" I tumbled onto the floor, knocking my head against the dresser.

He peered over the edge of the bed. "You're still learning your strength."

Grumbling, I picked myself up, slipped into my clothes, and headed for the bathroom.

While I was in there, I sensed someone in the common room. *Let it be Monroe.* I walked down the hall, making no effort to mask my sounds, my mind whispering *please, please, please* with each step.

In one of the overstuffed armchairs, Noah looked up from the book he was reading. I glanced at Monroe's closed door.

"Still no," Noah said.

I rubbed the aching spot on my chest. "What are you doing up so early?"

"I could not sleep." He took off his glasses and set them on the end table. "Regina kicks."

"I bet she does." I shuffled one foot behind the other, feeling awkward at the mention of his sort-of girlfriend, who had put her hands and mouth on me just a few hours ago. "What are you reading?"

He turned the book around so I could see the cover. "Camus's *La Peste*," I read aloud. *The Plague*. "Appropriate."

"French makes me drowsy." Noah opened the book to the place his finger was marking. "Sit. I will read to you."

I padded over to the sofa and sat down, curling my feet underneath me. Noah picked up his glasses and began to clean them with the tail of his long red, green, and gold cotton shirt.

"I've always wondered—why do you wear glasses? Vampires' eyes are perfect."

"They remind me of being human." He adjusted the dark frames on the bridge of his nose. "And they look good."

I couldn't help smiling. "They do. And at least you don't have to fool with contact lenses and all that cleaning stuff." I thought of Tina and her elaborate nightly ritual.

Huh. Wait a minute. Control Enforcement agents were supposed to have at least 20/50 uncorrected vision. How did she get assigned to that branch?

Family connections, of course, though they hadn't helped her achieve her dream of the Immanence Corps.

Thinking of Tina reminded me to check on Lori. She

and the rest of the civilian population had less than two hours of freedom before the indefinite quarantine took effect.

Using the common room's landline, I dialed Lori's cell. She answered right away. "Hey! How are you?"

"Getting better." I heard traffic in the background. "Are you still fighting the crowds for bread and toilet paper?"

"No, we're looking for Tina. I called her this morning to tell her about you, but there was no answer. Her mom hasn't heard from her, and now with the curfew, today is our last chance to find her."

I twisted the phone cord around my finger. My secret was out there, unsecured. After all we'd done to ensure Ken's loyalty, my cover could still be blown.

"For my sake, you'd better track her down."

"It's not just that." Lori's voice tightened. "I think she raised the zombies."

I almost dropped the phone. "Tina couldn't raise a lump of pizza dough. She bragged about every talent she thought she had. If she could raise the dead, she would've taken out a full-page ad in the *New York Times*."

Noah looked up from his book. "Who raised the dead?"

I couldn't answer him, because Lori's words were pouring into my ear. "You won't believe what we just found in her apartment. Books and papers on how to call the spirits, and all this ritual equipment. Her mom recognized one of her own texts, one that's forbidden to all but the top necromancers. Tina had stolen it from her."

"She was wearing a bandage on her arm the night of your bachelorette party. It was hidden by her sleeve, but I saw it when she took her coat off."

"It could have been from the blood ritual. Good eye, Ciara."

I paced as far as the phone cord would let me. "Tina doesn't live in Sherwood. How did you get past the National Guard to go to her apartment?"

"We got a Control escort. Tina's mom is pretty high up in the agency, and she convinced them there was cause, since her necromancy texts were gone."

I looked at the clock. Still daytime. I hadn't realized Colonel Petrea's wife was human. "What does Tina's dad say about this?"

Lori hesitated. "He's not with us." Her voice sloped up at the end of the sentence, which told me she was nervous, maybe purposely cryptic.

"Is Mrs. Petrea there with you?"

"Yeah."

"And that's why you can't talk about Colonel Petrea?"

"Pretty much," she said in a forced casual tone.

"So when you say he's not with you, you don't mean just because he's a vampire and can't go out during the day."

"Right."

Why didn't Petrea's wife want him to know their daughter was missing? Didn't she trust him? Or was she hiding something herself?

Lori continued. "You knew Tina in a different way than I did. Do you have any idea where she might have gone?"

I tried to think, but my brain was murky as usual. "Sorry. I'll call you if I think of anything. Good luck."

We hung up. I sat on the sofa and explained the situation to Noah. Then I asked him, "If you were on the run because you'd done something wrong, where would you go?"

"I would stay here." He lifted his hands to encompass the station. "I trust no one more than these friends."

"What if they couldn't protect you?"

"I'd be worse on my own. Vampires need community."

I hoped my chagrin didn't show. Before I met this odd little family, I'd only trusted myself. In Tina's situation, I would go far away from anyone I'd ever known.

But to get inside her head, I couldn't think like a con artist. Tina wasn't a vampire, but like most humans, she needed community. Her community, her coven, was the Control, and even they couldn't help her now.

Who did that leave? Her parents. Maybe they were protecting her, either because she really had raised the dead—or because they had done it themselves. They were necromancers, after all. But then why would Mrs. Petrea tell Lori about the missing books?

"I'll be right back," I told Noah, then went into Shane's room to fetch my research books on Romania. If I could understand the Petreas' people better, maybe I could figure out how this all fit together. Or at least I'd fill the time until our next zombie-shoveling party.

I lounged on the couch with a fresh mug of, well, breakfast and turned to the last chapter I'd been reading before I died. Before Aaron died. Before the whole world fell apart.

Under the chapter title appeared this pithy quote from Bram Stoker's *Dracula*:

"Every known superstition in the world is gathered into the horseshoe of the Carpathians, as if it were the centre of some sort of imaginative whirlpool . . ."

I let out a sigh. No wonder Petrea had hated my human self. I questioned everything, believed in nothing. My blood or my mind—my soul?—drained the potency of superstition, the very thing that had once made his class of people so powerful. In his mind, I was everything wrong with the modern world.

Further reading confirmed my suspicions—the Transylvanian and Moldavian noblemen had used the threat of vampires, ghouls, and other "fictional" creatures to keep the peasants in line. What was a little physical hardship, or a starving child, compared to the eternal damnation of the vampire's clutches?

"This is interesting," I told Noah. "A group of seventeenth century Carpathian noblemen claimed they had vampires in their thrall, that they could control their actions. So if you crossed these guys, they'd sic the vamps on you." I flipped the page. "Of course, this book has to claim vampires aren't real, or it would never get published."

"Do you think they truly had vampires in their thrall?" Noah asked.

"They were probably bribing or blackmailing them. We can't actually be controlled, right? Like those zombies?"

Noah took off his glasses and squinted at the ceiling. "There is a Haitian voodoo practice where a person is given a potion that make them seem dead. The witch doctor then brings them out of their grave. The zombies, if you want to call them that, have so much brain damage from the potion, they do anything their master says."

"But vampires' brains aren't damaged when we die, right?"

"Such is my point. If the resurrection is proper, we are not even dead a minute. Humans have drowned for longer than that without destroying their minds."

My chest grew cold. "I was dead longer than a minute. You said you thought you lost me." I put a hand to my head.

"My mind's felt sticky off and on ever since. I thought it was because I was sick, or because Monroe had left me." I shot Noah a pleading look. "Do I have brain damage?"

He shrugged. "If you do, it will get better eventually. We can recover from almost anything."

I stared at the page in front of me, checking for blurred vision or sudden lack of literacy. I could handle losing a limb, but not my mind. My wits had gotten me out of more jams than I could count. The loss of even half of them would be the End of the Ciara as We Know It.

I recalled how foggy I'd felt while the CAs were doing their cheerleading routine. *Shit.* What if the zombie spell had a hold on me? Was I half zombie?

The book's spine snapped in my hand.

"Watch your strength," Noah warned, "especially when you're upset." He turned back to his own book and continued reading aloud.

I couldn't hear his words over the roar of panic in my head. I knew I should tell someone my theory, but revealing my weakness could land me in a laboratory, away from the people who'd nursed me back to life. The thought of leaving the station turned me cold and empty inside.

Plus, it was impossible, right? Elijah said the zombie spell worked through blood magic, and it wasn't as if the necromancer had bled on my dead body or—

Wait. My thoughts lurched back to another problem, one that I might be able to solve.

I picked up the receiver and punched in Lori's number. When she answered, I said, "I know where to look for Tina."

30

Help Me

A grim-faced Elijah opened the door of his basement apartment and ushered me and Shane inside.

"Tina's in the bedroom." He joined me as I passed him. "How are you feeling, Griffin?"

"Fine," I lied. "Which is more than I can say for Tina. At least I had friends who would save me."

He held up his hands. "I don't make vampires. Period. I told Tina that, and I offered to call an ambulance. It was daytime, so I couldn't carry her to the hospital myself."

"But if she was dying—"

"That's the thing. She's sick, but she ain't dying. Check this out." He led us down the hall to a closed door.

I opened the door slowly, trying not to let the hinges creak, and took a step toward the queen-size bed.

Beneath a sweaty layer of sheets, Tina's form breathed deep and even. I could feel the heat of fever coming off her, and my predator's sixth sense (or seventh or eighth sense) told me she was weak and sick.

But Elijah was right—she was nowhere near death. I looked at Shane, and he shook his head to confirm my diagnosis.

This part I hadn't guessed. All I'd guessed was that if Tina had raised the zombies—or thought she had—she might turn to Elijah for protection. Believing their affair to be secret, she'd figure no one would look for her at his apartment.

Bingo for me on that deduction, which we'd verified with a phone call to Elijah an hour ago. But I'd never suspected she'd be looking for something much bigger than a hiding place.

A loud knock came from the apartment's front entrance. I stepped quietly out into the hall and shut the bedroom door.

By the time we got back to the living room, Lori and David had entered, escorted by Colonel Lanham, who'd had to drive them due to the curfew.

"Ciara . . ."

My best friend stared at me. I met Lori's gaze for only an instant, but it was long enough. I held back a whimper of pain as my fangs jabbed my gums from within.

Lori took a step closer, and Shane did the same on the other side, ready to tackle me in the event of a need to feed.

"You look . . ." Her breath blew out, then sucked in. "You look so beautiful."

"Thanks." I stared at her feet, at the clumps of mud on Elijah's beige carpet, tracked in by our shoes. I tried not to breathe. Every muscle trembled with the urge to pounce.

Once a donor, always a donor.

Lori stepped closer, heart pounding, blood rising to

the surface of her skin, her face and arms no doubt flushed pink.

I backed away into Elijah's kitchen. "Tina's sick but very alive. David, you should probably check her vitals before we question her."

They moved down the hall, everyone but Shane.

"You look like you could use one of these." He withdrew a meal from my thermos bag, popping the straw to a vertical position.

I took it and sank onto one of Elijah's dining room chairs. "No more double dates with Lori and David."

"Things'll go back to normal. You had nice control there, which is encouraging." He rubbed my shoulders as I stared at the carpet. Suddenly his hands froze. "No way."

I looked up to see him gaping at a framed print of a football team on the opposite wall, above the black leather reclining couch. "What's wrong?"

"That's Elijah *Washington*? Inside linebacker for the '76 Browns?"

"It used to be." I took a long slurp, clearing my head of Lori-chomping thoughts. "Now his last name is Fox."

"I have to get his autograph. My nephews are huge Cleveland fans."

"Just don't tell them how you got it."

"They don't even know I'm a vampire, so they won't suspect. This would mean a lot coming from me, since I hate the Browns."

"I'm glad your love for your family exceeds your love for the Steelers."

Except for the poster, the decor in Elijah's apartment was solidly modern. The Contemporary Awareness Division was doing a thorough job with Captain Fox.

Shane tore his gaze from the poster to focus on me again. "Feeling better?"

"Physically." I set the empty cup on the table and ran my tongue over my now-fangless gums. "I'm dreading every moment with my two other best friends."

"Lori and David will adjust to the new you."

"In time for the wedding? I'm pretty sure chowing down on the bride and groom is a breach of maid of honor etiquette."

"One day at a time, okay?"

I nodded. "First, avoid zombie rampage. Second, redo bridal party seating arrangement."

He offered his hand. "Ready to work on number one?"

When we entered the bedroom, Tina was lying on her back with a thermometer in her mouth, her eyes half open. David held a stethoscope to her chest, so the room was quiet except for her wheezing breath.

Tina's eyelashes fluttered apart. "Ciara, I thought you'd be dead," she mumbled around the thermometer.

"I was. Am. Undead." I fought to keep from screaming at the sound of the word. At least my bitterness distracted me from wanting to eat her.

Tina's lids lowered halfway. "Wish I had that option."

"Shh," David said, still listening to her heart.

The thermometer beeped. Colonel Lanham cleared his throat. David frowned, then took the thermometer out of Tina's mouth and showed it to Lanham. Even in the low light from several feet away I could see the digital numbers: *99.8.*

Practically normal compared to the fever that had boiled my brain. Why did she get to survive this disease when I didn't?

Lanham nodded to Lori, who sat beside Tina on the bed and patted her knee. "Can you tell me what happened?" she asked her.

Tina drew a melodramatic hand across her forehead, like she was Greta Garbo in *Cámille*. "It's all my fault."

Lanham reached inside his jacket, and I heard the small click and hum of a recording device.

So he'd decided to let Tina think she was dying, the better to get her confession. Cold but efficient.

"What's your fault, hon?" Lori asked her.

"I wanted to show everyone I could do it." Tina wiped her nose with the tissue Lori offered. "But I didn't even know zombies existed." She clutched Lori's wrist. "I wanted to raise a ghost. Not just for me—for SPIT, too. If we could prove Sherwood was haunted, think what it would do for us."

"Sweetie, you didn't have to. We were doing fine."

"You can't fool me. I'm the treasurer." She grimaced and put her fingertips to her temple. "God, it hurts so bad."

Elijah picked up a white bottle from the dresser. "Time for your pain meds." He handed the bottle to Lori. "Three of these seem to knock out her aches."

I caught the label on the bottle. Ibuprofen. That over-the-counter stuff wouldn't have touched the railroad spike in my head Saturday night. She definitely didn't have what I'd had.

Lori opened the bottle. "Tina, you told us you had chicken pox when you were a kid."

"That's what the orphanage said. They might've made a mistake, or maybe they just said that so I'd be more adoptable. It was so crowded, they were desperate to get rid of us."

Lori shook out three brown pills. "Can you tell us when you cast the spell for the ghost?"

"Last Sunday night. I was so mad about not making Immanence Corps, I stole one of Mom's necromancy books and went to the Sherwood cemetery to do the ritual." Tina took the ibuprofen and a long gulp of water. Then she ran her finger over the jagged scar on her left forearm. "I went back every night, but there weren't any ghosts. I was hoping if we all went the night of your party, we would see one."

So Tina had raised the creature that murdered Susan Haldeman, then infected Aaron. Twelve people had died because of her experiment. I was the only one still walking. My hands shook with rage, and only her obvious sorrow kept me from wrapping them around her neck.

Lori brushed the sweaty bangs off Tina's forehead. "You should've come forward sooner so we could make it stop."

"I tried to fix it." Tina coughed. "Saturday night I did the spell of undoing. But nothing undid and the zombies came back." Another cough. "I swear I was going to turn myself in, but then I got sick. I was scared I would die like everyone else, so I came here. Even brought a VBC form."

Elijah's eyes filled with sadness as he looked at her.

Tina heaved a hopeless sigh and cast her watery gaze at David. "How long do I have?"

"Best guess?" He looked at his watch. "About fifty or sixty."

Her eyes widened. "Minutes?"

"Years."

"But I have chicken pox." She gave a hacking cough

as she lifted her shirt above her belly button. "You saw my spots."

Sure enough, the telltale fluid-filled red bumps covered her abdomen. My own belly itched at the sight.

"I'm not a doctor," David said, "but you do seem to have classic chicken pox symptoms. It's a serious disease for someone your age no matter what. You should go to the hospital to make sure you don't get dehydrated." He folded up his stethoscope and placed it in his red EMT bag.

She frowned at him. "*Classic* chicken pox symptoms? I don't have the mutant supervirus?"

"If you did, you'd be dead by now. Ciara was in a coma less than an hour after the first symptom."

Elijah let out a long breath. "Thank God I didn't turn you, Tina."

She gave him a cold glare, which even in her weakened state had the impact of a buzz saw. "You didn't know I wasn't dying, asshole, so don't congratulate yourself."

Elijah looked at the ceiling. I realized that with their difference in size, strength, race, and metaphysical status, she could dish out a lot of crap and he'd never be able to fight back without getting in major trouble.

Tina took a long swig of water. As she wiped her mouth, it verged on a smile. "My spell worked. I really do have powers." She looked at Colonel Lanham. "You were wrong. I belong in the Immanence Corps, just like my dad always said."

"You belong in jail." I lunged forward, dragging Shane with me. "That zombie you raised ripped the arms and legs off an innocent woman."

Tina pulled the covers up to her chin. "It was an accident. I'm sorry."

"You're not sorry, you're proud. You know what else you are? Alive! You know who else isn't? Aaron, who got infected by your experimental corpse." I ticked off the victims on my fingers. "Turner Jamison. Me. Nine other people who caught that mutant virus."

Tina's eyes were wide and wet. "What are you—"

"You'll beat this lame chicken pox, and when you do, you'll go back to walking in the sun and eating food. You'll hang out with your friends without wanting to rip open their throats and chug their blood like cheap beer." My voice cracked. "Must. Be. Nice."

Lori inched away from me to join David, who put a protective arm around her.

"Is that true?" Tina turned her frightened gaze to Colonel Lanham. "The zombie started this chicken pox plague?"

"That's our current working theory, yes."

She put her hands to her sweat-sheened face. "God, what have I done?"

Maybe her remorse should have cooled my rage, but it was only Shane's tight grip that kept me from crushing her stupid head.

"What we don't yet understand," the colonel continued, "is how the virus got into the *cadaveris accurrens* in the first place."

As we pondered this question, the room fell silent, except for Tina's snot-clogged sniffles.

Then Shane spoke up. "It came from her." Not letting go of my arm, he used my hand to point to Tina's jagged knife wound. "The blood ritual."

"She didn't even have chicken pox then," Lori said.

"Yes, she did." Shane looked down at me. "Remember

all that research I did on the varicella virus before you got sick? I read that the normal incubation period is ten to twenty days."

"So when Tina did that ritual," Elijah said, "the virus was already in her blood?"

Lori gasped. "The blood she shed on the grave."

"Hang on." David held up his hands. "As the only person here with the slightest medical knowledge, I have to say this makes no sense. A virus can't infect a dead body, no matter how much magic is involved." He gestured to Shane and me and Elijah. "If you guys can't get sick, there's no way a corpse can."

"Why not?" Lori shrugged. "If blood magic can reanimate a human being, why couldn't it do the same for a simple little virus? It's an organism, right?"

"The only way that could work," he said, "is if the virus was already in the corpse. It would have to be part of the body that was being reanimated." He put his hand to his chin, brow furrowed. "Maybe with a virus that can't be cured, like HIV," he muttered, "or with a virus that had actually killed the person."

"Or with a virus that lives inside you forever." Shane shook his head at David. "Sorry, you don't know everything. The varicella virus stays dormant in our nervous systems after we get over the chicken pox. Sometimes later in life it comes back as shingles."

"Shingles?" I pictured a person's skin looking like the surface of a roof. "Gross." A glimmer of gratitude shone through my bitterness. At least I'd never have to catch a disease again. Whatever shingles was, I hoped one day Tina got the worst case ever.

Elijah smacked his enormous hands together. "That's

it! Zombies are all about the nervous system. The blood magic puts their spinal cords back together and gets them up and going."

Colonel Lanham, who had been making notes on his phone, said, "But it still had to mutate into the supervirus inside the CAs for them to spread it." He thumbed a few more buttons. "Fascinating theory. I'm sending it to our necrobiologists for their opinion."

"Isn't 'necrobiologist' an oxymoron?" I pointed out.

Before anyone could groan at my pedantic observation, the doorbell rang. Several times.

While Elijah went to answer it, Colonel Lanham beckoned me and Shane into the far corner.

"If Tina Petrea is responsible for the CAs," he whispered, "she's not working alone."

"I agree." I glanced over at her. "She seems way too young and incompetent to pull off something this powerful. I still say she's as mundane as a block of concrete."

"It's not that. It's the fact that they've risen on more than one occasion. Each episode requires its own spell."

"She could be lying," Shane said. "Maybe she did the ritual more than once."

"Tina!" A woman in black blew past me, streaking a mass of red hair and a long pearl necklace. She sank to her knees beside the bed. "Sweetheart, we were so worried. Why didn't you call?"

"I'm so sorry, Mom." A tear slipped from the corner of Tina's eye.

"You didn't tell them anything, did you? Without a lawyer present?" She glared up at Lanham. "Interrogating a sick woman with no legal adviser? Can you sink any lower?"

The colonel made no move to apologize—or to disengage the listening device. "You know the rules. Miranda warnings are not required for evidence admitted to internal Control proceedings."

I frowned. That meant Tina wasn't going to civilian jail.

"Daddy . . ." she whispered.

I turned to see Colonel Petrea enter, stopping at the threshold to stare at his daughter. His face was as white and rigid as Mount Rushmore, and just as imposing.

"Tina . . ." he whispered as he glided forward. He repeated her name, sinking onto the bed and grasping her hand.

"I did it, Daddy." Her tears flowed harder. "I got it wrong, but I did it. I have powers."

Her mother blanched. "Tina, don't admit anything."

My con artist's intuition awakened. Was Mrs. Petrea just being protective of her daughter, or was she worried the revelations would implicate someone else?

"I always knew you were magic, *draga mea*." Colonel Petrea brought Tina's hand to his cheek, then kissed it. "Now you need to heal, so that we can teach you everything."

I simmered at the idea of Tina unleashing her questionable abilities on the world. But maybe Petrea was just telling her what she wanted to hear, thinking it would help her recover. Either way, it was weird to see them together like this, looking so close in age.

Then Petrea turned to his wife and murmured in a hypnotic voice. She softened and leaned against his side. He slipped his other hand over her shoulder to comfort her.

From her profile, Mrs. Petrea looked about fifty years old—a beautiful, well-kept fifty, but from the outside, the apparent age difference was startling. His touch held the passion and devotion of a young marriage, with a hint of controlling possession. Their power imbalance was even wider than that between Elijah and Tina, unless Mrs. Petrea wielded a secret weapon equal to her daughter's bitchiness.

This was the best Shane and I could've hoped for, had I remained alive. Every morning he would have been confronted with proof of my mortality. Maybe that had been part of the appeal, that it couldn't really last forever.

Now we had forever in our hands. And as the Artist Formerly Known as the Artist Formerly Known as Prince once perceived, "Forever is a mighty long time" (at least several extra decades, if we lasted as long as the typical vampires).

"Forgive me," Petrea told Tina. "I never meant to make you feel less than perfect."

I couldn't see his face, but his voice told me his jaw was trembling. My own chin quaked at the thought of my father and the fleeting wish—just now unearthed—that he had been at my deathbed.

Would I be at his? What if he died during the day and I couldn't be there for him? Or for my moms? Would I even know when they died, the way I would Monroe?

Monroe. He would've returned to the station by now to avoid being shut out of town until the end of the curfew.

"I'll get your coat," Mrs. Petrea said to Tina. "We're taking you to the hospital."

Colonel Petrea slipped his arms under Tina's body.

"You've imposed on your friend more than enough." He glared at Elijah as he lifted his daughter as easily as a rag doll.

She pressed her face into her father's neck. "He was never my friend."

"Don't say that, Tina," Elijah said as she passed him. "You know it's not true."

Colonel Petrea turned slowly to face the younger vampire. "There will be an inquiry." He swept out the door, Tina in his arms.

"Fine." Elijah followed them. "I broke up with her before she entered the Control." His voice echoed back to us. "I followed protocol!"

A roll of thunder rumbled outside. I shot a worried look at Shane. "Dexter," we said in unison.

I turned to Lanham. "Our dog's thunderphobic. Can we go back to the station?"

"Please do. Stay there until we call you."

"You do have jobs." David stepped forward. "The station is in charge of disseminating information about the curfew."

I looked between him and Lanham. They needed to do some serious negotiating for our time.

"I'll keep that in mind," Lanham said icily. "Now please wait for Agents Griffin and McAllister in the living room, and send in Captain Fox."

David's nostrils twitched, but he took Lori's hand and left without a word. Elijah passed them on his way back into the bedroom.

"I didn't do nothing wrong, I swear," he said. "I covered my ass from here to eternity when it came to our relationship."

Lanham shut the bedroom door and turned to us. "If Agent McAllister's theory is correct, it means that every corpse in that cemetery that had chicken pox during its life is a potential *cadaveri accurrens*."

I looked at Shane. "Did it say in any of those articles how many people get chicken pox at some point in their lives?"

He grimaced. "Something like ninety-five percent of Americans have had it."

Elijah whipped out his radio. "I better tell my commander. There's over twelve hundred people buried there." He put a finger to his other ear and turned away to speak.

"So more than eleven hundred zombies," Shane said. "And there are how many agents in the ZC?"

"Forty-eight," Lanham answered. "But agents from other divisions can be called in for backup."

"Still." Shane sighed and put his hands in his pockets. "It's a bug hunt, man," he said in a strange redneck accent.

"Huh?" I said.

"It's a line from *Aliens*. Never mind."

I turned to Colonel Lanham. "Are you going to the cemetery?"

"I'll send Captain Fox in my stead. I'll be following the Petreas to the hospital." He lowered his voice. "I want to make sure they arrive safe and sound."

Or arrive, period. "Let us know if Tina takes a turn for the worse." I glanced at the rumpled, sweaty covers she'd left behind. "But I'll bet anything she's out of the woods."

I took Shane's hand and headed for the door, biting back tears of bitter envy. I'd be wandering in those woods forever.

31

The Red

The rain fell in sheets during our drive to the station, so I couldn't open the car window to dispel the scents of Lori and David. I tightened my safety belt, as if that would keep me from diving into the backseat for a quick, hot snack.

Noticing my discomfort, Shane switched on the radio. An old blues tune was playing on WVMP.

I gasped and cranked up the volume. "Monroe's back!" My heart pounded with relief, and more than a little fear. Had he returned only because of the curfew? What if he came back but ignored me? The thought hurt even worse than his complete absence.

The song faded, and Spencer's voice came on. "That was 'Just Walkin' in the Rain' by the Prisonaires."

I sank into the seat, folding my arms to keep my heart from dropping into my stomach.

"Once again, this is Spencer Wallace closing out Monroe Jefferson's *Midnight Blues* show. Thanks for your calls of concern. I guarantee Monroe'll be back just as soon as he gets over that laryngitis. Then we won't be able to hush him up." Spencer gave a soft chuckle. "He's probably listening right now, so I'll just say, Monroe, we all miss you. Come back real soon."

I took a deep breath, then wished I hadn't. Lori's and David's scents hit me harder than ever.

The moment we pulled into the parking lot, I dashed for the building as lightning snapped overhead.

Inside, every phone line was ringing, as frightened citizens called WVMP for emergency information. Jeremy waved at me from the lounge sofa, where he was patiently explaining to a caller that yes, even the liquor stores were now closed.

I stopped at the booth and mouthed my maker's name to Spencer through the glass. He shook his head sadly, then returned to his own phone call.

"I'm so sorry," Shane whispered, kissing me on the temple. "Let's check on Dexter."

The giant black dog greeted us in the common room with wild panting and circling.

"Poor little dude." Shane knelt in front of him and ruffled the dog's furry black cheeks. "It's okay."

"Don't comfort him, remember." I pulled off my soaking windbreaker and shook out the rain. "It makes him think there's something to be afraid of."

"Right." He stood up and patted his thigh. "Come on, Dexter, let's dig up some of your blood-basted bone treats. Make this a party."

"While you're in there," I asked him, "can you bring out my research stuff on Romania? It's two books and a stack of articles."

He headed into our room, where the door swung shut. I turned to the sink, ready to face the least glamorous part of being a vampire—washing out blood cups.

When I was alive I hated doing dishes, and not just because I was lazy. The moment a meal was over, food might as well have been toxic waste for all I wanted to touch it.

Congealed blood was even worse.

"Yuck." I shoved the open cup under the hot running water.

As I reached for the dish soap, a hand snatched the bottle.

"Allow me," Jim purred in my ear.

I stiffened, neck prickling, but forced my voice casual to avoid escalation. "You're more than welcome to do my chores."

He squeezed the bottle, which emitted a slow, suggestive squirt of liquid soap onto the sponge. "Nothing's a chore where you're involved." He pressed his face against my hair. "I didn't think it was possible, but you smell better than ever."

I tried to move away, but he grasped the counter on my left side, trapping me. A clap of thunder pummeled the air outside, echoing in my guts.

"So Regina's had her turn with you," Jim murmured. "Who's next, or should I take a number?"

I held my breath, fighting to steady my pulse. I had to stand up to Jim myself, and quickly. If Shane found us this way, they'd fight, and Shane would die.

"How's this?" I turned and pressed my fingers to the hollow of Jim's throat. "I'm thinking of a number between zero and never."

"We all saved your life." He took my hand from his

neck and rubbed it between his own. "You owe us." He breathed against my fingers, which were turning cold from fear.

"I don't owe you this." My brain scrambled for the self-defense techniques I'd learned in Control orientation. I vowed to practice them until they were second nature.

"You're still chilly," he said. "Let me bring you along to visit a donor. We could drink our fill," he ran his warm tongue along the center line of my palm, "then fuck all night."

"Get away from her."

Jim jerked, then went suddenly pale. He put his hands up and slowly turned to face Spencer, who was standing at the edge of the kitchen area, not five feet away.

"All right, man," Jim said. "Everything's groovy. You don't have to tell me twice."

Spencer bore down on him with a gaze of molten steel. "I won't."

Shane's door creaked open. He walked out with my books and papers.

"Dexter's happily chewing, and I think I found your . . . stuff." His pace slowed as he saw us. "What's going on?"

"Nothing." I moved toward him, breaking the triangle of tension. "Thanks."

"It's your shift," Spencer said to Jim.

"Yeah. Right. Good. See you guys." Jim hurried out without looking at us.

Shane watched him go, his body as still as a lion's before it leaps. Then he slowly turned his head back to me. "What did you want these for?"

"Petrea said something that sparked a memory." I took the books and papers to the table. "I don't know where it goes, and my brain is still foggy, so I'm just going to flip through this stuff until something jumps out." I hoped my babbling distracted him from thoughts of pursuing Jim. "How's that sound?"

"Sounds like you need coffee," Spencer said.

"Thanks!" I sat at the table. "Colonel Petrea called Tina *draga mea*, a Romanian term of endearment. It made me think of dragons."

Shane sat beside me. "He called her a dragon?"

"No, the Romanian word for dragon is *dracul*. Or at least it was in the old days."

"Like Dracula?" Spencer said, filling the coffeepot with water.

"Exactly. Shane, remember when we were in Saint Michael's church?"

"When you fell in the holy water."

I glared at him. "Remember the stained glass window of Saint Michael defeating Satan?"

"Depicted as a dragon. What are you getting at?"

I flipped through my stack of papers. "I was going to do my paper on the Legion of the Archangel Michael, aka the Romanian Iron Guard."

"The fascist guys."

I found the article I was looking for. "They were so extreme, the Nazis had to step in and tell them to ease up."

"Good grief." Spencer hit the switch on the coffeemaker and came to join us. "How's that possible?"

"They were killing Jews too fast, too openly." My nose wrinkled at the page in front of me. "The most infamous incident happened in Bucharest. They were pissed that their leader, Corneliu Codreanu, had been killed, so they rounded up dozens of Jewish men, women, and children and—" My throat tightened around the words. "They processed them through a slaughterhouse. Like livestock."

"Holy shit," Shane said.

"Unholy shit, actually, and they knew it. They knew they were going to hell for their deeds, but they thought their souls were a worthy sacrifice to purify the fatherland." I examined the photo of the leader who had ordered the Bucharest pogrom. "I always thought it amazing that people so religious would put anything above their eternal fates."

"Maybe they weren't that religious," Shane said. "How could you believe in God and do those horrible things?"

"Believing in God doesn't make you good, just like not believing doesn't make you bad."

"Whatever. Let's not have this argument again."

I resisted the urge to send him another glare. We were both clearly on edge, and being unable to discuss the Jim thing, our testiness was making us bicker.

"I remember the pictures." Spencer paged through my textbook, licking his finger with each turn. "I was thirteen when our boys liberated the concentration camps. All the papers carried the photos of those people." Lick. Turn. "They were like corpses. Not just from being skinny, either. Their eyes were dead." He stared off through the wall. "That was the day I figured out there was no such thing as the devil. Didn't need to be."

We sat in silence for a few moments. Then I glanced at the painting on the page where Spencer had stopped.

I gasped, and my mouth hung open while my mind smoothed out the words. "They knew they'd be damned for murdering humans, but what if they thought they could earn back salvation another way?"

Spencer looked down at the page. "By slayin' dragons?"

"Or the real-world equivalent."

"Wait," Shane said. "You think the Iron Guard hunted vampires on the side?"

The station phone rang.

"Jeremy'll get that." I turned back to Shane. "It fits. The Archangel Michael was their icon. Dragons, vampires—we're all devils."

"It fits, but that doesn't mean it's true. What evidence do you have?"

The phone rang again.

"None." I held up a finger. "Yet. But I bet the Control has a huge archive on unsanctioned vampire hunters of the twentieth century."

"What's it got to do with anything," Shane said, "other than a paper you can never turn in without being called crazy?"

The phone rang a third time. Spencer sighed and went to pick it up. "WVMP the Lifeblood of Rock 'n' Roll, this is Spencer . . . yeah, hang on. I can give you that information." He opened the emergency services binder on the end table.

I focused on Shane. "The Legion of the Archangel Michael would have been around when Petrea was alive and human. Maybe he was part of it."

"Ciara, just because you don't like the guy doesn't mean he's a fascist."

"He called me Gypsy scum. The fascists hated Gypsies. He also hates communists, and fascists—"

"Everyone who lived under communism hates communists. And all rich people hate Gypsies. Isn't Petrea supposedly from nobility?"

"Oh yeah." I gave a heavy sigh. "So he couldn't have been in the Legion. It was made up of peasants."

Spencer hung up the phone. "Unless he lied about that."

I squinted at him. "You were listening to us while you were talking to the caller?"

"I hear everything." Spencer came back over to the table. "How old is this cat Petrea?" he asked me.

"I think he'd be about ninety, in human years."

"Then Petrea's not his real name. He would've changed his identity at least once by now."

"And that identity might be on record with the Control. I'm calling Lanham." I picked up my phone. Zero bars. "Lightning must have hit the cell tower."

"Use the phone in the lounge," Spencer said. "Looks like I'm stuck answering this one."

I headed for the door, and Shane said, "Be careful out there."

"I will!" I said with what I hoped wasn't annoyance.

As the door closed slowly behind me, I heard Shane ask Spencer, "Do I need to kill Jim?"

Just as I passed the studio on the way to the lounge, the overhead lights went out. I peeked through the booth window. Jim's face was shadowed by the blue emergency light. The smile he gave me chilled my spine.

A moment later, in a distant corner of the station's basement, the generator began to chug. The lights came back on.

I hurried through the door into the lounge, stopping short when I saw Jeremy lying on the couch, eyes closed and shoeless feet propped on the arm.

"Sorry, I didn't know you were . . . here." He didn't respond. "Jeremy?"

His chest rose and fell in a slow, steady rhythm. Below the roar of the wind, I could hear his pulse.

I stepped closer, inhaling through my nose and mouth, like a cat, the better to take in his scent. Then I knelt beside the couch and whispered his name. No answer, not even a twitch.

I carved out his silhouette with my palm, floating my hand a few inches above his arm, feeling his heat, his life. Real life, not the facsimile that now moved my blood and bones.

When I got to his neck, I realized his eyes were wide open, staring at me.

I jumped back. "Shit! Sorry. I didn't mean to—did I scare you?"

He slowly reached up to his head and pulled out a pair of earplugs. "What?"

"I wasn't trying to creep you out. Or maybe I didn't. You seem so calm."

"I know not to make sudden moves around vampires." He rubbed his eyes. "I didn't hear you come in."

"I thought that was because of my new stealth." I looked away, feeling foolish.

He set the earplugs on the coffee table. "I put these in because the wind was keeping me awake. This building sounds like it's going to rip apart."

A gust roared outside, shaking the station's foundation. "It's quieter in our apartment. We've got the fold-out couch."

"I've gotta get back to answering phones soon. Besides, no humans allowed, remember? I'm not in the club." His eyes flicked up to meet mine. "Yet."

"Jeremy." I sat on the edge of the cushion, next to his outstretched legs. "You don't want to be in this club."

He scowled at me. "Would you undo it if you could, go back to living as a human?"

"In a heartbeat." The word drew my gaze to his chest, then his neck.

His mouth opened and moved, maybe asking me a question, but his voice was lost in the rush of his pulse. The thirst built on the back of my tongue, almost drowning me.

Jeremy snapped his fingers softly in front of my face. "Ciara."

"Huh?" I shook my head hard. "I'm sorry."

"Don't apologize." He nudged me with his knee. "Not to me. Not to yourself."

I kept my gaze on the nearest leg of the card table. For the first time, that missing paint chip bugged me. "I know it's not my fault. My only alternative was dying, and I don't regret it."

"So why do you feel guilty?"

Did I feel guilty? I'd certainly said *I'm sorry* often enough these last few days to last a second lifetime.

"I see everyone differently now. I see them the way the con artist Ciara saw people. As pawns, objects, sources of sustenance."

"Bullshit." Jeremy folded his hands behind his head. "If you really saw me as an object, we would've stopped talking two minutes ago."

I looked at him, his posture mixing a boyish innocence with calculated seduction. His need to bleed was almost irresistible.

"I can't drink alone." My voice verged on a whimper,

and my fingers kneaded the edge of the sofa cushion. "I could hurt you, and it would hurt me to hurt you."

"Would it kill you to kill me?"

Irritation overcame my hunger. I was Jeremy's next target in his endless campaign to become undead. "Don't ask that."

"What if I were dying?" he said. "Like you were."

"Please don't do anything stupid. Don't try to kill yourself."

"What if I were in an accident or got sick like you did? Would you save me the way Monroe saved you?"

I gazed into his hazel eyes, which looked jade green tonight, the color of a new leaf on a spring morning, something I'd never see again.

"No." I placed my hand over his heart. "Live your life, Jeremy. Stop waiting for it to end."

He put his hand on top of mine. His heart thumped into my palm. I shut my eyes and felt each chamber contract and expand, squeezing the blood through his body. He had no idea what a miracle that was, and how easily it could stop.

"Regina has a new donor," he said. "That stripper guy."

I opened my eyes. "He means nothing to her."

"That's not why I brought it up. I'm available now. For you, if you want."

"What about Jim?"

He tensed, his fingers spasming against mine. "Jim's scaring me."

"Me, too."

"Last time I donated, he—he played a game I didn't like. Didn't clear the rules with me ahead of time. I think he's developing a taste for fear."

I shivered at the turn of phrase. "We have to do

something about him. As soon as the zombies are gone."

Jeremy tapped his fingers against the back of my hand. "Think about my offer."

"I can't be like Regina. I won't . . . you know."

"Jerk me off? That's okay. I'm not into you like that."

"Oh." I was relieved but perplexed. I thought he was into every vampire like that. "Good."

"There's this girl at the coffee shop I've been wanting to ask out. But I felt weird about it while Regina and I were hooking up. So I'm looking for a totally platonic donation situation."

"Then, yes. Thank you." I wanted to fall to the floor weeping in gratitude. I also wanted to start our "situation" right that moment, but I had no idea how to safely bite a human. Maybe I could go get Spencer and—

Footsteps descended the stairs on the other side of the door. I pulled my hand into my lap so it wouldn't look like I was about to rip out Jeremy's heart.

Franklin appeared, carrying a pair of plastic shopping bags.

"Jer, which of these microwave soup thingies you want?" He saw me and dropped the bags. "Ciara."

I kept my focus over his right shoulder, in case the effect of being in a room with two humans overwhelmed my infant self-control.

"How are you?" I asked him. Had it not even been a week since Aaron collapsed in front of class? It seemed like years, but to Franklin the wounds must be fresh and oozing.

"Hanging in there." His voice was guarded, as usual. "You?"

I shrugged. "Can't complain."

"That doesn't mean you won't."

I looked straight at him and grinned. If anyone could be trusted not to treat me differently, it was Franklin. He never much treated me as a human being to start with. Best of all, I didn't want to drink him.

"It's good to see you," he said, with only a slight catch in his voice. Then he picked up the plastic bag. "And now that you're a vampire, I don't have to share my food with you anymore."

The door to the exit slammed open, and Regina and Noah came through, dripping wet.

"Shit, shit, shit." Regina squeezed the rain from the ends of her black hair. "This thunderstorm in April is bogus."

"Lights are out all over Sherwood," Noah told us.

Franklin jutted his thumb at the door. "Don't forget: the town is cordoned off. So the phone and electric will have to be fixed by whatever skeleton crew of technicians already happens to be in Sherwood. Could take days."

"It's like *Night of the Living Dead*." Jeremy looked at Regina. "Now you gotta make me a vampire to keep me safe from zombies."

I shook my head as I dialed the hospital. "I long for the days when that sentence would've sounded strange."

The nurses' station patched me through to Tina's room. Mrs. Petrea answered.

"Oh, Ciara," she sniffled. "It's nice of you to call. I never got a chance to thank you for finding her. Who knows how long that man would have kept her in his hovel?"

Hovel? Elijah's apartment wasn't exactly the Trump Plaza, but I'm pretty sure it had running water.

"How is Tina?"

"Already better now that she's had some fluids. Her

fever's gone, though she's itching like crazy. Did you want to speak with her?"

A flash of rage shot up my arm, as if it could snap through the phone connection. No, I did not want to talk to the girl who got me killed.

"Can I speak with Lieutenant Colonel Lanham, please?"

There was a muffled sound from the receiver, like someone's hand was over it. Mrs. Petrea came back on the phone. "Dear, he'd like to call you back from a phone in the waiting area."

Good thinking. Colonel Petrea's vampire ears would hear every word I said, even from across the room.

"Have him call me at the station's main number." I paused, dying to ask her a million questions about her human life with a never-aging vampire. But those answers were irrelevant to me now. "Thanks."

"Noah, if you could supervise the child—" Regina motioned to me "—around the humans, while I get a hot shower, that'd be great." She swept through the hallway door without waiting for an answer.

Noah sighed and crossed to the sofa, where Jeremy quickly moved his feet so the vampire could sit down.

The phone trilled. Lanham.

"What do you have for me?" he asked without preliminaries, which was the way I liked him.

I explained my theory about Petrea and the Legion of the Archangel Michael, and how they could've secretly been vampire hunters. As I spoke, Franklin, Noah, and Jeremy stared at me in disbelief. I felt like a conspiracy theorist.

Franklin leaned over and whispered to Jeremy, "Next she'll be blaming zombies for the JFK assassination."

"I heard that!" I snapped, which just made them laugh

louder. "Assholes. Not you," I hurried to add to Colonel Lanham. "So can you find out Petrea's original name?"

"I'll ask my counterpart in the Anonymity Division. She owes me a favor."

I had a feeling a lot of people owed Colonel Lanham favors.

"If Tina had help in raising the zombies," I said, "then they might keep coming, even though she's in the hospital."

"Yes, until all the CAs she spelled are destroyed or—" He cut himself off, probably checking that no one could hear him. "Or until she is."

My skin turned cold, and not just because I was due for a meal. "You can break the spell by killing Tina?" No wonder her parents had been so devastated.

"We are not in the business of killing humans."

"Except when absolutely necessary."

He didn't argue. "That's not the case here. Captain Fox feels that the CAs can be contained within the cemetery."

"And his forces can stop them from attacking the town, even if they all rise at once?"

"They are trained to do so."

I frowned at his non-answer. "So what about Colonel Petrea?"

Lanham got so silent, I couldn't hear him breathing.

"Are you still there?"

"Yes." He was almost whispering. "Petrea is very influential in the Control."

"But if he's really the zombie master and no one stops him, he could go to another town and do it again."

"I acknowledge that he or his wife probably have the ability, but what's their motive? Why would they risk their position by breaking such a taboo?"

"Maybe it's an Immanence Corps thing." I shut my mouth as soon as the idea was out, because I knew where it came from—Jonathan Fetter's Project Blood Leash memo. Which I had officially never read.

Colonel Lanham fell quiet again for several moments, then he simply said, "I'll be in touch," before hanging up.

As soon as my line disconnected, the phone rang again. I answered, "WVMP, the Lifeblood of Rock 'n' Roll. How may I help you?"

"Yeah, the 911 people said to listen to you guys for emergency information." A local.

"That's correct." I opened the binder that contained all the pertinent details. "Did you have a question?"

"How did you get that gig? I thought it would be the country station out on Route 32."

"We're technically inside the Sherwood town limits, which makes us the official local station. Did you need emergency assistance?"

"Sort of. Can you play some Trisha Yearwood?"

"I'll see what I can do," I told him, then hung up, reminding myself that even compared to the blood-drinking, zombie-wrastling, stripper-stroking life I now inhabited, the human world was very, very odd.

"I'll do the phones for a while," I told the guys. "You two sunnysides need to eat."

"Hoping to fatten us up?" Franklin said.

I started to say, "No need for that," making my usual dig at his paunch, but caught myself in time.

He halted beside me on his way to the microwave. "Don't stop insulting me just because I'm in mourning. I need it now more than ever."

I gave him a grim smile. "Me, too. A little normal would be nice."

"Good luck." He patted my shoulder. "You're not exactly a magnet for normal."

"You're proof of that." The phone rang, and I turned to answer it with a glow of hope. Franklin hadn't been afraid to touch me. My future work in the WVMP office would be only half insane.

The number on the caller ID made me yank the receiver off the hook. "Sir?"

"Developments." Lanham's voice was crisper than ever. "Tina has changed her story. She's confessed to willfully raising CAs."

"So it wasn't about the ghosts after all?" Tina wasn't a saint, but I couldn't imagine her knowingly risking people's lives.

"Also, she's pinned Captain Fox as her accomplice."

"Elijah? That's even more impossible."

"She says she was blackmailing him into helping her, threatening to reveal their relationship to his superiors. He's up for a promotion to major soon. Fraternizing with a human recruit would not have helped."

"I thought they broke up before she started orientation."

"Indoc," he corrected. "The details of the soap opera are irrelevant. What is relevant is that before the *cadaveris accurrens* rose in Sherwood, the CA division was on the verge of downsizing. Captain Fox's company was slated for disbanding. He's been detained by Internal Affairs pending an investigation."

The pieces seemed to fit (a little too well), except one. "Elijah's not a necromancer."

"According to Agent Codreanu-Petrea, if Tina's blood

was spelled, someone else would need only to scatter it and say a few words. Captain Fox had access to the cemetery during the crucial times."

"Wait. Agent who?"

"Codreanu-Petrea. Tina's mother. It's a hyphenated mouthful, but I respect a woman's choice to—"

"*Codreanu* is her maiden name?" I squeezed the phone so hard, the receiver began to crack. "Is she a descendant of the Iron Guard leader Corneliu Codreanu?"

"Even if she were, why would she put her own daughter in danger?"

"To control vampires. Think about it: if you were married to one, wouldn't you want an equalizer? Honoring her ancestors would be a bonus."

Lanham fell silent again, which I took as a good sign. "I'll look into it."

"What about Elijah? Other than Tina's accusation, which could be a lie, the evidence against him sounds pretty circumstantial."

"The evidential elements of Internal Affairs investigations are not your concern. What is your concern is this: according to Tina, the rest of the CAs will rise tomorrow night."

"The rest?" I blinked hard and fast. "All eleven hundred and some?"

"Correct."

I couldn't even picture that many zombies in one place. "What do they have planned this time? Touch football? Ballet? Maybe a Cirque du Soleil routine?"

"Nothing that elaborate. They'll be reverting to form, she says."

"What does that mean?"

"They're going to attack the town."

32

Rise

Wednesday morning, in the midst of helping the community cope with the quarantine and the worst spring nor'easter of the century, the radio station received, from the Control, the weirdest delivery ever.

Shane and I lined up the six gelatin torsos in the common room and passed out katana swords to the other vampire DJs—except Jim, who would stay at the station that night, as determined by unanimous vote (minus his own). We trained the others using the techniques Captain Fox had taught us.

According to Lanham, the IA investigators had found more stolen necromancy texts in Elijah's apartment. Tina signed an affidavit saying she had given them to him to complete her spell, to put the period at the end of her sentence, so to speak. I worried how the Zombie Company would manage without its leader, tonight of all nights—when we were expecting a CA rampage so big we had to call in civilian vamps from across the entire region.

Just after evening twilight, I arrived with Shane and the other DJs at the Sherwood cemetery, finding what looked like a giant vampire reunion party. I recognized a couple of Noah's and Spencer's friends, and Colin from D.C., Regina's old chum. By my best count, we were still outnumbered five to one. But we had several advantages: weapons, functioning brains, and help from the living.

During the day, human Control agents had erected a fiberglass barrier around the perimeter of the cemetery. Its height and emerald green color reminded me of a baseball stadium's center field wall. Not only would it keep the zombies in, but it would keep out the prying eyes of any curious, curfew-breaking onlookers.

The Control had briefly considered trapping the zombies inside the wall until sunrise. But the resulting fire could burn down the cemetery, and its smoke and stench would attract human attention. Besides, if enough zombies piled on top of one another, they could easily crawl over the wall. It was our job to prevent that.

Sergeant Kaplan had been called in from headquarters to train the civilian vamps. Her experience teaching clueless orientation recruits would no doubt come in handy.

"Remember," she said, pacing before the ragtag band of amateur sword wielders, "the only way a CA can kill a vampire is by tearing off your head. So protect your noggin at all costs."

Regina raised her hand. "I thought zombies were after human blood. Why would they attack us?"

"Good question." Kaplan repeated it so the whole line could hear. "Two reasons. One, you smell enough like us that a CA doesn't realize you're not human until after it's ripped you apart and started to drink. Reason number two." She shrugged. "You're in their way."

I looked up at Shane, waiting for the fear to weaken my knees or make my eyes shift in search of the closest escape route. But between the sword in my hand, the man at my side, and the new strength of my limbs, I felt invincible. Or at least ninety percent less vincible.

"Listen carefully." Kaplan looked each of us in the eyes before continuing. "You've been trained all your unlives not to hurt humans, to treat us as the fragile creatures we are." The corners of her mouth quirked at her words.

Then her face turned dead solemn. "Zombies. Aren't. Human. Some still look human. But don't be fooled. Not even by the children."

My stomach knotted as I remembered a Vietnam war movie where a soldier had stopped to help a child, only to be blown up by a bomb strapped to the kid's body. The next child his platoon came upon was shot on sight.

"They're dead," Kaplan said. "Not dead like you. Dead like a rotting log. They can't think. They can't cooperate. They're simply meat puppets, with a necromancer pulling their strings."

I raised my hand, unable to stop myself. "If they have strings, wouldn't that technically make them meat marionettes?"

Everyone stared at me. I continued to my second point. "Also, they seemed cooperative the other night with the pyramid."

"I saw the film you took," Kaplan said. "They were programmed to do a specific task until it was completed. They didn't think on their feet. They didn't improvise." The sergeant paused, then pointed at me. "But Agent

Griffin reminds me of a good point. We don't know what they'll be programmed to do tonight, and it could very well look like a coordinated attack. But it doesn't change our tactics or your role. The ZC and the Enforcement agents will take on the bulk of the *cadaveris*. All you have to do is guard the perimeter—that means the fence—and clean up any CAs that make it past the first line of defense. Understood?"

We all nodded, with varying amounts of enthusiasm.

Her voice became almost gentle. "You're doing these things a favor. If you don't destroy them, they'll roast come sunrise." She cast one last gray-green gaze over us. "Now get into position, and good luck."

We spread out along the inside of the iron fence surrounding the cemetery. Every light in the cemetery had been extinguished, so that not even aerial photographers could see what happened here.

But it was plenty bright for vampire eyes, even with a new moon. I could see the section to our right roped off with orange boundary tape. Colonel Petrea claimed to have undone Tina's work over those fifty graves. The spell of undoing required much more time and pain than the original spell, so he hadn't had time to neutralize the entire cemetery. But this at least allowed the ZC to move their forces inward.

We waited. For hours. Midnight passed, and I had lunch. When 2 a.m. arrived, I had a snack. By 4 a.m. a rumor spread through the ranks that Tina had been lying, that tonight's zombie rampage was a hoax.

"If it isn't a hoax," Shane said, "it had better hurry up."

I followed his nervous glance to the east. "Morning twilight is 6:09. Per union rules, all Control vampires have to be safely underground forty-five minutes before twilight, which would be 5:24. That barely gives us an hour to kill the CAs and clean them up before the humans take over."

Regina lit another cigarette. "Whoever the hell this zombie master really is, that's probably just what they want."

"Why?" I asked her.

"Humans can't fight these things as well we can, so with the right timing, the zombies'll come out of the graves maybe half an hour before sunrise. No vamps to stand in their way but plenty of time to kill humans." She pointed to the fence. "And when they get over that wall and flame out, they'll keep running. Bags of burning flesh, booking up and down the streets of Sherwood." Regina took another drag. "Kinda cool."

"Cool, except then the world knows that zombies exist. If we can't contain them, it won't just mean a few human lives lost. Not that that's not important," I hurried to add.

Noah nodded. "It means we could all be exposed. Vampires, the Control itself."

"You think people would believe it?" Regina said.

Shane looked askance at her. "People believe it now, when they haven't seen the evidence. Vampires are on TV, in books, in the movies."

"Fictional vampires," she said. "They've been around since *Dracula*."

"Not like now. I get calls every night from people who wonder if we're real, people who are otherwise clearly in touch with reality."

"They sense something," Noah agreed.

"Maybe someday we'll all have to go into deeper hiding," Shane said, "and the Control will be one big Anonymity Division."

My throat closed at the thought of living in the shadows in every sense. I didn't want to end up in a secret vampire coven, unable to work and go to school and see my human friends.

I heard the deep rumble of a diesel engine on the other side of the cemetery. In a moment, it was joined by another.

I turned to place the sound, but the rumbling seemed to be coming from all directions at once. Another early spring thunderstorm?

But the sky was clear. The stars peered through the branches of the budding trees. My feet turned cold.

The sound wasn't coming from the sky. It was coming from the earth.

You know those war movies where the troops proceed in orderly fashion, taking on the enemy as a single-minded unit? And then you know those other war movies where the battlefield is complete fucking chaos?

This was the latter. This was the undead *Braveheart*.

The zombies came all at once. The ZC and Enforcement agents struck, severing heads as the corpses emerged from the soil, but there were just too damn many.

The CAs broke through the line.

Shane blew his whistle. "Move!"

We rushed forward in pairs to meet the monsters. I followed Shane to the right, chasing a lone zombie heading for the cemetery's north gate. The trees, the sky, and the graves blurred in my peripheral vision as my new-found speed and agility kicked in.

We intercepted the zombie twenty feet from the gate, not far from the orange-taped area, where Petrea's spell of undoing seemed to hold.

I passed in front of the carcass, distracting him with a feint. He changed course to follow me, putting himself in Shane's path. Shane's blade arced, and the hairless head tumbled to the ground. I made a silent promise to come back later and apologize to it.

Shane turned to me. "Behind you!"

I spun around but saw nothing. Then I looked down. An old lady was crawling on hands and feet, her back hunched like a hyena's.

My sword descended, whooshing through the air in what felt like slow motion. I missed the neck, but the blade swept through her shoulders and slammed the hard ground. The impact reverberated up my arms and shook my whole body. I blinked back the pain and watched the zombie collapse without a twitch.

"You got her," Shane said. "I mean, you got it." He pointed to the corpse. "Spine severed, that's what counts."

Slowly I extracted the sword from the woman's flesh, the ache in my elbows fading.

"You okay?" He scanned the graveyard for our next target.

"I'll live."

"I'll make sure of it." He squeezed my shoulder. "Here comes another one. Do like we did the first."

The corpse of the approaching man looked fresh and young. I hesitated. "You sure that's not a vampire?"

The man veered to his left, tripping over the orange

boundary tape, tumbling so hard a piece of flesh ripped from his cheek, leaving a dull black gap in his skin.

"Guess not."

We caught up to the zombie as it struggled to its feet. It leaped straight for Shane, who swiped his sword in a perfect downward arc. The zombie's momentum carried it forward, so that it fell against Shane, then slid down his body in two pieces.

"Ugh." Shane leaped back, his light brown shirt splattered with pink embalming fluid. The strongest formaldehyde whiff yet stung my eyes. This one couldn't have been dead more than a couple of weeks—he had just begun to rot.

No more zombies were in our immediate vicinity. "Should we join the others?" I asked Shane.

"We should stay in our sector in case any—" He froze, the hair at his temple dripping pink liquid. "What was that?"

I listened, but nothing came through the distant shouts of vampires and thunks of swords through rotted flesh. "What do you hear?"

He held his breath, then whispered one word. "Digging."

My eyes darted back and forth, resting on the torn orange tape. "This section's supposed to be safe. Maybe Petrea—"

Something cold grasped my right ankle. My foot sank into the soil.

"Ciara!"

My leg snapped from the pressure. I shrieked.

Pain radiated up my body. The zombie twisted. Shane lunged for me. We crashed to the ground, but still the creature held on. Its other hand seized my left knee.

No. I flashed back to my childhood, bending a Barbie doll's legs the wrong way.

The zombie yanked down hard. My scream seemed to fill the universe. Red spots filled my vision, and I was only vaguely aware of Shane roaring in fury as he hacked at the limbs holding me.

The pressure eased suddenly, and Shane dragged me away from the grave, where stumps of two wrists waved. I sat up and saw that the zombie's hands still gripped my shattered legs.

"Stay here." Shane wrapped my fingers around the hilt of my sword. "You'll feel better soon." As he picked up his fallen sword, he put his whistle in his mouth and blew the help signal.

I tried to catch my breath, but my lungs were seized with pain. Then I felt a sudden shift.

My right shin healed before my eyes. The ends of the bone, protruding through a hole in my jeans, slipped back under my skin, then clicked together with a jolt.

I exhaled hard and looked up to see Shane whack off the head of the handless corpse as it struggled out of its grave.

The head fell to the side, and Shane drew back his foot as if to kick it.

"No. Ow!" I sucked in a hiss as my broken knee snapped into place. "They'll need to rebury it." A pale glimmer moved to my right. "Besides, you need to get that one."

He dispatched the new zombie as Regina, Noah, and Spencer arrived, swords in hand.

"We relayed your signal," Noah said.

"But everyone else is busy." Spencer pulled me to

stand on legs that felt miraculously normal. He pointed to the blood on my jeans. "One of 'em bit you?"

"Compound fracture."

"That explains the screaming."

"Uh, guys?"

We looked at Regina. "What?"

She stood immobile, eyes so wide they seemed more white than brown. "I think the word is 'incoming.'"

I held my breath and listened.

Thumping. Scratching. Digging.

Every grave around us was coming to life. Five of us against four dozen emerging zombies.

I took a step backward. "We're way outnumbered."

"It's not about numbers." Shane lifted his sword. "It's about timing."

We mowed them down as they emerged. I told myself I was whacking weeds. An old childhood rhyme came back to me, taught by a temporary friend in Iowa. We'd sing it as we kicked the heads off dandelions in the fields.

Momma had a baby and its head popped off!

We worked our way down the rows, but each zombie we beheaded was a little further out of its grave, and I knew soon we'd be overwhelmed.

Faster. *Momma hadababy and its headpoppedoff!*

Faster. *Mommahadababyanditsheadpoppedoff!* Not people. Weeds. Stop them from growing, running, breaking fragile human bodies that could never heal.

Headpoppedoff! Headpoppedoff!

I arrived at the grave of Robert William Tester. The marker was smaller than the others, and bore a cherub with its head bowed, legs crossed, and wings folded.

I read the dates etched in the pale granite.

"No," I whispered. "Don't make me do this."

The thing that emerged from the dirt, the thing that glared at me with dull resentment and bottomless hunger, had been five years old.

One small leg broke free of the soil, then the other.

"Please." I pointed to the earth. "Go back."

It halted as if it understood me, and then it tilted its head, wisps of pale brown hair peeking out under the layer of mud. The sunken pools of black might once have been blue eyes begging for an ice cream cone or one more bedtime story.

From deep inside me, my last vestige of humanity answered. I lowered my sword.

The child took a hesitant step forward, then leaped for my throat.

I stumbled back, expecting to feel its arms tearing off my head. But in the middle of the corpse's flight, a shadow came between us, then a thud to my left as someone tackled it, wrestling it to the ground.

"Cut it when I say!" Spencer shouted. He struggled atop the zombie, whose arms were snaking up to circle the vampire's neck.

I stepped over and raised my sword. With a yelp, Spencer flipped the child on top of him.

"Now!" His voice was strangled, air cut off by the zombie's choke hold. "Ciara . . ."

If I sliced, I could cut them both in half. So I changed my grip on the hilt, pointing the tip straight down.

"God, forgive me," I whispered as the tears burned my skin.

I stabbed. Spencer screamed.

I yanked upward on the sword, and the boy's body came with it, its back skewered on the tip.

I tossed the weapon and its victim away and knelt beside Spencer. Blood poured from his stomach where the weapon had pierced him. "Sorry. Are you okay?"

"I will be in a minute." He stuffed his hands against the wound and took a halting breath. "Thanks."

"No, thank you."

We turned to look at the zombie kid. It lay twisted, motionless, like a discarded doll.

I must have whimpered, because Spencer grabbed my shoulders.

"It's not real." He shook me, then took my face in his mud- and viscera-caked hands. "Ciara, listen. You didn't kill it. There was nothin' to kill. Okay?"

I stared into Spencer's eyes, as dark as the moonless sky. But my assent wouldn't come.

"They're getting away!" Regina shouted.

I looked up to see a group of maybe twenty zombies staggering up the hill, near the edge of the orange boundary. Then one by one, they disappeared.

With no one to order us not to, we followed, Shane in the lead. He lurched to a stop at the top of the hill, waving his arms for balance. I almost crashed into him from behind.

There was a hole in the ground, the width of a human body.

I stepped back. "I'm not jumping in there. There's no way to tell how deep it is."

"Yeah, there is." Shane dropped to his knees and put his ear to the hole. "I hear footsteps going that way." He pointed toward the fence. "So it can't be that deep."

"They're heading into Sherwood?" I looked up the

hill to the chapel. "The Underground Railroad tunnel! Lori says it used to lead to a church downtown."

We looked at each other, a quintet of amateur zombie killers, asking the unspoken question. Did we dare follow?

Way back in the heart of the cemetery, the ZC and Enforcement agents were well occupied. Based on the screams, a little too occupied.

"I'll go first." Shane slipped his sword into his scabbard, missing it the first two tries. Then he gave me a grim smile and lowered himself into the hole. We heard a loud "Oof!"

A moment later Shane shouted, "All clear. It's about a fifteen-foot drop. Ciara, you come next and I'll catch you. The rest of you are on your own."

I sheathed my weapon and hurried into the abyss. I tried not to scream as I dropped into Shane's arms, and mostly succeeded.

We stepped aside. Regina, Noah, and Spencer landed lightly as cats.

The tunnel was nearly pitch-dark even to my vampire eyes. I stepped on something soft and realized it was a broken patch of sod the size of the hole—a trapdoor for the zombies to fall through. No wonder their escape route hadn't been seen ahead of time.

I put out my hands to feel muddy walls that seemed to be reinforced with wooden beams. A few steps away from the hole, the tunnel's height decreased dramatically, brushing the top of my scalp.

"Watch your heads," I told them. "Well, not Regina."

"See, there's advantages to being short," she said. "Of course, this humidity will ruin my hair."

"Shh." Spencer stopped. "What was that?"

A flashlight flicked on behind us. "It was the sound of me not chopping your loud asses in half." Elijah stepped forward from the direction of the chapel. In the same hand as the flashlight, he wielded the biggest battle-ax I'd ever seen. "For now, at least."

"How did you get out of custody?" Shane asked him.

"Colonel Lanham sprang me right after midnight. Once he got Tina alone, she recanted the whole testimony, said her dad put her up to it. Lanham brought me here and then left to find Petrea."

"How do we know we can trust you?" Regina said. "You could've been helping your girlfriend raise those things."

"Trust this." Elijah shone the flashlight beam on his left arm, which was now a bloody stump. "All the zombies in my sector came after me. I couldn't even see, I was at the bottom of such a thick pile."

I shuddered. "Sounds like an assassination attempt."

"Felt like it, too. Three of my squad members died saving me. I bet those monsters were just a distraction for the ones who ran away." He pointed his flashlight at the tunnel's ceiling, then at the long dark expanse ahead. "Now come on." Elijah tossed Shane the flashlight and slung his battle-ax over his shoulder. "Time to catch some zombies and the man who called 'em."

33

Under the Milky Way

The tunnel got taller as we proceeded, until I could run without knocking my head on the ceiling. Ahead of me, Elijah and Shane hunched as they ran, the latter glancing back to make sure the rest of us were keeping up.

"Some reason why we're doing this alone?" I said. "Why can't we call for backup?" It always seemed like the prudent move on TV.

"Shh!" Elijah stopped and turned. "Who we gonna call?" he whispered. "Who we gonna trust? Someone in the Control is behind this. They want to make it go away quietly." He handed me the ax, then checked the chamber of his Control-issued Glock. "Fuck that shit."

I tore my gaze away from the dull black pistol, then looked down the tunnel. "So we're all that stands between the town and two dozen zombies?"

Elijah glanced among us. "Y'all are new at this. I won't hold it against you if you crap out now."

I thought of zombies crushing the doors of my fellow

Sherwoodians, ripping apart the bodies of real live men, women, and children. Then I looked at Shane, whose eyes held the chivalric fire of a medieval knight.

I traded him the battle-ax for the flashlight, then tightened my grip on my sword. "Let's go." I charged to the front to light the way.

While most of my brain was watching out for an ambush, part of it was delighting in the adrenaline pumping through my veins, stretching and strengthening legs that had been shattered only a few minutes ago. I wondered if the same chemical cocktail would give me the nerve to kill the necromancer if it came to that. Sure, I'd dispatched some zombies, but they weren't alive—or unalive—to begin with.

We slowed near the end of the tunnel. A wooden door lay in splinters, bits of gray flesh clinging to the frame. Beyond the door, a dim bulb shone, so I turned off the flashlight.

Elijah put a finger to his lips and crept sideways through the doorway, his gun raised. Then he beckoned us to follow.

Lori was right—the tunnel led to the basement of a small church. On the far cinder block white wall, a long paper banner proclaimed HALLELUJAH, HE IS RISEN! in several crayon colors.

I glanced at the small crucifix over the broken door. *Great, a Catholic church*, I thought. *Now the other vamps will be afraid to touch anything with their bare hands.* Not that I could blame them. If this place really was consecrated, maybe even the walls and doors could burn us. Though I had opened the door of St. Michael's without hurting myself.

I quickly assessed the size of the basement room. *A small Catholic church, within running distance from Sherwood cemetery.*

"We're under St. Michael's," I whispered to Shane.

Feet thumped and dragged on the floor above us. We crept to the foot of the wooden staircase, which, if I remembered correctly from our last visit, led to the sanctuary.

Amid the shuffling, a male voice rose and fell while an organ played in the background. If all the zombies we'd followed were in the room upstairs, we were outnumbered more than three to one—and that wasn't counting any humans or vampires that might be up there.

Elijah beckoned me and Shane away from the staircase.

"We can't go in until we know what we're dealing with," he whispered. "Without recon, it'd be suicide."

Shane indicated a cellar door at the back of the building. "I'll go out and around and try to see through the front window."

Elijah nodded. "Get their number and position and look for weapons and bystanders."

"Wait." I pointed to a small, high window facing the street, covered by a thick black cloth. "Faster to go out that way, rather than run down the alley to the next block and come around."

"But I can't fit through that window," Shane said.

"I can." I hurried over to the wall beneath the opening. "Boost me."

Reluctantly, Shane knelt and held out his hand for me to step into. With his help, I shimmied up the smooth painted concrete wall, then swept aside the curtain, unlocked the window and slid it ajar, silently thanking the church's maintenance folks for keeping the hinges lubricated and quiet.

Shane pushed me higher, and I slid through the window onto the sidewalk, into the snow.

Wait. Snow? It hadn't been cold when we left the cemetery.

A breeze came up, twirling the flakes into the air. I realized they were cherry blossoms, prematurely torn from the tree limbs by last night's storm. The sight made me sad, as if spring itself had been dismembered by a jealous, violent summer.

I stuck my hand through the open window. "Sword," I whispered. "Just in case."

"Be careful." Shane handed me the katana, then gave me a penetrating gaze. "Promise?"

"Yeah, yeah. I'll text you with whatever I see. Turn your phone on and make sure it's set to vibrate."

"It's already on, and yes, on vibrate."

"I'm so proud of you." I blew him a kiss, then stood up, brushing the cherry blossom snow off my butt. I crept up the front stairs and peered through the smoky glass window. As I'd hoped, the sanctuary doors on the other side of the vestibule were closed. I opened the well-oiled exterior door and slid inside.

On one side of the vestibule, the side without the confessional booths, a small diamond-shaped window opened onto the sanctuary. I crept beneath it and listened.

Colonel Petrea's voice, clear and cold as a starry winter's night, rang out over the insidious organ chords. He chanted in a foreign language, maybe Romanian. I thought of Aaron and felt a rush of vengeful rage.

When Petrea paused at the end of each line, other voices echoed his. If they were his Immanence Corps henchmen I'd seen two nights ago, they were human.

I opened up a new text message to Shane:

PETREA + HUMANS? I struggled so hard against the new compulsion to text in complete sentences, my thumbs cramped.

I sent the message, then started a new one:

CAS =

I slowly stood to bring my eyes level with the lowest tip of the diamond-shaped window.

Oh my.

Zombies filled the front church pews, facing Petrea as he chanted at the top of the stairs in front of the altar, gloved hands held palm up toward the ceiling. I almost expected them to pick up the hymnals and join him in song. I quickly scanned the rest of the personnel, confirming the identity of the IC agents, then ducked down and filled in the numbers before sending my text message to Shane:

24 + 4 HUMAN IC, 1 @ ORGAN & 3 @ ALTAR NEAR PETREA. HUMANS ALL ARMED.

I watched the mailbox icon appear on my phone and wondered if twenty-four had a special significance. Then Petrea's voice boomed out in his faintly accented English, stopping my heart.

"Come forward, Monroe Jefferson!"

My head jerked up, too fast and too far. I slid back against the wall to hide. A few moments later, my phone vibrated in my hand. Shane's hastily typed message appeared:

TJEY HVE MONRPE.

So Shane could hear what was happening in the sanctuary from the basement. Maybe he and Elijah and the rest had moved part way up the stairs.

I dared to put an eye to the window. In the choir box, Monroe slowly sat up. Then he shuffled out to stand beside the altar, head bowed. His signature white hat, usually immaculate, was crumpled in his hands. He clutched and grasped at it like a dog gnawing a bone.

I wrote back to Shane:

THEY THREATEN HIM WE MOVE OK?

OK, he replied.

Petrea was speaking in that language again, and as my brain tried to discern a pattern, it seemed to get sticky, like each thought was a step through deep mud.

I shook my head hard, wanting to plug my ears but knowing that would be dumb. With what felt like my last rational thought, I forwarded to Colonel Lanham all the text messages I'd just sent Shane. Elijah would be pissed, but I knew we couldn't handle this alone, especially with my mind feeling so . . . um . . . where was I?

I straightened up, examining my surroundings, wondering how I got there. Fear pulsed through me, alternating with serenity. Not real serenity but rather the kind that comes from nitrous oxide or codeine. Dental visit serenity.

The sanctuary fell silent. My phone vibrated again, but when I looked down it wasn't a text message. Shane was calling me. How sweet. Maybe he knew how I'd gotten here.

I tapped the green Answer box on the screen and put it to my ear.

"Don't talk," Shane whispered. "Petrea got quiet all of a sudden. Can he see you?"

My buzz vanished, as if my head had been doused in ice water. I realized that in my stupor I had moved in front of the window. Petrea was staring straight at me.

All my muscles froze, like those of a deer waiting to see if the wolf will give chase.

He shifted his focus to the front pew of zombies. With a curve of his gloved forefinger, he beckoned the closest one on his left, opposite Monroe. It shambled forward, a hulking brute of a corpse, a head taller than Monroe and twice as wide.

Petrea looked straight at me as he placed his hand on the zombie's shoulder and said, "Kill this man."

"NO!" I slammed open the sanctuary doors and hurtled down the aisle, unsheathing my sword as I ran.

The zombie reached for Monroe's neck. I shrieked again and launched myself through the air.

As I fell, my sword came down, slicing through the zombie's porous skull. Most of my body landed on the guck-spewing corpse, but my elbows bashed the floor, jarring the sword from my hands.

Petrea laughed, even as feet pounded up the basement stairs—feet belonging to my fanged cavalry. I scrambled to my hands and knees, slipping in what was left of the zombie.

Two shots rang out from the top of the basement steps, the distinctive *pap! pap!* of a Glock. Then four more. Shrieks of human pain cut the air. I resisted the instinct to take cover, trusting Elijah not to shoot me in the melee as I . . .

Petrea clapped his hands twice.

As I . . . what? What was I doing?

He clapped again, in a continuous rhythm that slowed with each beat. My brain felt like it was being wrapped in cotton candy.

His ethereal voice came from behind me. "Stand up."

I obeyed, turning to face the sanctuary (not a very apt name at the moment, I thought). Elijah and the vampire DJs stood near the basement stairs, frozen but looking pissed about it, unlike Monroe, who looked as scared and stoned as I felt.

On the floor beside me, one Immanence Corps agent lay motionless, a bullet hole in the center of his forehead. Beyond him, two more writhed on the carpet, trying to staunch the flow of blood from the multiple wounds in their torsos.

At the organ, a fourth Immanence agent lay slumped against the keyboard, producing a sustained dissonant chord that scraped my spine. Blood dripped in a puddle at his feet.

The zombies stood in the pews facing the center aisle, as if ready to line up for Communion.

Petrea began to chant, low in his chest, somehow in tune with that chord of death coming from the organ. The zombies shuffled toward the aisle, marching in time. I tried to move, but my muscles felt cold and sticky, like my blood had turned to maple syrup.

I heard everyone's voice at once, swirling in an incoherent cloud inside my head, but the only sound that broke through was Petrea's chant.

I looked at Shane. He and the other vampires were shouting and advancing, but an inch at a time, caught in the same slow-mo syncopation as me and Monroe, while the rest of the world moved at regular speed. Like *The Matrix*, only the opposite.

As I was congratulating myself on the analogy, Shane's voice broke through the storm.

"Ciara, wake up!"

At least, that's what I thought he said. His words were broken and staticky, like when he calls me on his cell from the mountains of western Maryland, where one of his donors lives.

My mouth wouldn't move to answer him, so I just thought, *Why is he in Cumberland? Didn't he visit Greg last week?*

"Ciara, he's going to kill us all!"

His sound came clearer, but his meaning did not. *Why would Greg want to kill us?* I'd never met that donor, but he seemed nice enough on the phone.

"Ciara, you're the only one who can stop Petrea. I know you can do it, so wake the fuck up!"

This time Shane's voice cut through my brain haze. I couldn't turn my head, but my eyes darted to the side to meet his.

"That's my girl," he gasped, his neck muscles straining with every word. "Show him what Gypsy scum can do."

I remembered who I was. Not a zombie, not any kind of monster with strings to pull. Petrea had called me a metaphysical bucket of bleach. He said lies made up the fiber of my mind.

But his was the biggest lie of all.

I lifted my thirteen-ton hand and slapped myself across the face. "Ow." I staggered back a step.

Petrea glared at me and kept chanting.

"You have no—" I stopped, my mind grasping for the words "—power over . . ." *Over what?* " . . . Me."

Petrea didn't break the rhythm of his chant, but his eyebrows twitched, showing a break in concentration.

The dead IC agent at the organ slumped to the floor,

leaving Petrea chanting a cappella. The silence only increased his voice's power.

"You're full of shhhhhhit." I sounded like I was underwater.

Colonel Petrea blinked rapidly, then backed up to the altar behind me, brushing past the paralyzed Monroe. I turned to face him, but my movements were stiff and slow, like an arthritic dog's.

From behind the altar, Petrea brought out a long black gun with a convoluted shape and a clear cylindrical bottle attached in front of the stock. A holy water pistol.

"No." My tone was no-nonsense, as if chiding a little kid.

"I'll show you what I'm full of," he said softly, and held the barrel to Monroe's temple.

"No." This time I was the little kid, whimpering.

Petrea pulled the trigger. Water spouted out of the barrel, splashing against Monroe's head.

My maker shrieked and fell to his knees, clawing at his smoldering scalp. The skin peeled back, falling in tatters, revealing the chalk-white bone of his skull, and underneath, the gray-brown folds of his brain. Petrea pumped the gun to refill the chamber.

That's when I caught up to time.

I lunged for Petrea, rage freeing me from the spell he had over all of us.

He intercepted me, curling his arm around my neck, then spinning me to press my back against his chest.

"Let her go!" shouted Shane as he flew forward to defend me. The spell was shattering in all directions.

Petrea shoved the pistol in my mouth. I struggled, gagging, but his strength overcame mine as easily as I could immobilize a mouse.

"Not one more step," Petrea said. "Now that she's a vampire, this holy water will burn through her sinuses and turn her brain to mush."

My eyes pleaded with Shane, begging him to trust what I was, no matter how little he understood it.

It's only water. It's only water. But when I looked at Monroe, flailing and frying on the floor, doubt stormed the door of my psyche like a battering ram.

Petrea tilted back my head, almost snapping my neck. My gaze shot to the stained glass window above the altar. I shoved my imagination beyond the golden-winged angel and the beaten, bleeding dragon, to the sky beyond, where nothing lay but the stars. Millions of spheres of burning gas.

That's all they are, I told myself. Whatever force created them, whatever name It went by on each continent of each planet, It did not hate vampires. It did not hate me.

I closed my eyes and prayed for lack of faith.

A sharp crack snapped the air. Petrea jerked. Holy water coated my mouth, throat, and lungs—hot, searing liquid flame.

I choked and heaved, grasping for stolen breath. Petrea released me, and I dropped to the floor. The carpet smashed my face. I tasted my own blood as I bit my tongue.

Then . . . nothing. No sight, no sound, no feeling. No pain. The holy water had burned it all away.

Petrea was right. I was a vampire vegetable.

But I was not alone. Something cradled my soul, long enough to calm me, long enough for me to remember where I belonged. And this time, It didn't ask me to stay. It let me go, in a release as loving as any embrace.

Only water.

And then, it *was* only water. Water that burned not with holy fire, but from the way it made my chest spasm in a desperate reflex to breath.

On my hands and knees beside the altar, I gagged and retched, bringing up the liquid that had no power over me.

Through the tears blurring my eyes, I saw the zombies charge.

Elijah and the vampire DJs lunged to meet them, swords flashing in the candlelight. Beside me, Petrea's feet twitched.

I turned to see him sit up, the bullet hole in his left eye healing with each blink. He reached for the holy water pistol, his focus on Monroe.

No. I fumbled for my sword, but it had landed out of reach, behind the altar.

"Griffin!" shouted a familiar human voice from the rear of the sanctuary.

I looked toward the sound but saw nothing but a trio of badly outmanned vampires. Fighting back to back, Shane and Spencer were surrounded by ten zombies, whose outstretched arms were almost around their necks.

A small pointy object flew toward me over the crowd of undead. I snatched it from the air.

I'd seen this polished ebony stake before, its needle-sharp tip pressed to my chest, the letter *L* carved on the bottom.

Behind me, Petrea pumped the holy water pistol furiously, reloading.

With my thumb on the end, and my fingers wrapped around the shaft in the textbook Control grasp, I slammed the wooden stake into Petrea's heart. Without pausing to admire my work or let the shock sink in, I yanked it out.

His eyes met mine as he began to die.

Instead of collapsing, he stayed sitting upright and merely lowered his chin to his chest. "*Smecher*," he gasped with his last breath.

I shook my head. "Not this time."

A chorus of dull thumps came from the sanctuary. I turned to see the zombies falling, even the uncut ones. The vampires lowered their swords, and beyond them all, Colonel Lanham stood at the end of the aisle, a female Control sharpshooter at his side holding a long, scoped rifle.

"I . . . saw . . . you."

At the sound of Monroe's voice, I crawled to him and clutched his outstretched hand. He touched my mouth, his eyes full of pain and bewilderment.

"You . . . burned," he gasped.

"Not for long." I laid my hand below the smoldering place on his scalp. How could he survive this? "You can stop, too."

"No . . ."

"Yes." I dug my nails into the back of his hand. "I'm part of you now. You can stop believing long enough to heal." I leaned close to his ear. "Monroe, it's only water. Say it."

"I can't."

"Say it!" I clutched his shoulder. I had no idea if he could live long enough for us to fetch my human blood to heal him. "Repeat after me: It's."

His breath heaved in and out. "It's."

"Only."

"Only."

"Water."

He licked his dry, cracked lips. "It's only water."

"Again."

We said it together, five, ten, twenty times, in a quickening rhythm. The others joined in, covering the sound of Petrea's body sucking into itself, folding into the hole in his heart, tendons stretching, bones snapping. I shifted so I wouldn't have to see.

"It'sonlywaterit'sonlywaterit'sonlywater. . . ."

Monroe's head stopped smoking. His skull re-formed to cover his brain. New skin swept across his scalp like an ocean wave over sand, a wave that never receded. Even his earlobe returned in a complex series of curves.

We kept up our chant until he was whole again. Everyone fell silent, and the only sound was that of the last bits of Petrea disappearing through his wound. His hair, his toes, his fingertips.

There was a soft crack, like the flap of a flag in a strong breeze, and Petrea was gone.

I sat back, my hands barely catching me in time. Shane moved forward.

"Don't touch her." Lanham strode down the aisle. "Her clothes are covered in holy water."

"I can't believe you shot him," Spencer said to Lanham. "He could've killed her."

Lanham reached out a hand to help me up. "Let's just say I had faith in her lack of faith."

I gave him a grim smile as I rose to stand on unsteady feet, then turned to Shane. He'd called out to me with that same faith, and it had saved me. Saved us all.

Regina gestured to the corpses strewn around the sanctuary. "What happened to them?"

"When the master dies," Elijah said, "the *cadaveris* are released from the blood magic."

I walked down the stairs away from the altar. The other vampires gave me and my dripping clothes a wide berth.

I stopped beside the body of a young woman clad in what must have once been a colorful dress. Now it was nothing but a patchwork of gray, mud-caked rags.

I tugged the skirt down over the woman's knees and gazed at what was left of her face. "Rest in peace," I whispered.

Silently I added, *enough for both of us*.

34

Heroes

The sky decided to piss all over Friday night's funeral service for the fallen Control agents. Walking in high heels through the mud of the IACMUCE headquarters' memorial garden, I didn't stumble or stagger. Human gracelessness was a problem of my past. I had plenty of future problems to replace it.

The stone markers for the six dead-undead vampires bore the Control logo, a sun with curved, flaring rays. Each was marked with a brass plaque with their original and assumed names, along with the dates of their turnings and final deaths.

There were no bodies to bury, of course, so the markers lay only a few feet apart. Hundreds of other markers lined up to our right, all for vampires who had died in the line of duty over the last century. The sight reminded me of the crosses stretching over the fields of France after World War One.

When the service was over, Shane and I stood before the marker of a vampire we'd never met.

"So this is our choice," I told him. "Die in the line of duty, or fade into obscurity."

Shane shrugged, his hands in the pockets of his dress pants. "We also get a tombstone somewhere with our human name and a fake death date, courtesy of the Anonymity Division."

"But our real selves can never be buried." I thought of the zombies, crawling, stumbling, moaning without sound. "Then again, we can also never be turned into running carcasses, so that's a bonus."

"You want to bag the reception?"

"No, let's stay for a little while." I looked at him. "I'd hate to waste that suit."

He grunted, twisting his upper lip in disgust. "Just half an hour, then I need to leave for the studio. Regina'll kill me if I'm late. We need to get on a regular schedule again, get life back to normal." He winced and brushed his fingertips over my back. "I mean, you know what I mean."

I forced a smile, though I knew he didn't need me to fake a good mood. Now that the zombie attacks were over, I would have plenty of time to focus on the new me. Oh joy.

We followed the others into the reception room in the basement of the Control headquarters. Black cloths covered every table, and a small buffet was set up on one side of the room for human consumption (consumption *by* humans, not *of* humans). There was a cash bar that offered a small assortment of booze, plus blood served at three different temperatures—iced, room, and body. We ordered a pair of red wines.

Spencer and Monroe stood off to the side, looking awkward despite being two of the best-dressed people in the room. I headed toward them, my stomach flipping at the thought of speaking with my maker.

Monroe had been staying here at headquarters the last two days, withstanding a slew of tests and questions. It seemed that the night my maker had walked out after my turning, Petrea had kidnapped him as a vampire test subject for his own undead-puppetmaster spells. He didn't know at the time that Monroe had made me, only that he worked at WVMP. Maybe he thought Monroe's advanced age would make him "undeader" and therefore more susceptible to suggestion.

"Hello," I said to him when we joined them. "It's good to see you."

He nodded, avoiding my eyes.

Shane turned to Spencer. "My band's looking to add some surf rock tunes to our set list. We want a really authentic sound, none of that digital crap. So what do you recommend as far as reverbs and pickups?"

Spencer brightened, and began to rattle off the names and models each of his favorite artists once used. I took a deep breath and used the opportunity to try again with Monroe.

"I heard they held you captive in a cubby hole in the church basement all week. I can't believe Shane and I were right there Sunday night, upstairs."

"I heard you," he said softly, "but I couldn't call out. When you got hurt . . ." He touched his chest. "I felt it."

"It was nothing," I added quickly, "not compared to what you went through." I kept my breath steady. "I didn't know why, but I had to go into that church. I must have sensed you there, even when I was standing in the street." My babbling came faster as I let my gaze wander over the gray walls, the polished floors, anywhere but his silent face. "I never really understood the blood bond before, even though I've seen it with Regina and Shane. I thought that was just them. So maybe we should—"

"What do you want from me?" he asked.

His eyes pierced mine, and I fought the urge to run away.

"Nothing, I just thought we could—"

"Little girl, I gave you life." His voice was low but hard as steel. "I brought you back from the gates of heaven and hell. I held your soul in my hand." He extended his hand, his thumb and first two fingers pinched together as if holding a small object. "I coulda let you go." He snapped his fingers apart, dropping the imaginary thing. "I coulda let you bleed."

I made my tongue work long enough to say, "Thank you."

"I don't want your thank-yous." He loomed over me, dark eyes gleaming. "I don't want anything but to get you out of me."

My throat froze. "What do you mean?"

"You changed me. You put your disease in me."

"My chicken pox?"

"No." He blinked slowly. "Your doubt."

Anger warmed me enough to release the words. "That *disease* saved your skin. Probably saved your life."

"Hah." He set his empty glass down hard on the table. "Some kinda life now."

He stalked toward the door, dragging what felt like half my blood with him. Spencer followed, shaking his head and muttering, "Just give him time. Give him time."

Shane slid his arm around my waist to steady me. "Listen to Spencer. Go slow."

I nodded hard and quick, hoping the motion would jerk the tears back.

"Griffin."

I let out a breath, grateful for a distraction from my emotional implosion, and turned to Colonel Lanham.

"What's the word, sir?"

He straightened the lapel of his dress blacks, which looked somber without the medals—eschewed, I assumed, for the occasion. "I'm sorry to say, Petrea was working under the aegis of the Control. Part of a black ops effort to find a way to control vampires. The *cadaveris accurrens* were simply practice."

Project Blood Leash resurrected. No doubt the cheerleading routine was a test for the spell's precision.

"His spell worked on all of us vampires in the church." Shane looked at me. "But it seemed different for you and Monroe, like Petrea had your minds and not just your bodies."

"It's possible," Lanham said, "that the chicken pox virus made Griffin—and by extension, Mr. Jefferson—more like a CA than the average vampire."

I wrinkled my nose. "So we were zombiefied?"

Lanham frowned at my phrasing. "In a sense. Until Petrea died and broke the spell that raised the *cadaveris*."

"That explains why I felt so brain dead, and why my head feels clearer now. I just figured I was defective."

Shane rested a reassuring hand on my back. "But a vampire can't carry a virus," he said to Lanham, "so how would Ciara's fogginess affect Monroe?"

"The answer, I believe, is more metaphysical than physical." Lanham looked away and declined to elaborate.

I decided to help him out. "When I died, I think the

virus had already changed my essence or my soul or what-ever, making me more like the CAs. Monroe shared my death and resurrection with me. I could feel him taking and giving back more than just my blood."

Shane gave a solemn nod of understanding. It was a vampire thing.

"What I don't get," I continued, "among other things, is why Petrea would act against vampires when he was one himself."

"That's exactly why they chose him," Lanham said. "Who would suspect the most senior undead member of the entire organization?"

"He was just following orders, then?" Shane asked.

"Hardly. His ancestors, that Romanian nobility"—Lanham said the word with a slight sneer—"have had such a goal for centuries."

So Petrea wasn't a fascist after all. I still wondered about his wife, though, who was now under investigation.

"Their biggest fear was the revolt of the unworthy," Lanham continued. "After Petrea lived through the nightmare of communist rule, he was more determined than ever to fulfill his family's dream."

Shane sighed. "Takes the self-hating vampire to new heights, huh?"

"That can't be all it was," I said. "Petrea told me that a rogue vampire turned him and killed his family. Maybe he wanted to control vampires to keep them in line. Keep *us* in line, I mean."

"A reasonable impulse, taken to unreasonable lengths." Lanham rotated the glass of whiskey in his hands, star-ing into its amber depths. I'd never seen him so subdued, almost broken. "The Control has always been split," he said, "between those who would take a heavier hand with the undead and those, like me, who prefer a rational, pragmatic approach. But this development could tear the agency apart. Some of the vampire agents are threatening a strike, or worse."

I noted that a certain one-armed vampire agent had declined to stay for the reception. "Captain Fox made it sound like there was a cover-up."

Lanham nodded without looking at me. "Petrea wasn't authorized to move forward with the project so soon. He took the opportunity when he saw Tina do the ritual."

"So did Tina have the power to raise the dead?"

Lanham shook his head. "He did his own spell over the same grave after she left the cemetery. Then he procured one of the blood samples she'd given during Indoc as part of the weekly health screenings, when she was already infected with chicken pox but not sick yet. He paid the cemetery manager to apply it to the graves, then activated it himself at night. At least, that's what his surviving IC agent claims."

Ah. Good thing Elijah didn't kill them all.

I asked Lanham, "Did the survivor say what Petrea planned to do that night in the church?"

"Originally he wanted to compare how the spell worked on CAs versus your maker, so that he could move on to the next stage of his vampire-control project."

"Then why did he tell the zombie to kill Monroe?"

"Probably because you arrived. At such a young age, your maker's death could have killed you, or debilitated you so badly your comrades would have focused on saving you rather than stopping Petrea." He tilted his head.

"That's just a conjecture, since he didn't survive to explain."

My gut twisted in a mixture of fear and guilt. "Do Tina and her mom know I killed him?"

"Only that he was dispatched by one of his fellow agents in self-defense. His subordinate was unconscious at the time, so your secret is safe with those you already trust."

I glanced at Shane and thought of Tina's words to me. *Blood is in our blood.*

"A counselor will be contacting you," Lanham told me. "Killing in the line of duty is never easy, even less so when it's a fellow agent."

"Okay." I swallowed hard and bit my lip to keep it from trembling. I hoped the counselor could help me erase the image of Petrea's dimming eyes and bleeding heart.

"I should get back to the families of the fallen." Lanham said. "Griffin, I'll see you in six weeks." He reached to shake my hand.

I blinked myself back to the present. "Maybe. Maybe not."

He lowered his hand. "Pardon?"

"My contract states that I'll join you when I finish college, or three years from signing, which would be this coming December."

"And you're graduating next month."

"Only if I can finish my last class at home. See, it starts at seven p.m., which is before evening twilight." I gestured to my flammable body. "Bad for vampires. I sent my request to the Office of Academic Affairs, but the campus is still closed from the plague. If they say no, then I'm afraid I won't finish school until December." I pinched my brows together in a phony show of regret.

Lanham's impassive face tightened. "I see," he said. "When will you know?"

You mean, when will I decide? "Soon."

He turned slightly and seemed to be studying the far wall, where the black-and-white portraits of the dead-undead vampire agents had joined the Gallery of the Fallen.

"It might interest you," he said, "that in the last six-teen months, our research division has garnered much intelligence by studying your blood. Answers to questions concerning your nature."

"Really? Like what?" Why hadn't he told me before?

"I regret that we cannot share that information out-side the agency." Lanham turned on his heel and marched away. This time, he didn't offer to shake our hands.

My face went slack as I watched him retreat. "Wait," I whispered, though I knew it was pointless. He'd dangled the bait, and now it was up to me to bite—or swim away, clueless as ever.

Shane leaned close to my ear. "He's bluffing, trying to suck you in."

"I don't think so." My gut burned with the desire to know what I was all about—or what I had been all about, when I was human. "Sherwood did give us the option of having our papers graded by another professor, rather than canceling the course with three weeks to go."

"Do what you want, but I'm going to boot camp this fall."

I tugged on his tie. "And when you come back, no one will mess with you. Not if they want to keep their unlives."

"Let's just hope I'm not too late." He took a sip of wine and cleared his throat, as if realizing he'd said too much. No doubt he worried, as I did, that by the fall, Jim would have long since lost control.

"Hopefully by then I can get the band off the ground," he said.

I gave him a smirk, glad to be off the topic of my protection. "Always about the music with you, isn't it?"

"Until the day I die. Again."

I sipped my own wine, relishing the chance to taste something other than blood. "Regardless, I'm finishing that paper on the Legion of the Archangel Michael. Maybe Franklin can burn it and scatter the ashes over Aaron's grave."

Shane fell into a pensive silence, the kind that always ended with weighty words. "I've been thinking about that stained glass window, the one in that little church where we almost had our heads torn off?"

"I remember the place. Vaguely."

"I bought into that idea my whole life, and my whole unlife. The idea that it's easy to see who's an angel and who's a dragon. Who's on God's side. But when I saw the way you healed Monroe—"

"Monroe healed himself. I just convinced him to stop believing for a few minutes." I lifted my glass in a virtual toast to my faraway parents. "Learned the art of persuasion from the masters."

"You didn't make him stop believing. You got him to believe in something bigger. Because *you* believe in something bigger. Something that won't fit in a box."

I felt the world tilt as I realized he was right. Something had given me the ability to believe, whether it was

Monroe or Shane or death itself. It had been there for me when I needed It most.

Shane looked up, as if seeing the stained glass window again. "So when Saint Michael asks the dragon, *Quis ut deus?* 'Who is like God?' maybe the answer isn't 'no one.'" He turned to me. "Maybe the answer is 'everyone.'"

"Even vampires." My voice stumbled. "Even suicides?"

His face darkened for a moment, and I sensed he'd reached the limits of his mind expansion.

"Maybe." His breath quickened as he took another gulp of wine. "Maybe even us."

I gazed up at his profile and wondered if he'd ever truly let go of the things that haunted his soul. But his ghosts were a part of him, and I loved them as much as I loved the music he made and the kisses he gave.

My phone vibrated in the pocket of my suit jacket. Lori. "Sorry, I better take this," I told Shane. "She's probably having a last-minute freak-out over what to bring on their honeymoon tomorrow." Lori and David had decided to keep their original travel dates and take their honeymoon before the wedding, to avoid the expense of changing tickets. With the quarantine lifted, airlines were no longer waiving their cancellation fees.

"I have potential good news," she said. "We found a place available for the wedding and reception on Saturday, May 1. It's the only opening before July. Can you make it?"

"Hang on." I pressed the phone against my shoulder and spoke to Shane. "Will I be people friendly in two weeks?"

"It'll be a challenge." He took my hand and lifted it to his lips. "But I've gotten to really like challenges."

I gave him a wide smile. "So yes?"

He nodded. "Let's go for it."

Lori squealed when I told her. My thirst surged at the sound, and I started a mental What Not to Do Around Your Vampire Best Friend list for her (#1: high-pitched prey noises).

We returned to the studio in time for Shane's show. Later that night, Regina took me to meet her least kinky donor, a forty-something lady who worked at the Social Security Administration and who made a perfect cup of Darjeeling tea. The experience was blissfully unblissful, and I hoped one day I could have my own collection of vanilla donors like her. But with my need for frequent drinks, I couldn't be choosy.

As Regina drove us home on the winding back roads, I rolled down the car window. The night filled my nose with the scents of new life—seedlings pushing through the ground, eggs hatching, animals giving birth. The breeze lifted my hair, threading its fingers through the flowing strands and sweeping them across my face.

I stretched out my arm, permanently pale, and rode my hand over the waves of air, up and down, like when I was a kid, as my parents drove through the flat, endless, sun-scorched fields.

Unlike Mom and Dad, Regina didn't tell me to stop. Instead she rolled down her own window and did the same with her left arm. We laughed at our winged car.

At that moment, it was almost like being alive. Much less, but also much, much, much more.

35

Hey Hey, My My (Into the Black)

"How much more?" Lori asks me.

"About half a glass for each of us." I pour the rest of the Cabernet, splitting it evenly between our glasses, then sit back on the station lounge sofa. *Ah, back in the Now, where I belong.*

"No, I mean, how much more alive do you feel now that you're undead?" She stretches out her legs beside me, their Bahama/Greece sunburn set off by her cute yellow wedding rehearsal dress. "You just said it was almost like being alive."

"I don't know. I thought the turn of phrase sounded good."

"A little too good." She takes a small sip of the wine.

"There's a lot to be grateful for." I flex my arm. "Check out these triceps. I never have to hit the gym again."

"You never hit the gym your whole life."

"And now I can stop feeling bad about it." I draw out a wisp of hair. "My highlights will take longer to fade, since

I'll be out of the sun, and since I don't need to wash my hair as often."

"Ciara—"

"Though when I do touch them up, the chemical smell will be nasty."

"Ciara—"

"But I can just stuff cotton up my nose."

"Ciara, you don't have to pretend with me. I'm self-ishly thrilled you're a vampire, because otherwise you'd be dead—"

"Another bonus."

"—but you can always tell me when it totally blows. When you can't tell Shane or Regina or any of the others because you worry they'll think you're weak and whiny, you can tell me."

My smile can show only a fraction of my gratitude. "That means a lot."

"You can also bite me."

My hand squeezes the wineglass stem so hard it shat-ters. "Ack!" Reflexes kick in, and my other hand grabs the glass's bowl before it spills. "Hey, this could be the next big thing—stemless glassware. If people can't put down their cocktails, they'll drink faster. It'll be all the rage at the trendiest bars."

She laughs. "I'll put a set on our registry tonight, for those people who wait until the wedding day to buy a gift."

I slap my forehead. "I forgot to get one. Will you take a check?"

"You have a good excuse. And yes, we'll take a check." She swings her foot over her knee. "Just not at the same time as you bite me. That would be prostitutey."

"We're not discussing that."

"You need blood, and you need it from someone you trust, someone who won't make you feel like a dog begging for scraps."

"But that's not your job."

"Please let me do this." She wipes her nose and sniffles. "I don't know how I could live without my best friend. I hyperventilate every time I think about you dying, whether it's three weeks ago or three weeks from now. The only thing that keeps me sane is the thought of helping you live."

"Since you put it that way . . . okay. Thank you." Between Lori and Jeremy, I now have two relatively normal donors. Too bad I'll need at least a half dozen more, some of whom are bound to be weird.

"Condition." She holds up a finger. "David is absolutely, one thousand percent off-limits."

"I know that." I shift my weight, the sofa cushion suddenly uncomfortable. "Of course I know that."

"Unless your life depends on it, according to a certifiably neutral party, not your oh-my-God-I'll-die-if-I-don't-drink-him gut feeling."

I change the subject. "So how was the food tonight at the rehearsal dinner? It all tasted like Play-Doh to me."

"Thanks for faking it so well. And the food sucked. You weren't missing much." She looks away, and I know she's lying for my sake.

I raise my stemless glass. "At least I can still taste drinks. Although that cosmo was horrid. I didn't realize I couldn't taste juice, since it's just mashed-up fruit."

"Ew, so all you tasted was the vodka and triple sec? Wait, isn't liquor made from food?"

"The fermenting changes it. Same with the caffeine in coffee."

She lifts her glass. "To chemistry."

We clink and drink as Shane's voice comes over the ceiling speaker.

"It's twelve minutes before the hour, here at 94.3 WVMP, the Lifeblood of Rock 'n' Roll. That was 'Until the End of the World,' one of the less exhaustively played tracks off U2's *Achtung Baby*. I've got a special request coming up after the commercial break, something I think you'll all enjoy."

Lori's eyes glint as they turn upward. "My mom told me Shane has the sexiest voice she's ever heard. She couldn't believe how hot he is in real life, too. Not a face made for radio, she says."

"How old is your mom?"

"Fifty-two."

I sigh. "She's six years closer to his age than I am."

"Only in petty human years." She cocks her head. "She's right about the voice. It's magical."

"Magical enough to bring me back from the dead."

She shares my grin, but then hers fades. "Wait a minute. That's it!"

"That's what?"

"You said you heard his voice when you were in heaven."

"The white place. Whatever."

"And then in the cemetery with the zombie cheerleaders, you kept feeling foggy."

"Because of Petrea's spell."

"But every time Shane spoke to you, it lifted the fog."

"Yeah." I stretch the word into two syllables.

"And in the church." Lori sets down her glass and flaps her hands. "Oh my God! When you were under Petrea's spell, Shane snapped you out." She scoots over and grabs my wrist. "His voice was the antidote, Ciara. His voice was life."

I stare into her fiery eyes and try to laugh. "You're such a romantic. It's really cute."

"This explains everything."

"I've never heard of a voice having magic."

"Maybe it's never happened before. And maybe it'll never happen again, now that the spell died with Petrea." She tightens her grip on my arm. "Listen. What if when Shane called you back the first time, it wasn't really magic but just you wanting to be with him more than you wanted to be in heaven. And then—boom!" She smacks her hands together. "Heaven fused the magic with his voice."

I reach for her wineglass. "You are officially cut off. Tell me you have a designated driver."

"It's not as left field as it sounds. The blood magic mutated that virus and turned you and Monroe and the zombies into puppets. So why couldn't blood magic also plant something inside you while you were dead—*after* Monroe drank your blood, thus not affecting him—something that would protect you against the bad part. It brought balance."

Balance is a concept I can deal with. Every reaction having an equal and opposite reaction. "Go on."

"Remember," she continues, "your blood gave Monroe the disease that made him vulnerable, but it also gave him a way to save himself. Every disease holds the key to its own cure."

My brain hurts just thinking about it. "I guess if it

were possible in any universe, it would happen in—in that place. Heaven or whatever."

"Heaven or whatever. HOW for short."

The door to the hallway opens, and Jeremy slinks into the lounge.

"Shane kicked me out of the studio," he says to me. "My shift starts in seven minutes."

"Why did he do that?"

"Shh." He points to the ceiling speaker. "He said to tell you to shut up and listen."

I look at Lori, who curls her lips under her teeth as if to keep from laughing. She just shrugs in response to my questioning look.

Jeremy turns a knob near the light switch to raise the volume, then crosses his arms and leans back against the wall.

The commercial ends, and Shane's voice returns.

"Special treat for you vampires and other night owls. At least, I hope it'll be a treat. Performing an acoustic number here in our studio tonight is, well, me. Not that special, I guess. I wrote this song for my girlfriend and played it before asking her to marry me a few weeks ago."

My heartbeat stutters. *He is* not *doing this.*

"She said yes. We were very happy for a couple days, and then some stuff happened. Some of it was me, some of it was—okay, most of it was me. Long story short, we got unengaged, if that's the word."

"Disengaged," I whisper, then cover my mouth at my compulsive correcting.

"Anyway, she gave me back the ring, which I have sitting here on the studio table in front of me. A ring without a finger is pathetic, so I'm hoping she'll fill it again. But first. This."

A series of guitar chords fills the lounge. I put my hands to my chest, feeling the vibrations deep within.

Then his voice comes, and I realize Lori was right. He was my Orpheus, leading me out of the underworld again and again. No matter how far I stepped into the land of the dead, he always found me.

But she was also wrong. Petrea's spell was broken, but not Shane's. Even now, life flows through me stronger and faster at the sound of his words of promise, words that mean more than ever on this side of death.

I stand slowly, my legs steady. Jeremy opens the door to the hallway for me. I look down at Lori, who jumps up to throw her arms around my neck.

"See you tomorrow night—I mean, tonight." She squeezes me, not realizing how close I just came to biting her. "Don't you two stay up all day and fall asleep at my wedding."

"Promise." I extract myself from her embrace and move away quickly, out into the hallway. The door closes.

In front of me, the glass wall of the studio muffles the sound of Shane's music. But he spies me through the window and tilts his head toward the studio door as he sings.

I creep inside, using all my stealth to avoid making noise that the microphone could catch.

He starts the third and final verse, and I realize that something sounds different. As he describes the Ciara of the future, the notes become infused with a new pain, a new uncertainty—and, to battle it all, a new courage.

The final chorus strides forth, the wood of the guitar resonating in Shane's hands. The floor seems to tremble at each chord's impact. As he sings the last couplet, his eyes close and his lip curls in a snarl of determination.

Fate doesn't stand a chance against this guy.

When the last note fades, he opens his eyes, meeting my gaze without fear. He pulls the microphone a few inches closer.

"Will you marry me, Ciara?"

As I step forward to the mike, I try to think of a clever answer to make this night memorable for his listeners.

But all that comes out is, "I will marry you, Shane."

Grinning like a fool, he reaches to take back the mike. I snatch it out of his reach and recite his trademark sign-off line: "Good morning, and good night."

Shane hits the button for the final track of the show. Accompanied by the opening violin strains of the Verve's "Bitter Sweet Symphony," he takes the ring from the table and slips it on my finger.

This time it fits perfectly. I realize why he waited two weeks to ask me again—the ring was at the jeweler's, getting resized.

I take the guitar out of his lap and replace it with myself. We kiss and sway to the slow-building, mesmerizing tune, one that I'm positive didn't come out until after Shane died.

Jeremy takes Shane's place in the studio, giving us a calm high five on our way out. We collect Dexter and our bags, then head for the parking lot.

Outside, the seemingly endless April drizzle has taken a slight pause, and even the stars are out. By this late hour, summer constellations are already rising. I shiver in my coat, dreading the long days ahead, when the glowing tans of humans will mock my new existence.

As Shane unlocks the car and gets Dexter settled in the backseat, I gaze up at the stars. In two hours the sky will change from midnight blue to periwinkle, and the stars will fade one by one.

I remind myself that they don't really vanish. They're even more forever than we are, which is somehow comforting. And like us, they'll be back again. Tonight.

"Did you change the song you wrote for me?" I ask Shane. "It sounded new, but maybe it was just the venue."

"Nope." He draws me close, sweeping my hair off my cheek with one hand and lifting my chin with the other. In his eyes I see forever. And for the first time, he sees it in mine.

"Same song," he whispers, on the verge of a kiss. "Different key."

**Here is a sneak preview of
Ciara's next adventure, coming from
Pocket Books in 2011!**

I avoid mirrors these days—not because they don't show my reflection, but because they do.

Three weeks ago, my skin and hair were full of warmth and imperfections. My fiancé Shane said I was like "walking sunshine." Now my highlights are ice blond and my face, a flawless porcelain. Even the blue in my eyes is purer, sharper.

All of which is great in theory—far be it for me to bitch about the increase in gorgeosity. Problem is, I chose this golden-yellow maid-of-honor gown back when I was a "summer." Back when I was human.

I tug the dress's back zipper up as far as I can reach, then leave the mansion's powder room to enter the parlor.

Lori is sitting at the vanity, a light blue smock over her ivory wedding gown. She's too busy examining her mascara in the magnifying mirror to look up when I enter. But Regina and Maggie check me out from the upholstered sofa.

"How do I look?" I ask them. "Be honest."

"Um." Maggie brushes an auburn curl off her forehead. "Well . . . I love what you did with your hair."

"You look dead." Regina flips her silver lighter between the long crimson nails that match her bridesmaid dress. "And not in a good way."

I turn my back. "Shut up and zip me."

After she lifts the zipper and fastens the hook, Regina's fingertips drift across my bare shoulders. "You're cold," she whispers. "Time for a snack."

"I don't want to have to brush my teeth again."

"You'd rather get the munchies in the middle of the wedding?"

"You guys don't have to whisper," Maggie says. "I know the score." She raises fingers to her lips to form fangs.

"My mom could come in." Lori's words are slurred by her application of lipstick. "Ciara, go drink. And you look fine."

I blow her an air kiss, which she catches with a flash of French manicure, and pick up my small thermos cooler from behind the ottoman. Lori told her family that I'm a new diabetic who needs frequent snacks to maintain my blood sugar level. Which is true, substituting the word "vampire" for "diabetic" and subtracting the word "sugar."

In the bathroom, I face away from the gilded mirror as I slurp a quick meal, then clean the blood off my teeth for what feels like the fortieth time tonight. The brush doesn't snag on my incisors—a sign that the fangs are behaving themselves.

Unless I'm starving, I only go into *grrr* mode around people who have been or would like to be bitten. Which is roughly two percent of the population, but some days feels like a hundred and two percent of my acquaintances—including my best friend Lori and my runner-up best friend (and boss) David, who are getting married in twenty minutes.

A shrill female voice comes from the parlor, hurting my ears even through the powder room door. I reenter the room, though I'd rather escape.

Mrs. Koski is seated at the coffee table, where the contents of Lori's bridal bag are arrayed in neat lines. As she inserts each item back into her daughter's ivory lace purse, she makes a check on a list. Regina stands alone at the stone fireplace, watching in silence.

I join her and whisper, "Didn't she already do that?"

"Twice. But Maggie interrupted her, so she had to start over. After she made the girl cry. Lori took Maggie to help her put on her veil."

"I was supposed to do the veil. I'm the worst maid of honor ever."

"All set!" Mrs. Koski snaps shut the purse. Her smile fades when she sees me. "Oh dear. That's not your best color, is it?"

"Not anymore," I say through gritted teeth.

"But Lori chose the style and let you girls pick your own colors. That way everyone's complexion would be flattered." She rises on her six-inch heels, her silver sheath making her look like an aging ice queen from a Euro-pop video. "You could've worn Tina's blue dress."

A shiver jolts my body at the sound of that name. To cover my reaction, I rub the back of my neck, pretending it's tickled by a stray hair or the clasp of my necklace.

"Tina's a lot shorter than me." Plus it would've been tacky to wear her dress after I'd murdered her father.

It was self-defense, I remind myself. Besides, Tina Petrea illegally raised the zombie who spread the disease that took my life. Even if her detainment awaiting a Control tribunal—at which I testify next week—hadn't conflicted with the wedding, her necromancy alone justified kicking her out of the bridal party. The wedding magazines probably all agree on that.

I edge past Mrs. Koski toward the window, telling myself that it's her cloud of perfume closing up my throat and not the memory of Colonel Petrea's eyes as his life leaked out, or the memory of sunken black pools, like twin tar pits, in a zombie kindergartner's face.

With a groan of painted wood, the window slides upward at my touch. I rest my forehead against the cool pane of glass. Outside, rain rattles on the back porch's corrugated roof, almost drowning out my mind's replay of cracking bones, snapping tendons, and the slurp of steel through a child's rotten flesh.

The soundtrack of my nightmares.

"Ciara."

I turn to see Shane. He's a long, tall drink of black—tuxedo, shirt, *and* tie—with his head brushing the frame of the parlor's open double doors.

I thought he'd look awkward in formal wear, what with his terminal grunge-boy slouch and unkempt light brown hair half obscuring his pale blue, couldn't-give-a-damn eyes. He hasn't touched a comb since 1991.

But rather than taming him, the tux only accentuates his wildness.

"Wow," Regina says to him. "Haven't seen you in one of those since the night we met."

Mrs. Koski makes a purring noise. "Dibs on first dance with the best man." She sniffs at me. "After you, of course."

He gives them a nod without taking his eyes off me. "How are you feeling?"

"Fine." I strut to his side to show him just how fine.

He doesn't know about the nightmares. No one does. "Shouldn't you be with the groom?"

"David wanted a minute alone." He takes my hand and leads me into the hallway. "Besides, he's worried about you, too."

"Worried I'll eat the guests. But I swear I just had a snack."

"I can tell." He runs his hand up my arm. "You're warm. Not to mention gorgeous."

"This yellow dress doesn't make me look washed out?"

He scrunches his brows. "What do you mean?"

For once, I'm glad he has the typical straight-male cluelessness about color.

Shane takes my hands and examines me at arm's length. "If anything, you make the dress look washed out."

For the millionth time, he has said exactly the right thing. "Ooh, tell me more."

"If I were a poet, I would say you outshine the sun, moon, and stars put together." He steps forward, pressing the length of his body against mine. "But I'm not a poet, so I'll just say that no matter what you wear, I always picture you naked."

"Pornographic poetry—my favorite kind." I lift my chin for a kiss.

Shane stops right before our mouths touch. "We shouldn't. I don't want to lick off your lipstick."

"Yes, you do."

He tilts his head. "Yes, I do."

He kisses me just as his cell phone vibrates through his jacket. To keep him from taking his hands off my body, I reach into his pocket and withdraw the electronic nuisance. Its caller ID screen shows a number I don't recognize, along with the word "UNAVAILABLE."

Shane takes the phone. "Probably a whacked-out listener. I need to change my cell number again." He puts it to his ear. "Yeah."

The string quartet in the foyer below ends their song. In the relative silence, my sensitive vampire ears catch the words from the phone speaker:

Code Black.

Shane's face freezes. My heart stutters and stops.

"Jim, tell me you're calling from a pay phone."

I dig my nails into the molding on the wall behind me.

"Yeah, I know where that is," Shane says. "Which room? . . . Okay, we'll be there in fifteen, max." He slaps his phone shut. "Code Black. Get your clothes and the other DJs and meet me in the parking lot."

"Now? What about the wedding? The bridal party can't just leave before the ceremony."

He grips my shoulders and stares at me with haunted eyes. "You remember what a Code Black means, don't you?"

I swallow past a rising clump of tears and whisper, "Yes."

"Then you know every second counts." He tucks away his phone. "I'll tell David there's . . ." He scans our surroundings, his gaze settling on the rain-splattered window at the end of the hall. "Flooding at the station. We have to save the equipment."

"Not all of us. If you and I leave, he'll know something horrible has happened."

"He also knows not to ask questions." Shane brushes a lock of hair from my cheek. "Sorry you have to go through this."

"I'm one of you now." My gut twists at the thought of what we'll find when we join Jim. "For better or for worse."

His eyes turn sad as he kisses my hand near the engagement ring. "Parking lot. Five minutes." He runs down the winding staircase, taking the steps three at a time.

I hurry back into the parlor, where Regina is leaning out of the open window, sneaking a cigarette.

Mrs. Koski passes me on her way out. She gives one final shudder at my dress, then leaves without a word.

I rush up to Regina and whisper, "Code Black."

She freezes mid-puff. "Jim again?"

"What do you mean, 'again'?"

"So it is Jim."

"Yeah, but—"

"Bloody hell." Regina takes a final deep drag of her cigarette, as if storing up the nicotine. "How many?"

"Huh?"

She arches an eyebrow. "Do you know what a Code Black is?"

"Of course I do. But what do you mean, 'How many?' How many what?"

"Duh." She tosses her cigarette out the window. It sizzles as it hits the falling rain. "Bodies."